MY
BROTHER'S
SPARE

Library of Congress Control Number: 2019918355

ISBN: 978-1-7341745-6-4 (paperback)
ISBN: 978-1-7341745-8-8 (hardcover)
ISBN: 978-1-7341745-7-1 (ebook)

This book is a work of fiction. Names, characters, places, and incidents either are the product of the author's imagination or are used fictitiously. Any resemblance to actual events, businesses, companies, locales or persons, living or dead, is entirely coincidental.

Cover design by ebooklaunch.com
Interior formatting by Formatted Books

Published by Lost Island Press
San Jose, California
www.lostislandpress.com

My Brother's Spare

Shira Behore

To my grandma, Safta Sara, who listened to the eight year old girl who wanted to tell a story.

Thank you for everything.

I love you.

Prologue

I COULD NEVER FORGET MY MOTHER'S touch.

The swift and gentle movements of her fingers as they loosened the stubborn knots in my hair, the faint scent of lavender that lingered in the air whenever she was near.

And her warmth, one that filled every crevice in our vast estate.

I exhaled heavily, her steady hands moving through my hair, tying the deep strands back with a silver ribbon and securing it tightly at the base of my neck.

"There." I could hear the smile in her voice long before I turned to face her. "Beautiful."

She was radiant, with eyes as deep and dark as the night sky and a smile so bright, even the sun stared down in envy. *The Viscount's jewel*, the people had called her. A young lady of noble birth, yet one passionate enough to sympathize with even the weariest of outcasts. She existed as a quiet and soft-spoken woman in the public's eye, but her warmth extended past her blood, leading her to the outer neighborhoods of Nieve with warm food for the hungry and clean clothes for the bare.

"A saint," they would say. *"A guardian angel for the poor and a voice for the forgotten."*

I stepped up on my toes, my hand moving to touch the dainty chain that clung to her neck. My thumb pressed against the simple flower charm that sat comfortably between her collarbones, tracing the ridges and dips of the petals as she pulled me into her lap.

"Pretty, isn't it?" A breathy laugh slipped past her smiling lips, and I nodded, finally meeting her eyes. Her warm hands found mine, squeezing them faintly.

"V, are you finished yet?" my brother whined from the center of the vast room. I slipped from my mother's grip, turning to meet Victor's excited gaze. He was my copy, the two of us sharing everything, from toys and clothes to a womb.

"Twins!" my father would exclaim as he retold the story. *"Out of all the surprising things I've come across in my lifetime, hearing the doctor say that was by far the most astonishing."*

Victor had spread himself out across the carpet like a sunflower, carefully placing the last piece of his toy track onto the floor, connecting the twisting and turning trail into one large extension.

"The train." He sat up quickly, pointing a finger to my right. "Grab it for me, will you?"

"I'm not your maid, Vic." I sighed but bent down to grab the toy nonetheless. My pale nightgown swished at my knees as I ran over to his spot on the floor and handed the small mechanical trinket to him.

"Of course you're not." He grinned, setting the train on its tracks. "You're more like my butler."

He burst out into a fit of giggles as I tackled him, trying to hide my own itching grin. I pinned him down face-first, easily holding his hands behind his back.

"No fair," he mumbled into the carpet, turning his face to the side. "I wasn't ready!"

"Please, I always win!" I snorted, releasing his arms and taking a seat at his right. He groaned, sitting up once again, but didn't argue. He leaned toward the track, one hand holding the bright red train in place while the other moved to wind up the key that sat at its rear. I hugged my knees, watching his eyes light up as the train came to life, its small black wheels chugging their way down the dark tracks.

"Amazing, isn't it?" He beamed, deep blue eyes meeting my matching pair. Father had brought the train set home about a week ago, and Victor had been obsessed with it ever since.

"I don't want to be Viscount," my brother had announced a few nights prior. *"I want to be a conductor!"*

Father had laughed, a deep and comforting rumble, ruffling Victor's hair. *"I'm afraid you'll have to manage both jobs, Victor."* My brother had pouted, whining about how he would much rather deal with trains than with criminals.

"You should have let your sister come out into the world first then." Father grinned, his pale eyes meeting my own. *"Viscountess Valeria."* He tucked a long strand of hair behind my ear. *"How does that sound to you?"*

"It's a little late, isn't it?" Our mother's soft voice rang from her seat, her slender form standing elegantly from the deep velvet chair.

"Can't we please wait for Papa?" I begged, batting my eyes at her. "We aren't even tired yet, I promise!"

"Your father won't be home for a while, darling. You know how busy he is." She took my hand in hers, squeezing it gently. "Maintaining peace isn't easy work in the least."

"Because of the fire, right Mum?" I had asked her, my mother stiffening at the mention of the recent tragedy.

"Yes." Her voice was just above a whisper, her eyes heavy with sorrow. "Especially after that disaster."

She had caught herself, pushing her sadness to the back of her mind, a small smile taking her lips as Victor groaned.

"But it's barely past ten!" He sulked, playing with the hem of his nightshirt.

"Is it ten already?" Her eyes widened, moving to the golden clock that sat above the fireplace.

I elbowed my brother in the side, the boy instantly regretting his words.

"Goodness. To bed with you two." Mother shook her head.

I stood quickly, eyes locking with Victor's before we raced to the big wooden bed across the room. I jumped, squealing as I felt him slam into my side, hitting the soft mattress a mere second before me.

"I won, I won!" He grinned, and I pushed him off my back, panting as I smiled.

"Wretched cheater!"

"How do you two have so much energy?" Our mother laughed, joining us on the massive bed. She noticed my small hands reaching for the glasses that sat at our bedside, each filled halfway with warm milk. My mother lifted them easily and held them out.

"Thank you, Mum." I murmured, bringing the warm glass to my lips, Victor grabbing his own. Mother had smiled and laid down on her back. A tired sigh escaped her, her hand moving to touch the necklace that clung to her neck as she stared up at the ceiling. She closed her eyes, taking in a deep breath before sitting up, her tender gaze moving to us once more. She leaned forward, pulling us into a tight embrace and peppering our heads with gentle kisses.

"Off to sleep now. You have an early morning tomorrow."

"It's a Wednesday, isn't it?" Victor groaned, falling back onto his pillow. "Do we have to meet with Lady Rosenfield *every* week?"

"Mum, couldn't we miss class just this once?" I pouted, sitting forward on my knees. "If I have to sit through one more piano lesson I'll dissolve into the wind!"

"Dramatic thing." I crinkled my nose as she tapped it gently, soft laughter leaving my mother's lips. "If you dislike it so fervently I won't force you, but bear through one more class for me, alright?"

I begrudgingly nodded, Victor sighing at my left, the exasperated sound morphing into laughter as our mother tickled his sides.

"Goodnight, my darlings." She smiled as we scampered under the covers, pulling the soft duvet up to our chins. She stood, leaning over us and planting soft kisses on our foreheads. "I love you both."

A few strands of dark hair had fallen out of her tightly pinned bun, framing her beautiful face like a piece of art. Her face moved to the nightstand to my right, lips blowing out the candle that flickered at our bedside.

"Love you, Mum!" Victor called out after her as she stood at the door, turning once more to smile at us. She shut the towering bedroom door behind her, the *click* echoing across the room.

I stared off into the darkness of the room, the warm glow of the fireplace steadying my tired body and chasing the imaginary monsters away.

"Are you asleep yet, V?"

"Of course not," I whispered, turning to face my brother. "I'm just thinking."

"About what?" I felt him shift, snuggling himself deeper into the pillow.

"Papa." I sighed, scratching at my cheek. "I wish he would rest more."

"Me too." Victor's voice was much softer then, his eyes fluttering shut. I turned to lie on my back once more.

Our father had always been a busy man, his tired figure stumbling the short distance to Nieve's Imperial Station at the first rays of light, only to greet us with a tired smile well into the dark of night. He was the Viscount after all, the King's authoritative hand and watchful eyes. The keeper of justice.

"Asleep already?" I whispered, my brother's calm and even breaths being the only sound that filled the vast room.

"No." He exhaled, eyes still closed. "Just thinking."

I grinned, turning my back to his sleeping form. My eyes watched the fireplace, how every shade of orange and gold seemed to spill into another, melting into each other like paints on a canvas. Burning steadily, strongly enough to scare any shadow away. I let my eyelids droop, feeling the heavy weight of sleep push down on them. I exhaled as Victor's hand found the back of my nightgown, squeezing the fabric as he often would as he drifted off to sleep, making sure that I was still there.

"Goodnight, Vic," I whispered, shutting my tired eyes as the night swallowed me whole.

"Goodnight, V."

It wasn't the bright morning rays streaming through our bedroom window that woke me up, nor was it my mother's soft voice as she nudged Victor and me awake.

No, it was the jolting sound of glass, glass shattering into hundreds and hundreds of pieces.

I jumped, sitting upright quickly, sleep still heavy in my blurry gaze. My body slumped forward, eyes squeezing shut at the throbbing pain that ran beneath my skull. My hands clutched at my aching head, the room feeling unsteady where I sat. I squinted in an attempt to clear my vision, noticing the darkness of the room. The fire had burned itself out, leaving us cold and alone in the dark of night. A sudden sense of panic flooded through me. My hands hurriedly reached for my side, moving around until they touched Victor's sleeping figure. A heavy breath unknowingly slipped past my lips as I relaxed, feeling the rise and fall of his chest. A loud thump echoed from outside our bedroom door, my limbs stiffening once again.

"V," Victor mumbled, shifting in his sleep. "What is—"

I clamped my hand over his mouth, his sleepy eyes now wide as they met mine. He sat up slowly, my hand slipping from his lips to sit in his shaky grip.

Something was wrong, the fear in the air shifting our bedroom floor, warning us that whatever lay beyond the dark wooden door of our room was not simply stopping by for tea.

I pursed my lips, pulling Victor closer to me as I neared the bed's edge, slipping from the mattress and letting my bare toes touch the cold floor. The room felt emptier without the fire, and somehow that frightened me more than the thought of something hiding inside with us.

"V, what is it?" he whispered by my ear, and I squeezed his hand tightly in mine.

"Something's wrong." My voice was barely audible over the deafening silence. "I heard a noise."

"It must've been a maid." His words shook, as if he was trying to convince himself more than me. "Please, let's just wait for Mum or Papa."

A shriek echoed throughout the house, and I winced as Victor's grip on my hand became painful. His eyes met mine, pupils receding back into the safety of his deep blue irises. My heart hammered wildly in my chest as I forced my feet forward, inching closer to the door.

"V, wait," he began again, eyes swimming with fear, but I squeezed his hand in mine, pulling my brother closer to my side.

"Just stay close to me."

The door creaked open, and I bit my lip at the cold chill that ran up my spine. The house was eerily dark. It must have been still well into the night, only a few hours after Mother had tucked us in for the evening, and yet it was as though nobody had walked down these halls for months. It held an emptiness so vast and heavy that my feet felt weighed down with every forced trudge forward.

I swallowed my fear, relaxing my shoulders at the feeling of Victor's trembling hand in mine. *Everything is fine, it has to be.* I turned back to look at my brother, tears barely contained by the edges of his eyes. *For his sake if not my own.*

We flew down the deep ebony steps like a pair of mice, our nimble feet barely making a sound as we reached the estate's first floor. I whipped my head around, putting a shaky finger to my lips. Victor said nothing, his eyes focusing on the wall behind me.

I took a tentative step forward, focusing on the silence.

The quiet was thick, *aching*, leaving my back sticky with sweat and my lungs heavy with unease.

I stopped, stiffening as I heard it. A thud, like the dull sound of a heavy book hitting the floor. Except it was followed by heightened whispers, ones much too sharp and hurried for this hour of night. A man's rough voice barked out words into the silence, followed by the hurried whispers of a woman.

We tread down the extended hall of the first floor, my vision blurring as we neared the flickering shadows that danced on the floor outside the common room. Victor dug his heels into the carpet, pulling me to a halt. I turned to him, mouth agape, but the fear in his eyes was enough to render me silent. He shook his head slightly before moving to shakily point his finger across the hall. I followed his gaze, reaching my father's study. My stomach dropped, a sick feeling filling it, as I backed into Victor's chest.

My father's study door was open, his coffee-stained cup from this morning still sitting untouched amongst his files, his fireplace unlit, and his coat hanger empty.

Father had yet to return home.

The sound of breaking glass startled us once more, our trembling arms moving to grip each other desperately. I swallowed, inching closer to the room, Victor attempting to pull me back toward the stairs. I didn't budge, scooting alongside the wall until we stood right beside the common room's entrance.

"Please." My blood ran cold at my mother's shaken voice. "You don't have to do this!"

My hand moved unsteadily to my lips, afraid that the sound of my erratic breaths would give us away. My heart thumped in my chest, so harshly that I feared it would rip right through my ribs and fall out onto the floor in front of me.

"I won't say a word, I swear it! Just, please." The hand over my face tightened at my mother's quivering words. "Don't do this, don't make me leave them behind."

I doubled over, squeezing my hands over my ears as my head throbbed, the world moving in and out of focus around me. Victor's quick hands caught me by the arms, pulling me into his steady grip. I gritted my teeth, my brother's racing heart screaming in my ear as he held me tightly.

"V—"

I clamped my hand over his mouth as tightly as I could, forcing myself to straighten up.

"Wait, wait!" The voice pleaded, my heart stuttering.

I whipped my head around, staggering toward the door and peering around the edge. My grip on Victor's hand became deadly, my brother stiffening in fear as I recoiled from the scene before me.

Up until that singular moment in time, on the first floor of our home, right outside the common room's doorway, I had never felt it. I had been afraid before, but this feeling, this pure terror, it ran through my veins like ice, grabbing me by the throat and squeezing.

"What—"

I yanked Victor back before he could take another step, one hand clutching his and the other pressed over his eyes. He held his breath, palm sweating against mine as I looked around the corner once more.

The man was tall, almost monstrous, with the build of a boat merchant, heavyset and strong. His shoulders bent forward awkwardly, hunching over as he tilted his head. The mask he wore covered the entirety of his face, leaving only two dark eyes exposed. The scruffy fabric was a deep grey, the lack of light making it blend into the rest of his face, darker streaks dragging along the space below his eyes, giving off the impression of a wild animal. Of a wolf.

But his nightmarish appearance wasn't what frightened me.

It was my mother's small frame in his grip, her beautiful eyes now wide and empty as a thin blade pressed against her throat. I stared unmoving, the sound being cut off from my world as my eyes bore into the image in front of me. Her silent mouth moved steadily as she spoke, her hands tense but her sharp eyes dry of any tears.

At least until she stilled and turned her dark eyes hesitantly to the door. We stared at each other, my mother and I, both unmoving, both seemingly trapped in the horror of the moment. Her proud posture trembled and slumped, her expressionless face reducing itself to nothing in an instant. I wanted to run to her, to grab her hands and take her as far away from here as I possibly could. Instead I froze, letting the frightened tears I'd been holding finally fall down my cheeks. My mother stumbled in the man's grip, his strong arms holding her up as she cried out, a horrible sound echoing through the empty halls of the estate. Nausea clawed at my throat as he pulled her head back, pressing the knife securely to her throat, resting right above her silver chain.

My nails dug into my brother's skin as the man moved the blade in one swift motion, slicing right through the soft skin of my mother's throat. He held her up as she writhed, thick crimson blood running down her neck, staining her pale nightdress a violent red. His gloved hands pressed her face into his neck as she choked, her jerking movements slowly coming to a stop. Her stiff hands went limp, one last strangled whimper bubbling past her lips before her lungs emptied out. The man crouched down, placing her leaking body onto the blood-soaked floor carefully, as if to not wake her from her permanent slumber.

She looked like a doll, the porcelain kind that were displayed in toy shop's windows, pale as the moonlight and eyes so wide and glassy, so beautifully lifeless.

And the blood, the steady pool that inched across the common room's floor filled the air with the sickly sweet smell of death. The sticky liquid that coated her skin shone like melted wax, still oozing, *still warm.*

My hands fell limply to my sides, Victor's eyes still glued shut beneath their ghostly grip. *She's dead.* I staggered back, my knees weak beneath me. *Dead, dead, she's dead.* I gripped at my hair, pulling at the roots as the heavy feeling in my stomach clawed its way up my throat. *Her heart stopped, the blood in her veins is now spilling across our home's floor, and the killer...*I brought a hand to my lips as I gagged, my horrified gaze moving from my mother's corpse and meeting one darker than any moonless night.

The killer is still here.

I lunged for my brother, nails digging into his arm as I ran, my staggering limbs carrying us both as we stumbled down the main hall. My head ached, bile burning at the back of my throat at the image of my mother's lifeless body. My mind had disconnected from everything but the ever-present sound of my pounding heart. I tripped over myself, slamming my side into the dining room table and hitting the ground with a hard thud. My vision blurred as the pain flooded through me, Victor grunting as he lifted the top half of my body, stumbling back at my dead weight.

There's no way out, no way for us to outrun the murderer in this house. I forced myself upright, breathing deeply as I tried to gain my footing. The room was twisting around me, falling into itself as my eyes tried to focus, moving quickly across the dining hall. I tightened my grip on Victor's hand, dragging us toward the mahogany cupboard that stood in the corner of the room. I swung the heavy door open, ducking my head in after Victor as he jammed himself inside, filling half of the bottom cupboard. My eyes fell shut, my feet giving out beneath me as I dropped onto my knees, crawling into the open space next to him. I swallowed hard, gritting my teeth as my little fingers grabbed the edge of the open door, pulling it shut with all my might. I bit through my lip as the door clamped shut over my fingers, my hands pulling them away quickly as they ached.

Victor caught my hands in his, squeezing them tightly to lessen the pain as we sat in the dark. My body screamed in silent agony, a blanket of sweat binding the thin fabric of my nightdress to me like a second skin.

My bones stiffened at the sound of it, the drag of heavy feet, unsteady and weighted, like a dead man walking. My head fell forward, hitting Victor's arm as a wave of nausea spilled over me. Victor gripped my shoulders, holding me still, but it was no use. I wouldn't last another moment.

"Victor." I barely breathed, my clammy hands gripping the fabric of his shirt. "Victor, don't let anyone in." His grip on me tightened, my limbs finally giving out, falling over my trembling brother's form. I didn't want to close my eyes, to leave him there alone, but my body had taken over my mind now, pulling me under a veil of darkness. "Don't—don't say a word. Don't let anyone find us."

A few stray tears burned at the corners of my eyes, running down the side of my face. My lungs stung with every inhale, as if the air were too thick for them to filter. My stomach convulsed and twisted violently, ripping itself apart as I tried to swallow what I had just seen. Somewhere in the dark, Victor's hand reached for mine, trembling fingers lacing through my own as we sat tangled ourselves in each other's arms.

*Please...*I inhaled raggedly the blistering image of my mother's bloodied body burning behind my eyelids as I slipped in and out of consciousness.

Please don't find us.

Chapter 1

T HE EARLY MORNING AIR WAS chilly, biting at the skin of my cheeks as it slipped through the cracks of the station windows. The familiarly dull sky stretched over the same worn buildings, welcoming another grey morning to the people of Nieve. The sound of honking cabs and feet echoed from below, children scurrying across the cobblestone streets, brown leather school bags swung over their shoulders. The tired murmurs of merchants floated to the rooftops with the smoke of their morning cigarettes, rolling their aching shoulders back as they opened shop for the day.

And the station—I exhaled, listening to the rustling of files and muffled yawns of drowsy officers and staff—*is coming to life once again.*

I stiffened as a shadow loomed over my shoulder, muscles relaxing as a warm mug of coffee was placed on the windowsill before me.

"Good morning, V." I turned to stare up at my brother, the soft smile on his lips the same as it always was. His brown hair was combed back, blue eyes bright and awake, the boy ironed and pressed neatly into his uniform of a white buttoned shirt, black tie, and the deep blue jacket that flashed through every hallway in the station.

"Good morning." I instantly brightened, lifting the warm mug in my hands and letting the dark stuff swish around the cup's rim. I blew at the steam, bringing my hands to my lips and letting the bitter liquid wake my body up. A smile tickled my lips as I raised an eyebrow at Victor.

"No sugar, light milk." He read my mind, shrugging, but could not contain his grin.

"You finally remembered!"

"Although I still don't understand how you manage to swallow that down." He shivered, eyeing the metal cup sourly.

"Dramatic thing." I flicked his forehead, my brother laughing at the childish gesture. The faint smell of smoke drew my brows together, and I grabbed the fabric of Victor's shirt, pulling him down closer to me.

"Stop! You'll wrinkle—"

"Have you been smoking?"

His body stiffened, pulling away from my grip, a sheepish smile on his face. "It was just one cigarette."

"Victor!" I groaned, glaring at him firmly, the boy slouching away from my hold. "I really wish you wouldn't pick up Papa's habits."

"I won't, really!" he said quickly. "It just helps with stress."

"It kills you is what it does." I narrowed my eyes at him, bringing my mug back up to my lips.

I couldn't ignore the tightness in my chest as my brother rubbed at the bright silver badge that clung to his blazer, the familiar outline of the crown worn by every Imperial Officer, every Silver Soldier in the King's prefecture. He brought his eyes up to me, the tension instantly forced from my stance.

"Speaking of Papa." He crossed his arms tiredly. "He wants me to sit in for a meeting this afternoon, but I'm not exactly sure what it'll be about."

My lips pressed together as I instinctively shrank into myself. The Viscount's office was where most of these gatherings were held, and where my father spent most of his time. There he and commanding officers from every prefecture in the kingdom would discuss top secret security measures, high profile investigations, and the abolishment of any illicit operations. Of course Victor would get to attend, it was only natural, after all. He was to assume the role of Viscount eventually. It was inevitable. He couldn't stay as one half of a set forever.

As for me…

My fingers dug into the fabric of my dress shirt.

Papa lost his confidence in me a while ago.

I pulled a smile across my lips in an attempt to shrug off the painful feeling that lingered at the back of my throat. Guilt was easy to read across my brother's features, his eyes darting away from mine, choosing to focus on the swirling patterns across the station's marble floor.

"Sorry, I shouldn't have—"

"Victor."

He looked up at me tentatively, his posture relaxing at my smile. He didn't have to feel guilt for his birthright. *Besides*—my eyes drifted back over to the window, focusing on the silhouette of a young boy, his dark eyes meeting mine through the foggy glass—*I've taken matters into my own hands.*

"It's fine." I shifted my focus back to my brother, his lips turning up gently. "Let me know if you hear anything interesting."

"I doubt I will." He leaned back against the wall. "The meetings have been so dull as of late. Most of our focus is on security instead of actual problem solving."

"Security and safety *are* two very important factors to consider when protecting the Capital City."

"Yes I know, but lately it feels more like we're easing Papa's paranoia rather than actually being productive." He rubbed at his neck.

"You remember the fire, don't you?" I said quietly, letting my arms rest across my chest as my brother sighed.

"How could I forget?"

The Nieve Disaster.

It happened one snowy winter's night almost ten years ago, the Seventh District engulfing itself in hellish flames as two rival gangs burned each other to the ground, killing hundreds of innocent people along with them. If the Imperial Force had only been prepared to deal with such a thing, if Papa had only anticipated such a catastrophe, then maybe it could have been put out faster. Maybe we could have saved a few more.

"Then that should be enough to justify his precautions." A heaviness settled into the air between us.

"I know," he said, voice softer. "It just feels like we aren't doing enough anymore. Papa's focus has shifted to the smaller things instead of the bigger problems."

"Those problems being?"

"The rise in crime!" my brother exclaimed. "Sure, it's not as bad as it was a decade ago, but we're seeing a steady rise in violent cases with no answers. It almost feels like we're being led by the nose, like every criminal in the Capital is two steps ahead of us!"

A pang of guilt struck me, but I played it off easily. *If only he knew, if only Father—*

No. I swallowed harshly, slicking the stray hairs away from my face. *Everything that I have done, everything that I will continue to do, is for justice.*

"I'm sure everything will work itself out soon enough." I rubbed at my neck, the tense muscles leaving me sore. "Just don't get too worked up about it, alright?"

He said nothing, staring off in thought. I moved my eyes back to the window, eyes scanning for the boy.

The hairs on my neck pricked up at the intense stare on my back. My muscles went rigid as I avoided Victor's prying gaze.

Relax. I exhaled, slowly turning back to smile at him. *He couldn't know.*

In truth, when it came down to it there was very little I could hide from my brother. We were one in the same, after all. *But I have always been the sharper twin.*

He sighed, clenching his jaw. "You're a liar."

I froze, lips parting to defend myself, but Victor cut me off.

"You didn't just get here. You were on the night shift again, weren't you?"

My shoulders relaxed at his question, the tension in my posture from just a moment earlier melting away completely as I flashed a sheepish grin.

"V, I really wish you wouldn't do this to yourself." He sighed, running a hand through his tailored locks.

"I'm fine." I pulled a stray strand of hair back, twisting it into my loose bun. "You don't need to worry about me, Vic. I just wanted to get some paperwork done. Besides…" I smiled, trying to lighten the mood. "Is it that obvious?"

"Have you taken a look in the mirror as of late?" He crossed his arms, still painfully serious.

Of course I had. The deep sunken circles that framed my eyes had become a familiar feature of mine, the sickly pale tint of my skin from restless nights as common now as the heavy fog that clung to Nieve year round. Sleep had not been a friend of mine since I was a child. For when I slept, I dreamt, and it was in my dreams that the masked man waited and watched.

"Well you don't look so dapper yourself." I set my mug on the desk and turned to leave, sighing heavily as his hand caught my wrist. I turned back to my brother reluctantly, my heart throbbing at the frown on his face.

"You know, part of the appeal of a desk job are the flexible hours and steady atmosphere."

I rolled my eyes. "I've never been one for those things anyways."

"When was the last time you slept, V?"

"I think I have a short nap scheduled for next Wednesday, why?"

"I'm serious, Valeria."

I frowned at the use of my full name, quickly making obvious the level of his concern.

"You need to take your health more seriously. You can't just keep chasing—"

"Understood." I cut him off, forcing my lips to stretch into a smile. I was in no mood to have *that* conversation again.

5

He caught himself, pursing his lips and releasing his soft hold on my wrist. A heavy weight sat in my chest, but I ignored it, standing on my toes and pressing a quick kiss to my brother's cheek, patting the spot playfully afterwards.

"I'm off then," I said as I headed for the exit. "Don't wait up for me!"

I entered the hall, picking up my pace as soon as I was out of his line of sight. *These lies*—I shook away the guilt, inhaling deeply—*I just have to keep them up for a little longer.*

The truth was, whether or not Victor ended up leaking what our father and his associates discussed in their meetings didn't matter. I would find out soon enough either way.

My hand trailed up to my collarbone, the cool metal of my mother's pendant resting comfortably beneath the fabric of my uniform. I inhaled deeply, a sense of comfort warming my tense limbs as I approached the window at the end of the hall, scanning the cobblestone streets.

My squinted gaze halted, focusing on the young boy, his unruly hair pushed under a worn flat cap. A pair of dark eyes stared up at me, his clenched fist flashing one finger, then four, then three, before shoving his hands deep into the pockets of his work trousers.

143. I nodded at him before turning on my heels to continue back from where I had come from.

The Blue Swan, a popular underground speakeasy on the corner of 14th street in the Third District. One known to be crawling with dangerous individuals and leaking with criminal intent. My father had never been able to lawfully raid the place—the booming crime lords that owned the establishment always slipped through his fingers. *Of course that's where he wants to meet.* I rolled my head back, loosening the tension in my gait.

Fair enough.

I met my brother's eyes from across the lively office, his face brightening as he noticed my presence. I lifted a hand to wave but stopped it midway. I was a liar, a fraud—that wasn't something that I could deny.

But—I swallowed the guilt, giving him a smile just as he turned to leave—*I am going to avenge her.*

I am going to avenge us all.

Dark, heavy jazz poured from the live band like melted chocolate, coating the speakeasy in a thick sheet of luster and mystery. I pressed my velvety lips together, gloved hands moving to smooth over the length of my flapper dress, the deep green fabric blending with the black strands that hung down around my knees.

Sneaking out of the estate was shamefully simple, my window serving as a virtually silent and efficient means of escape. The dead of night worked as a solid cover, the rooftops of Nieve proving to be an easy feat even in such a fitted dress.

The atmosphere was weighted, as if the room were not only packed with the masked people that filled it but with all they had done. My eyes trailed over the maroon walls, tracing over the golden details that laced their way up and down them.

Old money, I thought, walking toward the edge of the room. *Corrupt politician?* My eyes scanned the room. *No.* I couldn't help but smile at my deduction.

Drug lord, most certainly.

I turned away in disgust at the sight of the round man seated toward the bar, a hoard of reluctant young girls being pulled into his booth as he laughed, flaunting his money. The weight of the leather harness on my inner thigh felt heavier, reminding me of the unlicensed pistol that waited strapped to my lower body.

Filthy animal. I bit back my tongue, gloved hands clenching at my sides. *If only I were here on my own accord, then I'd really show him a good*—

I stiffened at the hand on my shoulder, turning quickly to meet the face of a black cat, the fine velvet mask stitched together plainly but elegantly, leaving a pair of tea-colored eyes to stare into mine.

"Pardon me." Flint's hushed voice took the tension out of my clenched fists. "My Lady, is that you?"

I nodded my head, watching his shoulders relax.

"I hardly recognized you, Miss."

"I'm glad to hear that." I ran my hand through the ends of the blonde wig, the short strands brushing at my ears. I could never risk coming out to a place like this undisguised. *The Viscount's daughter spotted at a midnight speakeasy*—the news would ruin my father's image, let alone shut down the entire case.

"I could only tell by the mask. You haven't changed it." He tilted his head as he stared. The blue silk mask I wore rested across my nose, leaving only my lips and eyes exposed. The fine fabric was lined with exotic feathers, shades of blue, brown, and green swirling over each other to create the illusion of a peacock. Truthfully I could not part with the mask, its intricate colors and artistic stitches unlike any other I'd seen before, but I'd never admit that.

"Yes, well it was far too much of a hassle to change masks every week." I sighed, pulling at my silk gloves once again. He grinned but said nothing, instead leaning in so close that his curls tickled my ear.

"Two o'clock." My eyes moved at his whispered words, resting on an empty booth, a single man sitting amongst the fine velvet curtains. "In red."

My eyes focused on the blond, a thick cigar clenched between his teeth as he puffed out clouds of musky smoke. Flint pulled back, extending an arm out to me. In this sort of setting, all dressed up and masked, he almost blended in. Nobody would be able to tell that this mysterious man was a child of sixteen, two years my junior. A twinge of regret ran through my bones as I laced my arm through his, but I quickly pushed the feeling back, ignoring the guilt. *This is for justice.* My hand squeezed his arm as we approached the booth. *Everything that I'm doing is for the greater good.*

I was greeted by a sharp grin as I took a seat at the booth, letting my hands rest directly across from J.P. Carrow. They called him a businessman in the Underworld, a clean-cut older man with deceitful eyes and a tricky way with words.

A crook. I clasped my hands over the table as he sat up straight. *The worst kind.*

"Lady Spider Lily." His serpent-like features narrowed as he smiled, extending a hand out to me. I swallowed my repulsion, placing a gloved hand in his, biting my tongue as he pressed his lips against the fine fabric. "Always a pleasure."

Spider Lily. I stiffened, sitting up in the deep red booth. *A flower rumored to lead one to death.*

I had earned the nickname after about two months of creating this persona. I was the leak, the one who knew the ins and outs of the Force, the person who could let you slip right through the law's tight grip for a very specific price. *Information trading.*

Treasonous? Possibly, but the past six months of going undercover and leaking tiny bits of harmless information had gotten me further in my case than the past nine years my father had spent investigating in the open.

I pulled away from his grasp and rested my hands in my lap, feeling the soft cushions shift as Flint took a seat at my right.

"I appreciate you meeting me here on such short notice. I'd imagine that the all-knowing Spider Lily has quite the busy schedule." Carrow's eyes wandered over the bare skin of my arms as he took another puff from his cigar, blowing the smoke out of his nose. I turned my face away, resisting the urge to gag at the thick smell of tobacco, a smile pricking the man's lips at my obvious distaste.

"I suppose I should get to the point." He sighed, leaning his elbows over the table as he stared into my eyes. "I will be receiving a shipment at the docks in a few days." He pressed the butt of his cigar into the ashtray, twisting the stub as it fizzled out. "One that I'd prefer not to be dissected by the Silvers."

He wants to know when the docks will be free of officers. I clenched the fabric of my dress in my fists, feeling Flint's eyes on me. I leaned in close to Flint's ear, whispering a few words, before facing Carrow once again.

"This shipment." Flint repeated my words, his sharp eyes moving to stare at the man. "What would it entail?"

The man's eyes never left mine, a smile creeping across his pointed features.

"Hallucinogens."

My hands stiffened, fingers going rigid as the word left his lips. I squeezed my thighs, trying to hide any sort of reaction, leaning toward Flint once more. His brows knitted together at my words but nodded nonetheless.

"*Dream Stitching,*" Flint said slowly, not understanding the words as they escaped him. "That's what they're for, isn't that right?"

"My, what a clever lady indeed." Carrow grinned in amusement, straightening the collar of his shirt. "If you must know, then yes, there seems to have been a rise in demand for"—he trailed off, looking around before meeting my narrowed eyes—"fantasy."

"You mean lies?" Flint repeated my words, his back stiff.

"I mean false realities, illusions." Carrow's voice had sharpened, the smile on his face twitching for a moment before recovering. "The world can be such a horrible place. What's wrong with dreaming a little?"

"Nothing." My words were sharp on Flint's tongue. "It's when those dreams are twisted into nightmares that a problem arises."

"The shipment." Carrow's fist slammed against the table, rattling it. I gripped the pistol at my thigh, finding Flint's hand beneath the table on mine, stopping me. The man paused, clearing his throat and brushing back blond strands of hair as he collected himself. "Will I be able to receive the cargo without intervention?"

My hand relaxed, sliding off the gun's cool metal. These people were dangerous—I couldn't forget that.

I swallowed harshly, regret twisting itself into my chest like a rusted blade. *Am I really about to help this crook? Help him smuggle drugs into the kingdom?* I looked over at Flint, his eyes staring ahead intently. He understood, that's why he was here. He trusted me completely.

"I couldn't tell you," Flint said, my breath tickling his neck as I whispered. "But your best bet would be to intercept the packages on a Wednesday, when the moon is high in the sky. The docks should be almost completely free of officers."

Carrow grinned, leaning back in his seat. My stomach was heavy, swishing with uncertainty as his slitted gaze ran down my figure.

"Now the payment," Flint said suddenly, his arms tense as he stared daggers at the man. Carrow's smile fell, eyes flitting between the boy and I before he leaned forward in his seat once again.

"Of course." He flashed a toothy grin, lacing his fingers together. "I had one of my men go through everyone's belongings at the White Rabbit."

I leaned closer at his words, my heartbeat quickening.

"They found cats, bears, birds…" He sighed, shaking his head mockingly. "But not a single wolf's mask."

I felt myself deflate, the guilt of what I'd done intensifying. It was disappointing, but what had I expected? It'd been nine years since my mother's brutal murder and I was barely any closer to solving her case. To avenging her death.

"Very well," Flint said, and I stiffened, feeling his hand hover over mine, barely brushing the fabric of my glove.

"Good doing business with you." Carrow's eyes never left mine as I stood, turning swiftly on my heel and following Flint's steady figure back into the sea of masked people. *A fool.* I bit my lip, clenching my hands at my sides. *A fool is what you are.*

Of course he hadn't found anything, just as the man before him hadn't, and yet I couldn't seem to let it go. I couldn't move on, not with the gaping hole in my heart. Not while my mother's killer was out there somewhere.

I stumbled back, a shoulder colliding with my own, pushing me aside as a man hurriedly forced his way through the crowd. I steadied myself, narrowing my eyes, the back of his head disappearing into the colorful mass of people. *How rude.* I gritted my teeth, a sudden anger flushing out my earlier disappointment.

"Are you alright, Miss?" Flint's hand caught my arm carefully, soft eyes meeting my irritated gaze. My hands slowly relaxed, my head turning back to the crowd to see that the man had completely vanished.

"I'm fine." I pulled out of his grip, taking a deep breath. "I'm just ready to leave. I hate these sorts of places."

He said nothing, standing quietly at my side as I pulled at my gloves once again. Another night spent beneath this facade, another day full of alibis and deceptions. I met Flint's waiting gaze, his posture straightening. *Another day of pulling him further and further below the surface.* I moved to stare at my feet, avoiding his undoubting eyes.

Flint had been by my side for two years now, unwaveringly ready at my beck and call since the day we first met in that dark and horrible place. I had dragged him along with me ever since, chasing any and every lead, in the dead of night and in the early moments of dawn, finding nothing over and over again. *And yet—*

"My Lady?" His soft voice caught my attention once more, forcing me to meet his furrowed gaze.

And yet he still trusts me completely.

My head snapped up at the sound of breaking glass, screams erupting from the speakeasy's entrance as the windows shattered. My hand gripped Flint's collar, pulling him to the ground with me.

"What's happening? What—" I put a finger up, his voice going silent as my narrowed eyes tried to focus between the cracks of running people. *A gang dispute? Not in a place like this.* I lifted my head a bit, blood running cold at the flashes of deep blue toward the front of the establishment.

"Bloody hell." I gritted my teeth, gripping Flint's arm as I crawled in the opposite direction. *Why the hell are there Silvers here? I thought Papa didn't have enough evidence of criminal activity to actually warrant an investigation!*

"Besides that..." I groaned as Victor's words played themselves over in my head *"Father wants me to sit in for a meeting this afternoon, but I'm not exactly sure what it'll be about."*

"Of course," I muttered to myself as I glanced back tentatively, watching as Carrow was slammed down onto his booth's table, hands bound behind his back. "Thanks for the heads up, Vic."

We reached the back wall, Flint's hands feeling across the fine fabric that lined it, stopping over a small ridge. He grunted, digging his nails into the gap, the narrow door opening with a *click*.

Back doors, I thought, slipping through the cramped space, Flint at my heels. *These sorts of places always have them.*

The cluttered room was foggy, the humidity of the space clinging to my exposed skin like a wet garment. *We're underground.* I scanned the dark space. The speakeasy could only be entered by going down a flight of stairs, meaning this room was still below street level.

"There," Flint said. I followed his gaze to the small window at the top corner of the wall. It was just big enough for us to slip through, but where it rested was a completely different problem. It must've led into the street, but we were quite a ways below. Flint and I were roughly the same height, him having a mere inch on me, and with the frame towering over our heads, there was no way for us to climb out.

Angry voices barked on the other side of the wall, the two of us stiffening at their proximity. They probably wouldn't find us, at least not for a while, but the thought of slipping back into the estate in the morning light made my stomach twist.

"Quick." Flint ripped the dark mask from his face, pushing his unruly hair back as he crouched in front of the window. "Just climb on, I'll hoist you up."

"Absolutely not." A laugh escaped my lips as I stared at the expectant boy. "I'm not leaving you here."

"You don't really have a choice, do you Miss?"

I crossed my arms over my chest as he stared up at me, his hands still on his knees as he crouched down by the wall.

"Flint," I said, an uneasiness filling my chest. "I got us into this mess. I always do. You can't expect me to just—"

"Please."

I froze at the tone of his voice. So quiet, the same as it was the day we first met.

"I know that what we do isn't exactly right, but I choose to follow you anyways. I do that because you care about these cases, and it's because you refuse to give up that I'm even here to begin with." His dark eyes met mine, the brown orbs squinting into a gentle smile. "So please go. I'll be right behind you."

I bit back my objections, the clatter of breaking bottles from behind us sending a shiver up my spine. He was right, I couldn't risk getting caught, especially not dressed up like this.

"Fine then." I exhaled, peeling the black heels off my sore feet. "Hold still now."

I held my breath as I stepped onto his back, the boy grunting softly as I found my balance. I bit my lip, stretching my arms, fingers reaching for the window's edge.

"Just a bit further." I gasped as he shifted beneath me, my feet moving to rest on his shoulders.

"I'm going to stand upright," Flint breathed, and I swallowed harshly, feeling his careful hands wrap around my ankles. He stood up slowly, fingers gripping my skin tightly. My hands clung to the edge of the windowsill, unclasping the simple lock that kept the frigid night air out. The window swung open, the space just wide enough for me to slip through. I huffed, jumping off his shoulders and hoisting the upper half of my body through the window.

"Careful," he called as my feet kicked through the air.

"I'm trying to be," I said through gritted teeth. I gripped the top of the wooden frame, finally pulling the rest of my body out into the cold night air. A tired breath escaped my lips as the hard stone street pressed against my limbs, a shiver rippling through me as the wind tickled my skin. I crawled back toward the window, sticking my head through, Flint's relieved expression staring back up at me.

"As soon as it's quiet, slip out the way we came in," I whispered, my hands gripping the frame. He nodded, a small smile on his lips as he stared up at me. My heart throbbed, the guilt of leaving him behind ready to swallow me whole, but I pushed it to the back of my mind. *There is no point in staying.* My grip on the frame tightened. *I would only cause more trouble.*

"Call the estate as soon as you're home, alright? Promise me."

A breathy laugh escaped the boy as he leaned against the stone wall of the hidden room. I pursed my lips, his soft eyes peering up at me beneath curly strands of hair.

"I promise." He rested his head against the wall, dimples appearing as he grinned. "Now go!"

I released the windowsill, standing to my feet slowly. *That boy.* I crossed my arms over my chest, the night air biting at my exposed skin. *I have to stop dragging him through the shadows. It isn't right.*

I stilled, moving my back to rest against the wall as voices echoed from the front of the building. *Damn it Vic*, I cursed at him internally, moving to peer over the side. *How could you not have mentioned the raid?*

I stared at the Silvers, their proud backs facing me as they chatted, blue uniforms pressed and neat.

They had obviously been planning this for a while.

I slipped past the edge of the building, bare feet moving soundlessly as I flitted from shadow to shadow, the exposed skin of my back running cold as it pressed against the outer wall of the next building.

Much too easy. I sighed, slightly disappointed with the lack of a challenge. *I have to talk to Papa about working on their awareness.*

A sudden chill ran up my spine, eyes widening at the sudden shift in atmosphere. I had frozen, my limbs completely still as my head slowly raised to scan my surroundings. I had felt it of course—that unnerving feeling that raised the hairs on the back of my neck. The unsettling sensation of being watched.

My wide eyes stopped at the rooftop of the building before me, focusing on a still figure that stood about a floor above myself. I didn't know how much time had passed before he moved, the silhouette of a trench coat blowing back in the wind. That's when I saw it. The dark shadow of something on his face, the outline of a mask. I knew the shape well—it visited me every night in my dreams, after all.

The sickening curve of a snout.

Chapter 2

FEAR WAS A FRIGID ENEMY, one that chilled my body to the bone much faster than the Nieve air. But it wasn't as strong as the kick of adrenaline that flooded my veins.

I hadn't felt my fingers move, trailing toward the inside of my thigh to retrieve the weapon. All I knew was that before I could realize it, the pistol was in my shaky grip, my hands cocking it in one swift movement.

My heart pounded in my chest, vibrating through my eardrums as I steadied my breathing. *Relax, relax Valeria.* I swallowed harshly, the figure still standing motionless. *You're in public. You can't act so recklessly!*

I forced my tense hands to move, slowly pointing the gun toward the ground. I needed to calm down, to get a grip on the situation. I couldn't shoot, not when there was a chance that I could be wrong.

The figure stared down at me, tilting its masked face as I coerced my shaking limbs to a standstill. I squinted up at the man, parting my lips, but just as the grip on my gun loosened, he was off, disappearing across the rooftops as if he had never been there to begin with.

"Hey!" I yelled, stiffening as the distant officers' voices grew quiet. I cursed at myself, my steps silent as I ran along the expanse of the building, following the masked man's faint shadow. There was no way that I was going to lose him, not when there was a sliver of hope that he could be *the one.*

My breaths were heavy as I picked up speed, the seams of my dress splitting as they stretched.

There, I thought, relief flooding through me. We were approaching the end of the rooftop, a vast sea of emptiness standing between the man and the next building. The moon came into view, the pale light reflecting off the figure's crooked grin, the man taking a moment to look down at me before leaping off the building's edge, his body suspended in the chilly air before reaching the ledge of another.

Impossible. I slowed, watching his back disappear into the dark of night. *No normal person would have been able to make that jump. It just isn't possible.* My heart raced wildly in my chest as he ran further and further away.

I'm going to lose him. My breaths were uneven as I tried to trail along the expanse of the building. Whether or not he was the killer, I was going to be abandoned here without the answer, left to dwell on it for the remainder of my restless life. I yelled out in frustration, gripping at the short wig that still clung to my head. My panicked gaze scoured the street anxiously, fixating on a metal ladder, one that led to the very same roof. It clung to the wall of the building, serving as an emergency fire escape that residents could let down if needed, but one far too high for anyone on the ground to reach. My gaze drifted to a loose end of rope, hanging from what looked like a locked merchant's booth, a wooden cubicle that sat right at the ladder's base. My shoulders slumped at the realization of what I had to attempt.

I have already come this far.

I swallowed my doubts, strapping the pistol to my thigh once again and running over to the wooden shop, trembling fingers tugging at the splitting rope. It was scratchy against my palms, the twisted strands worn and fragile.

Too much pressure and it will definitely snap.

I took a few steps back, wrapping the end of it around my hand and pulling tight.

"Here goes nothing," I muttered, running as fast as I could, keeping my grip stiff as I jumped, my feet hitting the hard wood of the booth and pushing the rest of my body onto its low hanging roof. I breathed out, momentarily relieved at my success, but quickly scrambled to my feet.

I grunted, gripping the cool metal of the ladder as I clambered to the rooftop. The icy night air whistled past my ears as I climbed higher, leaving my nose red and my vision blurry. My fingers took hold of the roof's edge, pulling my body over its ledge, my wild eyes spotting the tiny back of the shadowy figure. A heavy breath of relief fell through my lips, the cold melting away from my form as I ran, feet slipping in and out of the roof's ridges, keeping my soaring body from tumbling to the ground. My blood ran hot in my veins, oxygen searing through my lungs as I ran, the breath stilling in my chest at every jump.

The distance between us grew shorter and shorter, my squinted eyes making out the back of a trench coat as I closed the gap. The man's slender figure weaved its way across the uneven roof tops, moving so swiftly I could have sworn that he wasn't running at all, but floating, simply riding the wind's current, his heavy boots never even touching the smooth tiles that lined the roof. My eyes widened as his pace picked up, a strangled gasp escaping me as his foot propelled off the building's edge, hands gripping the ledge of another.

He barely made it. My feet sped up, watching as he hoisted himself up and over the roof. *He's tiring out.*

I held my breath, kicking through the air as I leapt, fear coursing through me as my body thrashed in the vast emptiness of the moment, before tumbling over onto the next roof. I winced, the end of my dress finally tearing to reveal an ugly scrape down my thigh. My limbs were heavier now, the dull pain pushing some of the adrenaline out of my bloodstream, but I stood to my feet nonetheless, gazing across the flat rooftop.

This must be a factory. I panted, looking around wildly. *Or something of the sort.* Most homes in Nieve had slanted roofs, making them much more difficult to climb.

It was silent, even the wind's howling taking a short intermission as my bare feet crept across the scraggly gravel roof. My eyes flashed across the wide open space, an uneasiness creeping up my spine as I stared into the thick nothingness.

Where did he go? My hand reached for my thigh, the rough slit in my dress now exposing the harness. *He couldn't have just—*

I stiffened, grabbing the pistol and pressing its barrel into something behind me just as a thin blade was held against my throat. A deep rumble of laughter erupted against my ear, sending vibrations down my spine.

"You've got sharp instincts." A grin was evident in the man's voice as he spoke, my gun digging into his abdomen as his blade touched the skin of my neck. "For someone senseless enough to chase an assassin."

Assassin. My grip on the pistol trembled as I tried to steady my racing heart.

The blade, the mask—I swallowed the fear that clawed its way up my throat—*this all feels much too familiar.*

My eyes searched the rooftop fiercely, looking for something, anything to give me the upper hand.

Calm down. Breathe, Valeria. I steadied my grip on the pistol, finger ready on the trigger. *At the end of the day, it's a matter of which is faster—the pull of his wrist or my trigger finger.*

My shoulders relaxed as an idea flashed through my mind, and I internally cursed myself before letting both of my hands go limp, allowing my knees to buckle beneath me. My head fell forward, his free hand instinctively gripping my wilting body. He stiffened, and in a moment of surprise moved the blade away from my throat. I swallowed my fear and in one motion switched the pistol to my left and grabbed the edge of his knife with my right, feeling the blade slice through my palm. His grip on my waist tightened as his hand tried twisting the weapon from my grasp, but it was no use.

Even as the blade ripped the flesh of my palm raw, I was not letting go.

"You're braver than you look," he said, his grip on the thin knife tightening. I sunk my teeth into my lip, my breaths strained as I resisted the urge to cry out in pain. "It's a shame you'll have to die so soon."

"You," I said through gritted teeth, feeling the sticky warmth of blood run down my arm. "Let me look you in the eyes."

"You know, for someone I've never met before, you seem to hold a lot of resentment toward me." His breath sent goosebumps down my neck, the pistol in my left hand trembling at my side. "So, *who was it?*"

My spine went stiff, his words sinking their teeth into my skin.

"A lover perhaps?" I flinched, shivering at the icy quality of his voice. "Or was it a family member I killed?"

I clenched my teeth, crying out as I twisted the blade fully in my hand so that I was now facing the killer, the trembling gun aimed at his head. He released the grip on my waist, the stinging pain of my palm fading to a dull ache as I met his eyes. A bitter taste sat at the back of my tongue, my strength abandoning me as my posture slumped.

It wasn't him. My trembling hand loosened on the blade, lips quivering as I repressed the pathetic whimpers that lingered at the back of my throat. *Of course it wasn't him.*

The man that stood at the barrel of my gun was far too young to have been my mother's killer, and his eyes—they were a deep green, the type of unforgiving shade that clawed its way through gritty snow every winter.

Full of hatred, but not the same as the pair I was looking for.

And framing them was not the thick grey of a wolf's mask, but the burnt orange of a fox.

Before I could fully process the situation I had put myself in, the gun was swatted out of my weak grip, a gloved hand gripping my neck and slamming my back into the hard brick of the chimney. A strangled gasp escaped me as I clawed at his hand, the decorative mask falling from my face at the impact.

A way out. My bulging eyes looked around wildly as the air was knocked out of my chest. *Find a way out!*

The short blade rested below my chin, just touching my skin when the killer froze, his grip on my throat loosening. I heaved, my burning lungs pumping air in and out greedily, the knife still pressed against me. My watery eyes met his, bones stiffening at the expression that stared down at me. I flinched as he raised a hand, his gloved fingers digging themselves beneath my pale wig and pulling out a few strands of brown hair. The dark brows furrowed behind his mask, murderous irises swirling with something between confusion and disbelief.

"Would you look at that," he breathed, and I sucked in sharply as the knife's blade pressed against my neck. "Even the Blue Bloods breed criminals. You're the Viscount's daughter, aren't you?"

My blood ran cold, crimson hands clenching at my sides. *This is bad. Very, very bad.* I swallowed quickly, trying to mask any evidence of shock on my features.

"You must have me mistaken," I said, stomach turning as the edges of his lips twitched into a grin.

"I wouldn't lie with a knife to my throat."

"You won't kill me."

He blinked at the sudden harshness of my tone, the killer momentarily caught off guard.

"My father would hunt you down to the last crevices of this earth."

"Are you sure about that?" He cocked his head at me, the thin blade drawing blood as it cut through the first layer of skin. "It looks to me like you're out looking for someone because no one else will."

My hands trembled at my sides, the truth in his words reminding me very quickly of why I had pursued him in the first place.

"Besides, I tend to be *very* thorough when cleaning my hands."

"Just make up your mind." I clenched my teeth, a faint flicker of anger burning through me at his mocking words. "Unhand me or slit my throat. I don't have all night."

False confidence, do not abandon me now. I held his gaze, the bitter cold numbing the fear in my bones.

22

His grin faltered, grip stiffening as we stared at each other. Either way we were both in trouble here. If he were to kill me, his life would get immensely more difficult, even if he could clean it up, and if I were spared I could just as easily identify him and have him arrested—or worse.

My shoulders relaxed as his hand loosened, the metal blade clanging quietly as it hit the ground.

"The Viscount's daughter," he repeated, muttering to himself as his eyes trailed over my face. "Kenneth Anson's little girl. I'm not expected to kneel, am I?"

"You're leaving yourself open and unarmed." I shifted my face away from his, avoiding the topic of my family name. "Not very bright, are you?"

"As if I'd need a blade to kill someone." He brushed my words off easily, hardly budging. "Now, isn't this the part where you try to keep my mouth shut?"

"What is it that you want?" I stumbled unsteadily, my heartbeat still erratic. He was a murderer, a crook—not the type of person who would do things simply out of the goodness of their heart. I'd have to buy his silence. "Money? Information? Just name your price."

"Money, hmm?" His stare never faltered as he spoke, unease creeping up my skin. "If it's Daddy's vault you're offering, then I'll admit, it's tempting—but not tempting enough."

I swallowed the disgust on my tongue as his eyes drifted down my face, taking in my tattered appearance.

"No, I don't think I'll have anything of that sort," he murmured, bile burning at the back of my throat at his prying gaze. "I was actually thinking that we might be able to help each other."

"You're wasting my time." Anger flared through me like a raging storm at his audacity, heavy and uncontrollable. "If you're letting me walk away, then move."

"It would do you well to hear me out."

"You're a criminal, a killer nonetheless." I gritted my teeth at the nerve of his words. "There is nothing in this world that I would want from you."

I pushed past the man, the mangled flesh of my palm aching as I flexed and relaxed my hand.

"You're hunting someone, aren't you?"

I paused, the air in my lungs coming to a standstill, my legs halting on their own.

"You're looking for your mother's killer."

"How could you possibly—"

"Oh please, don't be dense, *Your Grace.*" He scoffed, his dark hair blowing in the harsh breeze. "Your father's face is plastered in every paper alongside the King's, it would've been surprising if I hadn't recognized you at all."

I was silent, panic digging its roots into my lungs as I realized just how much trouble I was in. If I were exposed, if Papa were to find out what I had been doing every week in the dead of night, my life would be over. His leash on me would only tighten, and any chance of avenging my mother would be gone.

No matter what, I couldn't let that happen.

"I won't rat you out, if that's what you're thinking."

"Why would I trust your word?"

"Oh, you most certainly shouldn't." An eerie smile pricked his lips as he took a step forward, approaching my shaky figure. "But I won't, not when keeping your little secret leaves me something to gain."

I didn't like it—the smile that twitched on his lips and the sinister glint in his eyes sent my stomach turning.

"I think we could be very useful to one another."

"Out with it already." I gritted my teeth, the blood on my palms still warm. "Stop walking around your words and say it."

"Let me help catch your killer, and in return help me catch one of my own."

The wind around us howled, threading through the tears in my dress and chilling me to the bone.

"You…" I shook my head, losing my balance momentarily and stumbling back. "You really think I'm stupid enough to shake hands with you?"

"I must admit, I'm insulted." He leaned toward me, ghostly eyes drifting over my face as I clenched my jaw. "Don't be so arrogant, girl. Up until now you've been running in circles pursuing a hopeless investigation, all the while this masked man of yours is probably drinking a cold glass of scotch as he slits the throats of little children."

My hands went limp at my sides, the weight of his words pulling my heart into the depths of my stomach. I didn't like it, how upfront this crook was. That he could so easily speak of this case while my own father could not.

"This is not us *teaming up*. This is a bargain, one you obviously haven't understood the value of yet." He straightened his posture, looking down at me with whispered mirth. "After all, I should mention I'm not just *any* killer."

"Am I supposed to know who you are?" I spat, disgusted by the unnerving pride that radiated from him.

"No." He smiled a horrible grin. "I'd hope not. But working at the Imperial Station, I'd assume I cause your *dear old daddy* quite a bit of trouble."

"Nonsense." I blinked hard, my head pounding from the cold, the throbbing in my palm not helping my condition whatsoever. "My father solves almost every case he receives."

"*Almost.*" He tilted his head at me, my brows coming together before relaxing, my shoulders falling forward as I realized exactly who I had stumbled upon.

"*Alias Black.*" His name was vile on my tongue, the nausea of this man's sins climbing up my throat as I forced them back down.

"Very good, Silver," he mocked, leaning forward a bit, his eyes glacial. "Although a bit slow, I will admit."

It wasn't the cold that shook my limbs this time, but disgust and terror at the man standing before me, black and white images of carved-up bodies piled atop each other flashing through my mind like a roll of film.

Alias Black, Nieve's most renowned hitman—I took a shaky step back—*the reason people started locking their windows and doors at night.*

"Alias Black, huh?" I had asked my father one particularly stormy night in his study. The rain had hammered down relentlessly on the silent streets of the First District, only the faint light of a candle illuminating my father's face. *"Is he part of a crime syndicate? Owned by some rich bastard in the Underworld?"*

"No." Father had sighed, rubbing his forehead tiredly. *"As far as we know he acts on his own terms, taking jobs as he sees fit. And killing, because it's what he knows how to do."*

"How…" My voice was shaky, Alias Black's gaze unmoving as I struggled to regain my composure. "How do you know I won't turn around right now and out you to the Viscount? I hope your arrogance didn't let you forget who I am."

"Because you've had every opportunity to turn and run, yet here you still are." He stopped, letting his gloved hands rest behind his back. "Besides, you wouldn't risk them finding out about your little hobby, would you *Lady Spider Lily*?"

"Is that a threat, *Ripper*?"

"It's an opportunity." His words were clipped. "One I wouldn't let go to waste."

I swallowed hard, my lips trembling with the cold, the thin silk fabric of my dress leaving me practically exposed to the merciless night air.

He has a point. I breathed, thinking of all the sleepless nights disguised in silks and decorative masks. *I can't keep this persona up forever.*

Sooner or later I was going to slip up. I was going to get caught, and the consequences that would follow would be much worse than my father confining me to a desk, much worse than what happened the last time I had let my mother's murder swallow me whole.

For the first time that night, my eyes had dropped from the hitman's masked face, spotting the hilt of a second blade tucked behind the dark fabric of his coat. His hands wore tightly fitted black gloves, resting loosely at his sides, ready to strike at any given moment.

Until now I had been wandering blindly in the dark, feeling around for anything remotely related to the case and jumping headfirst at any sign of suspicion. *But a killer*—I shivered as the wind bit at my skin again—*a killer would know the ins and outs of the Underworld, where I barely knew where to find the front door.*

"Don't misunderstand. I'm not asking you to trust me," he said, the movement of his lips almost ghostlike. "I'm simply stating that if you want justice as badly as you claim, it wouldn't be wise to turn your greatest asset away."

"And what's in it for you?" I said, all common sense flushed out by the cold.

"For me?" He grinned, a horrible glimmer in his emerald eyes. "I'm looking for a man of my own, one that could very well be the same killer you're hunting."

"Why?"

He paused at my question, a hand twitching at his side.

"Let's just say that he and I have some unfinished business." He extended a hand out to me, eyes burning viciously into my own. "Well then? How about it, Blue Blood? *Won't you sell me your noble soul?*"

I tell myself it was the cold, that it was the fact that my lips had gone blue and my hands numb from the night's violent breeze that drowned out the last bit of my common sense, holding my conscience's head below the water. Because for whatever reason I had lifted my bloodied hand, resting it tentatively in the palm of his gloved one. He stared at me intently, not surprised in the least by my choice.

I gritted my teeth, crying out as he squeezed my mangled hand in his, pulling my shivering body closer with his constricting grip.

His gaze remained unchanged, even as my blood dripped down our hands and onto the roof of the factory, even as my empty one reached up, ripping the mask from his face in one swift motion. The silence between us thickened as the mask clambered to the ground, his eyes never leaving mine.

"Rowan Marrow." His lips twitched into a smile, the tanned skin of his exposed face glowing in the moonlight. "I'll be seeing you very soon, *Your Grace.*"

And with that he disappeared, jumping off the rooftop, only the tight presence of his grip remaining, stinging my palm.

The lying noble and the notorious killer. A bitter taste slid over my tongue. *How horribly laughable.*

Chapter 3

THE CLOUDS SHIFTED ABOVE MY head, letting a few scarce rays of light slip through, reminding the people of Nieve that beneath the thick curtain of grey that seemed to cling to the kingdom, the sun still existed.

I winced, flexing my bandaged hand and instantly regretting it. I had barely made it home the night before, stumbling across the rooftops of the First District and somehow managing to swing my tired body through my open window. I must've laid there for hours, hanging in the uncomfortable space between sleep and consciousness before forcing my staggering body to the bathroom to disinfect and wrap my mangled hand. I tugged on the brown leather glove that clung to it now, its thick fabric stopping just above my wrist and concealing the wound completely. *Explaining my injured hand to Victor would be hard enough*—I swallowed, a pillar of unease rolling in my stomach—*but trying to lie to my father? Impossible.*

Lies. I pursed my lips, digging my aching hand into the pocket of my coat, the other clutching a large paper bag. *No matter how deeply you try to bury them, they always find their way back to the surface.*

That killer had been right about that at the very least. I couldn't keep this investigation up, at least not on my own.

And besides—I pulled at the frilled collar of my shirt, the high neckline suffocating. *I can't keep dragging Flint down these shadowy paths anymore. This is my burden to bear, after all.*

I hadn't heard from him since the night before, my spent body passing out as soon as my wounds were clean. I had tried to phone him this morning but had no success.

I stopped, closing my eyes at the familiar pit of anxiety building up in my chest. Flint was a smart kid, I knew he was perfectly capable of making it home alone, *but still.* I exhaled heavily, letting the tension melt out of my shoulders.

I stiffened, narrowed eyes widening at the sudden silence of the street. I had sensed it—an unnerving tension in the air, as if I were being watched. My body remained completely still, injured hand moving from my pocket to rest at my hip out of instinct, reminding myself of my vulnerability when I found the unauthorized pistol missing.

I wasn't given a moment to recover, a gasp escaping my lips as I was shoved forward, two slender arms swinging themselves over my shoulders and gripping me from behind.

"Come on, Val."

I exhaled heavily at the familiar voice, catching glimpse of a few stray curls as I turned my head.

"Your reaction time is getting awfully slow."

"Heavens, Lou." I swallowed my surprise as she released her grip on me, her bright eyes meeting mine. "You startled me."

"That was sort of the point."

"Yeah well"—I let my shoulders relax, moving my hand back into the pocket of my coat—"I won't be needing a coffee then. You scared the sleep right out of me."

"As if you were ever one for sleep." She grinned, the scarce rays of sun illuminating the tan skin of her face. Lou was a pretty girl, with thick brows framing olive eyes, her quick hands slicking back unruly curls as she matched my speed.

"What are you doing up so early?" She linked our arms together, her feet falling in step with mine. "Isn't it your day off?"

"How do you manage to memorize my schedule yet consistently fail to remember yours?"

"It truly is a mystery."

"Papa left rather early this morning," I said, holding up the paper bag. "So I figured I'd stop by and drop off some breakfast."

"He left for the first shift again today?" Lou furrowed her brows, tilting her head at me. An unpleasant lump sat in my stomach as I thought of my father's state, the tension seeping back into my shoulders.

"Yeah, he's been doing that quite a bit lately hasn't he?"

I turned my head, meeting her soft gaze, her hands squeezing mine. Louisa Tate had always been an intense force of nature, her instincts as sharp as her tongue, the brazen girl speaking her mind without a filter and always keeping her fists loose and ready when needed.

And yet—I couldn't stop the small smile from spreading across my lips at her tender expression—*she somehow manages to look like that.*

My eyes shifted focus to the space behind her, a wave of relief washing over me at the familiar brick building that sat across the street, or rather at who was standing at its entrance. Flint's unruly figure was clad in brown work pants, a matching pair of suspenders clinging to his loosely buttoned shirt as he lazily leaned against The Wild Iris Bookstore's crumbling exterior, his tired eyes fluttering shut every few seconds. *Breathe, Valeria.* I sighed, my grip on the bag tightening at the sight of the scruffy boy. *He's fine.*

My attention was quickly caught by the bookstore's entrance slamming open, the well-kept shadow of Oliver Brightley slipping down the short stack of stairs after shutting the door behind him.

"Ollie!" Lou squealed, and I couldn't suppress my grin as the young man flinched at the sound of her voice.

"Good morning, ladies." He reluctantly turned to face us, the deep bronze of his skin nearly matching in shade with the sleek mahogany door.

"Ollie, dear," Lou sang, her curly hair bouncing about as she skipped across the short distance between us, my steps not far behind hers. "Won't you keep two beautiful women company on their morning walk to the station?"

"Louisa, please refrain from using that insufferable nickname." He sighed tiredly, running a hand over his shaved head, fingers grazing the short textured hairs. "We aren't children anymore."

"You're no fun," she muttered, ignoring his request completely. "But I guess that's what's so refreshing about you."

"Yeah Oliver, walk with us." I smiled, his brown eyes meeting mine through the thick lenses of his glasses. "I'll even treat you to your first cup of the day."

"Second." He smiled, digging his hands into the pockets of his pants as he caved, joining us. "I had my first cup of coffee about two hours ago."

"I'll never understand people who willingly wake up at the ass crack of dawn." Lou sighed, Oliver grinning as she crinkled her nose.

"Well I don't spend half of my nights in an office, so I guess it's a bit different."

"Don't look at me." Lou shook her head. "I've been getting my full six hours a night."

They both slowly turned toward me, staring intently.

"What's with those looks?" I laughed halfheartedly, instinctively digging my bandaged hand deeper into my coat.

"Nothing really," Oliver said gently, avoiding my eyes. "We just worry."

"Because you're starting to look like something out of the mortician's office." Lou shrugged, flinching as Oliver elbowed her in the arm.

"Gee thanks." I laughed, but looked away." They weren't wrong, after all. For the past few years I'd been drifting from one restless night to the next, rarely managing to get three hours of undisturbed sleep a night. Every time I closed my eyes, I kept seeing it. The masked killer and my mother's squirming body in his grip, the image growing more heinous every time it flashed through my mind.

"So Ollie, how's business been?" Lou chirped, changing the subject quickly but keeping her concerned gaze on me.

"Rough." He crossed his arms over his chest as we strolled. "I've got too much to do and too little time to do it. That Jones boy has been helpful though."

"Flint?" I perked up, Oliver smiling at me as he nodded.

"Yes, he's quite the fast learner," Oliver said, "and very diligent with his work."

"That's good to hear." My tense hands loosened at the thought of the boy working in such a quiet and secure place. Oliver's words had dispersed at least some of my anxiety.

"That's right." Lou leaned against my shoulder, the ends of her curls tickling my cheek. "Business should be picking up around this time of year, with the holidays just around the corner."

"Lou, it's barely November," Oliver said.

"It's never too early to be festive."

"I suppose you're right." A smile spread against his lips as he stared ahead, his hands disappearing into the beige fabric of his coat. "That reminds me, I'll be receiving a large shipment from Kairi in the next few days."

"Kairi, huh?" Lou pursed her lips in distaste at the mention of the port city, the bustling island out of Imperial jurisdiction yet managing to cause almost as much trouble as all seven districts combined.

"A shipment?" My head snapped up, the snake-like smile of J.P. Carrow forcing itself into my mind.

"Yes, of some ancient Greek texts." He sighed, and I had to physically restrain myself from slamming my face into the nearest brick building. "I offered to assist in their translation and somehow ended up agreeing to handle half the load myself."

"Hell, Ollie." Lou's shoulders slumped. "You can be such a pushover."

"It's my old professor. I couldn't just say no."

"So I assume we won't be seeing you anytime soon?"

He rubbed his neck sheepishly at her words, Lou groaning dramatically at his obvious answer.

Our steps came to a stop, the wind tickling our faces as we stared up at the familiar marble building. The twisting columns of the station's front entrance towered over us, holding up the weight of all that bustled on the other side of its thick wooden doors. I turned my head, eyes trailing up the towering statue that greeted me every day, King Alpheus' metallic face looking sternly over the streets of Nieve.

"One sugar yeah?" Lou's coat blew back restlessly in the wind as she took a few steps up to the building's entrance.

"Don't bother yourself with it," Oliver said, hugging his coat closer to his body as he stood at the stairs edge. "I'll fix myself a cup back at the bookstore."

"You sure?" I asked, his big brown eyes meeting mine beneath the rims of his glasses.

"Completely." He smiled, our bodies stiffening as the wind blew harder. "But bloody hell, don't you think winter is a bit eager this year?"

I laughed, a grin finding itself across my face as I climbed up the first few steps of the station, the thick fabric of my skirt swishing at my knees. A rush of warmth erupted from the building, chasing away some of the mid-autumn chill. One of the massive double doors hung open, a matching pair of familiar blue eyes meeting my own before moving to my left.

"Oliver! Perfect." Victor's eyes widened before squinting into a smile. "I was just about to head down to The Wild Iris. The Viscount would like your opinion on some texts."

"On second thought, I'll take you up on that coffee," Oliver whispered, his sharp cheeks lifting into a smile. Despite the gnawing Nieve cold, a subtle warmth flooded through me, running steadily through my veins as we stood outside. It almost felt like old times, the four of us terrorizing the neighborhood with our childish endeavors. My grip on the bag tightened as I swallowed the nostalgic feeling, leaving a bittersweet taste on my tongue. *But we aren't kids anymore. We haven't been for a very long time.*

I moved my eyes from Oliver's, my feet beating up the pale stairs to the station. Those times were far behind us now, and as much as

I hated lying to the three of them, I couldn't let them get too close. Oliver and Lou had been by our sides from the moment Victor and I discovered that we weren't the only ones in the world. *They're so kind, so intelligent and full of passion.* I stiffened, Victor's arm brushing my shoulder as I slipped through the station's door. *I can't risk them getting involved in the web I've spun for myself.*

I pinned my lips back into a smile as the station's staff greeted me, giving them a cheerful nod before hurrying down the expanse of the first floor and to the stairs. My empty hand trailed along the pale baluster as I trudged up the steps, my shoulders straightening once I reached the fourth floor of the Prefecture's station. The Viscount's private quarters occupied nearly a third of the floor, the remaining area housing meeting rooms where Papa would often discuss everything from planned raids and leads on terror organizations to security in the Imperial Palace. My posture instinctively stiffened as my free hand brushed the cold metal of the doorknob, pausing to knock twice on the white wooden door.

"Enter."

I bit the inside of my cheek, pushing the door open. My father's back greeted me, his proud figure standing hunched over a pile of paperwork that sat at the edge of his desk. A deep sigh rumbled out of the man, his hand moving to run through his greying hair as he straightened.

"What business?"

The familiar depth of his voice brought a smile to my lips as I walked around him, placing the bag onto his desk. My father's brows knit together before meeting mine, his features relaxing instantly.

"Valeria darling, it's your day off today, isn't it?" The bright light of the office reflected against Father's pale eyes, the blue a much softer shade than my own. "You should be resting."

"But you don't get any days off, Papa." I spotted the crooked black tie that hung lazily around his neck. "You hardly had time to dress this morning, let alone have breakfast."

35

"You can't really have any leisure time as the Viscount," he said, my gloved hands swiftly straightening the black tie, my lips pressing firmly as I ignored the pain in my right. "Especially not in a kingdom like this one."

I paused, pulling my hands away, the injured one receding back into the pocket of my coat. "Has something happened?"

"Things are always happening."

"Something of particular significance, I mean."

"Things haven't been going as well as we'd hoped." He exhaled deeply, walking around the edge of his wooden desk, sitting down in his chair with a quiet groan. "No matter what I do, or how much I plan, they always manage to slip right past my fingers."

"They?" I asked, leaning over my father's desk, my eyes scanning the many documents hungrily. The sudden silence between us stopped my prying gaze, directing it back to my father's frowning face.

Of course. I bit my tongue, swallowing the rest of my questions. *Of course he'd be hesitant.*

It had been almost a year since I had last been involved in a case, Papa cutting me off from my junior unit and appointing me as an office aide after the last time I let my mother's murder consume me. Unlike with my brother, he put a wall up between the Imperial Station and my restless hands, pulling me out of the ranks and even going so far as to speak with me predominantly as Papa and never as the Viscount.

He must've been frightened after all—I stuffed my hand deeper into the pocket of my coat—*unnerved by my obsession with Mother's case.*

I had never been soft like my mother, her tender words spun of gossamer and silk. No, my words were more reminiscent of iron and ice, of brittling brick and crashing waves. My father knew that well, and while his love for me never faltered, he was wary. Worried of where the raging embers in my bones would lead me.

"Colonel Silverstein will be visiting the station in a few weeks or so."

"Uncle Michaelis?" I perked up, a tired smile resting on Papa's features at my expression. Colonel Michaelis Silverstein was the brain behind Nieve's armed forces, working on international conflicts while the Viscount sorted scuffles within the borders. He was also Papa's childhood friend, earning himself the title of Uncle after countless birthdays and holidays spent at our estate.

"He's been given a leave for the holidays for the first time in a while, so he'll be back in the First District once again."

"Will he be bringing his dogs home too?" I grinned as my father sighed, already knowing the answer to that question.

"In the forty years that I've known him I've never seen him without them, so I'd assume so."

I shook my head before turning my attention to the big board that stretched across my father's office, various colored threads linking clues to all sorts of crimes.

He was usually a lot more careful with me here, taking the time to put most of his case-related things away before my arrival, but it seemed as though I had surprised him.

He hated my involvement in cases, dreading what could happen should I get lost in blind pursuit once again.

But still—my smile trembled and I took a breath. "I might've found something."

"Found something?" He raised an eyebrow, his gaze focused on the contents of the brown bag as he dug through it.

"Yes." I swallowed, meeting his eyes hesitantly. "About the masked man."

His hands froze, his body almost flinching at my words. His pale eyes struggled to meet my gaze, muddled by a chronic sadness so deep that I feared part of my father had drowned in it, locked away forever beneath the surface.

"Valeria—"

"Mother couldn't have been his only murder," I pushed on, his body drawing back into his seat as I rambled. "I might've even met someone who has a lead. He may even be a potential victim! We could bring him into the station and—"

"Valeria!"

I winced at my father's booming voice, my words tangling themselves on my tongue as I swallowed them whole.

"Please." He collected himself, his voice a pained whisper as his hands rested shakily on the desk. "Let's not start with this again."

"I never stopped."

"I wish you would."

"Papa," I said, frustration bubbling beneath my skin at his words. "How can you sit there and—"

"I have searched, Valeria." He was much quieter then, as if the pain of remembering held his words by the throat. "I've questioned every soul that's fallen into the palms of my hands and followed every lead to the edges of the earth. "And I found *nothing*."

"And that's an excuse to stop looking?" I bit back, the wound on my hand tearing open as I clenched my fist, the blood warm as it seeped through the thin bandages.

"No." A wave of regret instantly washed over me at the shakiness of his voice, my father's strong eyes pricked with tears as he avoided my gaze. "I could never stop looking. I will spend the rest of my life chasing the bastard that took her away."

My father's vast office seemed infinitely bigger, and I was once again reminded of the bitter truth. That as shiny and courageous as the Viscount appeared, my father was just a man. One just as lost and lonely as myself.

"Papa—" I said, eyes apologetic, but he shook his head, the deep wrinkles across his forehead pulling tiredly.

"I should have protected her. I should have protected you all, but I couldn't. You are such a bright girl, Valeria. I recognize that. But I won't sit here and watch you waste your life away because of my mistake."

"You can't say that, Papa. It wasn't your fault."

"How can you know for certain?"

He was right—that I couldn't deny. Being the Viscount meant being the King's hand in Justice, His Majesty's sword and shield. We had many enemies, more than we could ever know.

"I need you to abandon this hatred, Valeria." His voice was strained, tired, reminding me of the worn leather of my boots. "It will do nothing but gnaw away at you."

"*Abandon it?*" I staggered forward, anger hot in my veins. "I cannot *abandon* anything. This ache, this pull in my chest, it is not something that can so easily be discarded. You should know that better than anyone, Papa!"

"That is exactly why!" His voice echoed through the room, my lips pressing shut. "Hatred runs bitter through my blood every waking moment of the day, *and look what it has left of me.*"

I dropped my eyes from his, unable to meet his searing gaze. My father had always been a gentle man. One collected and cool under any form of pressure. But the past few years had chipped away at his calm exterior, revealing a man who felt out of place in his own home. A man shattered by what the world had done to him.

My father blinked hard as he stood, abandoning the paper bag and reaching for one of the piling towers of files that lay stacked in the room. I bit my lip, teeth pulling at the fragile skin as he turned his back to me, his heavy shoulders slumping forward once more.

He wouldn't even listen. The warmth in my right hand continued to spread, painting the bandages in every shade of red. Victor and I were similar in almost every way, but we held one defining difference. He locked the things that hurt him away, hiding behind his charm and cheerful grin. But I just couldn't let things go. I never have. And I wasn't about to start.

"I will not be so kind again." My father's quiet voice had steadied itself, my posture stiffening at the depth in this tone. "I will not have you throwing yourself into harm's way in search of something that you very well may never find. It is my burden to carry."

"Papa, please," I began, already knowing where his words were headed.

"I've always respected your decisions, Valeria. I've allowed you to choose your own path in life unlike many young women of your status."

I swallowed harshly, his strong gaze meeting mine.

"Don't be mistaken, this is not a threat. I could never marry you off unwillingly."

The tension in my rigid arms released for a moment, my focus shifting as I stared at my boots. Even if he had threatened me with marriage I wouldn't have taken him seriously. His heart was far too soft to send me away.

"But this is a warning."

My eyes shot back up to his, my father's face wrinkled with exhaustion as he stared past my skin.

"I'll send you out of the Capital if I must. I'll ban you from the station if that's what it takes."

"You wouldn't."

"I have not forgotten what happened the last time you let yourself sink too deeply into this madness." He snapped quickly, his deep voice filling the space between us. "I have tried to be respectful of your passions by letting you work here at my side, but if that isn't enough, your grandparents would be more than happy to have you up North."

"*Work at your side?* Papa, I'm chained to a desk five working days out of six!" Frustration seeped through my words, bitter and weighted. "I know you worry, but if you would just let me work alongside Victor, I—"

"You will be doing no such thing."

"Why not?" I stammered, tired of not being taken seriously.

"Because you and your brother are different!"

Although I had expected those words, that didn't make them hurt any less. *You and your brother are different.* I blinked away the stinging warmth in my eyes. *As if I don't already know that.*

"While your brother has decided to move forward in life, you stubbornly insist on staying in the past." My father's voice quieted, his expression softening at my sudden silence. "The longer you linger in what happened, the more it swallows you, and I will not sit here and watch my daughter drown. So if sending you away is what it takes to keep you safe, I will not hesitate."

My lips trembled, anger and humiliation pricking my eyes as my nails dug through the fabric of my gloves and into my palms.

Useless. I forced my shaking limbs to steady. *This was all useless.*

I closed my eyes momentarily, chasing the tension out of my posture. There was no use trying to reason with him. Papa loved his job and took a lot of pride in being the Viscount, but he was always reluctant to let my brother and I explore the field, knowing the brutal horrors of humanity all too well.

But Victor was his heir, he was the one with the potential, the one who would pass on the family name. Unlike my brother, my presence wasn't necessary in preserving the family title—my father proved that to me quickly when he stripped me of my junior badge and left me wasting away behind a desk.

In his eyes I would always be a liability, someone far too unstable to handle her own feelings, let alone take on the responsibilities of a Silver.

"Now…" He exhaled tiredly, rubbing at his neck as he faced me once again. "I will respect all that you have done up to this point, so if you would like to give me the gentleman's name, I will gladly bring him in for an interview *alone.*"

I paused, my throat growing thick. "The gentleman?"

"You said you found a lead, didn't you?" my father questioned. "That you spoke to a potential victim?"

The hitman's face flashed through my mind, his green eyes as piercing as ever. *I could out him right now, help the Silvers track him down and put the murdering bastard in his place.*

*And maybe then…*A pathetic swell of hope filled my chest as my lips parted. *Maybe then Papa would put his trust in me.*

But the hitman's name didn't leave my lips—in fact, nothing did.

Because as selfish as it was, Alias Black was my only lead. My only real chance at potentially finding the masked man that haunted my dreams every night.

"I never did get his name." My words didn't feel like my own, spilling out from a dark and twisted part of my heart as I lied to my father's face. "I doubt it was of any significance anyways. Probably some sick man taking advantage of my desperation."

That wasn't a complete lie. My eyes avoided my father's, focusing on one of the windows in his study.

"Very well." He sat down with a huff. "Please go home, Valeria. Get some rest."

I was silent, still not meeting his gaze as I turned my back, making my way toward the door.

"Valeria."

I paused, my hand hovering over the golden doorknob.

"Please take care of yourself. If not for me, then for your brother."

A twinge of guilt burrowed its way through my heart, but I ignored it, swallowing the painful feeling.

"Of course. Good day, Papa."

The door clicked shut behind me, a shaky breath wracking my chest as I laid my head against its painted wood.

All my life I'd worked, studied, and trained to match my brother's potential. *All of those sleepless nights I spent chasing any lead, all those lies I told for the sake of my mother's case.* My eyes fluttered open, focusing on the dim windows before me.

Was that all for nothing?

My mother's pendant burned against my chest, the weight of it suffocating me as my hands trembled.

He's right. My nails dug into my palms at the dark eyes that flashed through my mind.

I will never get answers like this.

The healing skin of my palm tore further.

I will never get justice like this.

Alias Black was a killer, one that deserved to rot in prison for all he had committed, but he got things done no matter the cost. And whether I chose to recognize that or not—he was what I needed to crack this case.

I straightened up at Oliver's lingering figure at the end of the hall, his observant eyes resting behind the thick lenses of his glasses. I plastered on a smile, my anger dispersing itself into my bloodstream.

I will do this my way. I exhaled as Oliver passed me by, brushing my shoulder with his.

Justice will be served no matter the cost.

"Val!" My steps halted at the stair's railing, Lou's voice filling the hallway of the third floor. Her loose curls bounced as she approached me, freckled cheeks pink with a smile. "You're leaving already?"

"That seems to be the case."

She relaxed her shoulders, specks of gold swirling in her green eyes as she pursed her lips, knowing my father and his words far too well.

"I found this on your desk." She gave me a small smile and pulled out a neatly-sealed envelope from inside her blue blazer, the standardized uniform riddled with loose threads and wrinkles. "I was going to drop it off at the estate."

My brows came together as I took the envelope into my gloved grip, turning it over to find no name or address written anywhere.

"Thanks, Lou." I nodded, eyes still on the envelope, before turning my back and taking the first few steps down the stairs. The cold Nieve air blew past my face as I reached the first floor of the station, reminding me to pull my coat shut. I pursed my lips into a tight smile as a suit-clad man held the front door open for me, my feet picking up the pace as I rushed into the chilly air.

My nose scrunched, the cold air pricking it with its prying touch as I turned my attention back to the paper in my hands. It was a plain white envelope, no family seal on the front, the wax that held it shut dripped from a candle and left to dry. I grunted, struggling to tear the paper flap open with my clothed fingers, finally bringing it up to my lips and tearing it open by my teeth instead.

I pulled out the folded white note, the creases light and ink fresh, as if someone had just left it on my desk. I went rigid, my eyes trailing over the page to find one short sentence.

2am, 87 South Aurore Street, 2nd District.

My eyes flitted up from the page, head whipping around as I checked for prying eyes. The station's front entrance was barren, only the steady hum of voices coming from behind its wooden front doors.

A shaky exhale escaped me, my hands crumpling up the note and stuffing it deeply into the pocket of my coat.

He was here. I steadied my breathing, eyes drifting around the perimeter of the building.

Alias Black was here.

A new sense of unease blew over me as the realization of the matter hit. He was somehow able to infiltrate the Imperial Station, the building where the Viscount himself resided, without a hitch. Without being seen by anyone.

That man, Alias Black—I pursed my lips, his unmasked face flickering through my mind once more—*or rather, Rowan Marrow.* If he could do this much, if he could murder hundreds and slip through my father's fingers every single time, that had to amount to something.

He was a criminal, the worst kind, but that didn't change the fact that he had results. I had tried doing this the right way, to let those who were qualified track the killer down, but my father and his Silvers had been on this case for almost a decade and had nothing to show for their work.

Maybe the right thing to do was to stray from the lawful path. My Spider Lily persona was never fully immersed in the shadows, acting as a mere skin suit, a disguise for a Silver looking for a crook. Maybe all I had to do was abandon the mindset of my father's daughter and look through the eyes of a real killer.

I buried my face into the collar of my coat as the frigid air blew my stray hairs back, reminding me of the heavy autumn weather.

Two a.m. in the Second District, huh? My boots scratched against the cobblestone streets as I made my way down the main avenue, King Alpheus' statue boring holes into my back.

Very well, Alias Black.

Chapter 4

T HE SECOND DISTRICT WAS ONE of the quieter neighborhoods in Nieve, residing not too far from the First, where the station stood and the nobility lived. I hugged my coat closer to my body, the night air particularly abrasive as I walked the empty streets. It was well past midnight, the only people out drunk past their wits and stumbling home.

He's smart, I'll give him that. I shoved my hands deeply into my pockets, my boots trudging across the worn streets. He had decided to meet in the Second District for my sake, choosing the second-safest and well-kept neighborhoods of Nieve. Somewhere I'd be familiar with, somewhere I wouldn't feel hesitant to show up at. After all, I knew these streets like the back of my hand.

I swallowed, a hand moving to rest on my chest, my mother's necklace steadying my racing heart.

"Let me help catch your killer, and in return help me catch one of my own."

At the very least, I knew we were on even footing.

He needs me, I reassured myself internally. *Maybe just as badly as I need him.*

My feet came to a stop at the flickering lights of Sal's Tavern, the dimly lit crack in a building serving as an all-night bar for tired eyes and broken souls.

87 South Aurore Street, 2nd District. I straightened up before letting my gloved hand grab the doorknob and twisting, opening the door with the chime of a bell. A shiver ran down my back at the warm air that enveloped me, chasing the prying hands of autumn out. The place was barren aside from a middle-aged merchant passed out at the bar and a bartender polishing beer glasses, the man momentarily lifting his tired eyes to smile at me. I nodded in his direction, pulling my cap down lower over my face. It wasn't that showing up to a bar to meet with a man was particularly suspicious, but I preferred to avoid any potential rumors, especially when they were in association with a killer. *Especially when he gets caught.*

My gaze moved over the expanse of the wooden tavern, the tension in my bones releasing at his absence.

I must've arrived first. A deep exhale slipped through my lips, my steps loosening as I approached the back of the tavern, pulling out one of the many worn wooden chairs and taking a seat. The fireplace raged in the corner of the room, every shade of gold burning into another as the flames licked up the brick walls of their cage, their warmth chasing the last bit of chill from my bones. I let the thick brown coat slip off my shoulders, the scratchy work pants and pale buttoned shirt beneath allowing me to blend in with any other working-class citizen trudging home after a drink or two. I tucked a stray strand of hair behind my ear, most of the long locks stuffed beneath the fabric of my cap, a simple way to further my disguise. I stared down at my ungloved hand, the injured one still tucked away under layers of gauze and fabric.

The anger that I had felt earlier fueled me enough to wait until the dead of night, motivating me to pull on some of Flint's clothes and slip out of my open window, but now that I was here, now that the burning frustration from earlier had died down, my hands trembled, heavy with the realization of what I was getting myself into.

Alias Black was not simply a killer. In fact, throughout the entire history of Nieve, there had never lived a monster quite as brutal as he. Fathers, mothers, sons, and daughters—all killed with an incessant amount of force, always enduring an unimaginable amount of torture. People didn't commission Alias Black to commit murder—no, it was more like paying the devil himself to crawl out from underneath the cobblestones and drag unfortunate souls back with him to hell.

And despite that, here I am. I swallowed hard, forcing my anxious hands to still. *Going behind my brother's back and going against Papa's wishes.*

Yes, I have not been fully transparent with them for months, but going this far? I shook the image of Victor's hurt expression out of my head, turning my face up quickly as the door chimed, a brutal gust of wind forcing its way into the bar, chilling me to the bone.

The hitman looked more distinctive to me now, the hazy image of him from the night before clearing up in the dim candlelight. He was older than myself yet younger than I had imagined him being, reminding me of the countless instances of station staff whispering amongst themselves, speculating the elusive killer's age between droning telephone calls and endless rounds of paperwork.

His dark hair was pushed back, exposing his sharp features, a pair of probing green eyes meeting mine instantly.

There was a strange, refined brutality in the way he held himself, the killer standing out yet molding into the flickering shadows along the tavern walls all at once.

The deadliness of him was palpable. Even without uttering a single word, as his sharp gaze met my own, I was certain.

Certain that he could lean forward and slit my throat without blinking an eye, to emptily watch me writhe and wither, only caring that my blood not soil his boots.

He is Alias Black, after all. I turned my face away from the door, focusing on the chair in front of me. *The Underworld's executioner.*

I should not take him lightly.

47

His feet dragged across the tavern's floor, heavy leather boots soundless as they padded through the room. The screeching of his chair disrupted the soft silence, the boy exhaling heavily as he took a seat, his gaze briefly lingering over my attire.

"Awfully dull around here, isn't it?" The killer's eyes glowed in the dim light of the room, vivid shades of green burning holes into my face. "The shadows don't seem to reach the bright lights of the Second. It looks like your father has every monster in the Underworld running scared."

"Everyone but you." My voice was harsher than anticipated, amusement crossing his defined features.

"Growing up the way I did, you'll find I don't frighten easily."

"So I've heard." I held his gaze, fists clenched in my lap. "Alias Black, the killer with no conscience. You must be a very convincing liar."

The bar's door opened abruptly, a violent gust of wind flushing the brief sense of warmth from the room. The killer tilted his head slightly at my words, the edges of his lips pricking into an unsettling grin.

"You've got a tongue on you. I can respect that."

"Your respect means little to me." The cool metal of my pistol pressed into my skin as I straightened my spine. "What I need is your criminal experience."

"And that you shall have, Your Grace." He leaned back with a sigh, crossing his arms over his chest. "I'm glad you made the right decision."

"I didn't really have a choice."

"You always have a choice, *Silver*." He clicked his tongue, the red scarf around his neck hanging lazily against the dark fabric of his coat. "The problem arises when it comes to whether or not you can live with the consequences of yours."

I flinched at the title, the killer managing to irritate me in the few minutes spent across from him.

"But enough of that." He leaned his arms over the table, the tavern's light illuminating his sharp grin. "You'll have plenty of time to mull over your sins later. Since we'll be working alongside each other, I have a few ground rules."

"Rules?" I snorted, the audacity of the man pricking my nerves. "The killer has boundaries?"

"We all have lines that shouldn't be crossed."

I was silent, crossing my arms as he gave me a tight-lipped smile.

"One," he started, pulling at his fitted gloves. "Once we hunt down this killer—"

"If," I cut in, annoyed by his blatant arrogance. His lips pulled back into a lopsided grin, sending chills up my back.

"*When* we catch this *impossible* criminal, and after this little arrangement of ours is over, my identity remains a secret."

My fingers curled into fists, my earlier plans disintegrating at his words.

"You and the rest of the monarch's dogs can hunt me down to your heart's content, but you'll do so as a doe-eyed little noble who has nothing on me. Secondly..." I couldn't help but shrink back under his gaze. "No secrets, no lies."

"No secrets—"

"If you expect me to dig through your family's background, tracing back enemies, friends, or maybe some who are both, I won't be left in the dark. You need to be completely transparent with me."

He has a point. I reluctantly nodded, the killer smug with my compliance.

"And of course, if you screw up, or get yourself caught"—my bones stiffened at his words, the smile on his face not reaching his eyes—"don't expect me to save you. You're getting yourself into this because you and I share the same thirst for revenge."

"It's not revenge." I held his icy gaze, the killer's irritating words making themselves a home beneath my skin. "It's justice."

"That's the same thing, and you know it." He rolled his head back to loosen the sore muscles. "Justice is just a title made up by those in power to make their hatred seem more noble than ours."

"Is that what you tell yourself after you slit the throats of the innocent?" I spat, his head tilting as he stared at me again, thick brows framing empty eyes.

"Everyone's guilty of something. We're all liars, cons, and cheats." I shivered beneath his stare, the words hard and unrelenting as they left his lips. "It would be foolish of you to think any different."

My fists clenched at my sides. He may have worn that charming expression and flashed that sharp smile of his, but he wasn't fooling me. His eyes were cold, holding a frightening hollowness, announcing to the world that no matter what horrors he would encounter, they would never tremble.

Seduce and destroy—those are the words that afflict the minds of his clients. *Murder and maim* are some of his victim's final thoughts. *Avenge and restore* are the principles I had been nursed on since I was a child.

He and I are not the same, but in one sense, we are on the same side.

Whether I liked it or not, Alias Black was useful to me.

"Fine." I cleared my voice, banishing any lingering uncertainties to the back of my mind. "I accept your terms."

His lips began to peel back into a grin, but I put a finger up, stopping them midway.

"But I have a few of my own."

"Oh?" He raised an eyebrow, leaning forward in his seat.

"This sort of thing…" I turned my head, looking over the tavern before meeting his gaze again. "It won't happen again. No meetings where I could be recognized."

"You do realize that eliminates half of the Capital, don't you?"

"I won't be forced into any criminal activity either." I ignored his snarky comment, eyes stone cold as I spoke. "I have no interest in breaking any unnecessary rules."

"I would expect nothing less from the Viscount's little girl." He grinned, eyes glinting as the words rolled off his tongue.

"And as for the letter," I said, pressing the crumpled paper onto the table's hard wood. "No more of these either. I don't know how you managed to slip into the station, but I won't let it happen again. You aren't allowed anywhere near there unless it's in handcuffs."

My heart stuttered as the assassin leaned forward, lips twitching in amusement. "Worried, are we?"

"I don't think you understand, so let me make this as clear as possible. If I get any glimmer of suspicion, or if something happens to anyone in my life that could be remotely traced back to you"—my tone was venomous as I spoke, my gaze burning intensely into his—*"I'll rip you apart and scatter the remains."*

"A charmer, aren't you?" He grinned fiercely, holding my glare. "But I suggest carving people up. It's much more exhilarating."

"Are we clear?" I gritted my teeth, a hand shifting to grip the pistol in my waistband.

His smile slowly vanished, the boy raising his chin as he leaned back in his seat.

"Crystal."

A heavy breath escaped me, the steady tremor in my hands loosening its grip. *At the very least my family will be safe.*

"Lastly." I lowered my voice, pulling the cap lower over my eyes as the bartender glanced in our direction. "How can I be sure that you won't stab me in the back?"

"You sure do worry a lot." He sighed deeply, massaging the back of his neck. "But I suppose that's how you've survived this long while mingling in the shallows of the Underworld."

"I warn you, very few would describe me as a patient person." My words were clipped.

"Killing you would only put a bigger target on my back." He looked at me dully, dark eyes blinking at my tight expression. "And frankly, I wouldn't want to go through the trouble of cleaning up such a messy murder."

I sat up in my chair at the disarming grin that broke out across his features, eyes as vacant as they'd ever been.

"And besides, only cowards go for the back." The dim light of the room flickered against his sharp features. "If I *were* to stab you, I'd stare you in the eyes as I do it."

Monster.

51

The word clung to the boy before me, thick and heavy.

And I'm about to let him into my world.

His gloved hands now sat on the table, gaze focusing on my right. I clenched my wounded hand, his eyes lingering on it for a moment— but he remained silent, turning his face back to mine.

"I don't understand one thing," I said slowly, holding his stare. "We're hunting my mother's murderer, a singular man who broke into our estate almost a decade ago and killed her. You haven't explained how that benefits you."

"That's completely irrelevant." He shrugged, interlacing his fingers. "My reasons won't interfere with you or your little vendetta, so you shouldn't concern yourself with the *whys*. All you have to know is that there is one thing in this world that drives me more than money, and that is revenge. Let's say, *hypothetically,* that this killer of yours is responsible for more than your mother's untimely demise. Having a pair of eyes and ears on the lawful side as well as outside of it might prove to be quite effective in pinning him down, don't you agree?"

I suppose. I stared at him long and hard, the hitman growing bored with my silence. But that couldn't be the whole of it. As big of a risk that this would be for me, it was just as bad for him.

Alias Black and the Viscount's daughter sneaking out under the veil of night. I swallowed harshly at the damning thought. *How ludicrous.*

"Are we at an agreement then, Silver?" He extended a gloved hand across the table, but my own had slammed down against the worn wood, the sound echoing through the silent bar.

"Would you quit calling me that? I'm not—" I bit back my frustration, the irritated words tumbling past my lips on instinct. "I'm not a Silver, alright? I'm not one of them."

He had blinked at me, not because of my outburst and not because of my anger, but because of the words that had so reluctantly rolled off my tongue.

"Are you certain?" The killer cocked his head at me, the sarcasm abandoning his voice if only for a moment. "You seem like one to me."

His words were heavier than I had anticipated, soaking into my skin and weighing down on my heart. This murderer knew nothing of me and yet he could sit there and call me a Silver with more confidence than my father ever could.

I hated it.

I licked my lips, suppressing the hesitation in my bones as I took his hand once again, his grip not nearly as tight as it had been that first night on the roof.

"Wonderful. Now then," he said shortly, pulling his hand from my grasp and slapping a photograph onto the table.

The black-and-white Polaroid stared up at the two of us. The man pictured was in his late forties, tucked into a fine suit, his dark hair slicked back, two ink-drop eyes glaring into the camera. A fine silver cane sat clenched in his grip.

"Raul Martin," Rowan said, tapping the photograph with his index finger as I stared. "High class business man from the South, but does a lot of work here in the Capital. Widely recognized for his sour personality and awkward limp."

"Yes, he seems familiar."

"I'm not surprised," Rowan snorted, eyes icy despite his smile. "The rich like to flock, after all."

"I don't know him personally." I ignored him, squinting back down at the photo. "I think I've heard my father mention his name at the station once or twice."

"That would make sense," Rowan said, leaning as he spoke. "Because when I say he does *business in the city,* I don't mean stocks. He's known for helping people *disappear,* that is, for the right price."

My eyes widened, realizing where this was headed. "So you think he might know who we're looking for?"

"I think he might have helped cover his tracks." He crossed his arms over his chest as he slouched back. "I mean, this killer must've had *some* sort of help being that an entire kingdom's Imperial Force couldn't track him down for so many years."

I couldn't help but still at his words, feeling a jab of shame. We had failed my mother after all, Victor and Papa choosing to ignore the gaping hole in their hearts and move on.

But I can't—my hands clenched—*not when I looked that killer in the eyes myself.*

"Tensing up already." I snapped my head up at his voice, the hitman watching me with prying eyes. "Don't tell me you're afraid."

The faint remains of a tremor ran through my hands, the clenched fingers slowly relaxing as my pulse steadied. *Afraid?* My lips parted. *No, what I feel is much more powerful than fear.*

"I will not be bested." The words were firm on my tongue, my mother's pendant searing through my skin. "Not by a coward in a mask."

The killer's eyes glinted, pupils blacker than any starless night. "Awfully prideful, aren't you?"

"Do you have any evidence?" I ignored his question, the chair's wood hard against my spine.

He raised an eyebrow at me, my hands restless in my lap.

"Any proof that makes you so sure of his involvement? Not just in this crime, but any?"

"I'm a hitman, not a detective. I get commissioned to kill, not to interview witnesses." He laced his fingers together. "But I have my sources."

"That doesn't help much." I slumped back in my seat, feeling defeated before we had even begun. "We can't question him without hard evidence or a probable cause."

A deep laugh rumbled out of the boy across from me, my body going rigid as his chest shook, the assassin flashing a horribly amused grin.

"Have you forgotten who you've associated yourself with?" He wiped at his eye, teeth still bared into a smile. "If we are going to do this, you're going to have to get your hands a little dirty."

My lips parted to argue, but I quickly stopped myself. Just being here, just sitting across from this heinous killer, was treasonous. It was without a doubt that I'd have to dirty my morals to get answers.

"But wait." I narrowed my eyes, the assassin squinting at the confusion in my voice. "If you already have a lead, then what do you need me for?"

"Because, doll." He lowered his voice, green eyes scanning over the bar briefly as he spoke. "If this really is the same man I'm looking for, you may be the only person left to have seen him in the act and lived."

I furrowed my brows, his words crawling under my skin. *If this really is the same man, what kind of demon did Victor and I encounter all those years ago?*

"Plus I have a hunch that having Daddy's little girl in my pocket will prove to be more than helpful by the end of all this."

"I'm not *in your pocket.*"

"Yes, yes, whatever helps you sleep at night." His hands disappeared into the brown leather satchel that sat at our feet. "Ah, before I forget. I'm assuming the guy we're hunting wore something like this?"

My eyes widened in horror as he slammed the fox mask onto the table, my body leaning forward in an attempt to hide it from potential spectators.

"Are you out of your mind?" I hissed, glaring at the boy. "If you want to get caught for murder, be my guest, but don't do it while I'm anywhere near you."

"What the hell are you on about?"

"That mask." I stared down at the burnt orange fabric. "You wear that when you"—I swallowed my nausea, disgusted with my words—"*work*, don't you?"

"Do you really think I'd be so foolish as to pull out something like that?" He snorted, a few strands of his dark hair falling over his eyes. "I wear this to get in and out of *private establishments* without a hitch. I don't wear a mask when I kill."

"You show your face?" I flinched away from the killer at his words. Something about him murdering people with his face exposed felt more sinister, more personal. "If you don't hide your face, then how haven't you been caught?"

"Sweetheart, I run circles around these districts every day, and I have yet to be put in handcuffs." His lips twitched upward as he spoke, eyes burning brighter as the fireplace raged at his back. "While it may be hard to believe, I'm not some psychotic serial killer, but more of an *entrepreneur*. One who sells revenge and kills for a price."

He leaned a bit closer, an unsettling gleam in his gaze.

"One who never leaves any witnesses."

In that moment we had stared past each other's eyes, trying to decipher what exactly it was that lurked beneath the surface. I could've asked him why. Why he did what he did. Why he chose to kill.

But that was the thing about Alias Black.

He never needs a reason.

Even without the price, without the gold, he killed because it's what he was made to do. Because it's what made him feel the most comfortable in his own blood-soaked skin.

"Tomorrow at midnight, outside the Violet Estate," he said lowly, grabbing the decorative mask off the table and stuffing it into his satchel. He threw the leather pouch over his back easily and turned to look at me once more, deep eyes cold and calculated even as he flashed a grin.

"Come cloaked."

Chapter 5

ISTRETCHED MY SORE LIMBS, THE deep blue fabric of my uniform jacket pulling tight as I groaned. My shift had just ended, and unlike most days where I'd be one of the last people to leave the vicinity, I had checked out on the dot. I had a long night to prepare for, after all.

"Finally, freedom." Lou yawned, kneading the base of her neck. "I hate paperwork days."

"Yeah well, welcome to my reality." I rolled my eyes, Lou letting out a chuckle, stuffing her hands into the pockets of her pants.

"I'd imagine that the Viscount would have loosened his hold on you by now. You have too much potential to just waste away as an office aide. Impulsive? Yes. Emotional? Extremely, but other than that you have the makings of a proper Silver." She laughed as I elbowed her side, crossing my arms as we walked.

It was not as if I could argue with her—I had a reputation at the station for being hot-headed, my brother usually talking me out of trouble as I plunged into cases head-first. But my instincts were rarely wrong, my eyes able to catch a criminal in a crowded room.

But even so, I'm not the heir. I ignored the discomfort in my chest. *No matter how great my interest in the Viscount's affairs is, I will only ever be acknowledged as an accessory.*

I licked my lips, the chill evening air as present as ever, passing through my uniform easily.

"Is it too late to turn around for our coats?" Lou read my mind, momentarily moving her ungloved hands from inside her pockets and flipping the collar of her uniform jacket up, a desperate attempt to shield her neck from the biting wind. In our hurry to leave the office we had somehow managed to leave our coats behind, only realizing the severity of our mistake halfway into our walk home.

"We've made it this far. It would be stupid to turn back now," I said, not a single protest leaving my lips as she linked her arm through mine, huddling our bodies closer together.

A familiar voice spoke faintly from the other side of the road, the two of us turning our heads in unison to see Oliver clambering down the steps of The Wild Iris Bookshop. My eyes lit up as Flint followed closely on his heels, carrying a large package wrapped in brown paper and tied with twine. Oliver slapped on his cap before taking the load from the boy, nodding at him with a smile before wincing, Lou's voice filling the evening air.

"Ollie, walk home with us!" she called out, her curls blowing in the wind as she waved.

My grin fell as Flint caught my gaze, his eyes glancing over at the others before giving me a questioning stare. Usually I would have called or met up with him somewhere to discuss my plan for the next week, the two of us plotting our next moves and searching for any potential leads.

I shook my head slowly, swallowing harshly as his brows came together in confusion, but he said nothing nonetheless, nodding his head at me before taking off in the opposite direction. I tried to suppress the tugging sensation in my chest, turning back to the grinning girl on my right.

"Ollie, you wouldn't happen to have a spare coat or two, would you?" Lou asked the boy as he jogged across the street, huffing at us.

"Honestly, how do the two of you function on the daily?" Oliver sighed, balancing the package in one hand and pulling off his scarf with the other, tossing it into Lou's waiting hands. "We can stop at my apartment and I'll lend you my spare."

His eyes then moved to me, arms shifting to take off his coat but I put a hand up, smiling at him. "I'm fine, Oliver."

He narrowed his eyes at my trembling form.

"But thank you."

He exhaled, pulling the brown coat back over his broad shoulders as we trudged forward.

"You've been at the station quite a bit lately," I said, the boy pushing up his glasses as we strode. "Papa isn't running you ragged, is he?"

"Not at all." Oliver laughed, smiling kindly at me. "I'm happy that my insight could be of any value to the Viscount."

"Keep this up and you could join the ranks." Lou grinned to my right. "I'll even write your recommendation letter myself."

"Like that'll mean much." He snorted, dodging the girl's fists expertly.

"I'm a lieutenant, you know." She crossed her arms, eyes narrowed. "It wasn't just my charm and good looks that got me the role either."

"Oh, you don't have to tell me twice."

I laughed out loud, the boy apologizing swiftly as Lou fumed.

"But in all seriousness, I'll have to pass on the badge." He shrugged, turning his eyes to the horizon for a moment. "Honestly, I don't think I could stomach it."

The wind steadied itself around us, our steps matching as we trudged along the slick cobblestones.

"Have you had any interesting cases lately?" I turned to Lou, the girl sighing dramatically.

"No," Lou groaned, dragging her hands down her face. "I keep begging Victor to give me a murder case or a serial killer file, but *no*, apparently I'm much more useful in the drug department."

"Lou, please don't be so openly excited about murder." Oliver exhaled tiredly, his glasses fogging up.

"Come on." A wicked grin overtook her, the girl's hands digging into her pockets. "You're telling me that you have no interest whatsoever in hunting down a killer like *Alias Black?*"

My blood ran cold, muscles tensing at the mention of the murderer. Of Rowan Marrow.

"A cold-blooded hitman known for carving his victims up like jack-o'-lanterns, their bodies often left unrecognizable." She leaned in closer, the hairs on my neck standing up. "You're telling me that you wouldn't want to work on a case like that?"

"That's *exactly* what I'm saying," Oliver said, Lou narrowing her eyes at him before pulling on my arm.

"They say you can smell him from a district away."

"Smell him?" I swallowed the hard lump in my throat at her eerie gaze, the image of the boy sending my stomach into knots.

"Yes, the stench of rotting corpses," she whispered lowly.

My fists clenched at my sides, muscles tense.

"Of blood."

"Lou, that's enough." Oliver's quiet voice was sharper now, the girl barely sparing him a glance as she turned to me.

"Come on, Val! Doesn't it get your blood rushing?"

"Not really, no." I avoided her eyes, feeling her grip loosen on my arm.

"You two are no fun," she muttered, tucking herself deeper into Oliver's scarf.

"How can you say that?" Oliver's jaw dropped, the girl's pout turning into a snicker at his reaction. "I've let you drag me out of my apartment every other night for the past two weeks just to keep you *company* while you drink yourself into the next dimension!"

"Oh yeah, Val you should come drinking with us tonight!" Lou beamed, gripping my arm snugly once again. "I don't remember the last time the four of us went out."

"Forget about Victor." Oliver grunted, shifting the bulky package in his grip. "That poor boy hasn't moved from the Viscount's office from morning to night for the past two weeks."

"You should see him when he gets home." I sighed, bitter at the thought of my brother grueling the night away on cases, our father's silver ashtray not too far from his reach.

"What about going out, just the three of us?" Lou asked, looking up at me with shining eyes.

"I wish I could." I avoided her gaze, turning to stare ahead. "But I've been busy."

The three of us had gone silent now, an air of discomfort floating between us as a question sat on their tongues, Lou being the one to ask it.

"This isn't about your mother again, is it?"

"What does that—"

"Because you know that we're here for you, always." Lou cut me off, her cheerful eyes completely serious for once. "I know how your father feels about the matter..." She trailed off, momentarily looking away. "But I'm ready any time of day or night if you need me. I just don't want you to take things into your own hands again."

A sharp pain throbbed beneath the fabric of my uniform, my lips forcing themselves back into a smile as the two people beside me stared with soft eyes.

"No." The lie was rancid on my tongue. "It's nothing of that sort. I've just been really tired as of late. Trying to regain Papa's favor hasn't been easy."

"He just worries for you. We all do." Lou's hand touched mine softly, her olive eyes swirling with compassion, the pain in my chest worsening.

"I know." I forced a laugh, brushing off the weight that inhibited the air around us. "Everything's fine. I promise. Nights out just haven't been on my mind, but I swear I'll make time for one soon. Now I better get going." I slipped my arm of her hold, stuffing my hands into my pockets as I jogged ahead. "Don't have too much fun without me!"

The wind blew harshly, a few loosened strands of hair swishing wildly around my face as I turned back to glance at the pair once more, Lou waving at me from behind.

I forced myself to swallow the guilt, my steps heavy as I trudged the rest of the way home, the sharp pain in my chest now a dull ache.

Liar. I shook my head in an attempt to rid myself of the thought, but it was useless. I had been the prisoner of guilt for most of my life, the weight of my mother's unsolved murder hovering over my neck as the years went on, but this was different. I was lying to my family, to my friends, to all those who trusted and believed in me.

I clamped my mouth shut at the sickening feeling that climbed up my throat.

The tall gate that surrounded our estate creaked open, the metal cold even through the fabric of my gloves. I shut the gate behind me, my feet rushing up the steps that led to the door of the grand brick building, desperate for the warmth of the fireplace.

A gentle breath left my lips as I pulled one of the big doors open, the cold melting from my limbs as the warm air enveloped me into an embrace. I slid the jacket off my tired body, hanging it by the door. My fingers gripped at my tie, loosening it with a gentle tug before padding through the entrance and into the estate. My eyes trailed over the familiar ivory walls of the common room, red cushioned seats lounging by the raging fire, their golden frames illuminated by the flickering flames. I let my hand wander, tracing the top of my mother's old piano as I made my way through the room, the instrument lying untouched for far too many years.

I miss the sound.

The rustling of papers caught my attention, and I made my way across the narrow hall to my father's study, finding Victor hunched over the dark wooden desk, his hair an unruly mess as he flipped through one of his many files. I pursed my lips, moving past the door silently, my brother completely oblivious to my presence. It was his day off, if I wasn't mistaken, his absence at the station making the building feel somewhat lonelier, and yet here he was working away from the confines of our home. It was well into the afternoon now, the sun beginning to set, and judging by his dull awareness and slouching figure, he must've been down here since the early morning.

My ungloved hand rested on his shoulder, softly squeezing, my brother's back tensing before he met my eyes.

"Goodness, V." He exhaled, a gentle smile spreading across his features as he clutched his dress shirt in surprise. "I didn't hear you come in."

"I noticed." A small smile overtook me despite the heaviness in my chest.

My gaze moved from his face, lingering onto the file before him, the papers scattered randomly across his desk.

"Another drug operation?" I asked, eyes trailing over the first few lines of text, Victor sighing heavily at my side.

"I just don't get it." He buried his fingers into his hair, looking up at me with frustrated eyes. "Father traces criminals so easily and his instincts have always led us in the right direction. But lately it feels like we're playing a losing game, like criminals know what we're going to do before we know ourselves. Father, he…" My brother paused, wrestling with the words on his tongue. "He even went so far as to suggest that there might be an informant among us."

My blood ran cold, fear blooming through the sticky liquid, stopping its flow in my veins. "Did he really?"

"Absurd, right?" He slammed his fists onto the table, jolting the papers. He paused, flinching slightly at his own behavior and taking in a deep breath. "I…" His voice was much smaller now, his eyes tentatively meeting mine. "I don't even know if I have what it takes to be Viscount, V. To fill Papa's shoes."

"Nonsense." I tried to laugh, still shaken by his earlier admission, but my brother's face remained unchanged. A heavy sigh escaped me as I released the tension in my stance, momentarily putting my own worries aside. "You're so hardworking, Vic, and you care so deeply about the people of Nieve. There isn't a doubt in my mind when I say that you'll be the greatest successor."

And I meant it. My brother had always had the biggest heart, always putting those around him before himself.

That's how he's always been. My shoulders relaxed as he cracked a small smile, his hand moving to squeeze mine. *Compassionate almost to a fault.*

"Besides, you still have a long way to go." I smiled, trying to lighten the mood. "By the time we finally get Papa to retire we'll be seniors ourselves."

He let out a breathy chuckle, nodding in agreement as he moved his gaze back to the files in front of him.

"You sure you don't want to be Viscount, V?" he said, grin widening as I snorted. "All the criminals in Nieve would be running for the hills."

"Why? Do you still plan on being a conductor?" I said, pulling my hand away from my brother and heading back toward the door.

"Maybe."

"Then you shouldn't have been so pushy when we were born."

He laughed out loud, a lighthearted rumble rolling off his chest and widening my smile. It felt good to talk to him like this, to ease his mind for a change instead of spinning more lies for my own sake.

He deserves so much better. I clenched my fists at my sides as I reached the door frame. *They all do.*

"Will you be having dinner with us tonight?" he asked, my body pausing at the door.

No. I closed my eyes. *I'll be running around Nieve with Alias Black.*

"I think I'm just going to get some sleep." I turned to face him once more, flashing a smile. "It was a long day in the office."

The edges of his lips lifted into a small smile, his eyes squinting lovingly as he nodded.

"Good. Get some rest, V."

I was silent, leaving him in the study and trudging up the dark mahogany steps to the third floor, eyes floating to the grand golden clock that hung at the base of the staircase.

Old Reliable, Papa had dubbed the clock, claiming that without it he wouldn't know night from day. It had been around longer than Victor and I, ticking through every second of every day since my great grandfather's time. Victor had always favored the heirloom, volunteering to polish it with the maids every morning when we were kids.

"I wonder who first invented the clock," Vic had asked me one early morning as I sneakily scanned through the morning paper. Our father didn't like sharing cases with us, not wanting to frighten Victor away from his birthright, but I had been drawn to the world of justice since I first learned to read, stealing our father's newspapers to get a sense of the weekly occurrences.

"Probably a man like Papa," I had said, raising my eyes momentarily to my brother.

Loud thuds were heard from above as our father scrambled out of bed, muttering about sleeping in yet again. We had both burst into a fit of laughter, Victor grinning up at the golden clock.

"Someone who's always late," he had said.

A melancholic smile sat on my lips as I turned away from the wall, climbing up the rest of the steps to the third floor, following the hall until I reached the last door. A deep breath left my lips as I entered my bedroom, ripping the tie from my neck and watching it fall to my feet. The door clicked shut behind me, my back resting against it, pulling off the brown glove from my injured hand. Only a thin layer of gauze remained, wrapped tightly against my skin. I untied the bandages, unraveling them onto the floor, the puckered wound stretching from one side of my palm to the other.

It will definitely scar. I pursed my lips, wincing slightly as I flexed and clenched my hand, the healing skin pulling tight.

My feet moved quietly to the vanity, pulling open the bottom drawer to reveal my first aid kit, careful hands retrieving the small bottle of alcohol and the thinning roll of gauze.

Everything will be fine, I thought, bringing the white fabric up to my teeth, grunting as I tore through it. *I'm finally going to get answers.*

I licked my lips, hardly flinching as the alcohol spilled over my palm, the scarring skin raised and angry.

65

And that starts tonight.

The stars were bright that night, somehow managing to cut through Nieve's eternal fog as they shone overhead, letting some of the pale moonlight through. The streets of the First District were empty at this time of night, all of its inhabitants either tucked away within their grand estates or still out for the evening in the Second or Third.

The Violet Estate was an empty mansion that sat on the outskirts of the First District, serving as a temporary home for the rich and noble passing through the Capital. It earned its name from the gorgeous purple violets that bloomed outside of the estate every spring, dyeing the fields in their bright shades and announcing that for a few short weeks, the cold weather would finally come to pass.

I adjusted the collar of my coat, the dark fabric oddly breathable but still warm. The thin white gloves that clung to my hands hugged my skin tightly, barely leaving room for the gauze. I momentarily closed my eyes, reaching for my mother's pendant, the cold metal pushing against the skin of my chest, the familiarity of it steadying my breaths.

"You want to break into his home?" I had asked the killer earlier in the day, sneaking off to a telephone booth during my break as per his instruction. *"You do realize that part of our agreement was no unnecessary criminal activity."*

"Technically he doesn't own the estate, so we won't be breaking into his home per se." I had clenched my jaw at his pathetic reasoning. *"And discreet infiltration is extremely necessary, especially if we want to keep this simple and clean."*

"We can't." I shook my head at his words, gripping the black frame of the booth. *"That goes against all of his rights."*

"Would you rather we storm the place?"

"No!" I yelled, stiffening immediately at the alarmed expressions of the people passing by.

"Then relax." Although his voice was distorted through the old phone, I could still hear the grin on his lips. *"We'll be in and out."*

"I just…" I swallowed hard, eyes lingering briefly over every passerby through the glass. *"I don't know. This feels wrong."*

"Probably because it is."

I clenched the phone with a tight grip at his blatant admission, my guilt intensifying tenfold.

"Allow me to put this into terms you'd understand, Your Grace." My eyes narrowed at his mocking tone, the killer taking care to enunciate each word. *"This alliance between us is like a waltz. It takes two individuals swaying to the same melody in order for it to work."*

"Then I'm afraid you'll find that I'm not very practiced in dance," I bit back, tongue sharp with annoyance. *"I might step on your toes."*

"Then let's agree to be forgiving of one another." His voice had sent shivers down my spine, sinister intentions not easily masked by innocent words. *"I've found that I myself am prone to taking steps against the rhythm."*

A chill pricked at the back of my neck, different from that of the cold, my hand finding the hilt of my pistol easily as I whipped around.

My muscles loosened at Rowan's amused gaze, the hitman's attire mimicking my own.

His hair was brushed back into a black newsboy cap, a few dark strands peeking out from beneath it, framing the green eyes that stared down at me.

"Would you look at that." His catlike grin stretched from ear to ear. "You actually showed."

"We had a deal, did we not?"

"Very true, but nobles aren't really well-known for keeping their ends of a bargain." His eyes dropped to the hand at my hip, the killer lifting an eyebrow. "I've been meaning to ask. How did a secretary manage to get her hands on something like that?"

"I'm an aide," I corrected, pulling my coat back over the gun. "And that's not important. Let's just say that when your father runs the King's Imperial Force, tools for self-defense aren't exactly hard to acquire."

The edges of his lips twitched into a grin, the assassin's gloved hands disappearing into his coat momentarily.

"Put these on." He opened his coat, the hilt of a blade flashing in the moonlight as he pulled out two garments.

I hesitantly extended my hand out, brows furrowing at the unsettling white mask I was given, the porcelain material stretching over the eyes and down the face, hiding half of the wearer's mouth behind it. But it was the uncanny expression that jolted me, the mask reminiscent of those in theatrical dramas, sunken lines near the eyes and half of a deep frown characterizing its features. His own mask matched mine, but instead of a tragic frown, it was half of a frightening grin that stretched up its cheeks.

"A bit dramatic, isn't it?"

"Were you expecting any less?"

"No." I rolled my tense shoulders back, taking the plain black cap from his other hand. "I can't say that I was."

"I would really prefer not having you there at all, as you aren't exactly difficult to recognize, but it seems like we'll have to make do," he said, pulling at the ends of his black gloves, eyes already focused on the estate before us. "You'll need to pull your hair into that cap and untuck your clothes. The less that can be deduced about us the better, especially since you're *so* adamant on leaving everyone alive."

"Because if we're spotted," I said slowly, putting his thoughts together.

"Which is certainly a possibility with you," Rowan muttered, gloved hands feeling up the gate.

"It would be best if they can't make any distinctive observations about us."

"Very good, Chief," His dark gaze met mine again. "So keep your steps light, and try not to breathe too loudly. Perhaps don't breathe at all."

He ignored my glare, the killer sparing me one last tight smile.

"Now, do try to keep up."

His gloved hands gripped the metal bars of the gate firmly, easily jumping and hoisting himself over, his feet landing soundlessly on the other side.

I swallowed harshly, watching as the assassin straightened his coat on the other side of the bars, his electrifying gaze meeting mine.

This is it. I breathed out, shaky hands gripping the hat firmly. *There's no going back after this.*

I slapped the cap on, pulling my hair back and shoving the long strands beneath it before gripping the gate myself. I pulled my careful body up and over with a grunt, barely making a sound as I landed onto the other side. Rowan cocked his head at me as if to say something, but remained silent, instead placing the grinning mask over his face.

My stomach turned as I mimicked him, the cold grip of my own mask constricting.

The two of us were silent as we padded across the vast greenery, making our way to the back of the estate. My eyes locked on a small back door, meant to serve as easy access for maids, butlers, and the occasional gardener. I looked over at Rowan, his gaze resting on the very same thing.

Or the perfect entry point for an assassin.

Our quick steps had our backs at the estate's wall in a mere few seconds, Rowan's gloved hands retrieving a hairpin from his pocket, bringing it up to his teeth and snapping it at the center. His hands moved skillfully, twisting the two metal ends in the keyhole, eyes trained ahead as he listened, only turning to look at me as we heard a faint *click.*

The door swung open quietly, our bodies slipping through easily. We were in a servants' lounge, the common tea sets and simple furnishing making it easy to distinguish from the rest of the grand estate.

I stilled, gaze intense as I tried to pick up any noise in the estate.

"Asleep," a warm whisper breathed against my ear, my body recoiling at Rowan's proximity. I swallowed my unease, bringing a shaky finger to point out toward the hall.

He shook his head.

No guards. The tension in my shoulders released a bit.

That made sense after all—the Violet Estate constantly had new inhabitants. The people visiting very rarely brought guards of their own or went through the trouble of finding temporary replacements for their short stays in the Capital.

That's a relief. The tension seeped out of my hands, clenched fists relaxing. *At the very least I won't have to worry about the hitman killing anyone tonight.*

A clean stealth mission—that was what the killer had promised. A silent operation that would lead us through Raul Martin's files and back out into the night air without stirring a single soul.

Whether I liked it or not, I had to trust this plan, trust his words. *Or at the very least, pray that he isn't as big of a liar as I am.*

Rowan moved ahead, the door creaking slightly as he pushed it open, the steady hand resting on the hilt of his blade and sending my stomach into knots.

Our bodies flew across the halls, disappearing from shadow to shadow like a pair of ghosts as we scaled the massive estate, climbing the stairs to the second floor. Rowan put a hand up, halting our steps, his eyes creeping along the closed doors of the second floor before shaking his head. I furrowed my brows, but followed him nonetheless, the two of us reaching the third and final floor of the mansion.

The Violet Estate was quite different from my own home, its luxurious elements and qualities overemphasized, demanding the attention of everyone in the room. From the gold-plated furniture and goose feather cushions to the crystal chandeliers, the towering estate was the epitome of all things lavish and aristocratic. It was almost unsettling.

I let my gloved fingers gently touch one of the extravagant rose arrangements that adorned the hall, a few red petals softly falling to the floor. *How pretty.*

"Quite the place, isn't it?" the hitman whistled from my right, my body jolting at the sudden sound. "Well, I'd imagine this seems like home to you."

"Focus, would you?" My words were barely audible, dread brewing itself in the pits of my stomach. It didn't matter that no guards were present—Raul Martin was still asleep somewhere within these walls.

"So tense." The darkness painted frightening pictures along his mask. "It's terribly amusing, really."

"Keep talking and you might just get us caught," I whispered harshly, irritated with his aloofness. "I wonder how amused you'll be when they string you up for your sins."

"Are you always this grim?" His voice quieted, narrowed eyes dragging over the line of closed doors, their wooden borders decorated with elegant carvings and designs. "Besides, I could never allow that. I plan to die buried beneath the weight of my own gold."

My lips twitched in disgust at the man before me, the killer flashing me half a grin before putting a gloved finger up. Rowan tilted his head, motioning for me to follow as we advanced down the next corridor.

The ideal place to look for evidence of the masked man would be his study, but between the twisting hallways and the endless doors, I wouldn't be surprised if it took us all night to find it.

He paused, our careful steps coming to a halt in front of one of the many massive doors, the killer's sharp gaze focused.

"Stop pausing for dramatic effect."

"I'm not," he whispered, hardly sparing me a glance.

I narrowed my eyes at his sudden seriousness. "Then what—"

"There's someone here."

My blood ran cold at his whispered words, pulse quickening. "How do you—"

"Shh."

My heart hammered erratically in my chest at the jiggle of the doorknob, pounding through my ears so violently I feared it would give us away. I held my breath, one of Rowan's gloved hands pressing my back into the wall, the boy following suit.

Click.

The door cracked open, my wild eyes staring holes into the side of Rowan's mask as a dark figure escaped into the hall, our own shadowy forms hidden only by the veil of night.

NOT GOOD. I screamed internally at the idiot assassin. *NOT GOOD AT ALL.*

For it only took a few short seconds for me to identify the mysterious man as Raul Martin, the silhouette of a dragging limp giving him away almost immediately.

What could he possibly be doing at this hour? My hand found Rowan's sleeve, squeezing it instinctively. *What on earth had to be kept until this late into the night?*

I could tell that Rowan pondered the same question, because as soon as Raul's back turned the corner, the hitman's hands were on the doorknob, twisting it soundlessly. Rowan cracked the door open, carefully slipping his body through, my own shaky limbs right behind him.

The room was dark, massive, characterized solely by the faint outline of a desk's frame and the towering bookcases that climbed three of its walls. *The study.*

"You can let go now."

I jolted at the sudden sound of Rowan's voice, releasing my deathly grip on the fabric of his coat.

"What the hell was that about?" I whispered fiercely, nausea thick at the base of my throat. "You do realize that was *Raul Martin,* the man we're currently investigating, the very man who almost discovered us *in his house* a few moments ago?"

"Yes, I was there."

"This isn't a joke!" I gritted my teeth, the killer sighing deeply. "Hell, I should have never gone along with this, never followed a crook!"

I should have never stooped this low—I couldn't stop my lips from trembling—*never gone behind my father's back.*

"You said this was a simple infiltration, that we wouldn't be harming anyone—"

"And so far we haven't." He turned sharply on his heel, my legs stumbling back. "Although you're certainly making me want to."

Despite his loose actions, there was an icy edge to his words, quickly reminding me of one of the few rules of our arrangement. He wasn't here to help me. He was using me just as much as I was using him. Should I lose my head and get caught, he would be gone with the wind, a mere ghost in the hall.

Rowan Marrow was not here to save me.

"I could start with his eyes first, or maybe pull out all his teeth?" He spoke lowly, watching me with burning eyes. "What about his other leg, hmm? Should I leave him with only his arms? Forced to crawl miserably across his velvet floors like a *maggot*?"

"Now you're just trying to scare me." I willed myself to still, hating the violent hammering of my heart.

"And why would I do that?" His words were strangely cold, their edges sharp. "I'm *already* Alias Black, my name *already* evokes a bone-shattering fear in the hearts of those who hear it. I needn't waste my time trying to frighten you when you should already be afraid."

My pulse was loud in my ears, a cool chill passing over my skin as I forced myself to hold his stare. The house was empty, its only present inhabitant a ways away, and I was alone. Alone with Alias Black.

And it terrified me.

"You're either on my side, or in my way." He held my stare, the hitman violently sincere. "And I can assure you that the latter isn't a place you want to be."

He raised his chin, staring down at me silently for a moment, waiting for me to tremble, perhaps waiting for me to cry. But I didn't.

I would never give him the satisfaction of seeing me falter.

"Now, the faster we find evidence of this masked killer, the faster we can leave," he said slowly, making sure every word made it past my skull. "So why don't you untwist your trousers and start looking?"

I bit back my words, knuckles white at my sides, the urge to strangle the killer a hard one to swallow. But I was already here, already an accomplice in this mess.

The faster we could find what we needed, the sooner we could leave. *The sooner I can wash Alias Black and his sins off my skin.*

"There's a lot of ground to cover, so we'll split the room into sections." His mask became more visible as the clouds cleared up, a few wisps of moonlight seeping through the thin curtains. "Your experience as a secretary should be plenty helpful."

"Do you *want* me to shoot you?"

"Too loud," he said, already trailing his fingers along one of the many shelves. "I'd be more than happy to let you borrow one of my knives though. I just had them polished."

"You know what? I might take you up on that offer," I muttered, brows furrowing at the faint smell of something strong, something familiar. "Perhaps I'll start by cutting out that tongue of yours."

"So she isn't completely stiff." I could hear a whisper of a grin in his voice as I rounded the desk, careful hands tracing its dark wood. "What a pleasant surprise."

"I'm just full of those, aren't I?" I opened the first drawer and ran a finger along some old contracts. *What is that smell?*

"Let's not get ahead of ourselves now, Silver."

"Do you smell that?" I ignored the killer's words, the boy raising an eyebrow behind his mask.

"Smell?"

"Yes, something burning, something…"

I paused, narrowed eyes stopping on a single ivory candle in the corner of the desk, one stubbed and overused. *One whose wax is still warm.*

"We won't find anything here."

"What?" Rowan turned quickly. "Why not?"

"Because Raul was sealing letters." I sighed, the burning scent of paraffin wax a common one in the station's office. "And whatever he had written, whatever he's hiding, was taken with him. He isn't keeping any evidence in here."

To be sealing letters at two a.m.—I pursed my lips—*that definitely feels secretive, but could it be criminal?*

"So we have to figure out where he went," Rowan said.

"That would be ideal, but how are you so sure this was anything illicit?" My arms rested tiredly across my chest. "He could be writing to a secret lover or something of the sort."

"Because I just do."

"That's a horrible answer."

"Yet it's the one I gave nonetheless," he said shortly, dark hair peeking out from under his flat cap as he approached the door. "Stay close to me."

"Wait." I stiffened as he swung the door open, slipping back out into the hall, my feet anxiously following. "Hold on a minute!"

"Shh."

"Don't shush—" I froze when he turned around sharply, a gloved finger hovering over my lips.

"*Quiet,*" he whispered, my masked face jerking from his. He straightened up, taking one more moment to look at me before continuing down the hall.

"Where are you going?" My words were softer as I trailed after him. "Raul could still be awake."

The killer was silent, his leather boots padding quickly across the carpeted floors without another word. It made me uneasy.

My eyes moved to trace the hallway of the grand estate, gold details adorning the carefully-painted walls. At least, I thought they were gold. It was much too dark to tell.

I froze as Rowan lifted a hand, the two of us coming to a halt near a secluded set of double doors, his gloved hands moving to grip the handles. *The room must be massive.* My brows knit together at the isolated space. *Almost as big as a—*

Panic sunk its claws into me first, the realization of what he was about to do a hard slap to the face.

"Wait—"

But the doors had already swung open, the killer slipping through them without a word, my own body close behind him.

The bedroom was dark, darker than the rest of the estate, the only motion being that of Raul Martin's chest, the man tucked into his regal bed and in a heavy slumber.

"Change of plans." The whispered words were barely audible, but I still heard them, my unsteady feet stumbling back. My heart stuttered in fear as Rowan met my gaze, his eyes as empty as ever.

You've already come this far, they seemed to say. *There is no point going back now. Turning back won't save you.*

My teeth sunk into my bottom lip, drawing blood as Rowan moved around me without a sound, unsheathing a singular knife out of the multiple strapped at his hips.

Fear struck me at the glint of the tiny blade, my hand reaching for his before my mind could fully process my actions. Rowan was silent, eyes burning into my own from behind the mask, but my grip on his wrist only tightened, my own gaze matching his intensity.

"You can't."

"*Let go.*" His voice was nearly silent, gaze venomous as I dug my fingers into his arm.

"Like hell I will," I whispered, careful so not to wake the slumbering man. "Do you even realize what you're about to do?"

"We need answers."

"*At what cost?*" My nails dug past his skin, but he didn't flinch, his eyes never wavering.

He was going to expose us, endanger our identities, and terrorize the sleeping man for answers he might not even have.

No. I swallowed the burning acid at the back of my throat. *No, this is wrong. This is so disgustingly—*

"So you don't want to solve it? You don't want to avenge your mother?"

"*Don't you dare even start.*" I bared my teeth, words dripping with venom. "That isn't it, and you know it."

"Then let me go."

My limbs trembled, something between fear and resentment boiling through my blood. Maybe it was both.

It was too quiet, my heartbeat too loud, and Rowan's stare too searing, burning, daring me to loosen my hold on his wrist and take the fall.

To rip the rotting wings from my back and join him in the blistering pits below.

My eyes fell shut, a shaky breath leaving my lips before I met his gaze again.

"Fine." It suddenly became very hard to swallow, the lump of shame in my throat refusing to go down. "Intimidate him if you must, but torture is out of the question. *Keep your hands off him.*"

He sneered, prying his arm from my grip, but I had given up far too much to be brushed off so easily. My hand found the stiff collar of his shirt and yanked him down to my level.

"You won't harm a single hair on his head." My words were more forceful now, my own pistol reflecting in the window's light. "*Or I swear* you'll be leaving this room a few limbs lighter."

"Those are some big words coming from an amateur at best. An imperial dog should wear its leash." His eyes had widened, but they didn't move from mine. "*Silver isn't gold.* Don't expect Brother Dearest to save you when I've decided you've lost your value."

"As if I'd take the threats of a faceless crook," I spat, challenging him. "And if you try anything, you'll find yourself sorely mistaken. My brother always comes for me." I held my tongue as the bed shifted slightly, the heavy man moving in his sleep. My eyes narrowed at the gloved fingers that gripped my chin, forcing my masked face to meet his.

"Keep up this insolent behavior and we'll surely see."

I pressed my lips together, angry, but conscious of Raul's body to our left. Reluctantly, I let the fabric of his shirt slip through my fingers.

Rowan turned his back to me, adjusting his collar with a tug before approaching the bed, knife in hand, and without hesitation clamping the other over the sleeping man's mouth.

Raul must've opened his eyes, his body jolting at the image above him.

"Make a sound and I'll slit your throat." Rowan's voice was low, completely emotionless as the man trembled silently. "Won't you join us for a bit, Raul?"

My hands clenched at my sides, nails threatening to tear through the fabric of my gloves. I was not like him—I was nothing like him. The fact that I stood here ready to vomit while he stared the man in the eyes was enough to prove that. *Then why?* I stared down at my hands. *Why am I letting this happen?*

"Am I understood?" Rowan said, the man stilling. A few silent seconds passed before Rowan motioned for me, my body complying on its own, moving to the veil-like curtains at the window and untying them, retrieving the thick silken rope that bunched the fabric together.

Raul was completely silent as I strapped him to one of the velvet chairs in the room, binding his hands behind the chair's back, his ankles strapped tightly to its golden legs. *A wooden foot,* I noted as I secured his left. *That explains the dragging limp.*

Based on the information we had on the man, I could imagine a plethora of ways he could have ended up losing the limb.

Rowan stood at the still man's back, one of his multiple knives held tightly against the skin of his throat.

It was strange seeing such a valued businessman like this, the distinguished man in his night robe and his dark hair a jumbled mess as he sat completely still. He was oddly calm, staring straight ahead as I pulled at the rope once more, making sure it held firm.

But I suppose that's what fear does to you.

I turned my face up, giving Rowan a reluctant nod, before standing to my feet.

"The blade stays. Remember that," he said slowly, Raul's eyes trembling as the hitman rounded him, moving to my side.

"Who the hell are you people?" he whispered harshly, eyes moving back and forth between us. "All the money is in the safe by my bed! Let me go and we can forget about this!"

"As tempting as that is, I'm afraid you won't be able to buy yourself out of this one, Raul." Rowan cocked his head at the man, his body stiffening under the killer's intense gaze. "But fortunately enough for you, we just need a few answers. Specifically on the subject of your past criminal activity."

"What on earth do you…" he had started, but stopped at Rowan's unwavering gaze. "Look," Raul exhaled tiredly, shoulders slumping. "I've dealt with men like you before, so just tell me what you need and we can work this out, alright?"

The hitman tilted his head at the man. "Oh, I'm counting on that. You're an influential man, aren't you Mr. Martin?" Rowan didn't give him a moment to argue, his voice as calm as the sea before a harrowing storm. "You have a lot of money and your name seems to hold quite a bit of power in these parts. Are you trying to tell me you've achieved all this through a few measly stock investments?"

Raul froze beneath his gaze, narrowing his eyes up at the killer.

"I'm a bit familiar with the market myself—not personally, but through a few colleagues," Rowan continued, his unsettling mask reflecting in the moonlight. "You don't own enough to rent a quarter of this estate, which begs the question—how did you manage to climb up the economic ladder with so little to your name?"

"It's luck." The bound man gritted his teeth.

"Crooked business is what it is." Rowan's expression remained unchanging, a lump of unease sitting in my throat.

"I have no idea what you're talking about."

"Then maybe I can help remind you." My stomach dropped as Rowan pressed the blade against the man's neck, my own hand moving to rest against the pistol at my hip.

I swear if he—

I stopped, Rowan turning his head back, staring me in the eyes long and hard before loosening his grip on the knife. I couldn't help but stare into the emptiness of his gaze, at the coldness of his eyes.

I wondered what he saw as he stared back.

Murderers are still men. The sudden thought manifested itself in my mind as the resistance in my bones relaxed, the stiff hand at my hip falling to my side.

He won't try anything, at least not while I'm here.

"Mr. Martin." Rowan turned his back to me, the man sitting up as the assassin leaned toward him. "You seem like a busy man, so I'll make this brief. *We know.*"

He didn't have to specify a thing. Raul's expression alone was enough to confirm our suspicions.

"But then again, how could we not?" The man's lips curled back at the killer's words. "Unlike your lackluster business ploys in the South, your illicit exchanges here have kept your name alive and well in the Underworld." Rowan grinned wickedly, the cheerful mask growing more sinister the longer I stared. "Not that you do much to hide that."

"Stop spouting rubbish." Raul forced the tension from his shoulders, his jaw firm. "While my means of income may be untraditional, everything I do is completely legal!"

"Ah yes, harboring criminals and money laundering. I'm sure the King would agree."

It was subtle, but I caught it—the muscles beneath Raul's shirt tensing, eyes flashing my way for a brief moment before he collected himself.

"I would be careful with your assumptions there." Raul was angry now, speaking lowly as Rowan leaned closer to him. "I am much more capable than you think. The King's Imperial Force couldn't sniff out a single misdeed of mine for years, so who the hell do you think you are?"

"*Oh*, but I'm not with the Silvers." A cold laugh escaped the killer's lips, the boy flipping his knife out once again and running a gloved finger along the blade. "Actually, if you *really* knew what kind of serpent had wriggled its way into your garden, you'd be spilling a lot more than just information."

A chill ran through me at his tone of voice. *If only he knew that Alias Black had slithered into his home, and that I had held the door for him.*

"So let's skip the petty banter and cut right to it."

"Or what?" Raul said slowly, a smug expression inching up his face despite his position. "I've been in enough of these situations to know

80

that you're holding back. You threaten me with that knife, but you have no intention of using it."

I stilled as the man's dark eyes left Rowan, burning past my mask and into my soul.

"Not with that one here."

We both jumped, my hand grabbing for my gun as Rowan slammed the blade down, tearing straight through the chair's armrest and missing Raul's fingers by a mere centimeter.

"Then let's switch things up, shall we?"

There it is again. I furrowed my brows, Raul's startled form peering over at me from the corner of his eyes, almost like a reflex.

No—I straightened up—*not at me, but behind me.*

"You have a lovely wife, don't you Mr. Martin? A real showstopper." Rowan didn't need to look at the man to know that he froze, his back rigid as he processed his words.

"She isn't here." His voice was quieter now, much more docile.

"Yes, you're right. She's out with a friend for a night out and about town. *Doloris*, wasn't it?" Rowan purred as he spoke her name, lips twitching into a smile.

He's been watching them. I crossed my arms uneasily. *And they've been oblivious.*

"I'd hate for something to happen to such a beautiful lady, and I think you'd agree, isn't that right?"

The man's posture had slumped, the confident edge in his voice diminished to dust as he peered up at the hitman.

"Please," he whispered, Rowan sauntering over to the corner of the room. "If you need safe passage, *I can help you.* But not like this. We don't need to get violent, alright? I've dealt with your kind before."

"*My kind?*" Rowan laughed, picking up Raul's silver cane. The head of a lion had been carved into its handle, its jaw open and teeth bare. "I wouldn't be so sure. But I see you've encountered at least one unsavory soul." He stopped in front of the bound man, tapping his wooden leg with the end of the cane. "You know, I'm a bit curious.

Was this a gift from a criminal you helped escape, or was it given to you by the family of his victim?"

He has him.

Raul's lips parted but not a sound escaped him, the man's eyes widening to an impossible degree as the puzzle pieces clicked into place. We weren't here for his services. In fact, we weren't average criminals at all. There was no way for him to slip out of this one.

"I don't know who you are, but think this through." Raul stumbled over his words, but they no longer held that same conviction. They were pleading. "You think this makes you strong? Powerful? There is power in mercy. So please, *leave me be.*"

If it had been just the two of us, if it were solely Raul and I in this room, I would have wavered. But mercy was not a word exercised by Alias Black.

Rowan stared down coldly at the bound man, the air around the hitman frigid and unforgiving.

"Then I suppose I'm weak."

Raul's shoulders fell forward, the man's breaths heavy as he tried to collect his bearings. I turned my eyes to the floor, guilt heavy in my lungs as the man struggled before me. I would not let any harm come to him or his wife, *but still.*

He couldn't know that.

"What..." His voice was quiet, hesitant. "What is it that you want to know?"

Rowan's lips twitched back, the boy straightening up in satisfaction.

"You work with quite a few crooks, don't you?" he asked, taking long strides as he paced slowly along the expanse of the room. "Help them disappear for the right sum of money?"

"No, I—"

"Raul." He stopped, clicking his tongue. "Don't make me have to soil my gloves so early into the evening."

"I help them leave town safely for a price, yes," he admitted, one word rushing into another, "but it's very rare that I do!"

"I don't like lies."

"What does this even matter? Just tell me who you two are looking for!" The man's patience had been spent, his eyes now blazing, caught between an expression of fear and anger.

I was ready for it now—his eyes flashing to the shelves at my left, my eyes following his quick gaze to the first row of books. I tilted my head at the deep ebony shelves, crouching down to the bottom layer.

"Hey, hey!" he called from behind me, his voice muffled as Rowan slammed his palm against his mouth in an attempt to silence him. "You can't go through my stuff!"

Too easy. I raised my chin, my fingers gripping the books to find them hollow, a mere cover for a hidden cabinet. My lips pressed firmly together at the disorganized hoard of documents, my careful hands sifting through them slowly.

From murderers to petty thieves—my fingers traced the pages slowly—*he aided them all.*

These documents, all signed in Raul's matching signature, listed large undocumented sums of cash streaming into the businessman's pocket from unknown sources. Even if it couldn't be used as hard evidence against him for aiding criminals, in my hands was a tax evasion case that, if discovered, would most certainly land him behind bars. *Not that they would ever be found.* I pursed my lips, setting the pile aside. *He would most certainly burn everything here the moment we'd disappear.*

But that wasn't the problem at the moment. All documents were left unsigned by the other party, making them anonymous. *Untraceable.*

Even if Raul could remember aiding the masked man all those years ago, I couldn't ask him. I couldn't risk exposing the case, exposing my identity.

My brows drew together at a much smaller stack of papers toward the bottom of the mess, the tiny slips tied together neatly with twine.

"Leave that alone," Raul tried again, his voice strained. "Those are personal loans, nothing more!"

I pulled at the strings, the tightly stacked papers coming loose.

Letters, I thought, the torn black wax of a seal still attached to a few of them. I set the pile at my side, opening one of the latest ones, the date listed being a mere month ago.

My head jerked back, Rowan's grip on the man tightening as I blinked wide-eyed, caught off guard by the words scribbled before me.

"These letters." The words slipped past my lips before my mind could process them. "They're from Laury James Young, aren't they?"

The man opened his mouth to speak, but no words escaped him, my eyes staring holes into his head as he sat completely still. "How could you—"

"They are addressed to you as Raumar, taking the first three letters of your first and last name," I said, eyes scanning the letter over once more. "And are sent from an individual named Lauyou. Judging from the politically-charged contents of this first letter, and of course the name, it's simple enough to assume that you've been busy not only with aiding criminals, but also talking conspiracies with Laury James Young, the most famous political voice in our papers today."

"Famous?" Rowan asked, narrowing his gaze at Raul's stiff frame.

"Well, of course." I straightened up. "He's the first politician cocky enough to take a public stance against the King."

Was this inherently criminal? Not really, but the way he froze at my realization—the color draining from his skin—told me that there was more there than what I was seeing.

Besides—I stood, making my way slowly to the tied up man—*a man so resentful toward the King could have easily pushed that hatred onto the Viscount.*

"Now." I crouched down in front of Raul, his gaze leveling with mine. "Why don't you tell me what a businessman such as yourself has to gain from talking Dream Stitching with an anti-monarchist like Laury James Young?"

Rowan went rigid at my right, the change of stance so severe that even Raul momentarily turned his gaze from the letters to the killer at my right. I swallowed my unease, watching him force his shoulders to relax. The assassin turned his back to us momentarily, retrieving what looked like an old pocket watch, his deep eyes staring at it for several seconds before tucking it back into his coat with a silent sigh.

How strange. I narrowed my eyes at the killer's back, the muscles tense beneath his coat.

How unlike him.

"I know how this looks." My attention snapped back to Raul's stuttering form. "But I swear to you, I have nothing to do with any sort of drug operation!"

"Then please." I motioned to the letter. "Explain what it is that I'm reading."

"Mr. Young and I were simply making an observation of what this country has become, of what that damned King Alpheus has let our country fall into!"

I flinched at the blatant slander of the King's name, my grip on the paper tightening. "Why were these hidden away then?"

"Anti-monarchists aren't exactly allowed to speak their minds." He was angry now, teeth gritted as he spat out each word.

"You do realize that the term *anti-monarchist* in and of itself is treasonous, don't you?"

"What?" He laughed bitterly, glaring knives at me. "Are you a Silver now?"

My lips parted, a burst of anger rushing through my veins, but Rowan had stepped in, Raul flinching as he rested a hand on his shoulder.

"We appreciate the honesty, Mr. Martin. My associate and I will be taking our leave."

The smile on Rowan's lips sent goosebumps up my arms. The expression dropped in an instant, Rowan's hand grabbing the fabric of the man's sleep shirt, lifting the chair forward until his mouth rested at his ear.

"A word of advice though." The man trembled in Rowan's grip, the hitman's voice just above an eerie whisper. "Stay out of the shadows, Raul. I have a creeping intuition that you won't last there much longer."

In one swift motion, he was out cold, Rowan's skilled hand hitting his jaw sharply and sending the man to sleep. I swallowed harshly, disappointed with myself, the letter now a crumpled mess in my angry fist.

"You need to learn to keep your emotions in check." Rowan didn't face me as he spoke, untying the man easily and hoisting him over his shoulder with a grunt.

"I apologize." I faintly touched the mask on my face. "I don't know what came over me."

"Senseless pride."

"Says the arrogant assassin."

"See, but I've earned *my* right to be arrogant." The hitman's tone was sharper now. "Whether you agree with my choice of profession or not, I have built a name for myself. What exactly have you done, *Silver?*"

I held my tongue, watching silently as the man's limp body was thrown onto the mattress of his bed, Rowan rolling back his sore shoulders before turning to meet my eyes.

He was right, after all. Even if I had any credit to my name from my time as a trainee, that was no longer my reality. Truthfully I was a glorified desk assistant, my father's fear of losing me to the chaos of the past keeping me bound to his side.

"Just don't let it happen again."

We slipped out the same way we had come, just two shadows flitting across the empty estate, morphing into every dark corner we passed. We hadn't found out much, nothing pointing even vaguely toward my mother's murder, but something still didn't sit well with me.

Laury James Young. I grunted, pulling myself back over the gate, landing with a quiet exhale. *What exactly are you up to?*

"What's with the glum expression?" Rowan and I walked ahead, disappearing beneath an archway, away from the eyes of any potential onlookers. "Don't tell me you expected to find him wolf mask in hand, confessing at your feet?"

"Don't be absurd." I narrowed my eyes at him, tucking my own frightening mask into the depths of my coat. "I never thought it was him."

I just wish we got more clarity on what could have happened that night.

"I want to investigate Mr. Young as well," I said, removing the cap from my head and freeing the long locks of hair that filled it.

"The politician? Why?" Rowan crossed his arms, leaning against the stone wall of the archway. "Must I remind you that I'm not part of your little justice league? Chasing down those who stand against the King isn't what I agreed to."

"My family is directly connected to the monarchy." I pulled at my coat, raising my brows as I spoke. "Don't you think that her murder could have been fueled by hatred for the King?"

Her death could have been the simple work of misplaced anger, the burning hatred of a desperate individual, one ready to risk it all for a shot at revenge.

"Fine," he huffed, his tone on the verge of annoyance. "If you're so adamant about it."

He turned his back to me before I could get another word out, tipping his hat as he walked away.

"Don't look for me. I will find you."

I had wanted to ask him that day about the way he had stiffened at the mention of drugs, how the calculated grin had trembled on his lips as he pulled out his watch and stared so intensely.

Instead I stood in silence, watching the mystery of a man disappear into the darkness, the cold night air promising yet another sleepless night.

Chapter 6

THE COMFORTING SMELL OF FRESHLY brewed coffee flooded my senses, slipping through the open door of a nearby cafe as Lou and I stood out in the cold. It had been a slow day on patrol, the two of us bickering back and forth to keep ourselves busy as we stood in the bustling streets of the Third District, the hours spilling into each other.

"What I wouldn't give for a hot cup of coffee right now." Lou looked longingly at the cafe's flickering lights, pulling her cap lower as the breeze picked up. "Actually, at this point I'd settle for hot water."

I snorted at her words, a smile spreading across her lips.

"It's way too cold for November," I agreed, my uniform clinging snugly to my body. While Lou despised morning rounds with a burning passion, they had become the most anticipated parts of my week. Getting my father's permission to leave my cramped office was rare, basic morning patrols being my only chance to use my training and work outside of the stuffy station, giving me a prideful happiness that not even the bitter cold could spoil.

"Ah, before I forget," Lou said, her curls bouncing as she turned to face me. "Nana asked if you and Vic would like to stop by for dinner."

"Asked? That doesn't sound like her at all." I raised an eyebrow, a sheepish grin spreading across Lou's face.

"Well, she *demanded*."

"Much better." I nodded, the girl letting out a lighthearted laugh.

Nana Tate had been a close friend of my mother, a sweet older woman who had taken it upon herself to tend to Victor and me after my mother's passing, father often slaving the nights away at the station. That was part of the reason why Lou and I had become so close—the girl becoming more like an older sister than my lieutenant. A subtle bitterness rolled over my tongue, my eyes moving from hers.

"While I'd love to stop by and visit her, I can't tonight." My smile wilted, Lou's expression drooping momentarily. "I have plans."

"That's a shame." Lou had smiled, but I could tell that it wasn't genuine, her sunny demeanor clouded over like the grey skies overhead. "But I guess that's to be expected. You must have your own affairs to attend to. We aren't children anymore, after all."

The undying hole within me ached, throbbing dully as I gave her a sad smile. We weren't children anymore. We were adults with secrets and lies, with responsibilities and loyalties. No matter how much we longed to linger in the past, time would never stop moving. The hands on the clock could never simply stop, destined to forever tick the years away.

"So, who's the lucky bachelor?"

"Oh god Lou, that isn't it at *all*." I scoffed, cringing internally as the killer's face entered my mind.

"What? It was a fair assumption." She grinned, smoothing her unruly hair into a low bun. "You've been a lot quieter lately, slipping away at random times during the day and always busy at night. I mean, it's either that or you've taken up a part-time job as an assassin."

Although I was well aware that her words were meant as a joke, I couldn't help but stiffen as the piercing claws of guilt dug into my back, clinging to me like a leech.

"Well, if you aren't seeing anyone, then I'm still betting on you and the Crown Prince." She did little to suppress the mischievous smile on her lips, my posture stiffening at the mention of the blond-haired boy.

"Please don't speak of Caelum in that light. It isn't proper."

"Of course you'd be on first name basis!" She laughed, my frantic hands moving to cover her lips. "Oh, to be of noble stature."

"Lou, he's ten years older than I am!"

"All the better." She clung to my wrists, batting her eyes dramatically. "If it were for His Highness, I'd gladly trade in a life of uniforms and guns for corsets and tiny dinner forks."

"You're a rotten liar, Lou."

Noble marriage. I begrudgingly pulled my hands away from her grinning face. *Unlike my brother's many duties, that was my only real responsibility.*

While I was fortunate enough to be born into a family that didn't rush such affairs, I couldn't put it off forever. As the second-born child, I was living independently on borrowed time. It was the matter of a few years until a ring would be forced onto my finger.

"I jest." She laughed at my pursed expression. "No matter how dashing the Prince is, I'd sooner wear a bear trap for an anklet than be caught powdered and pressed."

"Welcome back, Lieutenant."

Faint giggles had caught our attention, her teasing eyes moving from me to focus at my back. A surprised breath left my lips as my body jolted forward, a little girl tumbling onto the ground at the impact. I turned my head around, the child's big brown eyes blinking up at me as she sat on the cobblestone street.

"Goodness me." A gentle smile found its way to my lips as I crouched down to her level, offering the girl a gloved hand. "You took quite the tumble there. Are you alright?"

My smile grew brighter as her shoulders relaxed, taking my hand easily. She smiled bashfully, whispering a soft thank you, her friends waiting quietly up ahead, not wanting to leave her behind.

I turned my head back, my grin withering almost instantly as my eyes caught a familiar flash of green from over the little girl's shoulder. My arms fell slack at my sides, gaze now focused on one of the tables outside the warm cafe, a familiar head of black hair blowing in the wind, serpent-like eyes peering at me from over the edge of a book. The girl ran off, blond hair bouncing as she joined her friends, my attention snapping back to the giggling group of children.

I stood back to my feet, muscles tense as my eyes darted from the children to Rowan, the hitman holding my gaze.

Relax. I tried to steady my breathing, stealing a glance at Lou. *He wouldn't try anything in public. He's messing with you.*

My unease only accelerated as he flashed a crooked grin, his lips pinning back at the stiffness in my bones.

"Are you alright?" I flinched at the warmth of a hand on my arm, my wide eyes meeting Lou's. "You look like you've just witnessed a murder."

Or are about to. I swallowed the thought, relief flooding me as the kids ran off, disappearing into the bustling streets of the Capital.

"I'm fine." My lips pressed into a tight smile. Lou's brows furrowed as I turned my back to her, walking away from the cafe. "Let's go. You'll need to switch posts soon, and Papa will want me back."

She matched my steps, the two of us walking in silence as we rounded the corner, Rowan's piercing eyes still boring into the back of my head as we trudged. It was still hard for me to process the fact that he was a human being too, the killer a citizen of Nieve who went out and made friends just like every other person on the street.

The thought made me sick.

The walk back through the Third was a peaceful one, the towering shops and buildings making Nieve feel livelier than just the boring estates that lined the First. Our thick boots dragged over the cobblestones, Lou entertaining me with her usual level of eccentricity as we finally reached the First District.

"I heard from the Viscount that Colonel Silverstein is coming home."

"Yeah, in a few weeks if I'm not mistaken," I said, nodding slowly as I spoke.

"Gosh, it sure has been a while." Lou sighed, stuffing her hands into her pockets. "I think the last time I saw him I had just gotten my badge."

"That wasn't *that* long ago."

"A lot can happen in five years, kid. Let me know when you've worked at the station for three."

I grinned at her words, our laughter filling the square as our loose bodies turned the corner. My eyes instantly met the sharp metal gaze of King Alpheus, the statue overlooking the First District.

But his steady eyes didn't hold mine for long, my attention quickly grasped by the station's doors, loud cries erupting from the front of the building. My heart dropped, head turning to Lou, but she was already steps ahead, cheerful eyes now narrowed and steady, an unshakable hand resting on the pistol at her hip.

My legs had begun to move unknowingly, feet pounding silently up the steps to the station door, a massive breath of relief escaping me at the deep blue eyes that met mine. My gaze shifted almost immediately from my brother to the woman gripping the front of his uniform, her fur-clad shoulders shaking as hysterical cries escaped her.

"Please, let me see the Viscount. I demand that I speak to him!"

"Ma'am, if you could please take a deep breath and have a seat, I—"

"You don't understand!" She shook out of my brother's grip, eyes wide and wet with tears. "They were inside the house. They almost killed him!"

"Excuse me. Why don't I get you something warm to drink? Let's get you inside," Lou tried, but the woman recoiled from her touch, eyes wild.

"I don't need to be warm. I need the men who broke into my estate caught!"

"Where is it that you live?" Victor asked gently, hands hovering near her shaking frame.

"My husband and I are visiting from the South."

My muscles went rigid, realization hitting me like a ton of bricks as she struggled to speak through her tears.

"They broke into the Violet Estate!"

This is bad, very very bad. My eyes shot to Lou, then to my brother. This woman was Raul's wife, her attire and fine jewelry making much more sense now. She must've been horrified coming home after a night out and finding her husband's study a mess, his disgruntled figure panicked and afraid. Even though he wasn't completely free of crime, nothing warranted such treatment.

I did this to her. My chest throbbed beneath the layers of my uniform. *This is my fault.*

"Where is he? Where is the Viscount now?" Her thick red curls bounced as she stammered, hands pulling at my brother's coat.

Did Raul figure us out? It was dark in the room, but did he end up remembering anything distinctive? Or worse, did he somehow recognize me? By my voice? By my mannerisms?

Stop. I closed my eyes, trying to rid myself of the selfish thoughts. That wasn't what mattered right now. There was a frightened woman asking for our help. My worries didn't matter.

Silver or not, I was still a part of this station.

I swallowed harshly, straightening my shoulders back as I took her trembling hands in mine.

"Please, Miss." I smiled softly, her pale blue eyes moving from Victor to focus on me. "Why don't we go inside and I'll have an officer take some notes on your case?" I released the tension in my stance as her shaky hands relaxed in my gloved grip.

"Alright." Her big blue eyes were bloodshot from crying, the tears on her cheeks glistening in the cold. "Alright, fine."

I squeezed her hands gently, looking over at Victor from the corner of my eye. He nodded softly, moving to hold the door open for us as we entered, the warm air flushing the woman's cheeks a faint pink.

My eyes scanned the busy vicinity, the woman shrinking into my side as we entered, standing in the center of the bustling hallway.

She was afraid, distressed, and although the fear of being outed was great, the guilt of what I had done was greater. While I couldn't confess or help the investigation, I could temporarily ease her worries, and for now that was what mattered.

"Excuse me." My voice was much bolder than I felt, a few sets of eyes stopping to look at me. "Could I get an officer over here?"

The thick scent of firewood and booze flooded my senses, chasing the late night's chill away. A shiver ran through my skin, pricking down my arms and back as my cold body was enveloped by the warmth of the alehouse.

I flashed a tight smile, tipping my hat at the warm eyes of the tavern owner, his white hair peeking below a flat cap of his own. The bustling streets of the Third District had quieted down now, leaving my lonesome body to wander down the lit alleyways alone. The small inn was quiet, the gentle droning of whispered murmurs the only sound filling the room, weary groups of factory workers spread around the bar, drinking the hard day's worries away. And beyond their clouded gazes and quiet smiles sat Rowan Marrow, his soundless figure tucked into the corner of the room. His tanned skin and sharp features were illuminated by the fireplace's gentle glow, cold eyes staring at the swirling flames in contempt.

He was a handsome fellow—I gave him that. Even the gentle scowl on his features was charming in a way that I couldn't describe. His simple work attire was clean, far too clean for any *real* laborer, his pristine white shirt left partially undone, the simple black vest that covered it hanging open as he sat back, a hand lazily playing with the ends of his dark hair.

His face remained unchanged, even as he turned his head to look at me, perceptive green eyes boring into my own.

"How long were you planning on staring?" He turned back to the fireplace as I approached him and pulled out the chair across from his.

"Not long." I sighed, taking a seat in front of the assassin, his cool gaze moving to me.

"Daddy didn't give you any trouble?"

"Shut it."

"What?" He raised his eyebrows mockingly, snickering at my firm expression. "Am I not allowed to express concern for my colleague?"

"No," I muttered dryly, eyes drifting across the twisted bottles that sat behind the bar. "But if you're *so* eager to chat, what's your story *Alias*?"

The shift in the air between us was minimal, but I sensed it, the assassin's dark eyes narrowing slightly. *He's uncomfortable,* I thought, a strange sense of pride momentarily flitting through me. *Good.*

"I don't have one."

"Everyone has a story." I held his gaze, noticing the muscles shift beneath the fabric of his sleeves.

"Well, I doubt you'd favor it much," he said shortly. "Everyone in mine is dead."

"But somehow you're not." My words were much sharper, a flickering flame of anger burning through my chest at the sinful man before me. "Funny how life works that way."

His jaw twitched, teeth clenched as I held his stare.

"Laury James Young, as requested." He wasted no time, pulling a folded paper from inside his vest, sliding it along the table's rough ridges. "He's a well-known yet low-ranking politician."

"Oh, I'm quite familiar with him," I said, smoothing out the creases in the newspaper article, faint smudges of ink staining my fingertips.

Laury James Young had first emerged in the political world about fifteen years ago, starting off as a voice for the people, his ideals appealing mostly to those in the outer districts and slums of Nieve. But only a few short years after his emergence he had gained quite the following. In turn he became bolder with his opinions, not shying away from his thoughts on the problems within the kingdom and the issues within the monarchy. He made empty assumptions about the monarchy and those who operated under it, dubbing the Imperial Force as a corrupted means of government that worked solely to protect the privileged, ignoring the problems of the outer neighborhoods of Nieve.

"But before we go any further…" I swallowed, the hitman raising an eyebrow at me. "Raul Martin's wife showed up at the station this morning."

The indifferent boy paused, elbows leaning onto the table as he narrowed his eyes. "And?"

"She was completely hysterical, sobbing about how their estate was broken into."

"Broken into by *who*?"

"She wasn't too specific." I sighed, sitting back in my chair. "But I overheard her interview, and it sounded like she was addressing two masked thieves, describing the pair as a man and his son."

"A man and his son," Rowan slowly repeated to himself, my smaller frame and higher voice a solid argument toward Raul's bizarre analysis. His shoulders loosened, the hitman leaning back tiredly, arms crossed.

"Do you think we'll be found out?"

"Definitely not." His tone was annoyed, eyes narrow as he stared through my skin. "I just hate being sloppy."

I clenched my fists below the table, a burning flash of anger brewing within me at his words. "These are people, not inanimate objects that we're playing with."

"All the more reason to be thorough."

The way he said that sent a shiver slithering down my spine, his heartless gaze quickly reminding me whom I was dealing with. He and I would never see things in the same light.

"Alias Black kills for a price, for a copious fee." I stared him in the eyes and asked despite already knowing the answer, looking for a weak point, hoping he would falter. "Is money really worth more to you than a human life?"

"Most definitely." He didn't blink as the damning words rolled off his tongue.

"You *disgust* me."

"I bet I do, Your Grace." His eyes glinted eerily into the flickering light. "But when there is no noble blood running through your veins, you realize just how high the value of money really is. It is not just what keeps your mug full and your clothes clean. It is your tongue and lips, your right to speak, your right to be listened to. Your right to live is measured in the weight of your pockets. What would my soul get me in the slums of Nieve?"

The shadow of something dark moved across the killer's collected face, an underlying anger beneath his cold-blooded words.

"*Not even the core of an apple.* No, I'd much rather gamble something as trivial as my humanity than starve on the streets."

He said more than I had expected him to, and the faint gleam of bewilderment in his eyes told me he thought the same. The killer shifted back in his seat, running restless fingers through his dark hair.

Murderers are still men. The words fished themselves back out from the depths of my mind. *Yet at times, this one seems more like a monster.*

"While our talk with Raul was a fluke, I think it was much more valuable than any discreet snooping we could have done on our own." He laced his gloved fingers together. "We'll stick with it."

I bit back my protests, knowing the killer was right but still not liking it. Terrorizing citizens wasn't exactly in line with my moral code, nor was it a tactile means of investigation.

All it would take was one person to recognize my voice or decipher our questions, and I'd be exposed for the noble blood in my veins.

I'd lose everything.

"But in light of the recent progression, from now on we blindfold our people of interest." Rowan's words jolted me out of my thoughts.

"Blindfold them?" My voice was smaller than I would have liked.

"The less they know about us the better. Besides, it'll work for intimidation as well, since you're so adamant on leaving them unscathed. The average human relies quite heavily on their sense of sight."

"You talk as if they'll just let you tie something around their eyes."

"That's why we'll use an incapacitating agent first."

My brows came together, fists clenching at his criminal proposal. "We are *not* drugging people."

97

"I didn't say that." He shrugged, carefully walking around his words as he spoke. He groaned at my tight expression, rubbing tiredly at his eyes. "Look, we can't risk knocking them out with force. We need them completely aware and coherent for questioning and a little chloroform won't kill anyone."

He crossed his arms when I didn't budge, my lips pressed into a fine line at his words.

"You know, if you want to solve this case as badly as you let on, you'll loosen that death grip on your morality. No one gets anywhere in life without getting their hands a little dirty."

"That isn't true."

"Is it not?"

I paused, stopping myself before I could argue any further. There was no point in reasoning with a killer.

"I'm going to assume that the rest of your family isn't as naive as you are."

"What the hell is that supposed to mean?" I narrowed my eyes at his bland expression, my words more defensive than intended.

"Exactly what it sounds like." He tilted his head as he spoke, observing my reaction. "You pride yourself on that sickening belief that this world intended for all who live in it to be good. I bet you think that makes you superior."

"I know it does."

"I'd be careful, Silver. That heart of yours is both a spear and a shield." He clicked his tongue, sitting up. "Until it is a shackle."

"Back to the topic of Raul." My voice was sharp, blatant irritation in my blood. "Dream Stitching—I'd assume you know what that is?"

My nerves loosened at his reaction, the cold-blooded killer nearly flinching as the two words left my lips.

"Yes," he said steadily, recovering quickly. "A bit."

"Hallucinogens have been ruling the black market for a long time, but it's gotten worse these last few years. Now they're available to anyone who wants them, giving every petty criminal the ability to drug someone, putting their victim in a state of false reality." I kept my voice down as the tavern door blew open, inviting a few more tired workers in for the night. "My brother receives quite a few cases related to these drugs at the station, but I've found that they're rarely related to the actual act of drugging someone. Most of the cases pertain to what happens afterwards."

After being drugged, the victim would be trapped in a dream-like state, unable to distinguish reality from whatever their mind would conjure up. This would often lead to mass crime and murder, those under the influence claiming to have slain beasts and monsters in their fits of fear, only to later discover that they had slaughtered innocent people.

"It wasn't always like that." Rowan's eyes watched the flames flicker behind me as he spoke. "Dream Stitching was originally invented for the wealthy, a way for them to live out their impossible fantasies, a way for them to experience dreams with their eyes open. But of course, there are two sides to every coin." His empty gaze fell to the table, resting on his hands. "It wasn't long before people weaponized the drugs, using hallucinogens to terrify people and coerce them into committing crimes in their favor, all the while the unknowing victim believed that they were simply having a nightmare."

My gaze mimicked his, and I furrowed my brows as he slowly moved his fingers, his eyes resting on each one before moving to the next. "You're counting them, aren't you?"

He paused, a bitter smile twitching at the ends of his lips as he raised his head to face me.

"You seem to know more than you let on."

"Yes." He sighed tiredly, black hair falling in front of his eyes. "It's a tell."

"A way to prove whether what you're seeing is real or not," I murmured, watching him nod slightly.

"A way to determine if you're awake." His shoulders shifted as he spoke, our eye contact almost forced. "Or dreaming with your eyes open. Your brain can't process things properly in dreams, resulting in strange-looking reflections, jumbled gibberish in books, and—"

"Extra fingers." I cut him off, looking down at my own hands. I counted ten, five fingers on each hand, before looking back up at Rowan, freezing as he stared through me, eyes as sharp as his blades.

"Laury James Young," he spoke after a short silence, gaze unwavering. "He lives in a mid-sized apartment in the Third District but comes from a small neighborhood in the Sixth. His mother was a teacher, his father a factory worker who passed away on the job. No security, but he lives with his wife, one who doesn't seem to favor nights out such as Mrs. Martin."

"An apartment means less room to move around, and thinner walls," I said—more to myself than to him—clenching the fabric of my pants in my fists.

"We'll need to be careful," he agreed, pulling at his gloves and standing to his feet.

"And the entrance? How are we going to get in?" I stood up quickly, pulling the cap over my eyes as I scanned around us.

"His common room window. He keeps it unlocked."

"How do you—"

"Tomorrow evening, two a.m." He cut me off, threading his hand through his coat sleeve, pulling the dark fabric over his shoulders. "I'll be in the alley across from 278 Pissenlit Street."

He pushed his dark hair back, flashing a lopsided grin that didn't match his eyes.

"Don't keep me waiting."

And just as quickly as he was here, he was gone, disappearing out the door without a sound. I stared at my hands again, the raised scar on my right palm causing my fists to clench.

*Laury James Young...*I pressed my fingers against the fabric of my shirt, the flower pendant beneath it digging its defined petals into my skin.

You're next.

Chapter 7

THE HEM OF MY DRESS brushed my knees as I strained, fingertips tracing the hard spine of a book. I grabbed its back, retrieving it with a slow exhale, my eyes shifting across the dusty cover.

"Pandora's box?" I called out, lifting my eyes from the fraying leather cover.

Oliver's eyes peeked over from behind a bookshelf, the pale morning light that seeped through the shop's windows reflecting off his glasses.

"Pandora's *jar*," he corrected, my eyes drifting to the pages as I flipped through. "It's a Greek mythological story of temptation and human curiosity."

"Temptation, huh?" I tugged at the tight fabric of my collar, before tracing the time-stained pages gently with my fingers. Frightening pictures adorned nearly every page, the dark ink beginning to fade after years of wear.

"Yes."

He grunted, lifting a thick stack of newly dusted books and rounding the shelves to stand by my side. The thick smell of worn ink and paper that filled the air around us only intensified as he leaned over my shoulder, placing the books down on a rusted cart with a huff.

"Zeus ordered Hephaestus to create a woman from clay, seeking revenge after Prometheus stole fire and delivered it to the human race." He pointed to a smudged image, my eyes squinting at his words. "He named her Pandora. He and the other Greek gods each gave her a gift, Aphrodite giving her beauty, Athena wisdom, Apollo talent, and so on. But Zeus—Zeus made her mischievous and foolish, then gifted Pandora a jar."

I furrowed my brows as he spoke, eyes drifting over the strange letters.

"He warned her not to open it, no matter the circumstance, before sending her away, and she tried to listen, she truly did, but of course human curiosity is untamable. Although she struggled to resist the temptation, she opened the jar, unleashing all evils upon the world."

My posture stiffened at the next few images, dark blots of ink littering the page chaotically, ghost-like figures escaping the decorated jar, each wearing a face more horrible than the last.

"Hunger, hatred, sickness, and death slipped out before she could slam it shut." His voice had quieted, as if not to wake the fearsome images on the page. "The only thing that she managed to trap inside was hope."

I blinked hard, shutting the book quickly and turning my face away from Oliver's before he could gauge my expression.

Something about that story unsettled me.

"In a way you could say that Pandora herself is an analogy for the jar. Both made of clay, both the jar and a human containing all of these evil properties." He took it from my hands, his solid frame still hovering over my shoulder as he wiped at the cover. "And in another light, you cannot blame her, for we are what we are. Foolish and self-ish, impulsively pushing through our lives without thinking of the consequences."

I must have grown too quiet, because Oliver gently padded around me, placing the book on a creaking rack before facing me with gentle eyes.

"I'm sorry about this, by the way."

"Sorry?" I raised an eyebrow, hesitantly reaching for the next book on my assigned shelf. "For what?"

"Making you spend your day off sorting books with me." He sighed, taking a moment to wipe the dust from his glasses. "I know we were supposed to grab breakfast, but tomorrow's shipment came a bit earlier than expected and I couldn't let Mr. Jones sort through it all alone."

The tension in my muscles faltered at the mention of Flint, the quiet boy scuffling away somewhere on the second floor of the shop.

"I'm sure you get enough dust and loose papers on the daily."

"I really don't mind." I flashed him a smile, brushing the loose strands of hair away from my face. "Besides, I want to help. This amount of work is insane, even for you."

My careful hands retrieved the next book on my shelf, wiping the cover with my sleeve. *Greek Tragedies and Their Relevance in the Modern Era.*

"You usually do this alone, don't you?" I asked, cocking my head at the cover before raising my gaze back to the shelves.

He hummed, reaching over my head to retrieve a thickly bound book, the old leather cover peeling apart. He furrowed his brows, sighing heavily before placing it on the bottom rack of the cart, along with all the other books that needed sprucing up.

"Doesn't it get lonely?"

He paused, turning his gaze down to me. I had jolted him, his deep chocolate eyes holding a comfortable sadness as he smiled warmly at me. Vic and I had lost our mother when we were young, but Papa had always been there, working tirelessly to fill the hole left behind.

But Oliver had been alone from the start, losing his parents before he was capable of even remembering them.

"I'm never alone."

My grip tightened on the book, a familiar sorrow in his gaze as his eyes flitted from mine to the shelves around us.

"How could I be with the hundreds of thousands of people who live beneath these covers?"

My heart throbbed in my chest, lips pressing firmly as they threatened to tremble.

Out of every single person in my life, I believed I understood Oliver Brightly best.

For he held the same look in his knowing eyes. The same sense of empty loss, of child-like pain.

A longing for something you can hardly recall.

My silence must've dragged on for longer than intended because a breathy laugh escaped him, his hand moving to gently rest on my head.

"I appreciate the concern though, Valeria."

A loud crash echoed from the second story, followed by a muffled string of curses. A laugh bubbled past my lips as Oliver closed his eyes, lifting a hand to rub at his forehead.

"I'd imagine that Flint has been keeping you on your toes." I grinned, Oliver's deep laughs rumbling through my chest.

"He's a good kid, and a hard worker," he said, glancing up at the ceiling at the sound of heavy steps. "He's just a bit *rough*."

A gentle smile pulled at my lips, Flint's bright brown eyes flashing through my mind.

"You mean a lot to him."

I raised an eyebrow at Oliver's words, setting the heavy book onto a creaking rack. "Why do you say that?"

"He talks about you tirelessly."

A faint blush seared my cheeks at the laugh that escaped me, Oliver shrugging as he moved to reach over my head once again.

"You did save his life, after all."

My expression wilted slightly, the night we first locked eyes still as clear as yesterday.

Flint had been by my side for the past two years, the two of us meeting when I was a trainee, the night of my very first case. My father had been investigating a string of child trafficking operations, a ring of them flowing through the lesser neighborhoods of Nieve. It was my first time operating in a unit all on my own, a ragtag group of junior officers, and I sent out to investigate a minor tip while father and Vic chased after their own more promising trails. We had knocked on every door in the Sixth District, looked into every lead and came up completely empty-handed. But something had been off, the streets much too quiet for so early into the night. That's when I stumbled upon a creaking sewer, leading my unit into the underground tunnels of Nieve.

To this day I cannot forget what we had found down there, the rotting bodies of young boys and girls haunting my nightmares unrelentingly. But it was in that dark and horrifying place where I had first laid eyes upon a young boy, so thin and frail that he blended right in with the corpses.

Flint had been fourteen years old at the time but looked much younger, his malnourished body consisting of little more than bulging ribs and sunken eyes.

I had busted my first case that night, making the first arrests of many that would follow that week.

The surviving children had been whisked away by child protective services, their eyes heavy with an emptiness I could never forget. They had seen the worst of what humans were capable of, lived through it themselves. Nothing in this world could change that.

But there was one boy, the child who had hid amongst the corpses, who held my gaze, his eyes focused and fierce. Not with hatred for what the world had done to him, but with something almost forgiving. As if he were willing to give life another chance, as if he were waiting to see what I would do.

And for whatever reason, I couldn't tear my eyes away from his.

Flint had been by my side ever since that night, my father agreeing to take the boy under his wing if I took responsibility for his future. I had worked extra hard for the next few months, managing to pay rent for a modest apartment of his own in the Third District and spending every free hour with the boy, learning of his interests, his dreams, and his fears.

It was soon after that when Oliver, who had just received the keys to The Wild Iris, offered to take him in as an assistant, giving him a chance to start over. To rule over his own existence.

"He cares for you very much, Valeria."

I swallowed the bitter guilt that sat on my tongue, averting my eyes from his.

That's exactly why I can't involve him in my problems any further.

I'd been avoiding the boy completely since the night Rowan and I met, coming up with every excuse not to see him, and I could tell that he was hurt. Even now, he didn't make a single attempt to come downstairs, probably thinking that he had done something to upset me.

And while that pained me, it was for the best.

"Oliver." The words spilled from my lips before I could properly think them through. "How can you truly distinguish between what's right and wrong? Whether doing the wrong things for the right reasons is justified?"

"That's a tricky question." He paused momentarily, staring off before turning to look down at me. "I guess the correct answer would be that at the end of the day there is no right or wrong."

"But that isn't true," I said quickly, shaking my head as I spoke. "Murder, theft, betrayal—they are all innately bad."

"You're right." Oliver nodded slowly, his deep eyes finding mine once again. "To an extent, of course."

I furrowed my brows at his words, the boy taking a moment to let the books slip from his grip back onto their original shelf.

"Each side of a conflict does things that they believe are right, that they think are necessary. No human being is inherently evil, nor are they perfectly good. We are all selfish beings whose actions are based on a narrow view of the world around us. It would be a lie to believe any differently."

"Then…" My words were hesitant, uncomfortable as they sat in my mouth. "Redemption. Do you believe in that?"

"Of course I do." Oliver's response was quick, the steadiness in his tone surprising me. "Imagine how dark and dreary a world without forgiveness would be. I believe that every human being on this earth is capable of doing what's right in the end. It's just a matter of whether they choose to believe in that themselves."

Forgiveness, huh? I swallowed the heaviness in my chest. The piercing green eyes of Alias Black flashed through my mind, quickly erasing any trace of the earlier thought. *Some things could never be forgiven.* I dropped my gaze to my feet, focusing on the old black leather of my boots.

With all the lies I've told, I must be past the notion myself.

"You know…" Oliver sighed, my eyes flitting up to meet his. "I may not be the best person for advice, but I think I can listen pretty well. If you need to talk about something, anything at all, you can tell me."

The boy stared down at me warmly, the two of us similar in ways that even my brother was a stranger to.

"You can talk to me, Valeria."

A smile unknowingly pulled at my lips, a faint sense of warmth returning to my vacant bones.

"I'll keep that in mind. Thank you, Oliver."

His eyes softened at my tone, his shoulders relaxing.

"You know what?" I said suddenly, the atmosphere of the room losing some of its weight. "I bet we could still make it for lunch if we finish within the next two hours."

"Great." He grinned, reaching over my head once more. "I could use a break."

The stone wall of the archway was cold, seeping through my many layers of clothing as I sat against it. Sneaking out of the estate had been easier than usual, both Papa and Victor soundly snoring in the office downstairs, their files still open and coffee mugs partially full. They had been working a lot harder these past few months, the pair spending their nights bouncing ideas off the walls of our estate as the rest of Nieve lay sound asleep in their beds.

My gloved fingers traced the frowning mask in my grip, its smooth, porcelain-like surface cold to the touch.

What I was doing was wrong. I was sure of that, but wasn't the pursuit of justice more important than these trivial feelings of mine?

Or—my grip tightened on the mask—*is this just my own reckless selfishness?*

The subtle sound of feet interrupted my thoughts, soft clicks against the cobblestone street turning my eyes up from my lap.

"You weren't waiting long, were you?" Rowan tipped his hat, my eyes dropping back to my lap. Surprise pricked my shoulders at the gloved hand that extended out before me, Rowan staring off as he offered it. I swallowed hard, tentatively taking it and pulling myself to my feet.

"Laury's apartment is straight up the road. The first building on the second floor." He dropped my hand, turning to walk ahead as he spoke.

There was something off about the killer, his sarcastic jests and probing words toned down to a minimum.

I narrowed my eyes at his back but said nothing, shifting my focus to the biting cold.

"I'm assuming you've been stalking him for the past day or two." I brushed off my pants before matching his steps.

"Observing him, yes." He nodded, stuffing his hands into his pockets. "He keeps the main room's window unlocked. We'll trail up the emergency ladder to the fourth floor's balcony and climb down the windowsills."

"And to"—the words were heavy on my tongue—"incapacitate him?"

He pulled open his coat, the glass of a bottle glinting in the pale moonlight. I must've stiffened, flinching away from the hitman, because his empty eyes moved from mine, the killer turning away and putting some space between us.

"It'll be quick and painless."

I furrowed my brows at his words, his back shifting beneath the fabric of his coat.

"So don't worry so much." He slipped on his mask before I could ask any further questions, my cold hands mimicking his movements. "Try to keep up."

The streets of the Third District were much emptier now, the bustling neighborhoods nearly silent in the dead of night. Rowan and I shifted from shadow to shadow, disappearing completely beneath the sheet of night as we reached the tall brick building, the apartment complex towering over us, one of many in the district.

Rowan's stealthy figure slipped up the ladder, his quick feet leaping and landing soundlessly onto the fourth floor's metal balcony.

A breath escaped me as I clutched the ladder, the cold metal chilling the skin past my gloves. I hoisted myself up easily, fingers gripping each rung as I pulled myself up all four floors.

My eyes fell shut momentarily in an attempt to steady my racing heart before I leapt onto the balcony, crouching as I landed to minimize the sound.

Rowan waited for me to collect myself before stepping over the metal railing and clinging to the other side. The rusty metal bars groaned at his weight, and his gaze focused as he steadied himself.

"Quickly and quietly." His voice whistled into the wind, the boy taking one more second to look at me before dropping his lower body, gloved hands loosening their grip on the bars and sliding down, tightening again just in time to grab the ledge, the tips of his boots barely touching the hard brick sill of a third-story window.

He clenched his jaw, both balls of his feet now on the ledge, before letting go of the railing completely and steading himself on the bulging sill. I watched as he repeated his movements, the assassin scaling down the side of the building, his silent figure moving swiftly and surely.

I swallowed harshly, a heavy lump of fear sticking to the inside of my throat as I swung a leg over the metal railing of the fourth floor's balcony, my shaky hands gripping the rusted metal for dear life.

"Breathe, Valeria." My whispered words were pleading as I let my legs reluctantly hang below me, my tight grip slowly loosening on the bars and sending me sliding down.

I gritted my teeth, clamping on the bars again as I reached the ledge, my body jolting at the sudden stop in momentum. My feet searched the open air, the tips of my boots barely grazing the hard sill below me.

You idiot. I cursed at myself internally, realization hitting me just as the wind picked up, pricking my skin once again. Rowan towered over me, his height giving him the ability to reach each window with ease.

But I—a grunt left my lips as I swung my legs, gaining strength with each sway—*I would have a significant amount of trouble.*

It took every ounce of restraint I possessed not to scream as I released my grip on the bars, my body falling forward, face slamming against the glass of the third story window as I crouched unsteadily on the brick base.

I groaned in pain, eyes fluttering shut as I rubbed at the sore skin of my face. Despite the stinging of my cheek, relief flooded through me at my successful landing.

Alright. I peeked over the edge, staring down at the raven-haired bastard beneath me, arms crossed and eyes expectant, an irritating grin on his lips.

I repeated my earlier motions, this time gripping the brick slab at my feet before letting my body dangle into the chilling air once more. I was less frightened now, the presence of Rowan beneath me, while annoying, was strangely reassuring.

I exhaled, feeling the hard ridges in the bricks below my fingers, before swinging my legs forward again, letting go immediately. My feet hit the brick sill, but I had lost my balance, not taking the time to prepare for the rough landing. A gloved hand gripped the collar of my shirt, steadying my flailing upper body, my own hands moving to grab the thick fabric of his sleeves.

"Quickly and *quietly*." Rowan dropped my collar as I backed away, feeling the hard glass of the window at my side.

"Thank you," I breathed, my heart still hammering against my ribcage.

He crouched down slowly, silently gripping the bottom of the windowpane and sliding it open. Rowan slipped underneath the glass easily, my own body mimicking his movements, before he pulled it shut, faint whispers of wind slipping in with us.

I licked my lips, the cold night air all but cracking the fragile skin, my eyes scanning the quaint space around us.

We were in the common room of the humble home, a worn brick fireplace sputtering weakly as our silent feet padded around. Basic wooden furniture filled the warm room, the space proving to be a perfectly cozy home for a middle-class couple.

A gloved hand slipped into the pocket of my coat, the jagged outline of a matchbox finding my fingers. I pulled it out silently, sliding it open and retrieving a singular match, its wood rough and splintered. I struck it quickly against the box, a faint spark emitting from it before it caught fire. My shoulders relaxed, the faint flame banishing some of the darkness. A breath left my lips as two fingers quickly pinched the tip of the match, instantly snuffing the pale beacon out.

"I'd prefer if you wouldn't," Rowan said under his breath, my eyes narrowing.

"Not a fan of the light?"

"Not really, no." He gave me a tight lipped smile. "I've been told I have a greater affinity for darkness."

But his hard gaze lingered on the burned-out match in my grip, dancing wisps of smoke painting pictures in the air above it, and for a moment, I thought he might have grimaced. Perhaps it was just a trick of my vision.

I shrugged him off, tucking its remains into my coat and turning my back to the killer.

I squinted through the dark, a smile finding my lips at the countless picture frames that lined the walls. They all varied in sizes, each one either dyed a strange color or decorated in fabric frills or patterns.

My fingers reached out, grazing the festive ornaments that clung to one of the wooden frames, the black-and-white image of Mr. Young and a woman grinning brightly at each other in the snow coming into focus as my eyes adjusted to the dark.

The unwavering stare at my back sent a chill through me, and I turned to meet Rowan's sharp gaze.

He tilted his head in the direction of the door on my right, my nerves spiking again as my hand found the doorknob, twisting it slowly. The two of us winced as the door creaked open, Rowan's quick hand grabbing the frame before I could push any further. He didn't utter a word, his body slipping through the half-open door, my own figure moving accordingly and squinting into the unknown terrain.

A stiffness infested my bones at the rustled movement toward the other side of the room. One—no—*two* bodies rose and fell gently as they drifted through a night's thick slumber.

The subtle clink of glass raised the hairs on the back of my neck, my eyes wide as Rowan retrieved the thin bottle from his coat, pressing its open head against a plain cloth. I clenched my fists at my side at the curved silhouette of a woman, Rowan brushing the hair out of her face before carefully pressing the cloth to her nose. She barely moved, the only indication of her incapacitation being the deep exhale that escaped her, her body slipping into a deeper form of sleep. Some tension left my shoulders when he pulled away from her, his steps light as he padded across the wooden floor of the bedroom.

Mr. Young had been facing his wife in his sleep, chest moving steadily as Rowan pressed the cloth against his nose, my blood running cold as the man shifted, then went as stiff as a board.

Rowan's lips pulled tight, holding the cloth more firmly as the man's eyes opened, bulging as he struggled to wrestle Rowan off him. One of his shaky hands clawed at the hitman, the other searching the bed desperately, stilling only as he touched a strand of his wife's hair.

Rowan sighed, ripping the man's hand from his shirt as his eyes rolled back, going completely limp. I exhaled shakily, my feet stepping carefully toward the woman's side of the bed. My heart ached in my chest at her still figure, my gloved hand finding hers and gently squeezing.

"So troublesome." Rowan's voice was breathless, dark strands of hair falling in front of his eyes. He grunted, hoisting the sleeping man over his shoulders and trudging out of the bedroom. "Imagine how much easier this would be if we simply disposed of them when we were done."

"You're disgusting." My grip on her hand tightened, a new flower of resentment blooming within me at the killer's words.

"Careful, doll," he taunted, eyes completely free of any regret or remorse. "You might hurt my feelings."

I hate him. My hand trembled against hers, blurry eyes tracing her rosy cheeks. *I hate him so much I can hardly breathe.*

But you want answers, don't you? My grip trembled, my own subconscious mocking me. *You want to solve this case.*

I straightened my back, my gloved fingers slipping from the woman's hand as I turned to follow Rowan out the door.

I would beg for forgiveness later.

The door clicked shut behind me, my tense fingers slipping from its handle as I turned to face the tiny room. My eyes scanned the bookcases that lined the walls, various papers littering the worn wooden desk that sat in the room's center, and countless abandoned mugs spread out across the floor.

This must be his study, I thought, my focus shifting to Rowan, his hands pulling the rope tightly around the man's wrists. He was bound the same way Raul was, hands at the chair's back and feet anchored to the seat's wooden legs, keeping the man secure.

"Blindfold," Rowan murmured, eyes intense as he worked, tightening the hold on the man's right leg.

I pressed my lips together, the hitman's nonchalant attitude sparking a blistering desire within me to watch him crash and burn.

113

But he's good, far too good at being wicked, and vile, and nasty.

"You know, even if you're never caught by the Silvers, the universe has its way of balancing the scale," I muttered, fishing through the fabric of my coat and retrieving a black strip of fabric, one I had ripped from an old cloth rag.

"I don't believe in things as incidental as karma."

"I'd be surprised if you believed in anything at all." I tossed the strip to Rowan, his gloved hand catching it easily and securing it around Mr. Young's eyes, blinding him.

"Money has yet to fail me thus far in life."

He stood to his feet, tucking the hair out of his face, before digging a hand into the pocket of his coat and retrieving an old pocket watch. I watched carefully as it clicked open, staring intently at the rusted metal hands that ticked beneath its glass.

"That watch," I said, taking a small step in his direction. "It's the same one you took out in Raul's estate."

"Perceptive, aren't we?" Rowan mumbled, taking another moment to stare before pressing it shut. "Time has no value in dreams. Just as your brain cannot process numbers or recognize your own reflection, the concept of time is useless when floating in and out of reality."

He tucked the watch back into his coat, his hand lingering in his pocket, his eyes still avoiding my own.

"As long as the clock ticks correctly, I know that I'm fully awake. That what I'm seeing is real."

"You check it quite often," I said, his green eyes meeting mine from behind the frightening mask. "I don't think I've ever worried about such a thing."

"Yes, well"—he breathed out, rolling his shoulders back—"I've spent a considerable amount of time in false realities."

I nodded, turning my masked face to the ground, but didn't miss his last few words.

"I just…" His voice stalled momentarily. "I like to make sure that what I'm seeing is *real*."

A weighted groan rumbled from the bound man. We grew silent instantly, watching the politician slowly regain consciousness. It was easy to tell the exact moment he realized what had happened, because without warning the man lunged forward, the chair screeching with the force of his movements.

"Who's there?" he yelled, pulling vigorously at his restraints. "Where is Caroline? Where is my wife?!"

"Why don't you answer some questions for us first, Mr. Young?"

He stiffened, limbs going rigid as Rowan's words echoed through the silent room.

"I am not saying a *single* word"—the vein in his neck bulged as he bared his teeth—"until you tell me exactly where my wife is."

"Do you *really* want to—"

"She's in the bedroom asleep." I cut Rowan off, swallowing harshly at the man's fear for his wife. "Don't worry about her. We're here to speak with you."

A shaky exhale left the man's lips, his head slumping forward, pale strands of his blond hair gleaming in the faint moonlight that slipped through the curtains. "What is it that you want?"

"You're somewhat famous, aren't you Laury?" Rowan didn't miss a beat, crouching down in front of the man, elbows on his knees. "A politician of *unconventional* beliefs."

"We are all entitled to our opinions." His head perked up suddenly. "If you were sent by the King, then—"

"*Please* Laury, don't get too cocky now." Rowan laughed, the terrible grin that adorned his mask seeming all the more sinister. "We are just two curious individuals wanting answers to a few curious questions."

Mr. Young was still tense, but his shoulders relaxed, the man not pulling as hard on his restraints.

"Would you say that you disagree with the monarchy?"

"I don't hold any hatred toward anyone," he said strictly, every word holding some form of conviction. "I just believe that Alpheus has let Nieve fall to ruin."

115

"*King* Alpheus?" Annoyance was a sharp blade on my tongue. "What makes you say that?"

"Are you joking?" His laugh was bitter, the blindfolded man shaking his head in disbelief. "The outer districts have fallen to chaos! Entire neighborhoods and communities abandoned by the King as he continues to filter money into the higher class. He has neglected his people, neglected the responsibilities of being the monarch." He pulled his head back, a prideful motion for a man in his current predicament. "Why should we stand silent at such blatant disregard for the well-being of our country?"

"And those connected to the monarchy? The Parliament, Silvers, and Blue Bloods?" Rowan asked, tilting his head as the man stilled.

"*Blue Bloods,* huh?" A smile pricked the edges of Laury's lips, Rowan's eyes narrowing. "You're from one of the outer districts."

I stiffened, Rowan's slitted eyes widening slightly, the hitman standing back to his feet.

"I haven't heard someone use that term since I moved from the Sixth."

Rowan's posture had straightened, his jaw set in annoyance.

This man is much sharper than we first anticipated. I turned my attention to the rest of the room, trailing my gloved fingers across the endless rows of books as I rounded his desk.

It was old, definitely worn from years of use. I squinted through the darkness of the room, the gentle light from the window exposing ink stains along the second drawer of his cabinet.

"Raul Martin." Rowan's voice was as sharp as his blade, the grin dropping instantly from Laury's face. "What do the two of you have to talk about?"

"I have no idea what you mean."

"Don't be foolish now." Rowan slammed his hands down, gripping the sides of his chair. "Your wife may be in the other room, but I will not hesitate to bring her over here."

"I am a politician, am I not? I discuss my beliefs and opinions with the people." He spoke defensively, strands of Rowan's hair dangling in front of the man's blinded face. "Raul just happens to be one of those who agree with my views."

"You two talk about more than just beliefs," Rowan said. He turned to me as I pulled open the wooden drawer, the sound of rustling papers catching their attention.

"What are you doing?" Laury's voice picked up, wrists pulling at their bindings once again. "You can't just—"

Rowan clamped his hand against the man's lips, green eyes narrowed as my hands flipped through the papers.

The pages were fresh, all signed by Mr. Young and stamped with the seals of many influential families as well as the signatures of those of lower economic classes.

"All of these people," I said, words slow as I pieced together the information before me. "They're all your sponsors?"

Rowan's gaze caught my own, and I tossed a folded document to him, the corners of his lips twitching into a smile.

"Well, haven't you been busy?" Rowan whistled, eyes scanning down one of the many lists. "These documents are almost"—he stopped, looking up at me—"treasonous."

"Nonsense!" Laury yelled, finally free of Rowan's grip. "They are simple opinions, nothing more!"

This is impossible. I furrowed my brows, going over the mass of documents again. *If this is true, if all of these powerful people opposed the King, then—*

"Do you plan to overthrow His Majesty?"

The words were sour on my tongue.

"What?" he stammered, the veins in his neck bulging as he spoke. "Of course not! Unlike some of us here, violence is not something I believe in."

"How dull." Rowan's shoulders slumped, the man ignoring his remark.

"I plan to run for a seat on the adversary council."

The King's council. I pursed my lips, eyes lingering over the hurried signatures. *A select group of politicians who aid King Alpheus in his legal decisions and endeavors.*

"With so many people backing my stance, they won't be able to refuse me."

My grip on the documents loosened. He wasn't a bad man, and although I hated to admit it, he wasn't completely wrong.

*Maybe...*I set the files onto the floor. *Maybe the monarchy isn't as perfect as I like to believe.*

I would have left it at that. I would've stood to my feet and left right then and there if it wasn't for something at the bottom of the drawer that reflected in the room's faint light. I furrowed my brows, gloved hands moving to touch its wooden base, my blood running cold as my fingers slipped beneath it.

A false bottom.

"What..."

My stomach dropped at the black box that sat at the bottom, a stack of letters at its side, the thin papers held together by twine. Identical to the letters found in Raul's estate.

"What is it?" Rowan asked, my hands pulling the messages from the ripped envelopes.

They weren't all addressed to Raul, but to countless other people of influence, all of them listed on the documents.

I handed the stack to Rowan's waiting hands, turning my attention to the black wooden box. I pursed my lips, pulling it open with some effort.

The hinges had been rusted shut, the tiny crate sitting unopened for years. My brows drew together at its contents, the box holding more letters, their paper yellowing and worn.

I lifted one of the folded messages, smoothing the deep creases as my eyes scanned it over. A shiver ran through my spine, my crouching figure toppling back.

Wait.

I scrambled forward again, pulling out a few more messages, lining them up side by side on the floor.

"Who is B.D.?"

Laury had frozen before our eyes, his stiff body so still that I wouldn't have been surprised if his skin iced over right then and there. "I don't—"

"I won't ask you politely again."

Rowan turned his head at my words, my eyes blaring with an intensity that could have burned the study to ash.

"The letters here, a box of them, they are all addressed to you from B.D."

"He…" His voice was hushed, as if the air within him simply refused to let the words out. "He was a pen pal of mine. We discussed politics and—"

"Conspiracies," I finished for him, swallowing as I looked back down at the papers before me. While the words themselves unsettled me, it was the dates that chilled me to the bone. "These conversations all happened ten years ago. Where are the newer ones?"

"I don't have any more—not from him." His words trembled as they slipped past his lips. "He said that he needed to disappear, that he would be gone for a while after the tragedy occurred."

"The tragedy?"

"The fire," Laury whispered.

Rowan's stoic figure went rigid.

"My last letter from him was a few days after the Nieve Disaster."

The fire that engulfed the lower districts in hellish flames, killing hundreds of innocent citizens. I could tell that Rowan's thoughts matched my own, his gloved hands clenching at his sides.

The fire that raged a few days before my mother's murder.

"Who is B.D.?" I asked again.

By the contents of these first few letters they both obviously opposed the King, opposed the nobility, maybe enough to kill.

"I don't know."

119

I gritted my teeth, standing abruptly and pushing past Rowan, hands gripping the man's shoulders and forcing his covered eyes to face mine.

"Don't test my patience." I gritted my teeth, Laury's body going completely still.

"I don't..." Laury shrunk in my grip. "I don't know! I've never met him!"

"Dream Stitching." Rowan's voice filled the room, my hold on the man loosening. "These letters were written when the drugs were first being introduced, when they were less of an issue and harder to attain. Why does it seem like such a popular topic between you and your pen pal?"

"That's where you're wrong." Laury's chest rose and fell heavily with the fear of my sudden advancement. "Nobles were already using the hallucinogens for their selfish benefits. It was only a matter of time before one of them began dealing it to the Underworld. *He knew.* B.D. knew what it would become and tried to warn me."

He knew? Was he a dealer then?

"What do you know of the drugs yourself?" I asked, the man's lips pursing at the harshness of my tone.

"Nothing much. Only that their creation accelerated the corruption of this kingdom. It's just another thing that the King has failed us on."

My lips twitched back in anger, the man's glare seeming to burn through the blindfold.

"Dream Stitching was created for the nobles, after all," he continued, words slow but sharp. "Their materialistic lives weren't enough. They wanted the ability to buy fantasy. It wasn't *if* but the question of *when* the hallucinogens would fall into the wrong set of hands."

Rowan's fingers flipped through the old letters, his grinning mask gleaming in the faint light.

"To be eternally trapped in a dream or to never be able to dream at all." He murmured under his breath, gloved hands stilling on a paper toward the end of the pile. "I wonder which would be more miserable."

I wasn't given a moment to ponder his words, the hitman moving past me without a second to spare.

"You've been of great assistance, Laury."

I furrowed my brows, gripping Rowan's sleeve, the killer barely glancing at me as he pulled the moist rag from his pocket once again.

No, I'm not done here. My heart pounded relentlessly in my chest. *I need to know who B.D. is, where he's gone, what he's done!*

"Wait." Laury's voice was steadier now, the man's posture straightening as Rowan clenched the rag in his gloved fist. "I don't know who you are or what you're trying to do, but don't get caught up in these affairs."

I stilled, the words sounding more like an eerie warning than any sort of friendly advice.

Or perhaps a prophecy.

"This kingdom is drenched in the sins of the rich, in the lies of the powerful. Don't tread too deeply into the past." Laury swallowed uneasily. "Or you *will* drown."

Rowan's lips pulled back into some semblance of a broken smile. "We'll keep that in mind."

Mr. Young didn't fight back this time, even as the cloth pressed over his nose and lips. His breaths were steady and even, the man's body slumping forward after about fifty seconds had passed.

"I wasn't done!" I yelled, ripping the mask from my face. Rowan ignored me, crouching down, his quick fingers pulling at the man's restraints.

An intense heat boiled through my blood, my lips curling back in anger.

"I'm talking to you!"

"I had to." His dark eyes stared into me harshly, flitting to the man's legs once I had quieted down. "You're sloppy with your emotions, and it's going to get us both caught. You can't let your heart rule over your head."

My lips pressed together into a thin line, eyes angrily staring into the killer.

121

"You wouldn't have gotten any more out of him anyways." Rowan sighed at my silence, shifting to untie the man's hands.

"That wasn't your call to make!" My feet paced, hands clenched. "What if B.D. is the murderer? What if he decided to disappear because he killed the Viscount's wife? Because he killed my mother!"

"If that's the case, Laury still wouldn't be able to help us. They were anonymous pen pals. He doesn't know any more than we do now." Rowan's voice was strained, the boy concentrating on the task at hand. "Besides, I know who we have to see next—Nicolo Pines. His name was listed in one of the letters you handed me." His teeth sunk into his lip, fingers finally undoing the tough knot.

I swallowed my frustration, grabbing the pile of letters that sat at our feet. If we decided to take them, Laury likely wouldn't report them as stolen. It wasn't hard to tell that he had been hiding them from prying eyes.

"Who is he?" I reluctantly gave in, fingers tracing over the worn papers.

"A merchant of *various goods*."

"A drug dealer then."

"Same difference." He grunted, lifting the man over his shoulders. "Nicolo Pines was one of the first to start selling hallucinogens on the black market, specifically one of the first men in the Underworld to dabble in Dream Stitching."

"The Underworld," I repeated, following Rowan's figure back into the bedroom. "So what exactly are we going to be infiltrating? An estate? Hidden mansion?"

"No." He sighed, rounding the bed carefully. "I think we can just show up to his shop. He'll answer any question for the right price. I'm thinking that this guy—this B.D.—could be a dealer himself. Or at the very least, someone mixed up with the Underworld."

Someone angry and tired of injustice, someone willing to kill for revenge.

"Just give me a few days." He paused, taking a moment to face me. "We have a lead now. All that's left is to see where it takes us."

I said nothing in return, restless thumbs running along the crinkled letters, tracing every swirl of ink and pressing against every sentence.

We were silent even as Rowan slipped Mr. Young's sleeping body back into his bed, even as we climbed out of the study's window, the wind howling into our ears.

My boots scratched against the hard stone streets, the cold slipping through my coat no matter how tightly I pulled it against my body. I turned my head, looking back at the hitman, my brows furrowing as his eyes scanned the rooftops.

"Hurry on home now, Silver." Rowan didn't have to turn around to know that I had stopped walking. "It isn't safe out this time of night."

"And you?" My voice was picked up by the wind, leaving it faint and quiet.

"Me?"

His expression was a disarming one, a charming grin accompanied by eyes so cold and empty that they challenged the night air itself.

"I'm afraid I have a long night ahead of me."

Chapter 8

"**D**AMN IT ALL!" MY FATHER's voice boomed through the thick walls of his office, echoing off the station walls. I flinched at the sound, my grip tightening on the steaming mug in my hands.

The station had been solemnly quiet the entire morning, voices hushed and steps silent, the only sound being that of the Viscount's rage.

"Hey." I pulled at Lou's sleeve, the girl passing through with a fresh pile of paperwork. Lou's bright eyes were heavy with sorrow, a few loose curls framing her tired face. "Is everything alright?"

"Far from it." She grunted, dropping the towering stack onto my desk, a hand instinctively moving to rub at her sore neck. "The front entrance has been bustling with reporters, our resources are stretched thin for the morning, and I'm pretty sure your father's anger has reached biblical proportions."

I furrowed my brows at her words, noticing how vacant the second floor was for the first time that morning. Aside from the two of us, it was nearly empty, all on-duty officers scrambling to fill any empty positions.

"Lou." I met her eyes again, the girl's usually cheerful expression dulled and grave. "What happened?"

"More bodies turned up this morning." She shoved her hands into the pockets of her uniform pants. "And the press got hold of the crime scene before we could straighten out the situation."

"More bodies? Lou, what do you mean?" My brows came together at the solemn expression on her usually bright face.

"*He* struck again last night."

"He?" I demanded, a thickness in my throat.

"*Alias Black.*"

My hands went rigid, any warmth draining from my body and leaving me ice-cold.

"Two bodies were discovered in an apartment in the Third District this morning. The first was left partially skinned, its eyes and tongue carved out and throat slit. It took a few hours, but the corpse was soon identified as Oba Zivai, an influential professor from the South." Her face grew grim, eyes flitting from mine as she forced the vile words from her lips. "The smaller of the two bodies was left whole and was quickly identified as Kato Zivai, his five-year-old son."

His five-year-old son. The lights seemed to dim, the station floor going in and out of focus as I processed her words.

Rowan had murdered a child.

"Apparently someone had hired the killer to off the professor, for reasons unknown to us thus far into the investigation. The child must've heard a sound and woken up, finding his father and the killer." Lou's words were unclear to me, faint, as if she were talking through glass. "And as you know…"

The familiar words thrashed through my skull even before they rolled off her tongue.

"Alias Black takes no witnesses."

My blood was heavy, stilling in my veins as my hands went limp, the glass mug slipping from my grip and shattering at our feet.

"Val!" Lou had called out my name, lunging for me as the floor shifted beneath my shoes.

Last night's conversation tumbled through my mind at full force.

"And you?" I had asked him foolishly, before turning my back and walking away.

"Me?"

I gagged, a hand moving to clamp over my lips.

"I'm afraid I have a long night ahead of me."

"Val, wait!" Lou's voice was muffled as I pushed past her, staggering down the never ending hall and toward the nearest restroom.

He went to kill someone. I slammed into the marble wall of the bathroom, my weak body stumbling to the toilet.

He murdered a man and his son in cold blood.

I retched, the morning's breakfast splashing into the water as I vomited. My body trembled, knuckles white as I clenched the hard metal seat of the lavatory. I couldn't stop the image of my mother from filling my mind, the constricting feeling of that night flooding back to me in horrifying waves.

That child had woken up in the night, walking in on his father's gruesome murder. And instead of running away or bursting into tears he had stood and stared, stared as the dead eyes of Alias Black, of *Rowan Marrow,* cut him down without hesitation, without a single shred of remorse.

That could have been me—my brother and I could have reached that very same ending, but we didn't. We were spared.

I swallowed the rancid taste on my tongue, shutting my eyes tightly.

Did this make Rowan more monstrous than the masked man?

He's a killer—I've known this from the start. My lips quivered, something much deeper than anger pricking my eyes. *So why am I so surprised? How could I have expected any differently?*

A strangled sob escaped me, my head resting against the hard wall of the bathroom as I cried, arms moving to envelop my trembling body.

He and Rowan are no different. A tremor ran through my hands as they clenched the fabric of my uniform. *The masked man and him are one and the same, and yet I've been treating this killer as a colleague, all the while he continues to murder as he pleases.*

And I—I brought a hand to my lips as nausea climbed back up my throat—*I'm just as bad as he is.*

"Oliver was right," I croaked, my voice a weak whisper. "We are selfish creatures."

And I'm the worst one of all.

I buried myself further into my coat, a subtle tremor still running through my weak body.

It had taken me about an hour to collect myself, and for the first time since I started working at the station, I had checked out early, my sickly complexion and jittery nerves enough of a reason to excuse me for the day.

I shivered, the sky far too dim for midday.

Rowan and I were to meet tomorrow night at the edge of the Fifth District, or what he called *the shallows of the Underworld.*

And while we had a lead, something that I had been searching for all these years, the thought of linking arms with the killer made me want to keel over and empty myself into the street.

I could end our agreement and continue tracking B.D. on my own. I had grown up in the world of cops and crooks, after all. I was perfectly capable of getting information from here on out.

I didn't need him anymore.

I stilled at the sudden shadow that loomed over my shoulder but soon relaxed, knowing my brother by the sound of his breaths.

"You should head back inside, Vic." I turned my head to meet my brother's bright eyes. "I'm more than capable of getting home myself."

"I know." He shrugged, stuffing his hands into his pockets, his blue eyes gentle. "But I miss walking with you."

There was something hesitant in the way he stood, the way he spoke. As if he were dealing with a frightened animal.

I said nothing, choosing to shift my focus to my feet, counting our steps as we trudged along the chilly road.

He was my twin after all, and for some strange reason I feared he could see what I'd done simply by the expression on my face.

Feared he could smell it on me.

"Could I ask what's on your mind?"

"Hmm?" I turned my gaze back to him, my brother's hair blowing back in the wind.

"You've been silent all morning, and taking a sick day doesn't really sound like you at all."

I tried to swallow the bulging lump in my throat. "I'm just tired is all."

Victor, I messed up.

"I guess the lack of sleep is finally getting to me."

I've allowed something terrible to happen.

My brother said nothing, his kind eyes heavy.

"How have your cases been?" I avoided looking at his face, the expression he wore tugging at my chest.

"Tough." He sighed, shifting beneath his coat. "Aside from the usual murders and petty burglaries, the poisonings have been getting worse."

Poisonings. I stared ahead. *That's what they called Dream Stitching down at the station.*

They wouldn't dare give the occurrences a proper name. That would make the problem sound bigger, more threatening.

"The issue arises when the three mix. So many crimes are fueled by these drugs, and often the people under the influence who commit them were drugged unwillingly." I furrowed my brows at my brother's words, his hand moving to rub at his forehead. "I mean, how do you administer justice in such cases? It doesn't help that we rarely get any evidence or reliable leads to track down the sources of these drugs. If we could get just one big bust, I just know that we'd be able to stomp out a whole ring of them." Victor exhaled heavily, my lips parting at a sudden thought.

"A main distributor is what you need," I said quietly, the lavish lounge of the Blue Swan's speakeasy flashing through my mind, the image of a blond-haired criminal manifesting itself. "Have you heard of J.P. Carrow?"

"Jean Pierre Carrow? The Fifth District merchant?" He raised an eyebrow at me, my conversation with the man still fresh in my mind. If Vic could bust him, it would surely lead to uncovering more dirt on the distribution of Dream Stitching hallucinogens.

"During a patrol a few weeks ago I ran into a group of people exiting his shop," I said, avoiding his gaze as I lied. "I overheard them discussing some sort of shipment, one that arrived at their docks once a month in the dead of night."

"What makes you think it's drug related?"

"Just…" I couldn't tell him that I had sat with the man, leaking confidential information to the drug-harboring criminal. "Just trust me on this one, Vic."

My brother pursed his lips, but pulled out the notepad from his coat anyway, lazily scribbling down my words. I exhaled deeply, a weak smile taking my lips as his hand squeezed mine.

We rounded the corner of the street, the faint outline of our estate now visible.

"Maybe…" I turned my head at the softness of Vic's voice. "Maybe you should take tomorrow off work too? Father and I would really prefer it if you rested."

"I'm fine, really. I'll be back on my feet after a good night's sleep." I pulled my lips into a smile, for his sake if not my own. "Besides, answering civilian complaints and alphabetizing paperwork isn't exactly strenuous work."

"I still can't believe Papa stuck you behind a desk."

"You and me both, Brother."

Victor tucked my hand into his coat pocket, the warmth of his palm against mine reassuring. "V."

I winced, looking away at the softness of his tone, but his hand only squeezed mine tighter, demanding that I listen.

"Valeria, we're twins. As different as we are, we are one and the same. So if something happened…" He paused, voice wavering. "If you got yourself into a mess you can't fix, then please, *let me help you.*"

I swallowed hard at the sincerity of his words. He had always tried so hard to fix what mother had left behind, to protect me from what I had witnessed.

But he couldn't fix what I had done, what I had allowed to happen.

"Promise me you'll tell me if something's wrong."

A bitter taste sat on my tongue as I forced a smile. "I promise."

Liar, filthy liar. My hand slipped out of Vic's soft grip, my feet moving steadily through the door and up the stairs of our estate.

He deserved better—they all did—and once the killer was in cuffs, I swore to spend the rest of my life regaining their trust.

But for now, telling them was not an option. Not when they'd try to get involved. Besides, Victor would surely tell Papa, and I was sure that he'd send me out of the Capital this time.

I exhaled, climbing the remaining steps to the third floor, dragging my feet to the last door on the hall.

My bedroom was cold, the quiet flames of the fireplace now completely silent.

I fell forward with a huff, the cool mattress sending shivers across the skin of my cheeks. The coat slipped from my shoulders as I shifted, the thick garment falling limply to the floor of my room.

I traced my hand along the side of the thick mattress, slipping my fingers into the cramped space between the wooden frame and the soft fabric. My arms stilled at the smooth cold surface that grazed my fingers. I pulled the mask from its hiding place, moving to lay on my back. Its deep frown and tragic eyes stared through me, emitting a ghostly presence that crawled over my skin.

It would be best if Papa and Vic don't find it. I bit at the cracked skin of my lips. *Explaining it to them isn't exactly in my interest.* And now that Raul's case was being investigated, I wouldn't want to be caught anywhere near a theatrical mask.

Rowan Marrow. His name unknowingly dug its way back to the front of my mind. I swallowed my unease, a sickly feeling still churning within me at the thought of all he had committed.

Redemption, huh? My lips trembled at the thought of Oliver's kind eyes.

A killer like him could never be redeemed, just as I could never be forgiven for letting this happen, for not outing him the first chance I got.

My free hand traced my mother's pendant, the necklace cold against my skin. My grip on the mask tightened, tired hands tucking it against my chest as I turned to stare through the window. The sun was still high in the sky, but my body ached, drained from the countless sleepless nights spent with the hitman.

And yet, even as my eyes fluttered open and shut, I knew that I would be getting no sleep that night.

Chapter 9

IN THE PITCH-BLACK OF NIGHT, the Underworld awakened. As those who roamed during the day shut their curtains and locked their doors, the eyes of those who seized the night were just fluttering open.

I let out a heavy breath, shutting the window behind me before the frosty night air could flood my bedroom completely. I had been told to dress casually—no mask, no flashy disguises, but to cover my face just enough to hide my identity.

I tugged at the blue scarf around my neck, pulling the fabric up to my eyes.

It had taken everything in me to force my sickly body out of bed and out the window, the thought of seeing the killer making me sick to my stomach. But this had to be done. I had come too far to turn back now.

I was going to solve this case.

My steady feet danced from rooftop to rooftop, the watching moon cutting through the gloomy skies of Nieve. I held my breath as I leapt, the tough material of my boots leaving the slanted tiles of one roof and landing on another. The run from the First District to the

Fifth was a long one, the biting cold weighing down my lungs as I ran, my ungloved hands numb.

I stopped, my heavy pants coming out in white puffs of air as my eyes scanned the busy streets below me. The Fifth District was lively for this time of night, the streets full of both men and women of all ages.

The shallows of the Underworld. My eyes traced the worn buildings, not a single estate in sight.

The Fifth consisted of lower-status neighborhoods, its streets lined with crooked apartment buildings, each home roughly the size of our estate's common room. Tired men and women sat against the crumbling buildings dressed in old work clothes, spending their last coin or two on a warm cup of cider.

My brother and I had been here a few times before, the crime rate alarmingly higher than that of the First through Fourth. I stiffened, hugging my coat closer as the wind howled through the rooftops, my squinted eyes focusing on the lone figure who stood on the roof beside mine.

The air stilled around us, a silent breath leaving my lips as I stared at Rowan. His empty eyes looked out over the district, hands buried into the pockets of his coat.

I swallowed the lump in my throat, my shoulders slumping as the wind picked up once again, picking up loose strands of his dark hair.

How...

My lips twitched with a feeling I couldn't recognize.

How lonely.

It wasn't sorrow, nor was it pity. It was the quiet understanding that no matter what he did, no matter what would happen from here on out, Rowan Marrow was destined to be alone. To roam the earth in empty misery for the rest of eternity.

But I suppose that's what it means to be a monster.

My feet left the stability of the roof, landing with a huff onto the next building's hard tiles. Rowan turned his head quickly, his gaze unchanging as he met my eyes.

My fists clenched within the pockets of my coat, head turning away from his as soon as our eyes met. As much as I wanted to tear into him, I couldn't bring myself to speak a single word.

Not now.

"Nicolo Pines—his shop is down this first street on the left." His expression was as unreadable as ever, the hitman gripping the metal emergency ladder with ease and sliding down the side of the building before me. "He's one of the bigger bosses when it comes to drug dealing within these streets. Whether it's painkillers, something to smoke, or a hallucinogen or two, he has it all."

I stared at my boots, following his movements, only raising my head when my feet reached the uneven street below.

I could feel his eyes on the side of my face, but to my relief, he said nothing.

I didn't think I could stomach a conversation with the murderer.

I looked to my right, a frail woman stumbling against the wall of a cracking building, her eyes glossed over and confused as she clawed tentatively at the air.

She'd been drugged. I slowed my steps. *Dream Stitched.*

"Don't even think about it." Rowan's voice pricked the hair on my neck. "You're not on patrol. You're not here to help people."

I clenched my jaw, ignoring his words and taking another step toward her. I gritted my teeth at the hard grip on my wrist, the hitman pulling me toward him easily.

"Let. Go." My voice was venomous, the boy's brows furrowing.

"I said, we're not—"

"Let go or I swear *I'll kill you.*"

Rowan's parted lips pressed shut, his gloved hand slowly loosening before dropping my wrist completely. My head whipped back around, fists clenching at the sudden emptiness of the street, any trace of the woman completely gone.

"The shop is up ahead." Rowan had already walked away, hands stuffed deeply into his pockets. "Keep up or I'm leaving you behind."

I waited, watching his body shrink a bit further before taking in a shaky breath. I swallowed hard, staring down at my trembling wrist, red imprints of where his hands had been flashing through my mind.

Relax. I clenched my fist, reluctantly trudging at his heels. *Relax, Valeria.*

Our two figures were silent as we weaved through the twisted streets of the district's back alleys. We came to a stop outside a crumbling brick building, the surrounding booths and shops just as run-down. Rowan knocked twice on the wooden door, longer strands of his dark hair falling in front of his eyes as the wind blew past us again.

The door cracked open, a fur-clad woman peeking through the door, a cigarette at her lips.

"We're closed." She let out a puff of smoke, her pale eyes falling on me before drifting over to Rowan.

"Really? That's a shame." The edges of his lips pulled down gently, the assassin moving to lean against the doorframe. "I was hoping to get a word in with Pines. He wouldn't happen to still be in, would he?"

The woman's sultry eyes trailed down the boy, her posture loosening as she stared into his tempting gaze.

"Second door." She cracked the door open a bit further, Rowan flashing a charming grin. "Knock before you step into his office."

"Thanks, doll." He winked at her as entered the shop, my eyes narrowing at the manipulative bastard.

She hummed a response, her silvering hair reflecting in the shop's faint light.

Rowan's smile dropped almost instantly as we rounded the corner, the boy ignoring the woman's instructions and taking no time to twist the knob and push the door open.

"Tailor." Rowan tipped his cap as we entered, my face recoiling back at the heavy scent of tobacco that escaped the room. "Not too busy stitching up a dream, are you?"

"Rowan, it's been a while!" A round man roared from behind the desk, a wide smile stretched against his plump face. "Has the devil come to collect me so soon?"

"Not today." He sighed, pulling out one of the gold-plated seats.

The office was alarmingly different from the rest of the building, the vast room reminiscent of those in lavish estates rather than a hole in a worn shop.

"And the lady?"

I stiffened, moving my attention back to the two men.

Rowan's eyes briefly met mine, sharp but collected, as they always were. "An associate of mine."

"Come, take a seat." The big man leaned back in his chair, tapping his cigar before bringing it up to his lips. "What can I help you with, *Diavolo*?"

"My colleague and I have a few questions pertaining to a potential customer of yours."

"Questions, eh?" His eyes drifted between us. "I'm no canary boy. I don't like to spread personal information."

He shifted forward in his seat.

"Unless of course, you can *compensate* my conscience?"

My eyes widened at the velvet pouch that hit the fine wooden table, a few golden coins peeking through the fabric.

"That should help ease your guilt." Rowan crossed his arms, tilting his head at the merchant.

Pines's lips twitched into a smile, the man sliding the pouch off the table and into his grip, squinting as he peeked into the bag. "What is it that you want to know?"

"We're looking for a B.D." Rowan leaned forward, Pines's face staring off in thought. "He could have been a buyer or seller about a decade ago. All we know is that he knew a lot about the Underworld, the monarchy, and the business of Dream Stitching."

"I don't recall anything off the top of my head," he answered gruffly, blinking as he thought, "but I can have my assistant take a look at the records."

"You keep records?" I asked, the attention of both men turning to me.

"Why wouldn't I?"

"Isn't that too risky?" I furrowed my brows. "Since this business isn't exactly legal."

If this building were to suddenly be raided by my father, he'd have files bursting with evidence of drug trafficking and probably countless other crimes.

A small smile pricked his lips, the man blowing out a huge puff of smoke as he stared at me.

"Let me tell you a thing or two about growing up in the Underworld, *Topolina*."

I shifted uneasily at the pet name, the man stubbing out the cigar in a glimmering ashtray. Rowan sat up at my left, his hard gaze boring into the pudgy man as he leaned forward.

"In this world you survive with two things. Your own sweat and blood, and the favors of others. You either take advantage of those in need, or you become one of them. My records help me keep track of who owes me what, telling me how much longer I'll have a leash around their necks."

A shiver ran down my spine at his words, resisting the urge to glance at the man at my side.

"Get a few poor souls in your debt and you might just make it to your thirties alive."

"That's horrible."

"That's business." His eyes had darkened, any sliver of humor completely gone. "Any other details about the man in question?"

"We aren't completely sure if B.D. and the man we're hunting are the same person yet, but in case they are, we are looking for someone who wore a wolf's mask." Rowan's voice was cut like steel, obviously annoyed by the earlier topic of conversation.

"A wolf's mask?"

"Yes." My voice was breathless, the thought of the man's monstrous figure sending a cold feeling through my limbs. "Made of a deep grey material, with a black snout. A mask that looks almost real."

"Well I've seen quite a few wolf masks in the past decade." He sighed, leaning back in his big chair. "But if you're looking for someone who might be of more use to you, I'd stop by Elodie's shop."

Elodie. That name was oddly familiar.

"The mask maker." Rowan groaned, rubbing at his forehead before slicking back any stray hair beneath his cap.

That's right. I adjusted the scarf over my face, keeping it well above my nose. Flint had purchased both of our masks from the Fifth, Elodie's artistic ability unmatched throughout the kingdom.

"We'll take our leave now." Rowan sighed tiredly, seemingly put off by the mention of the woman. "You know how to contact me if you find anything in those records of yours."

"But of course." He flashed a sly grin, pouring the pouch of gold out onto his desk, Rowan standing to his feet.

"Thank you for your help." I nodded, the man's beaded eyes flitting to mine momentarily.

"Any time."

My eyes narrowed at the tone of his voice, watching his hands play lazily with the coins.

"And just a friendly word of advice." He paused, the air in the regal room becoming very thick. "Leave. Don't shake hands with the likes of us."

My lips pressed tightly, stance stiffening at his clean cut words.

"There are no such things as honest deals and sincere bargains in the Underworld. People down here know nothing but to stab you as they smile."

I didn't like how sincere those words sounded despite the lofty glint in his eyes.

"I appreciate the concern," I said firmly, holding the man's stare. "But I can manage myself."

The door clicked shut at our backs, my heavy steps sounding against the wooden floor of the building.

"Don't be out for too long." A voice purred from the side of the main room, the woman from earlier taking a long drag of her cigarette as she leaned against the wall. "It's an awfully cold night."

"We'll keep that in mind." Rowan nodded goodbye, not bothering to smile at her as we ducked out the door. I flinched at the icy air that rushed at us, the wind more violent than before.

"Elodie's shop is just past these two streets. We shouldn't be out for much longer." Rowan pulled his cap lower over his face as the wind howled, the two of us trudging along.

I remained silent, staring at the back of his head as we walked. The main road had twisted off into a few smaller ones, the musty smell of old bricks and cigarette smoke filling my nose as we shuffled through a narrow alleyway, the pale moon our only light. Any sign of life had now disappeared from sight, the bustling business of the main streets now a faint buzz at our backs.

"Keep those pretty blues covered." Rowan's voice was clear despite the wind, shoulders tense in the cold. "Elodie has a thing for eyes."

I turned my head down to my feet, an uneasy chill climbing up my spine at the casual tone of his voice. The uneven cobblestone streets were slick with a thin sheet of ice, winter now chasing the last few wisps of autumn away.

I gasped, my sturdy boots slipping on a loose stone, a strong hand gripping my arm with ease.

"Watch your step." Rowan's eyes cautiously met my own, his words quiet. "Be careful."

Even through the fabric of his gloves, I could feel the careful constriction in his grip. I could feel the ragged ridges in his palms, the calloused prints that clung to his fingers.

*His hands…*My heart stuttered. *They're warm.*

So warm.

Warm with the blood of all he's committed.

I pulled my face away as my stomach lurched, the thought sending me recoiling back from his touch.

"What are you—"

"Don't touch me." My words were breathless, a deep-rooted panic heating up my blood. The wind blew harder, my knees weakening and sending me stumbling back.

"Hey!" His gloved hand reached for me again, fingers outstretched, but they were *red*, bloody and tainted with the remains of the innocent.

"Don't!" I yelled, jerking away, my jolted body hitting the ground with a hard thump.

He froze, pulling his hand back quickly at my reaction.

My heart pounded ruthlessly in my ears, a desperate hand moving to clutch the fabric of my shirt as I tried to calm the racing organ in my chest.

No, you can't do this now, Valeria. I closed my eyes, fingers clenching as I panted. *You have to breathe.*

Every time the killer drew nearer, I felt it. A renewed awareness of how lethal he really was. His sins stained the air around him like an odor; they clung to his hair and his clothes, seeping out from under his skin. It was as though he wore a thin cloak to mask the darkness within him, a human skin suit he'd pulled on for my sake. As if not to reveal his fangs and claws to me so soon. As if not to frighten me.

But I would not be fooled so easily, not by his sly smiles and clever words—not anymore.

All the pain he had caused, all the lives he had taken.

He's drenched in them.

"Valeria." My name sounded so wrong coming from his lips, sending my stomach into knots. "Are you—"

"You killed them." My words were barely audible over the roaring wind, but he had heard them anyway, his own falling silent. "That little boy, along with his father. You killed them both that night, didn't you?"

My heart hammered in my chest at the deafening silence, the street cold beneath my quivering body. I flinched at his unwavering expression, the killer staring down at me hollowly.

"Yes." His gaze didn't falter as he spoke, tone unreadable. "I did."

"Do…" Anger burned through my blood as I staggered to my feet. "Do you even give a damn?! I realize that your life must not have been easy, that you and I didn't grow up in the same world, but *still*." My voice broke as the words escaped me, livid eyes blaring into his. "How can you be so indifferent?"

"I'm a hitman. I was doing my job."

"That child didn't have to die!"

"I gave him mercy." Rowan's gaze was hard, his lips twitching as he spoke. "He watched his father die right before his eyes. I am not so cruel as to let a kid live with that burden."

"That wasn't your choice to make!" My shaky hands gripped at the roots of my hair, my head dizzy. The ground shifted beneath my feet, my stomach twisting at his icy tone.

He had no remorse. He showed no guilt. *He doesn't care, so why do I expect any differently?*

"Don't you realize what you've done? Can't you see the blood on your hands?" The stars swirled above my head, my vision blurring as anger pricked my eyes. "Or do you just not care? Are you such a monster that these murders don't faze you at all?"

Rowan's lips pressed firmly at my accusations.

"You have the audacity to hunt down a killer, to want revenge on someone for taking something from you, while you yourself are no different. Hell." A bitter laugh fell past my lips, bouncing off the brick walls of the alley. "I guess it's hard to have a heart when you've stopped so many."

My ragged pants contaminated the street, blistering anger radiating onto Rowan like the sun.

It burned right through him.

"*Oh, I bet you relish it.* Do you get off on having your victims bleed to death in your grip?"

"And what if I do?" Rowan had grabbed my wrist, pulling me toward him in one swift motion, lips twitching upwards. "Tell me, *Your Grace*. What would you do then?"

"You…" I winced, resisting the urge to cry out as his fingers dug into my skin. "You heartless bastard!"

"You knew who I was when we shook hands. You knew of my capabilities before we made this deal." His callous gaze froze the blood in my veins, hand twisting my wrist with every word. "Don't pin your guilt on me."

"But I—"

He yanked at my arm, my back slamming against the brick wall of the alley. Black dots danced around my vision, his face coming in and out of focus.

"You what?" he mocked cruelly, bringing his face down to mine. "You thought there would be something waiting to be found? Waiting to be fixed? *Don't make me laugh.*"

I flinched as he raised his other hand, his fingers landing on his chest, digging into the fabric of his shirt.

"You see Valeria, *there's nothing here.*"

I swallowed harshly at his words, his nails sinking into my palm.

"I am a killer, nothing more nothing less."

"That child didn't have to die." My lips trembled as I spoke, the violent cold painting them blue. "You could have spared him."

"And what?" he spat, my hand going numb in his grip. *"Let him turn out like you?"*

The wind around us had fallen silent, the only sound filling the dark alley being that of my ragged breaths.

"A liar and a fraud? So self-obsessed with their vision of revenge that they'd go to any lengths to get it?"

My lungs burned at his words, teeth sinking into my lip as I tried to twist from his grasp.

"I can finally see the resemblance between you and those other rich bastards." His voice was lower now, his lips moving to hover over my ear as he spoke. "You can play the savior all you want, Valeria, but you are just as rotten as I am."

I gritted my teeth, forcefully swiping my free hand across his cheek. Rowan's face turned away from mine, three deep red scratches carved into the tanned skin of his face.

"I am *nothing* like you," I spat, watching a thin trail of blood slide down his jaw.

My heart hammered through my ears, dark strands of hair covering Rowan's eyes as he stilled, his body unmoving. The grip on my hand loosened, my throbbing wrist moving to rest against my chest as he brought a gloved finger up to his cheek, red spots soiling the fabric.

I tried to swallow the sticky panic at the back of my throat, adrenaline keeping my trembling legs steady as Rowan turned his back to me, taking a few steps ahead.

"You aren't stupid, Valeria." His voice was vacant, any remaining anger dissolving into the unrelenting wind. "The first thing that you should have realized is that my reputation did not write itself. Things would have been a lot easier for you to live with after that. Call me what you will, but at the very least, *I know what I am*, and I'd much rather be an honest killer than a self-righteous liar."

The gnawing wind swirled around us once again, my aching hand reaching into my coat and grabbing the pistol at my waist, aiming it at the killer's head without hesitation.

I could do it. The cold had shaken my bones, knuckles white as I gripped the trigger. *I could end all of this madness with one pull of my finger.*

"Don't be a fool, Valeria." I swallowed harshly as the words left his lips, the assassin's back still to me. "Even with all that hatred coursing through you, do you really think you could kill me?"

The killer had paused, his dark hair blowing wildly as he stood unmoving in the violent wind.

"You don't know anything about me, *Alias Black*." My words were viperous, anger hot in my veins. "Ending you wouldn't be much different than putting down a rabid dog."

He turned back to me, hands stuffed deeply into the pockets of his coat as two dead eyes met my own.

"Are you certain of that, *Your Grace?*"

My grip on the trigger tightened as his boots dragged forward, only stopping when the cold metal of the barrel pressed firmly into the fabric of his shirt. His eyes seared past my skin, my own trained on the steady rise and fall of his chest.

"*I wonder.*" I could feel the warmth of his breath, fear crawling up my spine at his whispered words. "Could you shoot me at this range? Let my guts paint the alley walls red, have my crimson blood splatter against your face?"

Bile burned at the back of my throat as his hair tickled my forehead, the pistol trembling in my grip.

"*Could you bear the weight of my lifeless body falling limp at your feet?* If you think you can, then please, entertain me." He bared his teeth into a horrible smile, the emptiness in his voice chilling me to the bone. "Take off that *pathetic* noble mask."

My lips quivered, vision growing blurry.

"And give me a taste of that vicious human heart."

The warmth that escaped my eyes was not one that I had expected, the surprise of the hot tears streaking down my cheeks mirroring itself in the murderer's gaze, his narrowed eyes widening if only for a moment as he watched them fall.

*Why...*The gun fell away from his chest, my arms limp. *Why can't I just pull the trigger?*

I forced myself to look him in the face, the expression staring down at my own unreadable.

"As I thought," he said dryly, vacant eyes unrelenting. "How disappointing."

I couldn't scream, couldn't yell. I could hardly bring myself to speak, but as I stared up at the guiltless monster, I made my decision.

This would be the last time. I would not waste myself away trying to find a flame within a blizzard of a human being. This was the last night I'd spend alongside Alias Black. I'd solve this case myself.

"*I hate you.*"

Rowan said nothing, turning his back to me without a sound, his coat blowing back in the icy breeze as it bared its fangs. I stood there in the night air, tucking the pistol back into my coat, chest heavy with the weight of my own weakness. I wiped at my face with my sleeve, angry at the tears that soaked into the thick fabric.

As much as I wanted to do it, to rid this world of the monster that was Alias Black, I was not a killer. He and I would never be the same.

The wind had quieted down then, but the air was cooler somehow, emptier in a way that left my bones cold.

My feet had begun to move all on their own, coming to a halt at a narrow door in the side of a building, the killer standing silently at my right. The shop was a hole in the wall, a dusty shack built into the corner of the alleyway.

I shivered as the door creaked open, a sliver of warmth emerging from the shop. Rowan was silent, not sparing me a glance as he slipped inside without a word. It fell shut behind him, my hand pulling the scarf up to my eyes before I gripped the handle myself, wrist throbbing painfully as I pulled the door open.

I swallowed the discomfort, shoving my way through the cracked opening and into the dazzling shop. My lips parted softly at the candles that hung from the ceiling, illuminating the room in a comfortable warmth, fancy fabrics and exotic feathers decorating all four walls of the shop. The strong scent of ginger and eucalyptus left me dazed, forcing the rest of the tension out of my shoulders.

"Can I help you?"

I jumped at the honeyed voice to my left, a woman appearing from behind a beaded curtain. Her thick curly hair was wrapped in a silk head scarf, deep shades of green and gold dressing her body, her deep chocolate skin luminous in the candle light. I averted my eyes from hers quickly, moving to stare at the ground as her shoes clicked their way to the dark wooden desk in the center of the room.

"Elodie." Rowan pulled on a smile for the woman, moving the cap from his head. "Aren't you looking as lovely as ever?"

"Empty words do little to impress me, boy," she purred, leaning her arms over the desk, dark eyes catlike as she spoke. "Besides, I don't need you to tell me that I'm beautiful."

I peeked back up at her, the woman's slender figure and lustrous skin resembling a princess in a storybook rather than a shopkeeper in the Fifth.

"What is it that you need? Not a mask, I'd imagine." Her eyes traced the scratches on Rowan's cheek, prying orbs drifting over to me.

"Information," he said shortly, her dark eyes rolling.

"I don't like to discuss my clients."

"A wolf's mask, made about a decade ago." He ignored her, the woman raising an eyebrow at the boy. "Deep grey material and a black snout. It looked well-made enough to be real. Have you made such a thing?"

"A wolf's mask, huh?" She narrowed her eyes as she thought, leaning her weight forward onto the table. "I've made a few, but ten years ago I think I do recall stitching together something of the sort."

"You do?"

"Yes." She tilted her head as she spoke. "I was paid handsomely for it too, which was strange since it was such a simple mask."

"Who was it?" Rowan pressed, the woman looking at him dully. "Do you remember who bought the mask?"

"Like I said, I don't like to talk about my clients."

"Elodie." Rowan's voice was much lower now, silken and demure, his arms moving to rest on the table as he leaned a bit closer. I stiffened, turning to look at my feet at the sudden change of ambience. *Please? I'm sure that there's something I can do for you to change your mind?*

A catlike grin spread against her lips at the boy's words, a breathy chuckle escaping her.

"Rowan Marrow." Her gentle hands touched the fabric of his shirt, undoing the first few buttons before stopping, eyes full of amusement. "I don't think I want you as badly as you think I do. Her, on the other hand…"

My muscles tightened, eyes not daring to meet hers.

"Why don't you let me get a good look at you, girl?"

"I'm afraid that won't be possible." Rowan dropped the act instantly, the molten shades of green that swirled within his eyes cooling to stone.

"And why is that?" Elodie smirked, sharp eyes staring holes through the fabric of my coat. "If you've been keeping her around, she must be a pretty little—"

"Drop it." The candles flickered over our heads at the icy tone of Rowan's voice, my own body going rigid. I hesitantly looked over, his vacant expression hard and unmoving. Elodie's lips curled into a grin, eyes narrowing in amusement.

"Fair enough." Her eyes drifted over to me once more before finding the hitman. "The buyer was a younger gentleman, came inside in a hurry and paid upfront for the fastest mask I could make."

My brows furrowed, Rowan's expression mimicking mine.

"He didn't have any requests, just that I be quick."

He was in a hurry, not caring what the mask looked like, just that he had one by the end of the night. *But what was he in such a rush for?*

I'd imagined that targeting and killing a member of nobility required some sort of planning.

"And this man, do you remember what he looked like?" Rowan pressed further, Elodie sighing tiredly as she crossed her arms.

"Pale, blond, but if I'm being completely honest, he seemed out of place."

"Out of place?" My quiet voice had filled the room for the first time since our arrival, the edges of Elodie's lips turning up into a smile.

"Yes, he hardly knew why he was here, much less what he wanted. Almost like he was sent here on the behalf of another."

Of course. My shoulders slumped. *Anyone planning to commit such a crime wouldn't want any trails left behind. He must've sent someone here to purchase the mask for him.*

"Do you have any documentation of him being here? A signature, a note, anything?" I asked, her lips pressing into a firm line as she shook her head.

147

"He paid a hefty sum to avoid any formalities."

"Would a drug dealer even have that much money?" I muttered out into the open, Rowan leaning tiredly onto the desk.

"Yes, especially when Dream Stitching was just becoming available to the public." I avoided his eyes as he spoke, nauseous at his every word. "He would have been more than capable to pay off any obstacle in his path."

"That's about all I can recall." Elodie sighed, dark eyes swirling in the warm light of the shop. I moved to adjust my scarf, pulling it higher over my face, my wrist sore as it moved.

"That was more than helpful." Rowan nodded a silent goodbye, pulling the cap back over his head before turning to the door.

I turned to the woman, nodding in gratitude, her gaze catching mine for the first time that night.

"You've got quite the gems, don't you?" Her feline gaze squinted at me, Rowan's figure freezing at the exit. "Much too beautiful for a place like this."

"Pardon me?" My brows came together, the woman rounding her desk to take a closer look.

"You aren't from around here, are you?"

I stilled, confused by her analysis.

"Your eyes," she murmured, thick eyelashes framing her sharp gaze. "They aren't like the ones I usually get down here."

"There are plenty of people with blue eyes."

"Not the color." She tilted her head as she spoke, voice much quieter now. "I mean, Marrow's eyes are beautiful too, captivating, seductive, but they're cold. All of them are. But you, your eyes are still—"

"We'll be taking our leave now," Rowan cut in, a sharp edge to his voice. I tore away from her bewitching gaze, swallowing the unsettling feeling in my bones.

"Yes," she said, eyes narrowed, a stray curl escaping her head scarf. "Have a safe walk home."

The blistering cold pulled any warmth from my body almost instantly, my face moving to bury further into the thick fabric of my scarf.

There had been someone here, someone who had purchased a wolf mask ten years ago and had worked thoroughly to cover his tracks. Someone with money, with influence, someone with enough knowledge of the Underworld to slip through the shadows without a trace.

Someone with enough knowledge of the nobility to plan such a murder in a night or two.

I swallowed harshly at the wind that stung my face, Rowan and I walking a great deal apart as we trudged through the back alleys.

But—I licked at my cracking lips, the action just making them worse—*was hatred for the monarchy enough of a motive? If he went through such lengths to kill off a high member of nobility, why settle for my mother? And why not kill Victor and me as well?*

I turned my head up, shoulders relaxing to see that I was alone, the hitman already disappearing into the night.

I pursed my lips, pulling my hand from the pocket of my thick coat, a prominent red ring circling my wrist. *It will most definitely bruise.* I groaned, the thought of wearing a glove at all times again giving me a headache.

"You knew who I was when we shook hands. You knew of my capabilities before we made this deal." My hands clenched into fists so tight my bones hurt. *"Don't pin your guilt on me."*

"Call me what you will, but at the very, least I know what I am." I blinked fiercely, a feeling I could not describe pricking my eyes as Rowan's words repeated themselves in my head. *"I'd much rather be an honest killer…"*

"Than a self-righteous liar." My words were nearly silent, overshadowed by the howling wind as my boots crunched against the thin ice that layered the streets.

Rowan had no right to jab at me. He was a murderer, the lowest, most disgraceful type of human being. But his words had planted themselves deeply into my mind, burrowing themselves a home within my wandering thoughts.

Everything I've done—my hands squeezed the fabric of my coat—*all the lies I've told, they were in pursuit of justice.*

Selfish or not, my reasons were justified. This was all for the greater good.

Drunken murmurs echoed off the streets, stumbling men heading back home for the night, the bitter cold sobering them up pretty quickly. It was late, well into the dark hours of morning.

Papa would be waking up in an hour or two, pulling his tired body to the station to get some early work done. A sad smile pulled at my lips.

I guess in that sense, we are pretty similar.

The walk back to the First was a grueling one, the whistling wind being my only company as I trudged back to the First District. I would never usually make the lengthy trip on foot, but finding a cab this late into the night was impossible.

A warm exhale slipped past my lips at the glowing lights of the First, the familiar neighborhoods relaxing my posture. We had lived here our entire lives, our noble status keeping us in the safe embrace of the First District, the closest to the Palace a person could get. While the King still resided quite a ways away, guarded by acres and acres of well-watched land, we were his second-in-command, his trusted right hand. Nothing comforted me more than that.

My fingertips touched the icy metal of the estate's front gate, but before I could go any further, a chill ran down my spine, raising the hairs on my neck. My head snapped around, narrowed eyes scanning the streets for another set of eyes. My cold hands were just about to grab the pistol at my hip when they froze. The familiar silhouette of Rowan Marrow stood on a rooftop a ways away, hands stuffed into his pockets as he disappeared back into the night.

*Has he...*I furrowed my brows. *Has he been following me? And if so, how did I not notice earlier?*

My hands gripped the gate firmly, hoisting myself up the familiar structure as I had countless times before. My wrist throbbed, the cold numbing most of the pain and leaving the ache dull.

I don't understand him. I huffed, landing soundlessly on the other side. *I don't need to either.*

We were done, finished.

A killer was a killer and nothing could redeem that.

And yet as my numb body climbed up the outer structure of the estate, my hands sliding the bedroom window open and letting in the night chill, I couldn't shake him.

I had wanted to do it, to pull that trigger and avenge the hundreds of lives lost to his filthy hands, but I couldn't, and no matter how long I dwelled on the fact, I couldn't understand why. Nobody would have blamed me for his loss. Nobody would have even known. The mangled bodies of victims would simply stop showing up, people would stop losing their loved ones, and Nieve as a whole would lose some of the darkness surrounding it.

But his words. I shut the window at my back, the glass cold even through the fabric of my coat.

"Take off that pathetic noble mask. And give me a taste of that vicious human heart."

No. My knuckles went white at my sides. *I will not corrupt myself for him.*

And while I had made my final decision that night, I found myself unable to sleep yet again. For the damning image of Rowan Marrow had etched itself into the front of my mind.

Chapter 10

My boots clicked against the hard tiles of the station floor, my wrist aching below the weight of my morning paperwork. I had managed to sleep through the last two hours of the night, my limbs still sore as I rubbed the sleep from my eyes. While it wasn't much, the rest had helped somewhat, clearing my racing mind to an extent.

My quick feet clamored up the stairs to the fourth floor, eyes widening at the familiar head of brown hair that bustled from desk to desk, delivering staff paperwork. I swallowed the unease in my chest, turning back quickly, but I had already been spotted.

"My Lady!" Flint's voice filled the space between us, my heart throbbing at the sound of his voice.

"Miss, I…" He dropped his load onto a desk, stumbling over his words as he approached me. "I've been so worried! I don't know what I did to upset you, but I am so sorry, so very—"

"Flint." My voice had abandoned me, the sorrow in his eyes deep enough to flood the floor of the station. "You haven't done anything wrong."

"Then why?" His words were breathless, shoulders tense and brows furrowed. "Why did you disappear on me?"

Look at what you've done. I gritted my teeth, my grip tightening on the papers in my hands.

You just can't help but hurt people.

"Flint, just trust me on this—you don't want to get involved." I turned to walk around him, but he stepped out, blocking my path.

"I trust you. You know that I do," he said, brown eyes soft as he stared at me. "But please, whatever it is that you're doing, don't do it alone."

"Move."

"Miss, *please.*" His hand gently reached for mine, my wrist throbbing beneath the fabric of my glove. "I don't know how, but I know something is wrong. I just feel it."

His gaze was too real, too trusting. He didn't deserve this. I had made a promise two years ago, swearing to protect him, to give him a second chance at life after finding him in those sewers. I wouldn't drag him in any further.

"It's not my place to tell you what to do." He swallowed, eyes momentarily flitting from mine. "But *please*, let me help you."

"Flint." My voice shook, nausea clawing up my throat at the words on my tongue. "I told you to move."

His hand stiffened, pulling away from my sleeve instantly. I forced myself to look him in the eyes, my heart cracking at the expression that stared into mine.

"Alright." His voice was just above a whisper, the hurt painfully audible in the words. "Alright, fine."

His shoulder brushed mine as he walked past me, the boy pulling his cap down lower over his eyes as he descended down the stairs, leaving my lips trembling.

This is for the best. I'd rather him loathe me in safety than end up getting hurt because of his loyalty.

I exhaled deeply, letting my eyes briefly shut before continuing across the floor, the Viscount's door waiting patiently at the end of the hall. *If Flint were here*—I swallowed the heaviness in my throat, pressing my elbow down on the door handle—*then Oliver is somewhere nearby.*

153

My thoughts were proven right away, my back pushing open the door to find both Lou and Oliver hovering over my father's desk, their hushed whispers falling silent as they turned to face me. My eyes drifted to the board set up in the center of the room, my father's tall figure stepping in front of it, avoiding my gaze.

My lips pressed together, papers creasing in my strangled grip.

"Please, don't let me interrupt." My words were bitter, hands angrily dropping the pile onto one of the many cabinets in the room. "I was just leaving."

"Val, wait—"

I shook my head at Oliver's voice, already out the door and slamming it behind me.

Useless, useless, useless. I gritted my teeth as I ran down the stairs, violently wiping at my eyes. *I can't protect anyone. I can't solve this case. Hell—I'm not even qualified to speak with my own father!*

As much as I hated him, Rowan was right. I was just a fraud, an unreliable piece in the game of life, one that constantly moved backward instead of forward no matter what it did.

"Val! Hold on a second!"

Lou's voice bounced off the walls of the station, my feet picking up as I burst through the front doors.

"Valeria." She grabbed my wrist, my teeth grinding together at the pain.

"Let me go, Lou."

"Like hell I will!" She was angry now, her thick brows coming together as I pulled at her grip. "Val, what is it? What's wrong?"

"I'm fine." I was tired, tired of all of this. No matter what choice I made, it was never the right one. The closer I'd get to answers about my mother, the further I'd drift from those I loved. There was no way to win.

"No, you're not going to lie to me." She shook her head fervently, pulling me closer. "When was the last time you ate? The last time you slept through the night? Val please, I know you're strong, I know you are perfectly capable of taking care of yourself, but something isn't right. I just know it."

"Why is everyone so concerned about me? I'm not a child for you to watch over!" I finally snapped, the chilling wind leaving me nauseous.

"We know that, but—"

"*Do you now?* Apparently I'm not even stable enough to listen in on a basic case!"

"You know how these things work." Her playful eyes were now narrowed and serious. "We can't let any information leave that room."

"Let go of me." I pulled at her hold again, panic shooting through me as Rowan's constricting grip flashed through my mind.

"Val, what is with you?!"

"Nothing is with me!" I burst, ignoring the pain in my hand and yanking it out of her grip. "I'm used to the fact that my father doesn't trust me, that my brother feels the need to protect me from my own recklessness, so please, *excuse me* if I didn't expect you two to be exactly the same!"

Her expression wilted, any anger slipping from her face as I breathed in and out, my heart pounding against my ribcage. My lips pressed together, regretting the words almost instantly.

She didn't deserve my frustration. At the end of the day, I had done this to myself.

I turned my teary face away at the sight of Oliver's figure, the man fast approaching us. I blinked hard, my feet feeling unsteady as the wind beat at my back.

"Valeria." Lou's voice was much softer now, but I wouldn't meet her eyes. "What happened?"

"I…nothing." I struggled with my words, my voice growing thick as the weight in my chest threatened to consume me. "Nothing happened! I just—"

"Val, breathe."

I squeezed my eyes shut, feeling sick to my stomach. "I said I'm fine. I just need to—" My knees buckled below me, two strong arms gripping me from behind. Oliver grunted, gently sitting us both down

155

onto the cold cobblestone street. My hands trembled, fingers moving to cover my lips as my stomach threatened to empty itself right then and there.

"Valeria." Oliver's voice was hushed, my body shivering as he laid his coat over my shoulders. "What is it?"

"Val, please—"

"I just don't..." I choked out, my throat thick and vision blurry. "I don't know what the hell I'm doing!"

Everything that I had bottled up—all of the guilt, exhaustion, and disappointment that collected itself over the past few years—had finally bubbled to the surface.

And although all I wanted to do was scream and cry, to come clean about all I had done and finally dispel the weight from my chest, I couldn't. I couldn't be that selfish. I wouldn't risk the safety of others for my benefit any longer. I closed my eyes, taking in the moment of comfort for one more second before parting my lips.

"It's Vic," I lied, my stomach lurching at how natural it felt. "I'm just not ready for him to leave me behind, to leave me alone."

"You're worried about him inheriting the title?" Lou's voice was hushed, my lips quivering at the tenderness of it.

"Valeria." Oliver sighed, laying his chin in his palm as he stared at me. "You know that's nothing to worry about, right? You're not going to lose him."

"It isn't just that," I whispered, some truth escaping from the depths of my heart. "Vic is so good. He's kind. He has patience and a way with people, while I..." My voice caught itself, Lou squeezing my hand as we sat there in the bitter cold. "I am my brother's spare. His extra. Without him by my side"—hot tears filled my eyes, threatening to swallow me whole—"I fear that I'll disappear completely."

"That would be impossible." Lou's thumb traced my palm, olive eyes warmer than the sun itself. "You have the biggest heart, Val, although I'll admit it seems to lead you into a considerable amount of trouble. You're hardheaded, rash, and stubborn almost to a fault."

Oliver glared at Lou, a gentle smile pulling at her lips as she spoke.

"But that's because you care so deeply about those around you. You never abandon anyone in need."

"But that isn't true," I whispered, fear and frustration streaking my cheeks with their warmth. "Every time I'm put at a crossroads, every time I have to make a choice that questions my morals, I never seem to do the right thing. Lou, I'm drowning in a sea of guilt and regret and no matter how hard I try to swim, I can never reach the shore."

"That in itself is proof enough that you're good." Oliver's words were soft, just loud enough for me to hear.

My trembling gaze met his, deep chocolate eyes squinting at me from behind the lens of his glasses.

"Your guilt may be heavy, but it shows that you care."

"I know things can be difficult at times." Lou's voice was quiet, as gentle as the hand that stroked my hair. "And you might not know who or what you can trust, but please, *lean on us.*"

The sobs that broke past my lips were real, broken and violent, shaking my body with the weight of them, but I was still nothing more than a liar. Even as Lou's gentle fingers ran through my hair, as Oliver's hand rubbed up and down my back, I couldn't be consoled.

If only they knew. My lips quivered, pressed against the fabric of Lou's uniform. *If only they knew what I did, that that child was murdered because of my negligence, because I chose to use Alias Black for my own benefits instead of turning him in.*

I swallowed the vile taste on my tongue, chest shaking at every inhale.

If they knew all that, if I laid every one of my sins out before them, would they still hold me as they do now?

I had drifted too far, too far into the darkness, my vision consumed so heavily that I couldn't even recognize my own hand in front of my face.

*But...*I swallowed hard, prying myself from their warmth. *Hard decisions have to be made for the betterment of the people.*

The crimes committed could not be taken back, not now. All I could do was stalk further into hell and pray that the flames wouldn't consume me before I could beg for forgiveness.

I will use you Rowan Marrow. I wiped at my nose, inhaling deeply. *And when you've served your purpose, I'll throw you to the dogs.*

I slammed another drawer shut, flopping back into my father's big chair with a huff. I had searched nearly every drawer and cabinet in his office, looking for a sliver of a clue or hint as to who B.D. might have been.

My father was the Viscount after all, the King's authoritative hand. He had to have *some* sort of lead, no matter how small.

I sat up, straightening the files on his desk back into their previous positions, careful to leave no trace of myself behind.

My father wouldn't like me snooping through his office, especially if he knew the reason why.

My hands froze, the familiar sound of the front door opening sending my stiff body to its feet.

The house was supposed to be empty until later tonight. I scrambled toward the door, countless excuses filling my mind as muffled footsteps approached the office.

"Papa, I—"

My words stopped halfway, the wide eyes of my brother staring down at me.

"Thank God," I breathed out, gripping Victor's shoulder as the tension left my body.

"What the hell?" he whisper-yelled, whipping his head around before gripping my arm and pulling me through the door. "You are *so* lucky Papa asked me to wait up here for him."

"Believe me, I know that." I squeezed his shoulder gratefully before ducking around him, hurrying down the hall to greet my father.

"Won't you take your coat off, Papa?" I leaned toward him, kissing his cheek.

"I wish I could." He smiled tiredly at me, pulling the cap off his head. "But I'll be running back to the station in a few minutes. I somehow managed to forget some files this morning."

"Files?" I asked over my shoulder, rushing into the kitchen to pour him a cup of coffee.

"Yes." His voice was muffled through the walls, my hands hurriedly pouring the dark liquid into a metal cup. "I have a few new cases regarding the past week's poisonings."

The past week's? I furrowed my brows, making my way back to the common room. *Are they happening that often now?*

"Here you go, Papa." Vic appeared from around the corner, a few tan folders clutched in his hands.

"Thank you, Victor." He sighed, taking the papers from my brother, turning to me with warm eyes. "And you too, darling."

I smiled softly at my father, handing him the steaming cup. The bright lights of the common room reflected off his greying hair as he turned his back to us, Victor tight on his heels.

"I'll see you for dinner, Valeria!" Papa's voice echoed from the front of the estate, faint wisps of the winter wind grazing my skin as he slipped through the door. I waited, hearing the door slam shut before turning back to his office.

That was close. I pushed the office door open again, heading back to his enormous desk.

If my father were to catch scent of what I'd really been doing, that I was spending every night out investigating my mother's murder, he would surely send me out of the Capital to my grandparents.

And I couldn't let that happen, not until this case was closed.

"So what is it exactly that you were looking for?" I jolted at my brother's voice, whipping around to see him leaning at the entrance, arms crossed.

"Nothing, just cleaning up a—"

"V, you don't even clean your own room. I do."

159

I pursed my lips, hands clenched behind my back. Questions were inevitable. Actually, I was surprised that Vic hadn't said anything sooner.

"Do…" I exhaled, my shoulders dropping. "Do the initials B.D. mean anything to you?"

"B.D.?" he repeated, laying his head against the wall as he thought.

"Yes, is there any file with those initials listed? Or maybe a suspected criminal with these initials?"

"That's a bit vague." He looked off in thought, eyebrows coming together. "I couldn't say so off the top of my head, but I could check the record room for you."

The record room. I perked up, eyes widening.

The Imperial Station's archive held a detailed report of every major arrest, an account on every busted case, as well as every lead my father and his predecessors had ever had. Before my father's restrictions I had practically lived in that dusty room, sneaking in to go over my mother's file into the early hours of the morning.

But I had more information now. I had a potential lead. *Who's to say that all the answers aren't locked behind the station's towering doors?*

"Could you get me in?"

"Definitely not." He scoffed, pulling his weight off the doorframe. "It's open to essential personnel only. Besides, if Papa knew you were sticking your nose into cases again, he might *actually* send you away. These aren't just empty threats anymore. He's worried for your wellbeing."

My chest ached, the image of my father's greying hair and tired eyes pulling my lips down into a frown.

"And I can't let that happen, V." Victor put a gentle hand on my head, planting a warm kiss on my forehead.

"But Vic—"

"It's a no."

I bit my trembling lip, clenching my fists at my sides as he walked out of the study, pulling on his coat as he passed the common room and approached the front door. I followed him soundlessly, arms crossed in silent dejection, my brother pulling on his cap without a word and moving a gloved hand to grip the doorknob.

He paused, a deep exhale escaping him. His head rolled back tiredly, my brother's hand dropping from the cool metal handle.

"I can't let you in myself, but I *could* borrow the keys and accidentally leave them in the door."

"Vic," I breathed, my lips pulling into a smile as I smashed into his back, wrapping my arms around him. "Thank you."

"Yeah, yeah." He turned to face me once my hands loosened. "This is because I trust you, okay?"

"Yes, I know. My instincts haven't failed me yet—"

"No. Not your capabilities."

My brows came together at his words.

"I trust *you*, V."

There it is again. That familiar tightness filled my chest, guilt sinking its ruthless teeth into me once more.

I swallowed hard, wrapping my arms around his chest and holding my brother close. He wasted no time, securing his arms around me, a loving hand stroking my head.

"Thank you, Vic," I whispered into his chest, the two of us silent in the moment. "And I'm sorry."

I furrowed my brows, grunting as I pushed the heavy door of the station's archive open. The key had been left in the door as promised, waiting undisturbed for my anxious hands.

Gaining access to the station wasn't difficult as the Viscount's daughter, but getting in and out unnoticed was a different story. Not when every pair of eyes were constantly on me.

I had waited patiently outside in the bitter cold for the first shift change of the night, where those itching to get home would rush out and those forced to stay the night would drag themselves in. It was a brief ten-minute period where the station was most jumbled, those entering and those leaving mixing into each other as they rushed about the first floor. It was a matter of skill after that, my soundless steps flying up to the third floor of the station, the hallway completely free of any prying eyes.

I stepped into the dusty room, shutting the door behind me before letting my eyes drift over the endless rows of information. It was much colder here, the station's heater warming all rooms except for this one. Some of these files were decades old, so the room was kept at a consistently low temperature to help preserve the documents. My boots beat against the pristine white tiles of the room, the seemingly endless wooden shelves rough beneath my fingertips. Up until recently we had hired a team to keep track of records, organizing the new files and cases alphabetically for easy access, but the past two years had been rough, much too busy for anyone to accurately keep track of every paper that shuffled in and out of the Viscount's office. Now the once museum-like room was a scrambled mess of paper and ink, cases disorganized and papers out of order. I pinched the bridge of my nose, the vast reality of the task at hand seeming more difficult than first anticipated.

I had just begun filtering through the first shelf when I froze, bones going rigid at the sound of the doorknob rattling.

No, no, no. I pushed the papers back to where they had been, eyes wildly scanning the windowless room. *Nobody is scheduled to be here until tomorrow!*

I held my breath, the door opening with a loud creak, my brows knitting together at the wide brown eyes that met mine.

"I knew it," the boy muttered under his breath, flinching at my livid glare.

"Flint, what the hell?" I whispered, wincing as he shut the door with a slam. "You can't be in here!"

"I'm sorry! I just…" He pulled at his suspenders nervously as he spoke. "I saw Victor snooping around all suspicious this morning and got curious."

I mentally face-palmed, no stranger to my brother's blatantly *inconspicuous* ways.

"I saw him leave the keys in the door and knew you'd be here."

"You couldn't have."

"Forgive me, My Lady." Flint walked past me, flashing his dimples. "But your brother isn't exactly the type to sneak around at his own expense."

Fair enough. I sighed, my heart still beating erratically. Still, I didn't want him getting involved. This never concerned him. It was my own selfishness that had pulled him out of bed and into the freezing air before. I couldn't let that happen again.

"Go home, Flint," I said tiredly, my arms crossing themselves over my chest. "I told you not to get involved."

"It's a bit too late for that." He grunted, grabbing a heavy folder off the top shelf, blowing the dust away. "So what are we looking for?"

"*I'm* looking for some files, older ones."

"From a decade ago."

I nodded at his words, his brown curls bouncing as he turned to look at me. I pursed my lips, my arms dropping to my sides at his persistence. *Fine.* I rubbed at my forehead. *But this is the last time.*

"The initials B.D."

"B.D.?" he repeated, sitting on the ground with a huff. He leaned his elbow onto his knee, eyes scanning the first few documents without another word. A soft chuckle escaped me before I could stop it. Flint turned his chocolate eyes up to me, blinking as I laughed, the smile on my lips small but more genuine than most. Because in his brown eyes was the warmth of an undying hearth, the rough wood that kept the faint flame in my chest burning, if ever so slightly.

Reminding me of home.

"Did I do something strange?" he asked, a pale pink tint inhibiting his cheeks at my warm reaction.

"Not at all." I shook my head, grabbing my own stack of files and taking a seat at his side. "I'm just very grateful to you, Flint. I don't think I tell you that enough."

"You don't have to thank me, Miss." He averted his gaze from mine, staring back down at his papers. "I help because I want to. I…"

I turned my eyes back over to him at his stuttering words.

"I care about you, Miss Valeria. Very much."

A bittersweet warmth laid itself over my skin, my warm gaze squinting over at him once more before turning to the stack of papers in my own grip. *That is exactly it, Flint.* I swallowed harshly, turning the first page of the top file back. *That's what I'm worried about.*

We must have been in there for hours because the next time I turned to look at Flint, he was fast asleep, his head leaning back on the seventh row of shelves, a fresh load of files sprawled half-open in his lap. We had searched paper by paper all night for a sliver of a lead, for any indication of this mysterious B.D., and came up empty-handed. I sighed, flipping the folder in my hands shut, wincing as I plopped my sore body onto the cold floor of the archive. Every criminal with the matching initials were either petty thieves or much too old or young to be the masked man. And as much as I believed in this lead, I couldn't shake the feeling that I'd been chasing a dead end. *What if this guy was never caught? What if he snuck in here and destroyed any existence of himself?* If he were capable enough to break into our estate, he must have been capable enough to get his hands on a few papers.

I dropped the new stack of documents onto the floor beside me, my eyes following the pillow of dust that erupted above them. If my mother were here, she'd tell me to take a deep breath, to calm my nerves and lay the facts out in front of me. To cool my head and look at the problem from another angle.

But she isn't here. I let my tired eyes close. *I am on my own.*

I had the initial facts of the murder—that I was sure of, but something had to be missing. People couldn't just disappear. I sat up at the sound of soft murmurs from a few shelves away, Flint shifting in his sleep. A sad smile overtook my lips, eyes heavy as I basked in the silence of the room.

Is this what she would've wanted? My hands clenched in my lap. *If she were looking down at me from somewhere overhead, would she be proud?*

I had been raised in a noble household, one where justice and doing what's necessary for the greater good had always been preached, always praised.

"Hard decisions have to be made for the betterment of the people." That's what Papa had always said, spending nights upon nights over at the station instead of at home with us. Wasn't I just doing what was necessary in the pursuit of justice?

*And if so, why are Papa, Vic, Lou, and Oliver...*I stood to my feet, grabbing my coat from the floor and approaching the sleeping boy.

Why are they so adamant that I quit? That I give up on the case?

My shoulders sagged, hands carefully laying the thick brown coat over Flint's sleeping body. The boy's eyelashes fluttered gently, the sudden warmth of my coat a warm embrace opposed to the frigidity of the room. I crossed my arms, taking a seat at his side. I had dragged him through the night yet again, and as always I had nothing to show for it. My disappointment soon morphed into frustration, the jumbled mess of a room nearly unsearchable. My eyes shifted from him to the crumbling shelves shoved into the left corner of the room. Away from the endless rows of evidence sat a section labeled *News and Press,* a forgotten division within the Imperial Station's record room. In all honesty, it was more of a formality, the climbing shelves doing nothing but collecting dust over the years. In most cases those musty shelves were of no use, but in a case like this one, where every factor was open to change, who was to say that the answer wasn't shoved between a few unkept newspaper pages?

What if B.D. wasn't a criminal at all? What if my mother's murder was a one-time strike? His very first offense? He had never been caught, so of course he had never been convicted, but he had to have some sort of public presence. Laury James Young wouldn't talk so freely with just anyone.

165

*What if...*I stood to my feet, eyes flashing across the back section. *What if B.D. held relevance in the media?*

It would make sense, after all—an up-and-coming politician exchanging treasonous letters with a writer or reporter, maybe even an extremist. One whose anger toward the King got the best of him, the man using his extensive knowledge of the nobility to successfully infiltrate the Viscount's estate. An angry man, not a seasoned criminal. One who couldn't bring himself to kill the children, even if they were his only witnesses.

"Come on," I muttered under my breath, hands skimming through the yellowing slips. *Please.* My lips pressed together as I reached the *D* section, pulling out all of the documents and dropping them onto the floor.

Just give me a sign. My hands tore through the files, papers scattering themselves around my shaking body. *Tell me I'm in the right direction!*

A cold breath slipped past my lips, trembling fingers gripping a yellowing column labeled *The Ace of Spades*, a small part of an old anti-royalist newspaper.

Rich Man's Money, Poor Man's Blood, the title read. I skimmed the article before stopping at the bottom of the page, the paper crumpling in my constricting grip.

Written by B.D.

I flipped to the next paper, finding another article, the same signature sitting at the bottom of the page. There were a total of eleven, each exposing and shaming the monarchy, each signed with the initials B.D.

I was right. My hands found my hair, fingers threading through my roots as I sat in disbelief. *I did it.* I pulled the evidence together, setting the torn columns neatly at my feet before shoving the rest of the papers back onto the dusty shelf. The dates lined up with the letters in Laury's office, the latest one dating back ten years ago, the oldest one published two years prior.

And the contents—I sat down again with a huff, flipping through the remaining papers once again—*they match the sort of conspiracies discussed in the letters too.*

I had straightened up at that point, moving to wake the sleeping boy, but something else had caught my eye. At the bottom of each article, in tiny letters, the words *The Black Press* were printed clearly.

The same publishing company that put the voices of lower-class politicians into the paper today. The same one that printed Laury James Young's articles now.

If that publishing house used to print B.D., who's to say they didn't know his real identity?

I bit my lip, scrambling to Flint's sleeping form and jolting him awake.

"What…" he mumbled, eyes heavy with sleep. "What happened? What is it?"

I took his disgruntled face into my hands, grinning as he squinted in confusion.

"I have a lead."

Chapter 11

LAUGHTER ECHOED OFF THE STREETS of the Fifth District. The early hours of night were accompanied by the sound of clinking bottles and drunken singing, the atmosphere bringing a smile to my lips. The winter wind soon drowned out the sounds of the street, my hands pulling the cap lower over my eyes. I had forgotten my gloves back at the estate, the excitement surrounding my lead leaving me sloppy and disorganized. I flexed and clenched my bare hands, the bitter cold leaving them numb.

"You know…"

I snapped my head up at the familiar voice, Rowan's figure sauntering lazily through the alley.

"You've got some nerve calling me out here like some delivery boy."

My lips pressed into a firm line, a shaky tremor running through my hands as he stepped closer. He must've noticed, his careless steps coming to a halt.

"I was pretty surprised to get a call from Nicolo Pines." He shifted his eyes away from me, staring off into the dark of night. "Even more surprised when he told me that the little mouse from earlier had returned, asking to reach me."

We were silent, the wind whistling between us. I hadn't expected that of myself either—not after that night in the alley. But this was bigger than me.

Rowan was a killer, a monster of a human being, but I couldn't deny the fact that he was useful.

"I didn't think…" His eyes finally met mine, green orbs hesitant. "I didn't think I'd see you again."

I stared through him, taking in every quiver of every one of his words. I would not be bested. Not by any beast and certainly not by any man. *That is why I returned.* I turned my face from his. *And that is why I'll solve this murder.*

"Yes, well"—I exhaled, forcing my tense shoulders back—"I'm not one to quit on things halfway through."

His lips didn't twitch back as they usually did. His smile wasn't a ferocious grin or a deceitful smirk. Instead it was a small smile, something as close to genuine as he could ever get.

"I didn't think so."

"The Black Press," I said, the pride in my voice not easily masked. "They printed an anti-royalist newspaper over a decade ago, among their articles being a monthly column labeled *The Ace of Spades.* Each entry discussed the shortcomings of the monarchy, some even going as far as to publicly discuss anti-monarchist conspiracies."

"Like the letters we found in Young's apartment." His eyes narrowed as he thought, our feet walking in step.

"And each one was written and signed by the same set of initials." I nodded, pulling the worn slip of paper from my pocket. "B.D."

"Okay, that's all good and well, but how does that help us track him down now?"

"The thing is," I started, the two of us coming to a stop. "The Black Press still operates today, and is the very same paper that prints for Laury James Young."

"Well then." He raised his eyebrows, a grin pulling at the ends of his lips. "I'll give credit where credit is due. Not bad, Blue Blood."

"Not bad?" I scoffed at the audacity of the man, but nothing could spoil my mood. We had a tangible lead, after all. "And don't act so surprised. My blood practically runs silver."

"I won't forget it again." I could hear the smile in his voice without looking up, a strange feeling of unease filling my chest.

How could this boy who laughs so easily be the same one who slits the throats of so many?

No. My face snapped to the side, my wrist aching in the pocket of my coat. *He is not a case for me to solve. It isn't my job to find a sliver of light within the endless pit that is Alias Black.*

That isn't my responsibility.

"Infiltrating the press wouldn't be good." He interrupted my thoughts, my brows drawing together.

"You can't do it?"

"Please." He scoffed. "I can slip in and out of any vicinity in Nieve. It just wouldn't be wise for you to be seen there."

I sighed heavily, hating the fact that he was right. There was no way that I wouldn't be recognized in a place like that. The Black Press's ideals stood firmly against the nobility, always watching, always waiting to jump at any mistake we made. They would tear my father apart in the papers if I were seen anywhere near the Fifth District unattended, especially if they knew what I was investigating.

"Aside from the fact that you're a walking cover page, their archive is impossibly large." He trailed off, tilting his head as he spoke. "Locating anything specific in that maze would take ages for an untrained set of hands. We need someone on the inside."

Someone on the inside, huh? I swallowed hard, my mind racing. The station was always swarming with reporters after bigger cases were closed—cases of murder, mass fraud, and nobility scandals.

*But...*I stopped walking again, brows furrowing. *There's always one kid who stands out rain or shine for the political cases, demanding to speak with Papa on the people's cries of injustice.*

"Rin Ryugazaki," I said, turning to Rowan. "He's the guy we need to meet with."

"Why him?"

"I've seen him outside of the station quite a bit," I said, my freezing hands clenching the fabric of my coat. "He seems knowledgeable and genuinely cares for the good of the people, not just a good scoop."

"A reporter then?" Rowan nodded slowly, the wind picking up around us.

"And a writer."

I had actually read a few of his columns before. His arguments were never forceful, written more to educate the masses rather than to shove any sort of ideology down their throats. For a man as young as he was, he had potential.

My shoulders slumped, a new obstacle arising.

"The only issue is, I don't know where we'd find him."

I should have thought of this earlier, I scolded myself internally. *Of course slipping in and out wouldn't be this simple!*

"He's from the Fifth, yes?" Rowan asked, strands of dark hair slipping out of his cap.

"I think so."

"And his age, how old did you say he was?"

"Looked about twenty." I furrowed my brows at his sudden questions. "Why?"

"Because"—he grinned, steps crunching against the icy streets as they picked up. "I have a hunch as to where he might be."

"A brothel?" My voice was hesitant, wide eyes trailing over *The Satin Serpent,* a towering silk-adorned building on the outskirts of the Fifth, thick sultry music pouring through its open doors.

"Not quite." Rowan flipped up the collar of his coat, turning to face me. "Think of it as a venue of *exotic performance.* That being said"—his green eyes caught the faint light of the street, momentarily seeming to glow—"you can get anything for the right price in the Underworld."

I took in a deep breath, letting the tension melt from my shoulders. This was for investigative purposes—there was no use getting worked up.

"After you."

I nodded at Rowan, stuffing my cold hands into the pockets of my coat and advancing toward the open double doors.

I was hit with an entirely new atmosphere the second I stepped in. Tattered fabrics of every color covered the brittle cracks in the walls of the building, the heavy smell of cheap cigars and strong booze constricting our senses. The lights were dim, the room illuminated by a few low-hanging metal chandeliers, but that didn't conceal the massive crowds of people who gathered beneath them.

Time-corroded tables littered the room, games of chance and others of luck splayed across each one, everything from cards to pairs of dice clenched in the tired hands of middle-class workers.

An old wooden stage sat in the forefront of the room. About ten women, each more beautiful than the last, stood atop it, performing a synchronized number. Their hands held extravagant feathered props, their curved figures clad in thin silks.

I tore my eyes away from the display in front of me, my focused gaze moving to wander across the crowd. The audience consisted of mostly men, ages ranging from mere teenagers to workers in their early thirties. I squinted up ahead, a smile breaking out on my lips at the familiar flash of a camera, Rin Ryugazaki's slender figure standing by the stage and snapping a few winning shots.

"Found him."

"That's all good and well, Silver, but how exactly do you intend to get to him?" Rowan leaned a hand on the worn wood of the bar, the woman mixing drinks pushing a shot glass full of clear liquid over to him with a wink.

The place was packed, people near the front crowded elbow-to-elbow. Even with my face covered, one wrong move could get me discovered, and getting caught in a place like this would undoubtedly make the headlines.

"We'll need a distraction."

"A bigger distraction than what's already on stage?" He grinned, eyes still glued to the entrancing performance.

"Rowan." I rubbed at my forehead impatiently, the boy freezing at the use of his name. I furrowed my brows, his eyes moving to meet mine before dropping to the floor, a deep sigh rumbling from his chest.

"Fine then." He turned to his right, grabbing the shot glass and downing the liquor without hesitation.

"Hey, we're on the job! You can't…" I whisper-yelled, stopping halfway through as he pulled his cap off, cheeks already tinting a warmer shade. "What are you doing?"

"Keep up, Silver." He pushed his hair back, an alluring gaze finding mine. "I'm being a distraction."

My eyes widened as the confusion left my features.

"You have two songs." His hands fumbled with his shirt buttons, fingers loosening the cravat that hung at his neck. "Be quick."

I pursed my lips, Rowan giving me a hesitant nod before stepping ahead, his back disappearing into the crowd. *Alright then, Valeria.* A shaky breath wracked through me, my hands pulling the dark scarf up to my eyes.

Your turn.

My lone figure slithered through the crowd, the soft fabric of my scarf tickling my nose as I stared down at the ground. Loud whistles and shouts suddenly erupted from the crowd, a smile pulling at my lips as I resisted the urge to glance up at the stage.

Rowan was efficient. I'd give him that.

The familiar back of Rin Ryugazaki came into focus, the boy grinning as he snapped a few pictures from the side of the stage.

"Ryugazaki, isn't it?" I asked, the boy not taking a second to glance up from his camera.

"That depends who's asking."

"Someone who needs some answers."

"Tough luck, kid." He laughed, eyes squinted into his camera as he spoke. "Gossip isn't really my specialty, and I don't give out information for free."

A price, huh? I groaned internally. "How much?"

"Oh no, no, no." He clicked his tongue, pulling the bulky camera away from his face and adjusting the flash bulb. "Nothing you can offer me."

"Are you sure about that?"

"Completely." He pulled his fingers through his hair, the dark strands falling back into place. "Unless you have the story of the century."

He may have been from humble roots, but he was no pushover. Getting his cooperation wouldn't be as easy as first anticipated. I closed my eyes, a reluctant breath leaving my lips as I realized what would have to be done. I had promised to do anything for the sake of the case, after all.

"What about…" My words were tentative, the boy raising an eyebrow as he brought the camera back up to his face. "What about the scoop of the decade?"

He paused, bringing the camera down, deep almond eyes finally meeting mine.

"And who exactly are you?"

I pursed my lips, his shoulders tensing as I pulled the scarf down from over my face. "Someone who may be of interest to you."

"The Viscount's daughter," he muttered under his breath, still frozen in place. He quickly dropped his eyes, obviously intimidated. "Sorry, I didn't recognize you."

"Glad to hear it."

"But no." He shook his head, turning his eyes back to the stage. "I don't work for the King's dogs. And no offense, but you being here isn't as important as you think it is."

"I wasn't talking about me," I continued, the boy sparing me another glance. "I am currently pursuing a private case. The case of my mother's murder."

His gaze sharpened, the nonchalant eyes of a boy hardening into the analyzing gaze of a reporter.

"I've been hunting down the killer for years but recently found a solid lead, one that points in the direction of The Black Press."

He raised an eyebrow, but listened nonetheless.

"Help me solve this case, and I promise that the scoop will be yours. I won't leak any information to the media before it's in your hands."

"Your Grace." He grinned, his dark bangs matted to his forehead. "I think we might just have an agreement here."

My posture loosened, a huge breath of relief escaping me at his willing words.

"I won't slip any of this to the public prematurely," he added quickly, pulling his camera's strap over his neck, "but I'm putting my trust in you. We're making a deal, after all."

"Yes, it seems I've been making quite a few of those as of late." A breathy laugh left my lips, a sense of solace filling me for the first time that day. "Ah, yes." I straightened up again, eyes wide. "Before we leave I need to collect my assistant."

"I'm assuming he's the fellow on stage."

"How'd you know?" I raised an eyebrow, the boy shrugging.

"Reporter's intuition."

We rounded the thick hanging curtains, my eyes widening at the sight before me. The performers had rearranged themselves on stage, laughing as they danced, a few leaning over the shoulders of a familiar black-haired boy. Rowan's solid figure sat at the worn brown piano, colorful strips of fabric hanging from his hips and his chest bare. His fingers bounced across the untuned keys, an uncanny melody blaring from the instrument.

"*My sweetheart's two feet are sewn backward,*" he sang, eyes closing as his fingers skillfully maneuvered across the keys. "*My arms splintered below and above.*"

"*We stumble and trip in the moonlight.*" The rumbling laughter of the crowd filled the room, voices joining in. "*But I guess that's just falling in love.*"

The room had grown warm, the booming laughter and burning booze chasing out winter's prying grip, leaving a pleasant feeling in the air around us.

Rowan's dark eyes had locked with mine, a question glowing in shades of vivid green. I nodded, arms crossed over my chest as I grinned, unable to tear my gaze from the stage. His shoulders relaxed, lips pulling into a smile.

There it is again. A heavy feeling filled my chest, eyes moving from his. *That feeling of unease that creeps up on me when I least expect it.*

"B.D. you said?" Rin's muffled voice sounded from somewhere in the archive, his slender form hidden between the towering shelves of information.

"That's correct," I shouted back, hugging my coat closer to my body. The Black Press was comically simple to infiltrate—all it took was a smile and a few short words from Rin and we were let in, no questions asked.

Rowan sighed at my right, cheeks still warm from the booze and his earlier performance. While he probably didn't feel the chill, I certainly did. If I thought the station's record room was cold, this one felt like an ice box in comparison. The Black Press's archive was constructed like a vault, all walls made of thick, insulated metal, only one massive door leading in and out.

"I'm surprised you revealed yourself," Rowan said, pulling at the ends of his gloves. "And to him of all people."

"I did what had to be done for the sake of the case."

"How noble of you."

"You seemed like you were having a swell time." I turned my shivering body to face him, a safe distance still lingering between us. "You make for a good distraction. I'll give you that."

"What can I say?" He shrugged, faint wisps of a grin on his lips. "I've been told that I can command the attention of any room."

"Must be a hassle with your chosen profession." I turned to face the shelves once more, the inklings of a smile tugging at my lips.

"I've learned to use it to my advantage."

"I found something!" Rin's voice echoed from somewhere within the vast vault. I snapped my face up, the boy rounding the corner of a comically large rack. My outstretched hand was met with a thin stack of articles, identical to the ones found at the station.

"Anything about the writer? Maybe a photograph or some sort of author's blurb?"

"Nothing." He pushed his bangs back. "All I managed to find was a publishing contract signed twelve years ago."

"Damn it," I muttered, my confidence deflating. Every time I got one step closer to the truth, I ended up taking two steps back.

"The only other thing I can think of is breaking into the director's office, but that would be basically impossible." Rin rubbed at his neck, Rowan's sly hands taking the columns from my grip. "Besides, most of his records are down here anyways."

"Think, Valeria," I murmured under my breath, turning my back to the boys. "Think of another way."

"You're an idiot. You know that, right?" Rowan's voice sounded from behind me, my lips pressing together.

"I'm in no mood for the comments of a drunk." I gritted my teeth at Rowan's voice, annoyance pricking my shoulders. "I'm trying to think. I mean, we must've missed something!"

"Yeah, you didn't flip through all of these pages."

"What?" I whipped my head around, brows knitting together at his lax expression. "They're the same as the ones from earlier though!"

"Except this one." His eyes widened in mock surprise, lifting the last article, a red outline peeking through its thin paper. "Has a letter tucked into it."

I gasped, pulling it out of his loose grip, eyes scanning through the handout. Sure enough, tucked between the thin pages of anti-nobility advocacy was the worn envelope of an opened letter, the date listed above being a mere day before my mother's death.

"*My apologies for my recent absence,*" I read out loud, Rowan's gaze hovering over my shoulder. "*Due to the escalating madness in the outer districts of Nieve I have had very few opportunities to sit down and write.*

"*I fear that all we know is not as it seems.*

"*Nieve is drenched in more blood than I've ever known, and it grows worse by the year. My final article will address this past week's tragedy, expect it soon.*

"*Do not try to reach me afterwards. For your safety as well as for my own.*

"*Best, B.D.*"

"This past week's tragedy?" Rin muttered to himself, crossing his arms.

"The fire." Rowan sighed, the familiar *click* of his pocket watch sounding behind me. "The murder and fire occurred on the same week."

"So he planned to write an article about the fire? That's all?" I furrowed my brows, reading the letter over again. Something was wrong, almost sinister about this whole situation. *I fear that all we know is not as it seems? Nieve is drenched in more blood than I've ever known? What does that mean?*

"He obviously feared for his safety." Rowan shrugged, eyeing the endless rows of files before us. "Maybe this was around when he planned the murder. This article would be his last because he planned to kill your mother and disappear afterwards."

"But that's the thing." Rin shook his head, eyes weary with uncertainty. "He never wrote that last article. He mentions at the top how difficult writing a letter would have been for him, so why did he go through the trouble only to not fulfill his claims?"

"What if he was in trouble?" We both turned to look at the assassin, his green eyes drifting down from the towering shelves. "Did we ever stop and think that maybe B.D. isn't the murderer at all?"

"Nonsense." I crossed my arms, shutting him down instantly. "He has to be."

"Well hold on now, Chief." Rowan put his hands out in front of him, tone teasing but eyes serious. "Just listen. What if, in some alternate reality, B.D. wasn't the killer? What would his role be in all this?"

"He…" I swallowed hard, eyes narrowing. "He could have known something, something that caught the eye of someone dangerous."

"Maybe something like what started the fire," Rowan whispered, more to himself than to anyone else. "Or rather, who."

"What are you talking about?" I scoffed, eyes narrowing at his lack of common knowledge. "The guy who started it died in the flames! It was an act of hatred, a tragedy brought about by a petty feud between two rivaling gangs."

"Is that what they feed you nobles?" He smiled as he spoke but his eyes were hard, cold to the touch.

"It's the truth."

"Yes, it makes *perfect* sense that a man would set a building full of his own colleagues aflame."

"Well he *was* a criminal! What did he care?" I spat, furrowing my brows at the assassin.

Rowan's lips parted to say something, but he swallowed his words, turning his face away from mine.

"I don't know how much help this would be"—Rin's voice was quiet, eyes tentatively moving between us—"but I could introduce you to Marvin Reese."

"And who the hell is that?" Rowan's voice was sharp, aggravated for a reason I couldn't decipher. I gave Rin an apologetic look, his posture loosening.

"Well…" He pulled at his suspenders, the straps stretching. "He's a survivor. The only survivor from the first building that caught flame."

"Impossible." Rowan whipped his head around, and for the first time since we had met, a look of pure shock had overtaken his stoic features. "That's impossible! That fire burned half of the Seventh to the ground, killing hundreds of innocent people. You're telling me that someone from the first building, *someone who witnessed the start of the fire,* is still alive today?"

179

"Alive is a very generous word." Rin shrugged uneasily, gaze falling to the ground as he spoke. "And very few know of him because he's become quite paranoid, for reasons you can imagine."

"How soon can we see him?" I said quickly, ignoring Rowan's stunned figure.

"I could get you a small window of time in the next few days."

"Rin." I grinned, pulling the reluctant boy into a hug. "You really are the very best."

"I'm well aware," he muttered, patting me dryly on the back.

The walk back from the Fifth was silent, Rowan completely lost in his thoughts as we trudged through the bitter cold.

We had gotten so many answers, and yet my mind was heavy with new questions. *Who is B.D.? What did he mean in his last letter? And if he isn't the killer, then who is?*

*And...*My eyes drifted to the boy at my right, his silent figure towering over my own as we walked.

"The fire," I said, the wind carrying my voice high above us. "That's what you're after, isn't it? You want revenge on the guy who started it."

"Those are some award-winning deduction skills, Chief."

"I'm being serious." I shrunk back into my coat as the wind howled. "How are you so certain of your theory? That it wasn't caused by a gang dispute?"

"It's not a theory." He turned to face me. "I know it's true."

"How?" I pushed, burying my hands deeper into my pockets. "How can you possibly be so sure?"

"Well..." His eyes had changed again, a faraway look swirling within the green irises, like a seabound ship lost in the fog. "I suppose that's because I was there myself."

Chapter 12

MY EYES FLUTTERED OPEN, A warmth that I hadn't felt in years enveloping my tired body. A deep inhale filled my lungs, a hand running through my unruly hair and forcing the remnants of sleep out of the brown strands.

When was the last time I slept through the night? I rubbed at my eyes, stretching my back as I sat up straight. I had slipped back through my bedroom window at the premature hour of three in the morning, peeling the thick layers of clothing from my sore body and allowing myself to be swallowed whole by the waiting embrace of my bed.

I pulled back the heavy blanket that covered my skin, letting my bare legs hang over the side of the bed as I rolled my aching shoulders back. A bath was what I needed, the lingering scent of alcohol and cigarettes from the night before faint but ever-present.

My washroom was vast, the connected entrance to my bedroom making it my most private corner in the entire estate. I flinched, the water that spilled into the regal tub ice-cold. I pursed my lips, fearing that the boiler wouldn't be operating so early in the morning, my shoulders relaxing in relief as the steady stream gradually warmed. I sucked in a breath, my legs slowly stepping into the tub, a chill running across my cold skin as the hot water reached my stomach.

A soft sigh escaped me, my sore body lying back and soaking in the steaming bath. My eyes shut, the heat chasing away the last few whispers of sleep.

"How?" My eyes moved beneath their lids, replaying the scene from the night before. *"How are you so certain of your theory? That it wasn't caused by a gang dispute? How can you possibly be so sure?"*

"Well…" Rowan's gaze had changed then, empty eyes squinting, as if confronted with a painful memory. *"I suppose that's because I was there myself."*

I opened my eyes, staring up at the pale ceiling. He hadn't elaborated any more after that, forcing me to drag my feet the rest of the way home with untamable questions swimming through my mind.

Rowan had been there? I sat up, soaking locks of hair sticking to my back. *He couldn't have been more than a child.*

Does that mean he was from the Seventh District? My hands reached for the white stool at the edge of the tub, grabbing a floral bar of soap. If that were true, then I couldn't downplay his words. *As crazy as it sounds, who is to say that the criminal didn't get away?*

That would explain why he had proposed our alliance in the first place. The dates lined up, the fire raging just a few short days before my mother's murder. If he believed the arsonist was never caught, never brought to justice, linking the mysterious criminal to the killer in my story wouldn't be that far of a stretch.

It wouldn't be impossible.

My bare feet padded down the stairs, hands fiddling with my tie as I hurried to the first floor. I stopped at the last set of stairs, fingers gently resting on the wooden railing as I stared up at the big golden clock. I watched the seconds tick by one by one, shoulders softening. I pushed the image of Rowan's pocket watch to the back of my mind, a loud rumble from my stomach reminding me that I hadn't eaten yet today.

A yawn escaped me as I entered the dining room, the bright chandelier illuminating the towering walls. My brows came together at the man before me, my father's quiet figure sipping his morning brew, papers in hand. He was rarely home this late, opting to head out of the estate's double doors before the sun itself appeared in the sky.

My thoughts were interrupted by a muffled bark from across the hall. I stiffened, hand pulling away from the dining room's doorway as I jogged down the first floor's expanse, my feet coming to a stop at the common room's open doors.

My shoulders dropped as a brick of realization hit me, four giant wolfhounds crowded onto our sofa, scratching at its wooden details.

"There she is!" The booming voice of Michaelis Silverstein echoed throughout the hall, an impossibly large smile taking over my features.

"Uncle!"

I laughed, running into his outstretched arms, the giant of a man lifting me into the air without losing a breath.

"I'm so sorry! I didn't realize you had come so soon!" I rambled once my feet touched the ground, his pale eyes squinting kindly at me. "I would've greeted you sooner!"

"Don't worry about it, darling." He smiled generously. "Your father hardly remembered, himself."

"That isn't true and you know it!" Papa's voice echoed through the walls, sending the two of us into a laughing fit.

"So how does it feel to be back home in the First?" My smile was steady as we walked through the large halls, approaching the dining room.

"Better than you can imagine."

Uncle Michaelis was the corporal of Nieve's army, spending months upon months overseas or in training facilities. It was rare to have him home for more than a week at a time.

"That estate of yours has probably been collecting dust like you wouldn't know," Papa commented, flipping to the next page in his paper.

"Eliza has taken care of things wonderfully." He waved my father off. His thick Northern accent pulled at every one of his words, drawing them out. "But enough about me, what have you and your brother been up to?

I swallowed a lump of unease at his words. The last time Uncle Michaelis had been home was nine months ago, before my father demoted me from a junior on the force to a desk aide.

"It's been…" I glanced over at my father, his eyes still buried within the weekly articles. "Good. I'm just happy to help Papa however I can."

"You don't need to lie to me, Vally dear." He glanced over at Papa, "I know what a pain Kenneth can be."

"I would prefer if you didn't slander my name to my daughter."

"*Slander.* Okay, Sir Pretentious." He stroked his white mustache, his thinning hair matching its color.

"Our father does run a tight ship, but that's part of the reason he's been so successful." I shrugged, Papa lifting his eyes to give me a kind smile, but it was half-hearted. He had been strangely quiet that morning, his usual jests and hurried steps slowed to a crawl.

"Have you two had breakfast yet?" I asked, moving to pour myself a cup of coffee, a drop of milk splashing into the black abyss that filled my cup.

"Yes, we were just finishing up," my father said, flipping the page in his paper.

"If you can call what you Capital folk eat breakfast." Silverstein snorted, heavy arms crossing over his chest. "Why must everything be so sweet and buttery?"

I grinned, moving to grab a jar of jam from the polished wooden hutch that clung to the wall.

Northern food was always too salty for Victor and I, their pickled vegetables too sour and the wild fish jumping straight from the ocean onto their plates. We'd been raised in the subtle sweetness of the First District, after all—on the gentle flakiness of morning pastries and the privileged warmth of afternoon tea.

My hands gripped the jar's smooth glass, the deep red of autumn's last strawberry harvest a welcome sight. I popped the lid open, moving to grab a fresh slice of bread when my hand stopped, hovering mid-air. For right before my eyes sat my father's calendar, something he had started using to help with his forgetfulness. And past his scheduled meetings and investigations sat a blank square, the twenty-first of December.

The day my mother had been taken from us.

That's it. A heavy weight sat at my chest, my appetite abandoning me completely.

He's like this because that day is approaching again.

Father had always worked hard, putting his heart into every case that found its way into his hands, but since my mother had passed, he had buried himself completely in work, using it as a distraction from his empty half of the bed.

December would always be when he was the hardest on himself, working even harder and using every excuse in the book to not come home, leaving us with Lou and her Nana for nights on end.

I swallowed hard, turning back to my father, his tired figure standing to its feet.

"We'll be heading out to the station. Michaelis wants to terrorize some new recruits," my father said, folding his paper. My uncle brought two fingers to his lips and whistled, the clamoring of paws sounding off the walls in the estate as the giant hounds ran through the door.

"As great as it is to have you back, I would have really preferred it if you left your *horses* at home," my father said.

"Come now." Silverstein scratched one of the massive beasts behind the ear. "They don't mean any harm. Besides, they're my security."

Michaelis Silverstein was a military man, a corporal of high esteem and honor, but in all my years working at my father's side I had never met anyone more paranoid than he was. His estate was guarded at all times by trained soldiers, the man owning seven enormous hounds, three of which never left his estate. I was sure he had his reasons, but still, it was strange to think of the jovial man in that light.

"You two go on ahead." I smiled, pulling the long strands of my hair back into their usual ponytail. "My shift isn't for another hour."

My father nodded, pressing a kiss to my forehead before grabbing his cap and disappearing out the dining room door, Silverstein and his dogs not too far behind. My hands fell loosely to my sides, the estate much colder in their absence despite the raging flames of the fireplace.

I jumped, two hands wrapping around me snugly from behind, my shoulders relaxing at the familiar scent of my brother's aftershave.

"Any particular reason for such a heartfelt hug?" I joked, but my heartbeat had steadied once more, Vic's chin resting on my head.

"Nope," he said, loosening his grip so I could turn to face him, his kind eyes squinting into a sad smile. "You just seemed like you needed one."

Victor's gaze drifted to the calendar, his arms shifting below the fabric of his uniform. He was always careful with the subject of our mother, my brother able to compartmentalize his emotions far better than our father and myself. I suppose a part of him felt guilty, remorseful that I had protected him that night. That I had covered his eyes while my own had watched our mother violently fade away.

"You aren't busy today, are you?"

"Not especially." I shrugged, pulling away from him, my hands finding my piece of bread once more. "Just the usual file sorting and paperwork back at the office."

"Well…" I groaned as he grabbed my arm, taking a huge bite out of my breakfast. "How would you like to investigate a case?"

My eyes widened, Victor's face smug as he munched happily.

"Poisoning chains have been getting much worse. Criminals are becoming more bold and more people are being killed due to the illegal use of hallucinogens." He wiped at his lips, words unclear as he chewed. "Lou and I are going to investigate a case down in the Sixth today, and while she is amongst the most accomplished Silvers on the force, I would feel much more secure if we had another pair of observant eyes at our side."

I blinked hard at his words, still not fully processing them.

"But Papa—"

"I convinced him." Victor smiled softly. "He is well aware of your capabilities and I swore to keep you at my side for the entirety of the day."

I pursed my lips, trying to suppress a smile, my brother struggling to conceal his own.

"What do you say, V?" His eyes squinted warmly as they stared down at me. "Just for today?"

I nodded fervidly before burying my face into his chest, vibrations running through me as he chuckled.

"Dramatic thing." My heart ached at the familiar endearment, the beating of his own steady against my ear.

"Thank you, Victor." My words were soft, muffled by the fabric of his shirt.

"What are you thanking me for?" He laughed, but squeezed me nonetheless.

For everything, I should have said. *For being the tether that holds my unsteady feet to this earth.*

But I didn't.

"For believing in me."

A car blared by, the old hackney carriage honking as it tried to pass through the narrow streets of the Sixth District. The outer districts, from the Fifth until the Seventh, were the lower-income neighborhoods of Nieve, the streets consisting of bigger factories and traction. I scrunched my nose at the pillowing cloud of soot that filled the sky, the factory fumes mixing with Nieve's heavy fog, completely blocking out the sunlight. It was easy to spot the differences between the Sixth and First—in some areas the two places clashed like night and day. There wasn't a single estate in sight, clotheslines strung across the streets from apartment to apartment, the crumbling buildings consisting of whole families in unrealistically tiny rooms. Even the children playing in the street seemed different, dressed in plain and simple clothing, boys and girls as young as twelve taking shifts in one of the many textile or leather factories.

A group of young children laughed a ways away, their giggles almost drowned out completely by the rumblings of machinery. A makeshift ball rolled out onto the cobblestone streets, the tightly-wrapped fabric covered with dirt from playing outside. Victor bent down, picking the ball up gently, a little boy jogging out from behind a building before coming to a stop. He stiffened, pulling at the strings of his shirt, before tentatively approaching my brother. Vic's eyes were honeyed, my brother handing the boy the ball with a sweet smile, tipping his hat when he stared up with wide eyes.

A soft smile smoothed the worry from my face, the child disappearing off with his friends again. I had never doubted that my brother would be an amazing Viscount, but it was these moments that only reinforced that belief. He would be good for the people.

"Val!"

I raised an eyebrow at the familiar voice, turning to see Lou jog up to us, file in hand. Her usually-cheerful lips were pressed into a fine line, the girl scanning the district with gentle eyes. I was sure she had felt it too. That unexplainable sense of guilt that came with patrolling these parts of Nieve.

"It's good to see you on the field." Her eyes were kind as they met mine, a deep-rooted warmth swirling within her olive irises.

"The file?" Victor asked, taking it from her outstretched hands.

"Following our earlier investigations, the violent chains of poisonings followed by harrowing crimes all lead us back to the Sixth." She went over her report, eyes moving between my brother and I. "One particular crime that happened just yesterday has yielded some new insight as to how these drugs affect its victims mentally."

"*A man. Age thirty-two*," Victor read, flipping through the file, nodding at Lou to continue.

"He was drugged sometime between seven and eight in the evening yesterday." She sighed, moving her hands to rest at her back respectfully. "An hour later he was found speaking incoherently, drenched in the blood of two women, their bodies lying stabbed and dismembered at his side."

"Hell," I exhaled, Lou nodding solemnly.

"He was obviously not in his right mind, and after about six hours had passed he seemed to have regained his awareness. He was horrified to hear of what he'd done, going completely hysterical and rambling about how *the shadows had peeled off the walls and attacked him*, taking the shape of two serpent-like creatures."

"When in reality it was just two innocent women walking home." Victor rubbed at his forehead, the sheer horror of the case enough to make my skin crawl.

"I don't understand." I crossed my arms over my chest, both sets of eyes turning to me. "The drugs, they just jumble up your mind a bit. You're telling me that this man couldn't distinguish the fact that what he saw wasn't real?"

"It's trickier than that, V." Victor swallowed, his eyes troubled. "Apparently you are encapsulated in a sense of false reality, the drug overlaying your brain in fog. Your fear becomes so amplified that you can hardly focus on your own breaths. It's not hard to believe that he couldn't focus on the fact that what he was clearly seeing could not be real."

I shivered, the cold hardly the reason for the raised hairs on my neck. I could understand him now—Rowan's constant need for validation in what he was seeing, his anxious hands grabbing for the rusted pocket watch as if his life depended on it.

How many times has he been trapped in such a nightmare?

"Nicolo Pines. He's a merchant in the Fifth," I said abruptly, my brother's brows furrowing. "Known for supplying"—I thought back to the assassin's words—"*various goods.*"

"A drug dealer then?" Vic asked.

I shrugged, nodding slightly. "Same difference. He's known locally as the Tailor. You can imagine why."

"The Tailor, huh?" Victor laughed, but it was humorless, a bitter smile on his lips. "A stitcher of dreams. *Isn't that something?*"

I avoided my brother's eyes, blistering waves of anger and disgust barely contained by his collected exterior, his skin pulling tight as the emotion raged beneath it.

"He must be the big supplier that crook in the Fourth was talking about," Lou mumbled, a gloved hand slipping into her coat and retrieving a notepad. "Nicolo Pines, you said?"

"Yes."

I felt my brother's eyes on me, his deep blues narrowing the more I spoke.

It's fine, I reassured myself, nodding as Lou jotted down my words. *Slipping them some useful information here and there won't give my case away.*

"I'll take Val with me to get a few interviews here in the Sixth," Victor said. "We'll meet you back here at—"

A harrowing scream echoed through the streets of the Sixth, the hairs on my arms standing stiff. Victor turned sharply to his side, calling out to a few deputies, but I had already taken off, my feet flying through the icy roads of Nieve.

"V, wait!" Victor's panicked voice called from behind, but there was no point in stopping.

I breathed in and out heavily, listening for the woman's voice again, Lou tight on my heels, pistol drawn.

My eyes scanned the area around me, finding a low-hanging emergency staircase leading to the roofs.

"You continue on ahead, I'll take the roofs," I yelled, Lou's running figure nodding as she passed me. I held my breath, taking a running start before jumping, fingertips gripping the cold metal of the retractable staircase, the steps hitting the ground with a loud clang as I pulled.

My feet clamored up the hard steps, the wind intensifying as I reached the roof. The tiny outline of officers ran ahead on the streets below me, my own body following them from above, eyes scanning the district for anything suspicious. I grunted, leaping from the roof of the apartment complex, my feet hitting the next one steadily before picking up their pace again.

Come on, come on! I huffed, my feet maneuvering across the metal roof skillfully. *Someone is hurt, maybe even dying.* I jumped onto the next roof, not taking a moment to rest.

We have to find—

I gasped, my foot slipping on an icy tile, my body toppling off the roof and straight down toward the bustling streets below.

I cried out, a tight grip latching onto me, the bruised skin of my wrist throbbing at the sudden pressure.

"Now, now, Chief." A familiar voice sighed from above me, my panicked eyes meeting a pair of green ones. "Don't go getting yourself killed just yet."

I gritted my teeth as he pulled my hand up to the ledge, my wrist aching intensely. "Rowan, how—"

"How do I always manage to appear when you need me?" My fingers dug into the crumbling bricks, a cry escaping me as the assassin released his hold, letting me dangle by the strength of my arm. "I guess I'm just too good."

I grunted, pulling my other hand to grip the ledge, clenching my jaw.

"It would be smart of you to stick to a group in these parts."

"Are you saying that I'm not capable?" I strained, muscles trembling as I pulled myself up.

"Why, I would never. I'm simply looking out for my colleague." He buried his hands into his pockets, watching me squirm. "Oh I'm sorry, are you struggling there?" He crouched down in front of me, his eyes glinting in amusement. "You know I'd be more than happy to pull you up if you ask politely. Go on, say pretty please. Make it flowery."

"Arrogant bastard," I said through gritted teeth, finally getting my elbows over the ledge, kicking my legs as I pulled myself up. He grinned, eyes moving to scan the streets below.

"It looks like you're back in action."

"I doubt that." I panted, laying my head back onto the roof's cold tiles. "It's just for the day. I'm not even allowed to carry a weapon."

I could play Silver all day if I pleased. The reality was that tomorrow morning I'd be chained back to my father's side, sorting through civilian complaints and filing paperwork.

"We have a meeting with Marvin Reese tomorrow night, a bit earlier than when we usually meet."

"It shouldn't..." I huffed, still catching my breath as I sat up. "It shouldn't be a problem."

His eyes drifted down to my hands, one clutching the other, my wrist still purple and agitated from our earlier confrontation.

"Glad to hear it, Chief." He turned his back to me, taking a few steps back the way I had come.

"Val!" A voice echoed from below, Lou's small figure appearing below. "Valeria!"

"You should go." He avoided my eyes even as he looked over his shoulder, my brows furrowing at his sudden change of behavior. "Try not to fall down any more buildings. I can't say I'll be there to catch you next time."

"Yeah, yeah." I sighed, pulling myself to my feet. "Thanks, I guess."

He nodded, dark hair blowing wildly in the wind as he sauntered away from where he had come.

"Val!" I snapped my attention back down to Lou, her jogging figure coming to a stop as her eyes met mine.

"I'll be down as soon as I finish my round!" I yelled, watching her posture relax, but it was only temporary.

"Don't bother. Corner of Sixth and Seventh Street," she called, running ahead. I furrowed my brows, happy that they had found the girl but confused as to why she had come all the way back here.

"And?" I yelled, Lou's form shrinking as she ran ahead. She turned back then, meeting my eyes once more as she yelled out four words.

"We've got a murder!"

Chapter 13

I BRUSHED THE HAIR OUT OF my face, hands fidgeting as I stood alone in the silent dark of night. Marvin Reese still lived in the Seventh District, Nieve's outermost neighborhood. I had only been here twice before, both times accompanied by Papa and Vic. On each of those occasions we had to handle multiple murders and more crimes of theft than our forces could manage. The Seventh was not somewhere anyone would want to be caught alone.

The faint sound of boots jolted my tense body, the familiar silhouette of Rowan Marrow materializing from the shadows. My eyes fell to his hands, the boy wiping them on a dark cloth, tucking it into his coat before I could dare to ask.

"You're…" My voice was unsteady, my fists clenching in my pockets. "You're late."

"Long day at work."

I swallowed the lump in my throat, turning my eyes away from his. We stared up at the run-down apartment complex that towered over us, the building a few wrong steps from crumbling to the ground.

"How'd you manage to get here on your own?" he asked, glancing at me briefly.

"I told you not to doubt me." I glared at him, the bitter cold stinging my cheeks. "And I told my father that I'd be helping Flint out at his apartment."

"Ah that's right, your pet."

"I'd watch myself, *Alias*." I gritted my teeth, the assassin's lips twitching at the name.

"Touched a nerve, did I?"

"I'm about to rip out all of yours."

"Tsk tsk, Silver." He shook his head, taking a few steps forward. "Violence is never the answer."

Anger was hot on the tip of my tongue, but he had already walked ahead, not sparing a moment to look back.

"Shall we?" he asked, ducking ahead, feet carefully stepping up the rusted metal steps. I was silent, following on his heels as we climbed up the building. Every floor that passed us by was worse, my face recoiling back at the heavy scent of urine and rotting meat that filled the air at every other turn.

"How can people live like this?" I whispered, swallowing the rancid taste on my tongue.

"Yeah, well…" Rowan didn't turn back to me, his steps speeding up as we approached the fifth floor. "Welcome to the Seventh."

Marvin Reese lived on the fifth floor of the building. While his door seemed well-kept and the area surrounding it clean enough, the apartment next to his had been smashed apart, the doors and windows boarded up with rotting pieces of driftwood. Rowan had avoided looking around since he had arrived, eyes trained at his feet. While he didn't seem too fazed by the state of these homes and the Seventh itself, there was something off about him, his cold and insensitive nature propped up on its toes.

I pursed my lips, pulling the cap down lower over my eyes before knocking twice on the wooden door, the two of us waiting in silence. A few hurried steps were heard on the other side of the door, the thin walls doing little to insulate a woman's muttering.

My posture straightened, my hand pulling the thick blue scarf higher over my features as multiple clicks were heard, followed by the door being cracked open.

"Yes?" An old woman's frail voice slipped out from behind the door, a flash of white hair hiding behind the thick wood.

"Hello, Mrs. Reese," I said gently, eyes squinting into a smile. "We're Rin's friends. We're here to talk with Marvin."

Silence filled the space between us, only the faint echo of a crying baby sounding from the streets below. My lips parted to speak again but the door slowly creaked open wider, revealing an old woman, her snowy hair pulled back into a loose bun, the blue nightdress she wore faded from years of wear.

"Please, come in." She smiled softly at us, my shoulders relaxing a bit. I slipped through the half-open door, Rowan tight on my heels. The wooden walls had been stripped of any decor, yellowing strips of wallpaper still clinging on here and there. Clothing racks were hung in the entrance of the house, my feet cautiously stepping over a bucket of soapy water.

"Do close the door after yourselves. You'll let the cold in," she called from further in.

Rowan turned to abide by her wishes.

"Please, have a seat." We reached the center of the apartment, her voice coming from a small backroom that must've been the kitchen. "I don't have much to offer you, but I have hot tea."

"Tea would be lovely." I nodded, smiling gently and taking a seat on the worn floral sofa.

My eyes drifted around the space, landing on a crooked cabinet at the couch's side, its legs uneven. This apartment only had three separate spaces, the main room right by the entrance—where we were—a side room for the kitchen, and a door at our backs, probably a bedroom. My chest ached, a fraying nightdress peeking out from one of the cabinet's drawers. *This must be where she sleeps.*

"Here you are." She smiled, returning with two metal mugs, the type that Papa would use to take his coffee from home to the station.

"Thank you." Rowan offered her a smile, bringing the cup to his lips. I nodded, taking my own cup, the hot metal warming my hands.

"So." She huffed, taking a seat on the single dining chair, its wooden legs unstable and worn. "What district do you two live in?"

"I live in—"

"We're from the Fourth," Rowan said, his green eyes less intimidating now that they were directed at the woman. I pursed my lips, choosing to go along with his words. It wasn't that being from the First was necessarily bad, but I didn't want her to know that I was in any direct relationship with the Viscount or the Imperial Force.

"Ah I see! I've heard it's a lovely place to start a family."

I jumped as Rowan choked to my right, breaking out into a fit of coughs as he pulled the scalding cup from his lips.

"Yes, it's really nice." I smiled, her worried gaze focused on Rowan as she offered him a hand towel, the boy accepting it with a strained nod of gratitude. I tried to shift the conversation and speed things up. "Is Marvin in?"

"Oh! Yes, he's in his room. Give me a second to let him know you're here." She waved her hands as she stood to her feet, the woman giving us one last warm look before disappearing into the back room.

"So have you decided how many you want?" I asked, Rowan's brows furrowing as he wiped at his lips.

"Hm?"

"Kids."

His eyes widened, a grin overtaking my features as he tensed. "*None.*" His voice was firm, his head shaking vigorously as a laugh left my lips. "Well I'll be."

I raised an eyebrow at the killer, amusement glinting in his eyes.

"Did Sergeant Uptight just let out a genuine laugh?"

"Don't be an idiot." I scoffed, but could do little to conceal my grin.

I could still feel his eyes on me, even after I turned my focus to my hands, watching the murky liquid swirl around the cup's rim. It was strange how at ease I was around him, especially at this proximity.

Especially after all he had done.

"Take off that pathetic noble mask." My fists clenched instinctively at the memory. *"And give me a taste of that vicious human heart."*

No, no. Alias Black is still the same. I squeezed my eyes shut, swallowing the unease in my throat. *He is still the same ghastly killer.*

Is it me then?

The thought made me want to vomit.

Am I the one who changed?

"You two are welcome to come in now!" Mrs. Reese's voice was soft, sounding from the room behind us. My eyes jolted open, tense hands placing the steaming cup at my feet before standing up, Rowan following my movements.

"Marvin dear, here they are." She smiled graciously as we approached the open door, the woman taking my hands in hers, her calloused palms wise with decades of labor.

I slipped through the opening, the smile from my lips withering as my eyes met a pair so dark and empty they challenged the night itself. My bones had gone rigid, unsteady feet stumbling back into Rowan's chest. The entirety of the Seventh District emitted an eerie atmosphere, the horrors of what had happened here whispered in every hungry child on the street and every decomposing body left to be found. But there was something about this specific place, this room, *this man*, that chilled the air with the clawed touch of death.

It was as if the man named Marvin Reese had died that night amongst the flames and what was sitting in the corner of this room was just his skin.

A steady hand rested on my shoulder, momentarily stopping the fearful tremor that ran through my limbs.

"You're trembling." Rowan's voice was low, his words warm against my ear.

"Am I?" I barely whispered, the hand gently squeezing.

"Terribly."

I swallowed hard.

"Relax." His breath sent goosebumps down my spine, my bones releasing their tension. "The most frightening thing in Nieve is already on your side."

I shut my eyes, inhaling deeply before opening them once more.

He is right. I straightened up, swallowing harshly before taking a step forward. *There is nothing left to be afraid of.*

Marvin Reese was not at all what I had expected. The image of him in my mind was linked to that of an old man, one paranoid and afraid, hiding within the confines of his mother's worn apartment as he tried to cope with what he had witnessed all those years ago.

Instead I found a man in his late thirties, his frail body confined to a wheelchair, half of the skin on his face completely burnt and waxy.

"Hello, Mr. Reese." I offered him a gentle smile, his dark eyes unmoving as they stared past my skin. "My name is Val, and this is my friend Rowan. We were wondering if we could ask you a few questions."

He stared long and hard, his lips twitching before his murky eyes blinked twice.

"That's a yes, dear," his mother said softly from our right. My lips parted, quickly understanding the situation before us. Rowan's posture slumped, the boy's usually-unreadable expression riddled with frustration.

"Great, thank you." I smiled brightly, crouching down to take a seat on the floor across from the man. Rowan crossed his arms, leaning on the wall behind me. "I think you know what we're here to discuss."

He blinked twice again, my shoulders relaxing a bit further.

"We are looking for a man, masked as a wolf. He committed a heinous murder ten years ago, but we think there's a chance that he was linked to the fire somehow too," I started, his eyes expressionless as he listened, Rowan's eyes burning into the back of my head. "We've been tracking letters from an old news reporter who disappeared after the fire. The probability of him being the killer is pretty large, but we came here because there is a sliver of a chance that he isn't the criminal."

"So do you"—I stopped, swallowing the weight of the question—"do you remember anything from the night of the fire?"

The four of us were silent, Marvin's mother wringing her hands nervously as she stared at her motionless son. Rowan sighed from behind me, my hands clenching the fabric of my pants.

A heavy breath wracked through me as he blinked twice, Rowan's posture straightening instantly.

"You remember?" Rowan asked, stepping forward and dropping to my side. "Do you know who started the fire?"

"Rowan," I tried, but his eyes had widened, the boy tense enough to shatter. "Did you see who lit it?"

Again, two blinks. Rowan's hands found his hair, his eyes staring off in disbelief. My stomach twisted, lips trembling as a question sat on my tongue.

"It wasn't a gang member that did it"—Rowan's eyes drifted back over to me as I spoke—"was it?"

My heart leapt, sitting in my throat as Marvin blinked once, holding my gaze.

How could they have missed it? How could the police get that wrong? My mind raced, all the possible reasons flashing through my mind like a reel of film. The evidence must've been burned away, or someone extremely skilled could have covered their tracks. *But who?*

"A name, a face, what did you see?" Rowan asked. "You were in the first building, right? Was it a man? A woman? A kid playing around with some matches?"

"Rowan, let him—"

"Tell me!" His voice boomed, Mrs. Reese flinching at the sound. "Please." Rowan's hands fidgeted as he collected himself. "Tell me what you saw."

"Was it a man?" I asked softly, Rowan exhaling as Marvin blinked twice. My eyes fell to Marvin's hands, watching them twitch. His index finger tapped the arm of the chair, my squinted eyes counting seven times.

"Seven? Eight?" I struggled, Marvin's eyes blank.

"A group of men?" Rowan asked, the two of us growing silent as he blinked twice. "What did they look like? Did they wear masks?"

One blink.

"Do you remember what they wore? Maybe a piece of jewelry or a specific color?"

He blinked twice, Rowan leaning in closer.

"Color?"

One blink.

"Jewelry?"

Two blinks.

"A brooch? Necklace?"

A group of men, I thought, my brows knitting together. "A pin?"

Marvin blinked rapidly, the two of us jumping forward at his validation.

"What was on it?" Rowan asked, hitting his forehead as he realized his mistake. "Uh, flowers?"

One blink.

"Feathers?"

One blink.

"A jewel of some sort?"

One blink again.

"Damn it!" Rowan ran his hands over his face, my lips pressing into a fine line at the sight of him. No matter the situation, he had always maintained an empty glare and stoic expression. *But now*—I swallowed the weight in my chest—*he's almost like a different person, like a frightened child.*

"An animal?" Rowan sighed, rubbing at his brows.

Two blinks.

"Really?" he blurted, quieting down at my sharp glare.

"An animal." My mind filled with the only answer that made sense. "Was it a wolf?"

He paused, dark eyes narrowing a bit, before blinking twice.

So there is a connection! My shoulders tensed, eyes widening.

"A group of men, all wearing pins with a wolf on it," I repeated, hugging my knees as I leaned forward. "Was there anything else? Anything distinct?"

Those next two blinks would send us into a downward spiral of random questions, the night sky growing darker and darker by the hour.

"Should I get you all another cup of tea?" Mrs. Reese popped her head back into the door, the old woman half-asleep.

"We're fine. Thank you, ma'am," I said softly, my back aching from the hours spent on the floor.

"Okay." Rowan laced his fingers together, closing his eyes as he thought. "Were they blond?"

Marvin's fingernail scratched at the armrest, the sign we had created to answer questions he didn't know.

"Did they smell a certain way? Was that it?"

He blinked a single time again, Rowan burying his face in his hands.

"Maybe we should call it a night? Let Marvin sleep," I said softly, the man's eyes drooping heavily every few minutes.

"But we're so close." Rowan whispered, dark bags of his own forming beneath his eyes. "I just know we are."

"We can come back," I reassured him, still shaken by his change in demeanor.

Rowan pressed his lips into a line, his sharp features illuminated by the pale moonlight of the window.

"Fine." He exhaled heavily, running a hand through his hair. "You're right."

The edges of my lips softly turned up, eyes squinted as I leaned toward Marvin.

"Thank you so much for your time." I gave him a warm smile, the man's eyes staring into mine. We couldn't push him any further. As desperate as we were for answers, it must've been hard for him to relive that night over and over.

We had stood to our feet, my hand just grazing the doorknob when we heard it.

"D, d—"

I froze, Rowan scrambling back to the man and kneeling in front of his chair once more.

"What? What was it that you said?"

"D—" His lips pulled slightly as he struggled, fingers digging into his armrests.

"Drug? Disc? Dent?" Rowan gripped Marvin's arms and searched his eyes wildly.

Our breath hung in the air of the cramped apartment, Marvin's lips twitching as he attempted to speak once more.

"D—dog."

Chapter 14

Dog. That was the only word Marvin Reese had managed to utter that night.

"Dog?" Rowan had muttered to himself, our tired feet clambering down the rickety metal steps.

"Dog," I repeated, rubbing tiredly at my eyes.

"We really just spent *five hours* trying to decipher the word dog?" He pulled at his face, sharp features clenched into a scowl.

"Well what the hell did you expect?" I snapped, agitated by his sulking. "For him to start spouting a detailed eye witness description?"

"That would have been nice, yes."

I groaned at his answer, hugging the coat closer and walking ahead.

We had known that whatever clue we'd get would have been a vague one, but that didn't make figuring this out any simpler.

"Okay, okay. I take it back. Dog I can work with." He sighed heavily, his long legs catching up to me easily. "We're just tired. I'll go home and sleep on it."

"Well you have fun with that. I need to somehow get to the Fourth."

"The Fourth?" He stiffened, brows coming together. "I hate to break it to you, Chief, but we aren't really a couple—and frankly, you're not my type."

"Don't be dense. I'm spending the night at Flint's." I narrowed my eyes at him, stuffing my hands into the pockets of my coat. "And *oh no!* It's a shame I'm not a psychopathic killer." I flung my hands up dramatically, a grin twitching on his lips. "I'm sure that's what gets you all hot and bothered."

"A good guess, but no." He shrugged, expression smug. "I'll leave that up to your imagination. But why is it that you can't go home? You never had a problem sneaking in and out before."

"Why do you care?"

"I don't." He pulled on his flat cap, dark hair tucked loosely beneath it. "But please, entertain me."

I sighed tiredly, the killer back to his usual irritating behavior.

Rowan's core—the reason for his murderous actions and empty eyes—still remained unclear to me.

But I felt as though I was beginning to get a sense of his edges.

"There's a big chance that my uncle's over at our estate."

"Your uncle?" He raised an eyebrow, and I stiffened, cheeks tinting at my informal word choice.

"Not *really*. Colonel Michaelis Silverstein," I said quickly, Rowan nodding slowly. "He's back home in the First, which means he and Papa probably spent the night drinking themselves silly. I bet they're both passed out downstairs at this very moment."

"That doesn't explain why you can't go home." Rowan tilted his head at the ground, kicking a glass bottle as we strolled through the dark veil of night.

"Michaelis is a very *anxious* individual, to say the least."

"Paranoid Imperial leader—sounds about right." He shrugged, my eyes rolling at his snarky comments.

"If he's home, then so are his hounds, and if they get one whiff of me smelling like the Seventh, I'll be a late night snack." A lighthearted chuckle escaped me, but the smile quickly left my lips as I turned to my right, noticing that Rowan had stopped walking.

"His what?"

"His wolfhounds." I furrowed my brows at him, the boy's conflicted gaze never leaving mine as he approached me once again. "But they're more like horses, if I'm being fair."

"Valeria." He shook his head, hands gripping my shoulders firmly. "His *what*?"

"First of all, *don't touch me*," I spat, the boy instantly loosening his hold. "And are you *a brick*? I said his hounds—his dogs—damn it!"

My clenched fists had stiffened, realization letting them fall limp at my sides. My eyebrows came together, feet taking a strong step back as I stared up at the boy's reluctant gaze.

"No," I said slowly, hands instinctively moving to touch the pendant around my neck. "Rowan, no."

"It's a lead."

"No, it *isn't*," I said sharply, crossing my arms over my chest. There was no way that was true, that that could *ever* be true. "You're just trying to find something to run with because you're just as lost as I am."

"Just hear me out, Chief." He pinched the bridge of his nose, green eyes fluttering open to meet mine. "Marvin said dog—that's all we've got."

"Exactly, so—"

"And I will *personally* break into every single dog owner's home in the Kingdom of Nieve until I find the culprit." I swallowed harshly at his words, a sharp pain in my chest. "We might as well start with Silverstein."

That conversation had taken place the night before, the two of us sitting in silence out by the old train tracks until five in the morning and boarding the first train back to the Fourth. My tired body had stumbled its way to Flint's flat soon after, passing out on his snug mattress while the boy headed to his opening shift at the bookstore. The station had been bustling with life by the time I arrived, overworked and sore but still kicking. As tired as I had been, my dreams were infested with images of Silverstein, the man's jovial smile and kind eyes refusing to mold with the word *arsonist*.

205

It would make sense for a man such as Silverstein to have his dogs with him if he were to ever commit a crime, and they weren't exactly discreet creatures, so it wouldn't be hard to believe that Marvin would remember them.

But still. I rubbed my eyes, the thick stack of files on my desk seeming more and more threatening at every second that passed. *There is no motive! No reason why a distinguished man like Michaelis Silverstein would go out of his way to set the Seventh District ablaze!*

A passing shadow caught my sleepy gaze, eyes widening as my father's busy steps clicked by.

"Viscount!" I called out, my father's hurried figure freezing. His pale eyes were wide, surprised by the title, but he approached me nonetheless.

"Yes, Ms. Anson?" He raised an eyebrow, and I pursed my lips at the words on my tongue.

"Papa," I corrected myself, a smile forming on his lips. "I wanted to ask some questions about Uncle Michaelis. About Silverstein."

"Oh?" He scratched at his scruffy cheeks, looking off in thought.

"Yes, if you aren't too busy." My gloved hands gripped the wood of my desk, Papa's hair glinting in the station lights as he nodded. "When did the two of you meet? And what makes our families so close?"

"Well Michaelis and I met when your grandfather was still the Viscount." He sighed, crossing his arms as he thought. "Back then the crime rate was much higher, rules less enforced, criminals let off more easily—and so on. I always had a very strong sense of justice growing up, and when I met a newly-drafted soldier who shared my same ideals, we quickly became very good friends."

"Ideals?" I brought the steaming mug at my side up to my lips.

"That the pursuit of the greater good was what would pull our kingdom out of the slums." He gave me a tired smile. "That hard decisions have to be made for the betterment of the people."

Papa's words were familiar. He had raised Vic and me, after all.

"But it's also up to those given the burden of power to bear the troubles of the people. We bear the weight of this kingdom so that its citizens can feel safe and protected. That's the leash that comes along with being Viscount."

A subtle warmth pulled at my lips, my father always inspiring me without knowing it.

"Silverstein is a good man, one who believes in the betterment of the people." He nodded to himself, kind gaze finally meeting mine again. "Can I ask why the sudden interest?"

"Just curious." I shrugged, turning my head as the mug was pulled from my grip, the lingering warmth tickling my palm.

"Ugh, that was a mistake." Victor's face scrunched in disgust, pulling the cup away from his lips. "I swear, you're made of steel or something. Put some sugar in that for heaven's sake!"

"Any other questions, reporter?" Papa sighed tiredly at Victor, my brother straightening up instantly.

"Yes, actually. The fire," I said, clenching my fists at my back. "Do you remember anything about it?"

If I am going to do this—if Rowan and I are going to infiltrate Silverstein's estate—I need to be sure. I need at least an inkling of suspicion toward him.

"How could I forget?" Papa swallowed, eyes clouding over. "We were so ill-prepared for such a tragedy. I remember officers as well as civilians running into surrounding homes, returning with buckets of tap water in an attempt to weaken the flames as we waited for reinforcements to arrive."

Victor stiffened at our side, my own hairs standing upright as my father stared off.

"There were so many screams, and the smell"—he exhaled deeply, hands gripping the edge of my desk—"of gas and charring flesh. The heat was so intense, they could feel it in the Sixth District. I still feel it now."

"That's"—Victor swallowed, voice unsteady—"horrifying."

"It was." Papa rubbed at his forehead, a few wrinkles deepening as he spoke. "But that's how it is with criminals. They think of themselves and their petty feuds, never the bigger picture."

"So you think the people responsible died in the fire?" I said quickly, leaning over my desk.

"Of course they did," Victor said, crossing his arms. "It's common knowledge!"

"And you, Papa?"

Tell me that it's true. My nails dug into my palms. *Tell me that you're sure without a doubt.*

"I have no reason not to."

My heart dropped to my stomach.

"There was never any evidence to suggest any differently. Everything pointed to the two ruling gangs, one of them growing tired of the other and sending their buildings ablaze."

"But the two gangs lived together." Rowan's words found themselves on my tongue. "It's just hard for me to understand how someone could light their own family and friends on fire."

"We can't understand. They're murderers, barbarians—their humanity has been flushed out to the point where they exist only as shells." My father's words were strong and unwavering, and if he had spoken them to me a few months ago, I would have accepted them, no questions asked.

But he hadn't, and hearing them now sent my stomach into knots. Yes, criminals were bad, and they deserved to serve time for all they'd committed, but that didn't make them inhuman killing machines. Even Rowan, as coldhearted as he was, smiled warmly at Mrs. Reese, laughed out loud at *The Satin Serpent*, and was patient with me at the start despite my vendetta against him.

"So there isn't even a *sliver* of a chance that the killers didn't burn up in the flames?"

"I didn't say that."

My nails dug into my skin at his words, the lump of dread in my throat growing larger by the second.

"But both the Investigative Unit and the Forensics Unit found nothing to suggest any differently."

They aren't one hundred percent sure, and yet all these years we've been told that gang extremists committed the crimes. I pursed my lips. *How many people were forced to flush out their doubts, to accept the Imperial Force's truth, and move on with their lives?*

"Thank you for your time, Papa." My heart was heavy in my chest even as my father smiled down on me.

"Of course."

I watched his back grow smaller as he disappeared through the crowd of bustling Silvers, leaving me to dwell on his words. There was no evidence to prove any differently. Technically that meant that their theory could be valid. But there was a survivor—one man alive who saw the crime occur.

That alone invalidated the Imperial Force's investigation.

"What was all that about?" Victor's words were unsure, his brows furrowing as I took my mug back from his hands. I wouldn't drag him in any further—I was already in much too deep. The sickening grip of the truth tightened its hold on my neck the more questions I asked, threatening to suffocate me completely.

"I was just a bit confused about something, but I'm certain now."

I'm certain that something here isn't right. I gave my brother a smile. *And whether I like it or not, I feel like I'll end up in the center of it soon enough.*

Michaelis Silverstein's estate sat at the edge of the First District, one of the last estates built in the neighborhood, making it the most modern and secure. The four-story estate towered above the street, a tall metal gate and an acre of open grass separating the cobblestone streets from the gleaming mansion.

Four guards were stationed outside at all times, two guarding the front entrance and two at the back. Three of his hounds also resided outdoors, their ears sensitive to the slightest of sounds.

But inside—that was a whole different chess match.

I had been in the estate once before, but hardly remembered its inner workings. Just that his dogs roamed the halls freely and that Silverstein himself was an awfully light sleeper.

Four days had passed since our chat with Marvin Reese, three since my father and I had our talk about the fire. Now I stood at the outskirts of the First District, the dark-haired assassin rustling at my side.

Rowan and I had decided to avoid questioning the man, the chances of him recognizing my voice too large and the risk of us getting caught far greater than the reward. This would be a simple infiltration mission, the two of us working only as eyes and looking for any sort of evidence that painted Silverstein as the arsonist.

"You know, the more I thought about it, the more it made sense," Rowan said, folding up his coat and throwing it behind a particularly large bush. "Silverstein is a corporal, and in war hard decisions have to be made for your troops to reach their desired outcome, for your side to win. Criminal activity was bad—the Silvers were having a tough time—so a radical group of soldiers decided to take matters into their own hands and exterminate the problem themselves."

"That's a stretch." I shivered as I shook my own coat from my body, the two of us clad in tightly-fitted pants, our skin-tight shirts made of the same dark material. Rowan had asked for my measurements some time ago, resulting in a sharp punch to the nose, but once I received the tightly-wrapped package of clothing on my doorstep, it made much more sense.

"But it makes sense, doesn't it?" His voice was hushed, green eyes illuminated by the moonlight. "They decided to kill the two rivaling groups at once, slapping on their little cover story and disappearing back into the shadows. They probably didn't expect the fire to spread as it did, panicking and leaving before the cops arrived."

"The fire. You said you were there." I felt him pause at my side. "Were you..." I swallowed hard, staring at my hands as I pulled on the dark gloves. "Were you in one of the buildings?"

"Yes." I didn't need to look at him to know that he was tense. "And that's all you need to know about that."

"I looked back on the dates"—I changed the subject, Rowan shifting at my left—"and Silverstein was in the city at the time of the fire. But we need to get something clear before we go in there."

I pursed my lips, the weight in my chest that had been resting there since the day before aching.

"You aren't going to harm him."

"If he's innocent I'd have no reason to," he said shortly, tightening the belted straps on his wrists, securing his glove in place. Rowan had no problem killing—I knew that far too well—and while the crime in question was horrendous beyond anything I could ever imagine, Silverstein was still a man, someone whom I cared for.

"Rowan." I swallowed, a hesitant hand resting on his arm. His eyes had gone vacant, as empty as they had been the first time we'd met.

"If he really is"—my voice shook, his sharp eyes meeting mine—"what you think he is, he'll get what's coming to him the right way. Through the law. Promise me you won't take matters into your own hands."

A soft smile had begun to take shape across my lips, but it soon fell completely. For Rowan's gaze was no longer his own, but filled with the sinister anger of hundreds of people, all those who had burned away in the flames.

"I have waited almost ten years to kill the man responsible for that fire, the man responsible for ruining my life and giving me a new one."

Rowan pulled his arm away sharply, my own recoiling at his deadly gaze. There was no way to reason with him—if Silverstein had really done it, if he was guilty of the crime at hand—he was a dead man.

"And while I've grown to somewhat value your opinions, my feelings are not so trivial that they can be changed by a few nice words and misplaced morals." His words weren't angry or forced, but firm, his voice even and calm as he stared past my skin. "If he's guilty you better find a way to restrain me yourself, because I swear to you now, I will kill him and everybody else in that estate."

This was a mistake. I shivered as he passed me. *I should never have brought him here.*

211

As much as we had done together, Rowan Marrow was still Alias Black, still a ruthless assassin that killed for a favorable price. He had always murdered without any real motive, killing because he was good at it, but now he had a fire lit under him. Who knew what he was capable of?

I didn't get to utter another word, for Rowan had approached the towering metal gates of Silverstein's estate. I pressed my lips together, pulling up my hood and following his silent steps. The gate and the lawn weren't the issue—it was finding a way to scale the estate that was difficult.

"Rubber shoes?" I had asked him, the two of us meeting in a bar the night after our discovery in the Seventh.

"Rubber outsoles," he had said, pulling out the world's ugliest pair of shoes from his satchel. They were two bulky things, thin and narrow at the top with large uneven soles. *"Some assassins prefer them, some do not."*

"And how exactly are they going to help us infiltrate the estate?" I had narrowed my eyes at them, taking one into my speculative grip.

"Look here." Rowan took the shoe from my hand, his finger running along the lumpy bottom. *"These rubber ridges help climbers grip to surfaces such as bricks, marble, concrete, and so on. Because of the tight guard on the estate, we won't be able to slip in through a door or take too long scrambling into a window. That's why we'll wear these and use them for extra support as we climb up the side of the estate."*

"The side of the estate? You mean climb up the walls?" I furrowed my brows, the boy rolling his eyes at me tiredly. *"Have you lost your mind?"*

"No, you dunce."

I clenched my jaw at him, Rowan sighing deeply before pointing at the shoe again.

"I've broken into quite a few estates before, and what do they all have in common?" He had raised an eyebrow, lips twitching. *"Cracks. Even the newest ones have jagged cracks through their outer walls. Giving a prepared assassin a perfect field to cross."*

We caught our breaths, my heart pounding wildly in my chest as we reached the brick walls of Silverstein's estate. We had climbed over the front gate easily, feet beating soundlessly across the cold grass, not a dog in sight. Rowan's eyes met mine, the boy giving me a slight nod before his hands gripped the ridges in the bricks.

"Quickly and quietly." His words repeated themselves in my head as the assassin's quick feet buried themselves into the cracks of the building, the boy advancing up the wall like a spider.

The trick was all in our fingers. Once we had a good grip, our feet would follow without an issue. I gritted my teeth, digging my fingers into the closest crack, my arms trembling as they pulled the rest of my body up. My feet scraped against the wall, finding an uneven ridge and lodging themselves into it.

The shoes worked! My shoulders relaxed a bit at the tiny success. I took in a deep breath, hand straining, looking for another dent in the bricks before repeating my actions again.

By the time I had made it to the third story, Rowan was sitting at the ledge of a window, the curtains pulled shut and obscuring our view of the inside. I held my breath, swallowing a scream as I leapt from the wall, my face slamming into Rowan's chest as I landed on the ledge. He didn't make a sound, his heartbeat soft against my ear as I regained my balance. We were up high now, the whistling wind threatening to grab my ankles and pull me off the narrow ledge. The hairs on my neck raised at the gentle murmurs from below, a tired guard rounding the corner below us. Rowan put a finger to his lips, the two of us sitting completely still as the guard walked by, the assassin relaxing once he was out of sight. Rowan shot me a look, the words *it would be so much easier if we just killed them* blatantly written across his features, before his hand moved to his waist, pulling out a thin blade. The same one he always carried, the same one that had probably claimed the lives of hundreds of people.

His brows came together in concentration, a gloved hand carefully resting against the locked window as the fine blade traced a circle into the glass, big enough for a thin wrist to pass through. We sat in silence, the boy tracing the circle with the knife over and over again, until he pulled away, two fingers gently tapping the glass, the circle falling clean off. I winced at the sound of it hitting the ground on the other side, two of us stiffening as the seconds ticked by. A sigh of relief escaped me when no guards came running, my lips coming together as I stuck my hand through the tiny opening, straining as I reached for the window's clasps. Rowan pressed his leg at my back, stabilizing my shifting body as I teetered on the ledge.

The first satisfying click loosened my shoulders, the second clasp much easier to reach.

Okay—I pulled my hand out carefully, Rowan moving to grip the window's base—*maybe this won't be as tough as we thought.*

I slipped through the window as soon as it slid open, Rowan tight on my heels, shutting it silently behind him. We dropped low, crouching as our eyes scanned the floor. The walls of the estate were a deep blue, matching my bedroom, the floors covered in a pale carpet, muting our hurried steps.

Rowan brought a finger to his lips, then brought up a second, pointing to the right wing of the estate.

We need to split up. I nodded, the boy taking one last second to stare at me before pulling his mask over his face, turning his back and disappearing into the left side of the estate.

My hands were shaky as I pulled on my own mask, the weight of guilt just as heavy as the fear of what we might find.

Dog—such a strangely specific word, yet vague enough that we could knock down the door of every dog owner in Nieve and only find the culprit at the end of our lifetimes.

Rowan's theory wasn't bad, but it was flawed. It left way too many factors open. Why would a military man involve himself in inner-city affairs, and wouldn't someone as experienced and knowledgeable as Silverstein think of another way—any other way to have the gangs arrested?

Look at you—I clenched my fists at my sides—*you're thinking as if he's already guilty.*

I stiffened at the sound of feet coming from around the corner, my back finding the cold wall of the hallway as I waited, my heart pounding in my ears.

"And what if we're caught?" My nerves had gotten the best of me the night before the break-in, meeting Rowan at a bar in the Second District.

"Then I get arrested for infiltrating the estate, and possibly for a few other crimes." He interlaced his fingers as he spoke, his words trailing off. *"While your dear old papa sweeps your mess under the common room rug and sends you out of the city."*

"I am not leaving, not until I catch my killer." My hands slammed against the table, the two of us stiffening as a few pairs of eyes glared over at us.

"Then let me do you one better." His twisted gaze had found mine, lips twitching into a grin. *"If you get spotted, just take this rag and hold it to the guard's face."*

My hands found the moist rag, the strip of fabric tucked into my belt.

"I can't wrestle a grown man, Rowan!" I had said, staring at the assassin with a dull expression. *"If I had a pair of cuffs or some equipment, sure—but not hand-to-hand."*

"Fifty seconds, Valeria." His words echoed in my mind now, the heavy steps approaching my waiting body.

"Just be strong enough for fifty seconds."

As soon as my eyes met the soldier's gaze I was on top of him, the two of us falling to the ground with a heavy thump. I pressed the cloth to his nose with one hand, the other attempting to stop his flailing arms.

No gun? My wild eyes scanned his belt, the absurdity of it not hitting me soon enough. My legs had successfully pinned his lower body down, but his grip was a strong one, and once his fingers found my neck all I could do was clamp down harder on his face as the air was squeezed out of me.

215

You said fifty seconds, damn it! I cursed Rowan internally, my eyes bulging as the man's grip became desperate. I gasped, his fingers twitching as they grew weaker.

There. I took in a burning lungful of air as one of his hands slipped from my throat. *Now just close your—*

I had just let the tension in my shoulders loosen when a searing pain erupted from my right, wide eyes focusing on the guard's trembling fist, a bloodied knife in his grip. His eyes rolled back, the sudden attack not meant to stop me and save himself, but to slow me down. To get me caught.

"Damn you," I whispered, my tired body slumping over the man as he finally gave out. I heaved in and out, pulling the rag from the unconscious man's face.

This isn't good. I placed a shaky hand at my ribs, the fabric of my shirt cleanly slit, letting warm blood run down my side. I didn't know how deep the cut was, just that the blood gushing from the wound was too much. But I didn't have time to worry about something like that.

Adrenaline had taken its hold, and despite the blood spouting profusely from my side I managed to stagger to my feet, dragging the soldier's body to lay it against the wall.

We have a time limit now. I pulled the blazer off the sleeping man, tying the fabric around my ribs. *Our mission needs to end before this guy wakes up or gets discovered.*

I stumbled down the hall, my once soundless steps now heavy and uneven. I was hurt, I knew that much, but I refused to turn back then. Not with all the answers just a few doors away.

My eyes lingered over the walls, elegant swirls and golden details covering the ceiling above my head. We had entered on the third floor, and if the structure of this estate was anything like my own, then that's where all the bedrooms were.

My best bet for finding evidence of any malpractice would be in his study—I swallowed, careful not to touch anything with my bloodied hands—*which should be a floor or two below.*

216

I crept across the hall's expanse, my steps speeding up at the sight of the regal staircase. I stopped, hesitantly pulling the crimson gloves from my hands, before descending down the steps, my body crouched and low.

How many holidays had we spent together, Uncle Michaelis' booming laughter mixing with Papa's gentle chuckles? The four of us singing carols as we waited for Lou and her Nana to arrive with the roast? He'd been there for it all—from our mother's funeral and our school graduation to our first training days at the Imperial Force. He had been a jovial presence in our dark and murky lives, even lighting up Papa's face during his hardest weeks. I refused to believe that such a man would have committed such a hate-driven crime.

You say that—I tucked the soiled gloves into my belt—*and here you are nonetheless.*

I had paused, feet finally reaching the second floor of the estate. The hall before me was much wider than that of my own home, giant golden picture frames decorating the wooden walls, various medals and awards also hanging at their sides. My eyes lingered across the pictures, heart aching at one of the carefully-framed images that rested against the wall. My feet staggered forward, desperate fingers touching the glass, my vision blurring. Hanging there was a picture from our eighth birthday, Victor and I clinging to one another, grinning wildly on Uncle Michaelis' shoulders. My lips trembled, the gentle figure of my mother in the background, her eyes squinted into a smile, her beautiful hair worn down and free.

That was our last birthday with her, her death coming a short few months later, leaving our family broken and detached. I wiped at my eyes, a heavy exhale wracking through me as I cleared my head. We would solve this first, then I'd be back on track. Then I'd avenge her.

My feet padded soundlessly down the hall, my ears pressing to each door and trying to listen in. I had reached the fourth door on the floor, cracking it open as I had done the others, and slowly peeking in.

Jackpot. I slipped my body through, closing it soundlessly at my back. I had successfully stumbled into Silverstein's study, the room twice as large as Papa's.

The wooden walls were lined with leather-bound books, the shelves extending from the floor to the ceiling, the room reminding me of The Wild Iris more than any office I had ever seen. I licked my lips, slowly advancing across the room, my careful hands opening and closing every cabinet I came across. A breath of relief filled my lungs as I came up empty handed, the endless documents of military reports and tax documents leaving Silverstein as clean as they got.

I straightened up, side stinging as I looked around the room once more, eyes falling on the desk toward the back corner of the study. I had taken a step in its direction but stopped, my blood running cold at the sound of clamoring feet coming from the other side of the door.

They must've found the guard. I panicked, scanning the room wildly for something, anything to hide behind. I cursed myself, opting for the desk as the doorknob jiggled. I dove behind its fine wooden frame, my panicked body knocking over a glass in the process. My heart jumped into my throat, trembling hands catching the mug just before it shattered across the floor. I held my breath, the door creaking open.

Please, just leave. I tried to steady my racing heart, fearing that it would give me away. As if my selfish prayers were personally answered, the door clicked shut, the guard probably doing a vague sweep of the room before deciding that it was secure. I sighed, the pain emitting from my wound leaving me shaky.

There. I swallowed hard, the fabric of my shirt growing stickier by the second. *We came, we saw, and there was nothing here.*

I moved to sit up slowly, placing the empty mug back onto the desk, but my vision was caught by a small dent at my feet. Peeking out from beneath a poorly-placed rug was the thin outline of a hidden latch. My blood ran cold, trembling hands moving to peel back the strip of fabric, revealing a space in the floor about the size of a briefcase.

What is...

My hands stiffened, fingers gripping beneath the wooden slide and pulling it back.

No. My body stumbled back, hands pulling the fabric from my face as I struggled to breathe. *No, this doesn't make sense!*

My trembling fingers reached toward the open storage box, hundreds of bloody badges filling it.

"The battle of St. Mordue, Caveer's Peak, Mt. Astrae," I whispered, gloved hands tracing the dried blood on each of the artifacts. All of these pins, all of these patches—they were trophies. Reminders of his conquests and victories against neighboring kingdoms, likely ripped from the uniforms of dead soldiers. My stomach lurched, fingers digging deeper at the sight of one particularly filthy pin. I turned it over in my hands, the fabric of my gloves wiping away some of the dust.

The bright silver of a wolf glinted in the pale moonlight that seeped through the window, the grime I had wiped away black and charred.

Soot and smoke.

The pin fell limply from my hands, my chest tight with what I had uncovered.

This can't be. Something is wrong. My fingers threaded themselves through my hair, my lungs pumping in oxygen desperately. *Nobody would be so careless. Silverstein wouldn't be this sloppy!*

My eyes scanned for the pin again, shoving its cold metal into the pocket at my hip, desperate hands throwing the rest of the bloodstained trophies back into the floor. *It was Silverstein. He really did it—all the proof was here, after all.* My nails dug into my palms as I tried to steady my breathing.

Then why does this feel so wrong?

A crash down the hall jolted my dazed body, sending me stumbling to my feet. *Rowan.* Fear coursed through me at the thought of him finding his own proof, the vivid image of Silverstein's decapitated head enough to make me gag.

I have to get us out of here. My shaky fingers gripped the doorknob. *I'll show him my findings once we are a safe distance away.*

The door barely made a sound as I slipped through and carefully closed it behind me. All I had to do was sneak back up to the third story and climb out the window. Rowan would surely meet me there. *But getting there will be easier said than done.* I swallowed harshly, a steady tremor running through my hands as my palm pressed against my side, the fabric of the guard's blazer now completely soaked through. I was losing too much blood.

My steps were hurried as they stumbled across the pale carpet, the heavy sound of boots on my right jolting my aching body.

Screw this. I clenched my fists, taking a deep breath before running up the stairs, my ribs screaming in pain at the sudden movement. *I don't need to be stealthy anymore. I just need to get out.*

My panting body reached the third floor, the pounding of feet behind me no longer a warning, but a threat. They knew that someone was here. I whipped my head around, looking left and right before heading back in the direction I had come from.

Come on, I pleaded internally, the hallway suddenly seeming never ending. *Just get me out of here!*

I froze, the looming shadows of two men rounding the corner, blocking off the left wing completely. My eyes were frantic, my slamming heart torn between making a break for it and trying to climb down faster than they could grab me—or looking for another way. The tips of their shoes came into view before my hands gripped the first doorknob I saw, shutting myself into the room.

I breathed in and out desperately, my body sticky with sweat as the clicking of boots got louder.

Breathe, breathe Valeria. I closed my eyes, my bloody hand moving to rest on my chest, my heart racing against it.

This isn't good. I furrowed my brows, trying to steady my trembling limbs. My little stunt by the stairs had surely raised their suspicions. *I won't be surprised if they break down the door any minute.*

The hairs on my neck stood, my closed eyes now as wide as saucers. Because as my heart quieted down and my breathing cleared, I noticed something that would monumentally affect my escape.

I wasn't the only one breathing in this room.

I turned around slowly, my heart falling into the pit of my stomach. Not at the woman sleeping soundly on the bed, but at the massive hound that slept at her feet. There had been a reason why I hadn't run into one until now. It wasn't coincidence or luck—they had been guarding their masters, sleeping closely at their sides.

It was a miracle that the massive dog hadn't woken up yet, the scent of blood and my pounding heartbeat enough to give me away. *Okay, think.* I clenched my fists at my side, body going rigid as its furry ear twitched. If I slipped out the bedroom door, it would surely wake up. It came down to how fast I could scramble down from the window. I swallowed my fear, my hand gripping the doorknob once more. A loud thump from outside jolted my body back, wide eyes turning to the dog, its mighty head lifting as it rubbed at its snout.

Not good, not good, not good. Fear grabbed hold of my throat, my wild eyes flitting to the only viable option at this point. The woman's bedroom window.

The dog was drifting in and out of consciousness, its sharp teeth glinting in the faint light of the room. I squeezed the tension from my hands, shoulders squaring. There was no use being afraid now—it was a matter of taking that leap or staying behind and dealing with the consequences.

My feet flew across the floor, gloved hands unclasping both locks on the window at once, the loud click jolting the dog awake. I refused to look behind me, both hands pulling the window open with all my might, the icy wind blowing the white curtains back wildly. The dog's barks boomed across the room, vibrating through my chest as I slipped through the window, leaping from the frame without a second thought. My hands grabbed desperately at the estate's outer wall, a searing pain ripping through my shoulder as my fingers dug into a narrow ridge. I suppressed my cries as my arm trembled, any sound drowned out by the dog's alarming barks. My shoes scratched wildly at the wall, but there wasn't a crack anywhere within reach, my grip slipping by the second.

It is no use. Panic coursed through my veins at the faint voices that echoed from above. *There's no way out of this one.*

My arm burned with the strain of my weight, eyes shutting as a brutal wind passed over my skin.

I was going to be caught, the evidence destroyed, and the entire case—everything I had worked for—would be shut down permanently. Papa was going to send me out of the city for sure this time—he was going to separate Victor and me.

*And Mum…*My eyes stung as my fingers loosened their grip. *She will never truly be at rest.*

A few lights flickered on within the estate, my eyes squinting at the sudden brightness. There was no way for me to survive this fall, not with the injuries I'd already sustained inside. Even with the pain of my side dulled by the adrenaline in my veins, I had bled through the jacket, the skin of my side torn open raggedly.

If I can just hold on long enough for the guards to spot me, then maybe they could pull me back up. I could explain myself and—

"Are we at an agreement then, Silver?"

Rowan's words echoed through my mind, etching themselves into the front of my brain as I hung there, a heaviness filling my chest. I had made a deal—made a promise, after all—to catch my mother's killer and to bring his own monster to justice.

I had been a liar for most of my life, the act of spinning excuses and stitching false alibis becoming as natural as breathing these last few months. And yet, as I hung from the third floor of Silverstein's estate, with guards at my back and answers in my pockets, I couldn't bring myself to lie to him. I refused to go back on my word to Rowan Marrow.

I swallowed harshly, a labored breath leaving my lips as my fingers reluctantly released their hold on the crack, my body falling from the third floor of the estate. My eyes squeezed shut, the air getting knocked out of me as my side scraped against a loose stone in the building's side, a cry escaping me as I hit the ground harshly. My head rang, vision unclear as I lay on the cold grass, my body throbbing, but somehow still alive.

The porcelain mask I wore lay in fragments around me, the theatrical frown now a mess of broken pieces. My side felt warm, much too hot compared to the rest of my freezing body. I had lost too much blood—I knew that much—but that wasn't important at the moment.

I needed to get out of here, to put as much distance as possible between the estate and myself.

I struggled to my knees, bending over as my stomach lurched. My hand pulled away from my ribs, the skin of my palm now warm and wet. A familiar metallic scent clung to my hands, my teeth gritting at the extent of the wound.

This isn't good. I struggled, managing to straighten up. I stared out, eyes narrowing at the tall metal gates that sat across the big open lawn. There was a good chance that I wouldn't make it, that I would stumble and not get up again, at least not until I was in the hands of Silverstein's guards.

Still—I staggered to my feet, my legs aching at the sudden strain—*I have to at least try.*

My heart pumped wildly in my chest, thumping through my ears as my feet beat against the grass, the dog's violent barks echoing across the field as the estate lit up behind me. *They are well aware of us now.* My lungs burned as I grabbed the freezing metal of the gate. *They'll be upon me in a few minutes.*

I cried out, my side erupting into a sea of pain as I pulled myself up the metal gate, arms burning in exhaustion. I gritted my teeth, warm tears filling my eyes as I reached the top, my battered body screaming in agony as I swung it over to the other side. My eyelids were heavy, the tight grip I had on the gate loosening. I didn't even scream as I fell the short distance, my body falling off the gate and slamming onto the concrete below like a straw doll. My head pounded, fingers twitching as they quivered against the cool stones of the street.

I did it. My body convulsed as a shiver passed through it. *I took a gamble and won.*

But I wouldn't be able to last long in this condition. My eyelids had already begun to droop, heavy with the loss of blood. *I need to get out of here.*

The ground beneath me was cold, and the world around me warped and melted into itself, leaving my ears ringing. Somewhere within the haze, a shadow extended over me, and for whatever reason, for a fragment of a second, I was so sure it was *him*.

"Vi…" My voice was hoarse, ragged. "*Victor?*"

The figure paused.

"Sorry to disappoint, Chief." I furrowed my brows at the words, feeling the shadow shift. "You've certainly looked better."

The voice above me sounded distant, my tired eyes squinting as a pair of ugly rubber boots came into focus.

"Hey? Hello?" Rowan's face came into view as he crouched down in front of me, his tone sarcastic but eyes serious. "Don't fall asleep on me now."

"Rowan?" My voice was barely audible, my throat still thick with panic.

"Don't worry, Your Grace. We'll get you fixed up." He sighed, pulling the gloves off his hands. "Let me see where you're hurt."

He had already retrieved his coat, the thick material completely covering his little heist getup.

"We…" I tried to move, but my body was spent, every muscle I possessed wincing as the world swirled around me. "We have to leave."

"Let me see the wound first."

Two gentle hands gripped my quivering body, slowly leaning my back against the gate. It was cold, my spine stiffening at the sudden contact. Rowan looked up tentatively before touching the ripped fabric of my shirt himself.

"You're bleeding," he murmured, moving my sticky palm out of the way. "Quite a bit actually."

"It's fine, but we have to—" I tried to speak, but didn't make it far, a bloody hand clamping over my mouth as a sudden wave of nausea hit me.

"It's really not." His hands moved to grip my shaky body once again, but I recoiled, groaning as my back slammed against the gate.

"Keep those…" I panted between words, my head heavy. "Keep those filthy hands to yourself."

"I'll have you know that I wash my hands thoroughly after every job." He tried to jest, but all sarcasm had been taken up by the wind, the boy pressing a hand to my sweaty forehead despite my protests.

"I can get home from here, just…" I took in a slow breath, moving away from his touch. "Just give me a second."

"Seriously, Valeria." Rowan was blurry to me now. "You need a hospital."

"I said I was fine."

"You know, it wouldn't kill you to listen to me for once."

"I wouldn't be so sure."

His lips twitched into a grin, his shoulders loosening at my banter. I swallowed harshly, black specks dancing around my vision as Rowan turned his back to me, the boy crouching low at the ground, his hands resting at his back.

"What the hell are you doing?"

"If you don't want a hospital, fine, but we need to get you somewhere soon." His dark hair blew wildly in the wind. "So go on. I'm offering you a free ride."

"Are you sure you didn't hit your head somewhere in there?"

He turned his head to look back at me, a few strands of hair falling in front of his eyes. The amusement had slipped from his face completely, eyes trained on the beads of sweat that had begun to trickle down my neck.

"I'd take the offer if I were you." He moved his eyes from mine, turning his face away once again. "Who knows if my generosity will extend into the next minute? Besides, I can't let you hobble home like this."

I raised an eyebrow at him, his back shifting as he shrugged.

"You're basically a walking bag of evidence."

Despite the weakness in my bones, a weak smile pulled at my lips. I let out a shaky sigh before throwing my arms over his shoulders, allowing him to hoist me up with a quiet grunt.

"I guess that's fair." I winced, lightheaded at the sudden change in position. "Go on then, my trusted steed. Flag down a cab to the Fourth."

"You don't want to go home?" he asked, standing still as I adjusted myself, fingers digging into the fabric of his coat.

"No." He stiffened as my arms wrapped around his neck, a pained groan leaving my lips. "Not like this."

I could get patched up at Flint's and tell Papa that we had a late night over at his apartment. My lips dipped down, a stab of guilt tugging at my heart as I imagined the boy's face when he'd open the door.

"You're definitely heavier than you look."

"You know what? I change my mind. I'd rather crawl."

"Kidding!" he said quickly, his sharp movements jolting my aching body once again. "I hardly feel a thing."

Our silent bodies came to a stop at the bush from earlier, Rowan messily rewrapping my wound with fabric before helping me slip on my coat. My head swam at the throbbing pain at my ribs, every muscle in my body aching from the strain of the night. I had lost a lot of blood, and no matter how tightly Rowan pulled the cloth at my ribs, the bleeding wouldn't slow.

"That should hold for now," Rowan murmured, pulling the tight fabric of my shirt back over the makeshift bandage. He stared me in the face long and hard before bringing a thumb up to his lips and wiping it firmly against my cheeks.

"Rowan, that's vile."

"Stop complaining," he said, wiping his sleeve across my sticky face once he was satisfied. "You can't get into a cab with blood on your face."

I can't be seen getting into a cab with you at all, I wanted to say, but the look in Rowan's eyes told me he understood that already, the boy removing his cap and slipping it over my head.

"The main road is up ahead." His voice had toned down, a strangled cry leaving my lips as I was lifted to my feet. "You're going to need to stand for a bit."

I held my breath, the legs beneath me feeling foreign. Unlike my own. "Rowan, I can't."

"You can't?" He raised an eyebrow, his hair unruly in the icy night air. "That doesn't sound like you at all."

I swallowed my protests, lips twitching back as I struggled to steady my feet. The assassin watched me carefully, my hands trembling as they clung to him. He pursed his lips, sighing at my pathetic form before gently securing an arm around my waist.

"Come on, Chief." His words were picked up by the wind as I dragged my feet a few steps forward. "It's just until we hail a cab."

My vision blurred as the pain intensified, the insanity of my earlier stunt finally hitting me. I must've bled through that entire estate based on the severity of the cut. How I managed to escape through the window and rush the field to the gate must've been a miracle.

My teeth tore through the cracked skin of my lip as we staggered along, the bright street lamps of the First District's main road coming into view. *We have to leave.* I struggled to keep up with Rowan's steps. *It won't be long until Silverstein's men start looking for the perpetrators.*

The blinding headlights of a black cab came into view, Rowan lifting an arm to signal it. I squinted at the sudden light, the car slowing down as it approached us.

"Just a bit longer," he whispered under his breath, my heavy eyes trained on the even cobblestone street as the creaking vehicle came to a halt. "Good evening, sir!" I could hear the smile in Rowan's voice, wincing at the booming sound.

"Evening?" the cabbie asked through the car's half-open window, his voice rough from years of stale cigarettes and burning liquor. "I'd say it's a bit later than that."

"I'd have to agree." Rowan laughed easily, the sound hollow. "Do you reach the Fourth?"

Please say yes. My legs shook violently at my weight, cold beads of sweat trickling down my spine.

"I don't." My jaw clenched at the cabbie's words, Rowan stilling as my body trembled in his grip. "I rarely go further than the Third."

I had figured as much. The people of the First rarely went further than the Third District, the lesser neighborhoods holding nothing of interest for the nobility.

"Do you think you'd be able to make an exception? Just this once?" Rowan asked quickly, the two of us stilling at the gruff voices that sounded around the street's corner.

*If we're seen here, if we get caught, I...*My racing heartbeat momentarily steadied, Rowan's hand finding my back beneath my coat, his palm warm against my thinly cloaked skin.

"Please sir, it's getting a bit late."

A worn exhale left the driver's lips, Rowan parting his own to speak just as my legs gave out, the blood soaking through my makeshift bandage and leaving my shirt sticky beneath my coat.

I held my breath, the arm at my side tightening its grip on me instantly, Rowan's hand tucking my face into the crook of his neck and out of view. He had noticed the shift too, after all—the driver's tired eyes now narrowed and pinned on me.

"Is she alright?"

"Just fine." Rowan's pulse was fast against the skin of my face, the voices at our backs growing closer.

"You sure?" Dread filled me at the sound of the car door opening, the driver's voice clearer.

No, no, no. He can't come over here.

"Very." The smile in Rowan's voice disrupted my thoughts, the boy pulling me closer into his chest. "My wife here just had a little too much to drink."

I stilled, the assassin's hand tightening on my back as three men rounded the corner, dressed in grey military uniforms.

"The Fourth then?" Rowan asked, pressing my face further into his skin. "I'll be sure to express my gratitude with a favorable tip."

His heart hammered against my ear, the instinctive reaction so unexpectedly human. I exhaled into his shirt, every ounce of strength within me focused on stilling my shaking hands.

"Alright." The driver huffed, Rowan squeezing me gently. "It's getting late and I wouldn't want the two of you stumbling home drunk. You have no idea what sorts of monsters lurk at these hours of night.".

Rowan's heart slowed, my fingers clenching the fabric of his coat as it steadied. "You're right. Thank you sir."

"In you go then." The old man turned his back, rounding the car back over to his seat, Rowan lifting me easily into his arms and swinging the car door open.

"Wife?" I muttered quietly, wincing as Rowan lifted me into the cab, pulling himself in alongside my limp body. "I thought I wasn't your type."

"You're not." A pair of deep green eyes briefly found my own before the cap was pulled lower over my face. "But somehow sister felt less appropriate."

My head had fallen against his shoulder, holding the weight of it requiring more strength than I had left. Despite the roughness of the road, my aching body, and the murderer beneath me, I found myself in a peaceful state of mind, my eyes falling shut as I drowsily rested against Rowan.

"Hey." His voice was stern, a hand tilting my heavy head toward his. "Keep those pretty blues open."

"Can't."

"It's not a request."

"I don't take orders from you." My words were barely audible, lips cold to the touch. Rowan fell silent, his hand moving to rest against my neck, fingers pressed gently at my pulse.

"Alias Black." Lou's words pushed their way to the front of my mind. *"They say you can smell him from a district away.*

"The stench of rotting corpses.

"Of blood."

229

But as we drove through the cold streets of the First District, the bright lights of the Second steadily approaching, I didn't sense that at all. Instead, as my head lay against his coat and my tired eyes fluttered shut, it wasn't the smell of death that stung my nose, but of soap and the faintest scent of whiskey.

Chapter 15

"C HIEF?"

A familiar voice called out from somewhere, my aching body shifting uneasily.

"Valeria?" The voice said, a bit more urgently, my brows furrowing as my body jolted up. "Valeria, I swear. If I paid to transport a corpse, I'm going to kill you."

"Shut up," I murmured against Rowan's coat, my nose twitching as the ends of his unruly hair tickled my face. "I'm resting, not dying."

I was no longer in the cab, my spent body now cradled in Rowan's strong grip.

"Glad to hear it," he said flatly. "Because you're bleeding onto my coat and it's starting to smell."

"Like what?" I winced, moving gently in his arms.

"Like death. Now rub the sleep out of your eyes because we're here."

My tired eyes squinted into the dark of night, confusion morphing into panic at the unfamiliar buildings in front of me.

"Where are we?" I said slowly, head whipping around. "I told you to take me to Flint's!"

"And I tried to ask you where that was, countless times I should mention." He huffed, tapping his foot impatiently. "You didn't respond and you're bleeding out pretty quickly, so I told the driver to bring us here instead."

"Here being?" I winced, my chest sore from moving around.

"My flat."

I recoiled, my lower body slipping from Rowan's hold and sending us both to the ground, his frantic hands catching the back of my head before it could hit the cobblestones.

"Have you lost your mind?" he whisper-yelled, eyes moving around frantically. "Are you *trying* to kill yourself tonight?"

"There is no way in hell that I'm going in there!" I winced, my body throbbing. An assassin's home was his most secure space. He knew every crack in the wall, where every knife was placed. He'd be at his best while I would barely be able to stand to my feet. I'd be a lamb in a lion's den.

"Oh, so you trust me enough to handle your unconscious body, but not enough to patch you up?" He laughed, but there was no humor there. We were both tired, sore, and over each other's frustrating company.

"That's because I told you where to go!" I gripped at his hair, the boy wincing as I pulled angrily. "There's this thing called trust and consent!"

"Yeah, well there's this thing called abuse." He groaned, my grip on him finally releasing.

My teeth sunk into my lip, a strangled groan escaping me as my side burned. Rowan stilled above me, a tired sigh leaving his lips. The street was cold against the bare skin of my hands, Rowan's dark hair swirling in the merciless night air as his body hovered above my own. I shrunk back into my coat as the wind picked up, chilling us both past our clothes.

"Look," Rowan tried, holding back his irritation by the teeth. "If it makes you feel any better, I'll ring up the kid once we're inside, but you need medical attention. Besides, even if I was going to kill you, it wouldn't be in my house." He winced as he shifted to sit on the ground, turning his back to me. "Blood is a pain to wash out."

"How reassuring."

"Although it looks like I'll have my work cut out for me regardless of whether you die or not," he muttered to himself, his wet coat a testament to that. My arms hesitantly draped over his shoulders, the assassin standing with a huff, my side stinging at the sudden shift in position. "Bear with me now."

I bit back my protests as we made our way up the first few steps of the towering brick building. We were silent as Rowan's boots slowly clanged against the metal stairs that led up to his apartment, the distant lights of the Third District brightening the murky sky. We came to a halt at the fifth floor, one of Rowan's hands moving from my thighs to his coat pocket, the man grunting as he pulled out a key, twisting it into the door before staggering in. A rush of warmth greeted us, chills running along my arms at the sudden change in temperature. The apartment was quaint yet surprisingly spacious, especially for the Fourth, its simple interior keeping it cozy and practical.

I squinted as we trudged through the entrance, Rowan's heavy boots dragging across the wooden floors. *For a hitman who kills for a price, I expected something a bit more lavish.* My eyes dragged across the plain walls, the furniture of the common space well-built but simple.

I suppose it's for familiarity.

"Sit tight." Rowan gently set me on the couch that filled the center of the main space, its black leather smooth beneath my fingertips. He spared me one more glance before disappearing around the corner, leaving my bleeding body to fidget anxiously until his return.

My eyes wandered over the barren walls of the flat, the floors swept and clean, the gentle scent of soap in the air, and not a single article of dirty laundry to be seen. *How bizarrely clean.*

It was strange to think of the killer as a normal man, one who lived in an average building, and did everyday pedestrian things. My brows furrowed at the big board shoved into the corner of the room, eyes widening as I recognized the little notes as leads in our case. He was treating this like a real investigation, after all.

I stiffened at the flash of black hair that peeked into the room, the boy now changed out of his stealthy getup, his thick hair tied back. My eyes drifted to his hands, one gripping a tin first-aid box, the other a rotary telephone.

The hitman grunted as he plugged its wire into the wall, placing the old thing onto my lap.

"Go on then," he said, crouching at my feet. "Call the little prince."

I pursed my lips, a shaky finger moving to dial Flint's number. The phone was cold against the sweaty skin of my cheek, the breath in my lungs holding at a standstill as it rang once, twice, before a click sounded on the other end.

"Hello?"

Stinging tears unknowingly pricked the corners of my eyes at Flint's groggy voice, the boy's words heavy with sleep. I felt Rowan shift at my feet, my face turning away from his, eyes focusing on the front door. I swallowed harshly before parting my lips.

"Hey, Flint."

"Miss Valeria?" All remnants of sleep abandoned him at the sound of my voice, my heart throbbing in my chest. "My Lady, where are you calling from? Why aren't you home?"

My hands clenched, nails digging into the couch's leather. *How selfish could I be?*

"I…" My lips quivered, cold lines of sweat dripping down my back as I bled. "I'm just out for a stroll. I stumbled across a phone booth and thought of you, so I…" I swallowed hard, trying to steady my breaths. "I figured I'd call."

I had felt his eyes on me, yet Rowan said nothing, the boy sitting silently, careful fingers clicking the tin aid kit open.

"A stroll? At this hour, Miss?" Flint asked, confusion evident in his voice. "Do you need me there? If so, just tell me where you are and I'll—"

"Flint." My voice cracked as his name left my lips, the boy falling silent on the other end.

"Valeria, where are you?"

Nowhere you should be.

"I just…" I collected myself, straining as I brought a hand up to wipe my eyes. "I wanted to say goodnight."

"Are you certain that's all?"

No.

"Yes," I whispered, trying to steady my voice. "That's all."

I wouldn't bring him here, not while I was bleeding out on Alias Black's couch. Not looking like this.

We were silent, only the sound of our breaths echoing through the phone.

"Okay." The word was hesitant, the boy immune to my lies but choosing not to push me any further. "Alright, Miss. Call me if anything changes, okay?"

My throat was thick, the boy waiting a few seconds before parting his lips again.

"Goodnight."

I slammed the phone down, forcing my quivering lips to steady. *I'll tell him. I'll tell him about all of this, but not now. He doesn't need to see me this way.*

"You sure you don't want him here?" Rowan asked, eyeing me carefully. "This is going to hurt like hell, and I'm not exactly the comforting type."

"I do." My voice was quieter than I would have liked, weak. "But he deserves better than that."

Rowan didn't ask about it again, brushing a stray strand of hair out of his eyes before leaning toward me.

"Your wound. Let me see it." I was silent as Rowan sat himself down between my legs, his eyes briefly meeting mine before moving to my right. His quick hands rummaged through the orderly box, pulling out a roll of gauze followed by a needle, some medical scissors, and a small bottle of alcohol.

"Aren't you going a bit overboard?" I cleared my throat, trying to lighten the atmosphere. "It can't be *that* bad."

"You've basically soaked through my coat in blood, not to mention your own." He gave me a tight smile. "The least you can do is let me see why."

I bit the inside of my cheek, reluctantly moving my trembling palm from my side. Rowan was silent, carefully cutting through the makeshift bandage and peeling back the tight fabric so that it stopped just below my chest.

The gash was ugly, stretching from the bottom of my ribs up to the side of my chest. While I hadn't felt the pain inside the estate, that guard had torn into me without remorse, leaving me to bleed through every hall I stumbled through.

"You know, you're a lot more trouble than you're worth." He sighed, my posture stiffening as his thumb grazed the skin below my cut. "This will need to be sewn up."

"Sewn up?" My shoulders tensed, the killer giving me a look.

"Consider yourself lucky that it isn't worse."

A heavy feeling settled in my chest as he momentarily turned to the first-aid box, rolling up his sleeves as his eyes scanned for a needle.

"Care to explain how exactly this happened?" he asked, fingers grabbing the cursed thing and drenching it in alcohol.

"It might as well be your fault."

"How could it possibly—"

"I was on the floor wrestling with a guard, as *you* suggested, and ended up getting scratched by his knife." I winced, his thumb pressing against the wound.

"*Scratched?* This is borderline impaled."

"It feels pretty near that now." My shoulders tensed at the throbbing pain, strands of hair now matted to my sweaty face. "But at the moment it didn't seem this bad."

"You can thank your adrenaline for that."

He placed the disinfected needle at our side, picking through the tin box once again.

"You didn't meet me back at our window. I would have waited if I knew you were going to be so clumsy."

"I know." I sighed, watching him tentatively. "I got anxious and made some big mistakes. Long story short I was cornered and ended up locking myself in a room with Silverstein's mistress and one of his dogs. So I had no choice but to"—he lifted his eyes momentarily, staring up at me as I spoke—"*take a leap of faith.*"

"Out her window?"

"That's correct."

"Isn't that something?" he mocked, but a smile twitched across his lips nonetheless. I swallowed harshly as he grabbed a clean rag, drenching it in the alcohol. "I leave you alone for thirty minutes and you go and get yourself so banged up. Honestly, I'm surprised you managed to claw your way up that gate."

"So am I." I held my breath as he brought the wet fabric to my skin, nails digging into his couch.

"Relax, would you?" He laughed, loose strands of hair falling in front of my face as I strained. The lighthearted expression slowly slipped from his face, hands much more gentle as they brought the wet cloth to my wound again.

"But I gave us away." He paused at my words, my eyes hesitantly meeting his. "Between the guard I knocked out in the hall to all the noise I made in the bedroom, they'll surely open an investigation."

"Don't forget the trail of blood you left behind."

"How could I?" I winced, Rowan's own hands now covered in the sticky stuff. "And knowing my brother, he'll be on our heels in a week or two. He's been really determined to solve the recent break-in cases, so it's only a matter of time before he connects the dots."

We fell silent, his careful hands working diligently as we sat in the stillness of the moment. My tired eyes fell shut for what felt like the first time in ages, the night's events draining me of my last bit of strength.

"Don't worry about it too much."

My eyes opened in surprise, the boy refusing to meet my gaze as he wiped at my skin.

"You did…" I furrowed my brows at the softness of his tone, the sudden shift foreign to me. "You did well, Valeria."

My lips parted, as if to speak despite not knowing what to say, but he lifted his head, beating me to it.

"Did you manage to find anything of interest?" He changed the subject easily, a sudden surge of panic running through me at what I had uncovered.

I swallowed the fear in my throat as the question hung between us. What I thought about Silverstein didn't matter anymore, not with the evidence against him. An exasperated sigh left my lips, a sore hand moving to the pocket of my pants and retrieving the pin. His eyes hardened, but he didn't say a word, hands clenching the wet rag in his grip.

"I couldn't believe it." My voice was just above a whisper, Rowan's eyes avoiding mine as I spoke.

"Why? Because he's from the First? Because he isn't the *criminal type*?"

"No." My hand found his, taking the bloody rag from his clenched hands. "Because it felt too easy."

The muscles in his back stiffened, his eyes meeting mine.

"A man as paranoid as Silverstein wouldn't have been so careless with such a thing." I sighed, swallowing as I dabbed at my own wound, Rowan listening intently. "The only thing that makes it easier to digest is the fact that this wasn't the only piece of damning evidence in his possession."

I was going to elaborate but quickly fell silent, an unexpected sense of dread filling my lungs as Rowan reached for the needle. His eyes met mine, the boy freezing at my anxious gaze before standing silently to his feet and disappearing around the couch.

"Rowan?" I called out, the sound of clicking bottles echoing from my back.

"Just a moment, Your Grace."

I held the moist rag to my side, the boy appearing a moment later, a corked bottle at his lips, teeth pulling it open easily.

"Here." He extended the bottle to me, the clear liquid sloshing inside.

"What is that?"

"Your lifeline."

"I don't drink," I said quickly, a strong scent leaving the bottle and burning my nose.

"And I'm not about to force you to, but believe me—you're going to want a hit or two of this before I get to work."

My eyes fell to the needle in his grip again, shaky hands reluctantly taking the bottle from him. He sighed heavily as he crouched down at my level once again, pulling a thick thread through the needle and tying it off. I crinkled my nose, slowly bringing the bottle to my lips, the clear liquid burning my throat as I swallowed it down.

"Easy there, Silver." He laughed as I held the bottle to my mouth, forcing one last gulp before Rowan took it from my grip. I burst into a fit of coughs, the liquid instantly chasing any remnant of the cold out of my system. "Hand up."

I followed his orders, resting my sore arm onto his shoulder, his eyes briefly meeting mine before dropping to the cut.

"Is that thing even clean?" My words were weighted, slurring into each other as my brain slowly fogged over.

"Cleaner than you deserve," he murmured, rolling his neck back before leaning in closer. "Now just try to relax."

"Relax?" I blinked hard, the alcohol settling into my bones. "How the hell am I supposed to—"

My sentence was cut short as a searing pain erupted from my left side. I cried out, nails instinctively digging into the bare skin of his neck.

"Not drunk enough, huh?" He winced as I bared into him. "This might sting a bit."

"I'd say I agree." I gritted my teeth, squeezing my eyes shut. "Son of a—"

"You know, for a noble you've got quite the sailor's tongue." Rowan drowned out my incessant curses, my face burying itself into the crook of his neck as he pulled the needle through again.

My breath was warm with alcohol, his skin pricking with goose-bumps at my every exhale.

"You're awfully comfortable," he mumbled, his words sending vibrations through me as I clung to him. "Does this not get your heart racing, Blue Blood?"

"Please," I groaned, my eyes falling shut at the pain. "I've been in worse positions with men like you."

"Pardon?"

"Mind out of the gutter, idiot." He winced as I tugged on his hair, his careful fingers pulling the string tight. The pain was intense, more than I could have ever imagined. I'd gotten stitches before, Victor and I getting into our fair share of mischief over the years, but I had always been numbed, handled carefully under my father's anxious watch. Never like this.

"Could I ask you something?" He broke the subtle quiet between us, my ragged breaths being the only other sound in the lonely flat.

"I don't see why not." My words were taut, fingers digging into his shoulders. Beads of sweat rolled down my face, soaking easily into the fabric of his shirt as I waited for him to continue, grateful for any distraction from the stabbing pain at my side.

"Why do you do this to yourself?"

My eyes fluttered open, eyelashes tickling the skin of his neck.

"This world of shadows—you repeatedly claim to not belong to it yet you plunge headfirst into the darkness for the slim chance of finding a clue, of finding a lead." His words were slow as he clarified. "Why do you care so much about justice?"

Of all the things that could have escaped the killing bastard, I hadn't expected something so candid. So sincere.

"I could ask you the same thing."

"No, you couldn't." He looked up briefly, giving me a firm look, but his hands were gentle, careful as he pulled the needle through my skin. "It's different. It's more than just hatred with you, yet I still can't seem to understand it." A weak laugh left his lips as he pulled his sticky hands away from me for a moment, wiping my blood on a rag. "It's as if you were born without a sense of self-preservation."

"Are you calling me heroic?"

"I'm calling you an idiot."

I couldn't stop a small smile from pulling at my lips, the expression wilting instantly as Rowan reached for the needle again, his fingers grazing my ribs.

"My mother, she…" I paused, swallowing the pain as the thick medical thread ripped through my bleeding skin. "She was everything to me."

"Just because you watched her die doesn't make you responsible for avenging her." Rowan's words were hushed, mumbled, almost as if he were speaking with himself. "The choices that spring themselves along the path of revenge are violent and unrelenting."

"I don't doubt that." I winced, the hitman stopping briefly and giving me a second to collect myself. "Some choices are hard, but they still have to be made. If someone has to carry the weight of her death, I'd rather it be me. I can bear it." I swallowed harshly, my brother's soft eyes flashing through my groggy mind. "Why force it onto someone who can't?"

His hands froze, the boy pulling away and forcing my head from his shoulder. I blinked wearily at him, frizzed strands of hair sticking to my sweaty neck as he held my gaze.

There was a silence as we stared at each other, the rigidity between us rippling through the air like the screech of a violin's bow across its strings. Sharp and aching.

There was something cavernous in the way his eyes seared past my own, and for the life of me, I couldn't figure out how to decipher it. In truth, I wasn't sure I wanted to.

I flinched at the blistering pain at my ribs, my half-stitched skin red and angry. His face jerked back, the boy snapping out of whatever thoughts sat gnawing at his brain and crouching down near my wound again without a word. I didn't question him any further, not due to disinterest in his sudden shift in behavior, but because I feared that if I parted my lips to speak again, I would likely scream from the pain.

"Damn it, Rowan." I struggled to keep the tension from my ribs, not wanting the pain to further. "Would it kill you to be more gentle?"

"Trust me, I'm trying."

"Well try harder."

"For a girl who chased me across the rooftops of the Third in a dress, you're pretty soft." An unexpectedly warm rumble of laughter shook his chest, rippling through my sticky body.

That night—my fingers slowly clenched, twisting themselves into the fabric of his shirt—*it felt like a lifetime ago.*

I didn't like thinking about how I'd changed over the last few weeks. How easy breaking rules had become to rationalize. More than that, I didn't want to think of how familiar Rowan Marrow had become to me. How easily my head rested against him as he wiped at my skin.

"Just hurry up, would you?" I said softly, a whisper of sorrow lingering at the edges of every word.

"Sure thing, Chief."

"All done." He finally sighed, wiping his bloodied hands on a towel. "That wasn't so bad now, was it?"

I would have cursed at him if I had the energy, but my body ached in ways that exhausted me to my core. The excruciating process had lasted no more than thirty minutes, but it might as well have been the whole night.

"I'll be a gentleman and clean it again in the morning, but after that it's up to you." He stood to his feet as he stretched, his own limbs probably sore.

"What…" I tried leaning forward, but stopped, wincing at the sharp ache in my ribs. "What do you mean in the morning? Aren't you taking me to Flint's?"

"I want to monitor your wound tonight before I set you loose again." He rolled his shoulders back as he spoke, the muscles stiff from hunching over my bleeding body. "I don't think you have any internal bleeding, but I'd rather be safe than sorry. I mean, just imagine what would happen to my nursing career if you died in my care."

"But my father—"

"Your father will ask where you've been, why you reek of blood, and who the handsome bastard who lugged you home is." He leaned in once more, eyeing the tightly wrapped gauze at my ribs. "I think he'd be much more understanding if you show up tomorrow well-rested and alive than if you showed up tonight half-dead after trying to expose an arsonist."

My retorts fell silent, the hollow realization of what would happen to Silverstein heavy on my heart. We would expose him tomorrow, sending the pin in with an anonymous letter as well as a testimony we wrote for Marvin Reese. No questions would be asked after that. Silverstein would be in cuffs and the media would be booming.

Rowan sighed, turning his back to me, his tired hands moving to collect the medical supplies that littered the space around us. The silence of the apartment was thick, coating my sweaty skin like an itchy winter coat. The alcohol had reached its full effect, numbing some of the pain as well as most of my clarity as I stared at the boy's back.

"Rowan." My voice filled the emptiness, words still weighted with the alcohol. "Do you know how many people you've killed?"

He paused, his hands stilling as my words sat between us. I pressed my lips together, regret mellowing out the liquid courage in my veins.

"No." I turned my eyes up at the sound of his voice, the boy slowly standing to his feet. "I lost count a few years ago."

"So they mean nothing to you?"

"Those people and their lives are irrelevant to my own." His words sent a sharp pain through my chest, his gaze unapologetic as it met my

243

own. "If I were to dwell on every life I ended, there would be nothing left of me. Hate me for that if you must—I wouldn't blame you—but I cannot help what I am."

As sad as it was, he was right. I did hate him for what he had done, for what he continued to do, but hating Rowan Marrow for the blood on his hands was like hating a knife for being sharp. No matter how hard he tried, he could not help his nature.

"Five hundred and thirty-two," I said, the killer turning his eyes to me. "Does that number mean anything to you?"

"Not particularly, no."

"That's the number of people who died in the fire." The ache I had felt then was different, echoing from the depths of my heart instead of the stitches at my ribs, for his eyes had filled with an image of childish grief that I knew all too well, even if it was only for a moment. "Doesn't feel like just a statistic now, does it?"

His grip on the bloody cloth tightened, his knuckles going white. "No," he exhaled tiredly, loosening his hold on the rag. "I suppose it doesn't."

There had been a few quick moments since we'd met where the monster Alias Black faltered, revealing a twisted boy behind his grisly mask. But Rowan Marrow had bloodied hands of his own. They clenched and tore, ripped and wrapped. They slit the throats of women and children just as easily as they cleaned my wounds. Seeing him as anything but a killer was as dangerous as willingly pressing one of his blades against my throat. And yet as the weeks flew by, it was something I couldn't help.

"Valeria."

I blinked drowsily at the use of my name, his back shifting beneath his shirt as he wiped the rest of my blood off his hands.

"It's getting late. You should go ahead and tuck in for the night."

I was silent, staring at him carefully as he lifted his head to me.

"Do you need me to carry you?" He raised an eyebrow, slouching back against the wall.

"I can manage." I winced, shifting forward to my feet. "But where should I go?"

"Back room." He didn't look up at me again, my pathetic figure hobbling over to the door behind him, where he had disappeared to earlier. My weak hands gripped the doorknob, eyes widening with confusion as the door creaked open.

"Isn't this your bedroom?"

"Why? Is there something wrong with it?" He straightened up, cocking his head at me.

"Not at all." My grip on the doorframe tightened, legs still shaky. "But where are you—"

"You sure have a lot of energy for someone who just narrowly avoided death." He sighed, crossing his arms over his chest.

I fell silent, giving him a small nod before entering the room and locking it at my back. The bedroom was quaint and warm, four deep brown walls encasing the space.

I was lucky that Rowan had found me when he had, that he didn't decide to disappear into the night without me. If it weren't for him I would have surely been caught either by the guards, the dogs, or Silverstein himself. I was sure he wouldn't have harmed me in any way, but the evidence would have been destroyed, and Papa would have sent me away without a doubt.

I'd have to thank Rowan again in the morning.

I limped over to the bed, my clothes still sticky as I struggled to lie down, much too tired to worry about changing them. I turned over to my right side, wanting to avoid any contact between the freshly-stitched wound and the mattress.

I would head over to Flint's in the morning and explain everything to him. The deal, the drugs, the break-ins. Other than exposing Rowan's identity, I would lay it all out onto the table.

I wouldn't involve him—I would never allow it—but Flint Jones was the one person in the entire world who could see right through me. I could not lie to him any longer.

As heavy as my heart felt with the night's discoveries, my eyelids were heavier, my aching body drifting off to sleep under the blankets' warm embrace. The subtle scent of soap and linen sent me off into a gentle slumber, the nightmares that visited me almost every night failing to appear. And while my body ached and my head hurt, in that moment in time, the fleeting sense of bliss was enough for me.

The quiet sound of rustling shook the sleep from my throbbing limbs the next morning, my eyes opening to find a room that wasn't my own. I sat up sharply, crying out in pain as my stitches stretched.

"Hell," I muttered, wincing at my own impulsiveness. I was at Rowan's apartment in the Fourth. I rubbed at my forehead, my head throbbing worse than the night before.

While my knife wound felt less sensitive, my aching muscles were sorer than they'd ever been, deep bruises appearing all over my body from my valiant fall. My feet reluctantly swung over the side of the bed, touching the cold wooden floor. It was easier to observe the bedroom now that the faint morning sun peered through the window. His room consisted of a big bed, a dresser, and a cramped work desk.

Plain and to the point, I thought, shakily standing to my feet.

My eyes widened at the pair of metal scissors at the wooden desk, my aching body limping in its direction and taking the tool into my shaky grip. I had fallen asleep in my stealthy getup, the tightly-fitted fabric heavy with the scent of sweat and dried blood. I sucked in a sharp breath, careful to avoid my bandages as I stuck the edge of the scissors beneath whatever was left of my shirt, snipping through the fabric easily. I peeled the tight material from my body, dropping it onto the floor in strips. The specially-designed suit was ruined either way, torn and bloody from the night's adventure. My body, however, was surprisingly clean, most of the grime and blood that had surrounded my stomach skillfully wiped away by Rowan's diligent hands.

I struggled over to the pale dresser, the piece of furniture fairly new and well-kept. It felt strange to dig through his stuff, Rowan and I still more strangers than anything else. My fingers traced over the neatly-folded clothing, tentatively pulling out a thick green worker's shirt.

I wouldn't want to stain anything white. I pursed my lips, eyeing the endless rows of white buttoned shirts. Besides, as warm as the flat was, the wind still slammed against every window, sending a chill up my spine.

I carefully stretched my arms out, sucking in a sharp breath as I wriggled my arms through the shirt, keeping my balance with some difficulty. *There.* I wiped at my forehead, a light sweat on my skin. At the very least, I was functional enough to dress myself.

I limped toward the door, my legs still burned out from the night's strain. The sound of metal clanging jolted my bones, my hand moving to grip the doorknob firmly, pulling it open in one swift motion.

I staggered into the main room, eyes met with the image of Rowan, the boy's eyelids heavy as he sat upright on the couch, hands carefully dabbing at his arms with alcohol. I swallowed hard, noticing the cuts along his arms and chest, some old and puckered, others fresh and bloody.

"You know, it's rude to stare." Rowan didn't have to look up to know I had been standing there for a good few seconds, my eyes dropping to the ground. "Glad to see you're still alive."

"You're hurt too," I mumbled, suddenly embarrassed by my vulnerability the night before. "You should have said something last night."

"While seeing you all flustered is refreshing, don't worry about me." I narrowed my eyes at the grinning boy, his fingers skillfully twisting the gauze over his bicep. "I'm used to patching myself up without a hitch."

He saved your life. My fists clenched at my sides, the boy focusing as he worked. *You owe it to him to show some compassion.*

I swallowed my pride, forcing my aching body to his side, taking a seat at his right and pulling his arm into my lap. His shoulders stiffened, my hands hesitantly moving to trace the fresh cuts on his skin.

"Chief, I said I…" His words stopped midway, my eyes turning up to meet his, my gaze as gentle as I could manage.

"Just let me do this for you," I said quietly, reaching for the wet rag and slowly dabbing the bloody cuts. "Your arms must be sore from stitching me up anyway."

The two of us sat in silence, his eyes staring steadily past my skin as I patched him up, hands gentle as I wrapped his wounds.

"Thank you." My voice suddenly filled the comfortable serenity of the room. "For last night. For saving my life. I shouldn't have given you such a hard time, and I'm sorry for that. Truly."

"Does that mean I've finally won your favor?" His dark hair tousled itself as he teased, the smile wilting slowly as he realized that I wasn't jesting.

"It means that I…" I swallowed harshly, looking back at him gently. "I am very grateful to you, Rowan. We may not agree on a great deal of things, but whether you choose to acknowledge it or not, there is good in you." His eyes left mine, jaw clenching at my words. I pursed my lips, squeezing his hand in mine softly. "You just need to be more accepting of it."

"You should head back to the station soon." He pulled his hand from my grip, my eyes narrowing at his obvious defense.

"You really ignored everything I just said, didn't you?" I sighed, sitting back with a heavy huff. "Men are so difficult."

"I didn't ignore you." He gave me a smile, one not as forced as I had expected. "I just wish you wouldn't say such nonsense. You're setting yourself up to be disappointed. Good people are stories of fiction."

"I don't believe that."

He raised an eyebrow at me, my hands no longer shaky but resting steadily in my lap.

"As conflicted as you are," I said slowly. "I just know you'll find the right path. We might even end up as friends someday."

"Friends, huh?" A breathy laugh escaped him, his deep eyes glinting as he grinned. "The renowned hitman and the aspiring Silver? You should write a book."

"Shut up before I *accidentally* reopen your wounds." I groaned as I stood to my feet. Rowan followed suit, his gaze a bit different than before. Not necessarily warmer, but less restrained, more comfortable.

"Understood, Your Grace." There was a strange glint in his eyes, something gentle, something soft, however faint it was. "But again, you should really head down to the station."

"You know, if you want to kick me out, just give it to me straight."

"No, that isn't it." He grinned, his hair falling in front of his eyes. "I delivered the evidence last night, as well as the letter from Reese. Silverstein should be taken in any minute now."

"You…" My words caught themselves in my throat, Rowan already disappearing into his room. *He walked all the way back to the station while I was asleep?* My brows furrowed, following the boy into his room. *He probably hasn't slept at all!*

"Why didn't you wait for me?" I blurted, the boy buttoning up his white shirt, the smooth bandages hidden beneath its sleeves.

"Because as heartfelt as our moment just now was, I needed to make sure this was done properly."

"You think my feelings would get in the way of justice?" Anger bubbled through me, amplifying the pain in my side.

"No, I think that you were hurt and disoriented last night, making you unfit to make such decisions." He slid by me and moved toward the front door. "Now wipe that bitter look off your face. The little prince'll be here in a few minutes."

"Flint?" My brows knit together at the mention of the boy, my side stinging as my posture jolted upright. "Why? How did you even…" I stopped, the hazy memory of Rowan's prying eyes the night before answering my question for me. "You memorized his number last night, didn't you? As I dialed it."

"I had a feeling it would be useful eventually. Plus if you died I'd need help transporting the body." He shrugged, the wool fabric of his coat heavy as he pulled it over his shoulders. "I'm heading out. He'll be here with spare clothes soon." Rowan turned to face me once more, sharp eyes drifting down my body for the first time that morning. "Unless you intend to take on the nobility without your trousers."

He huffed, narrowly dodging the wet rag I aimed at his face.

"A simple *no* would have sufficed." His voice was muffled, the assassin pulling on his thick leather boots with some effort. "Oh, and when he gets here, refer to me as *Dr. Marrow*."

"You must be joking."

"A pretty honorable cover, if I do say so myself." His hair fell in front of his eyes as he straightened up, a catlike grin on his lips. "Yes, Her Grace was so *incredibly* lucky to have stumbled onto a doctor's doorstep after being scathed by a car last night."

"You're despicable."

"I prefer *criminally creative*." His voice echoed from the other side of the flat.

I repressed the urge to snap back at him, my hand finding the pendant beneath the fabric of his shirt and squeezing it. *This is it.* The tension in my shoulders faded at the flower's familiar ridges and dips.

The beginning of the end.

I had never thought the day would come when one of my own would be dragged away in handcuffs. The station was swarmed with press, the familiar eyes of Rin Ryugazaki somewhere toward the back of the bustling crowd. Rowan's package was found by forensics this morning, the pin run through the system as evidence, Marvin's testimony verified, and Silverstein's estate swarmed all in a few short hours. He had been dragged out of bed by a team of five Silvers, his little trophy collection found soon after and used by the prosecutors in his case. The jury eventually pronounced him as guilty and sentenced him to death.

Now there was nothing left to do but cling to my brother's side as cameras flashed, a sea of chattering voices rolling over us with waves of questions. It was almost like the week of our mother's death all those years ago, Lou's nana keeping us inside and away from the media's prying eyes and burning questions.

My eyes dropped to my feet as the tired figure of Michaelis Silverstein was pulled down the stairs of the station, his hands bound by handcuffs and eyes wild with panic.

"This isn't right. I swear, I didn't do anything wrong!" he yelled, the swarm of reporters turning away from us and closing in on the guarded man. "Listen to me!"

His wild gaze found my father, Papa's pale eyes clouded over with a sorrow and anger that I hadn't seen for many years.

"Kenneth! Kenneth, just listen. I swear to you, I..." His eyes found my own, my stomach twisting at the tears in his. "Valeria, you don't seriously believe—"

"Don't you *dare* speak to her," Papa boomed, moving to stand in front of us. His gaze fell to the reporters, the crowd stiffening beneath my father's intense glare. "The rest of you are not welcome here. This station is not somewhere for you to flock and collect gossip." My father's voice was firm, the crowd reluctantly dispersing. "Leave."

"What did you say last night?" Rowan had asked under his breath earlier that morning, Flint's anxious eyes watching us carefully from the doorway of Rowan's apartment. *"About how finding that pin was easy?"*

"It was poorly hidden." I winced, digging my nails into the couch as Rowan unwrapped my bandages, gentle hands moving to clean my wound once more. *"The pin was just sitting there blatantly at the top of the pile, almost as if it wanted to be found."*

Rowan was silent, Flint's eyes boring into the back of his head as he dabbed at my stitches.

"I sound insane, don't I?"

"Usually yes, but not at this very moment," Rowan said, my hand swatting at his hair, a cry escaping me as he pressed harder against my side. *"You better pray that I never catch you gravely injured, because I'd be sure to be just as gentle."*

My nails dug into his shoulder as he pressed harder, gritting my teeth.

"Hey kid, do you mind grabbing me another rag?" Rowan called over his shoulder, Flint stiffening. *"You should find some in the backroom, counter on the left."*

Flint's eyes had met mine, the boy tense with the state of me. He had practically run through the streets of the Fourth after receiving Rowan's call, arriving in the unknown apartment to find me clad in a stranger's shirt, hobbling around like a drunk with my side sewn shut. He had been glued to me since then, eyeing Rowan venomously every time I winced or complained. I gave him a soft smile, the boy nodding with gentle eyes before reluctantly disappearing into the back.

My tired eyes had shut, a question on my tongue now that Rowan and I were alone.

"What about you?" I had asked, sucking in a breath as he tore off a long strip of gauze, wrapping my ribs slowly. *"Are you content?"*

He had paused.

"You found your arsonist, and while you didn't get to exact your own revenge against him, he'll be facing justice today."

"Your notion of justice does little for me." His eyes were trained on the task at hand, fingers moving swiftly. *"It doesn't fix the past, nor does it relieve my burning anger. But I can't really do anything else about it now."*

I pressed my lips together, moving my eyes to the window as he finished up.

"It just all feels a bit strange, forced."

"What do you mean?" I asked, my hair bouncing as I turned to him again.

"This all happened too quickly. Almost like we were led into a trap and given the opportunity to walk out mostly unscathed." His dark gaze turned up to mine, cold shades of green melding into one another. *"And there is little I hate more in this world than being played with."*

Rowan's words repeated themselves in my head as I sat at my desk, the cold winter air flooding through the station at every creak of the door. It had been almost a week since the fire's origins had been exposed, the lower districts falling into a frenzy over the truth. There were rallies in the streets, hate crimes spread out across the first three districts, and constant anti-royalist propaganda in the papers. Silverstein's betrayal to the monarchy was catastrophic, Nieve's Colonal exposed to be a ruthless killer in battle as well as an arsonist. Despite all the happenings, the station was emptier than usual, most available Silvers dispatched to districts Seven through Four in an attempt to quiet the crowds. Flint had moved into our estate, my father agreeing that the streets were no longer safe enough for a sixteen-year-old boy to navigate himself.

*And Rowan…*I sighed, rubbing my forehead tiredly at the thought of the boy.

We hadn't spoken since the day of Silverstein's arrest, the assassin making no efforts to contact me whatsoever. The thought of trying to get in touch with him had crossed my mind, but I had quickly shut it down. He and I were very different people. Regardless of what happened after the infiltration at Silverstein's estate, that was still the truth. He could not erase his sins just as well as I could not abandon my guilt. These burdens were tied to us and would be for the rest of our lives.

I thought that catching the man responsible for the fire—the man who had burned his childhood to the ground—would have eased his mind, if not just a bit. Instead it only seemed to push him over the edge, the arrogant assassin disappearing completely.

I sighed deeply, the stitches on my side no longer a nuisance but just another common ache in my daily life. I'd resume my own investigation soon enough, my leads a jumbled mess of nonsense once again.

B.D. wasn't the killer—I was sure of it now. He must've known of the origins of the fire, Silverstein taking matters into his own hands to keep him quiet. I was back to the start, dealing with the image of a monstrous masked man and a heinous murder.

My thoughts were interrupted by the heavy sound of feet, my eyes widening as they met my brother's teary gaze.

"Victor, what—" I winced, my brother slamming into me, burying my face into his chest, his heart thumping erratically against my ear.

"What happened? Vic, what is it?" My voice grew panicked, the worst possible case filling my mind. "Is Papa alright?" Fear coursed through me, my face pulling away from him. "Is Lou—"

"They caught him."

My heart throbbed in my chest, brows coming together as the words left his lips. My palms trembled, the air in my lungs too heavy to carry. Victor's tear-streaked cheeks trembled into a smile so full of sorrow and relief that my own vision blurred.

"They caught the killer, V."

Chapter 16

I N ALL THE YEARS SPENT solving my mother's case, there was always a bead of doubt that existed in the back of my mind. Even as the weeks spilled into months, and the hatred within me brewed deeper beneath my skin, there always lived the thought:

What if I never find him?

And that question, that uncertainty, is what gave me the ability to stand fearless and stare death in the eyes. But hearing that the killer was caught, that he was in custody at this very moment, shattered that persona completely.

My knees gave out beneath me, Victor catching my collapsed body in his arms.

"He's…" My words were strangled, breathless as my brother gripped my trembling body. "He's caught? Is he caught?"

My grip tightened on the fabric of his shirt as he nodded, heavy tears streaming down his face.

They found him? But how? When did this happen? Where is Papa? So many questions swirled through my mind, my head throbbing as my vision blurred.

"Is this real?" I whispered, fingers digging into Victor's shoulders as warm tears streamed down my face. "Am I awake? Am I…"

I struggled, heavy eyes searching the room for a tell, for a sign that what I was seeing was real. My shaky body relaxed in my brother's arms as my eyes found the clock, broken sobs escaping me as it ticked by evenly. *This is real. They really did it.*

"Papa is down at the prison now. We didn't want to risk bringing him into the station. He's being held in a cell until trial, but everything lines up."

"How did…" Years of heartbreak and stress untangled themselves in my brother's arms, the sheer exhaustion of the case finally falling from my shoulders. "How did you even know where to look?"

"We didn't have to." He wiped at his cheek with his shoulder, the smile on his lips still trembling. "The fire was the key, V."

The fire was the—

"Val! Victor!" A muffled voice echoed from the stairs below followed by the hurried sound of feet. Lou's teary gaze appeared, the girl's uniform a jumbled mess and curly hair unruly.

"Give them space, Tate!" Oliver was hot on her heels, the boy coming to a stop as he spotted us on the floor.

"This…" My voice was hoarse, ragged hiccups escaping me as I faced them. "This is real."

They didn't miss a beat, the pair running across the tiles of the second floor and slamming into our crying forms. I had let myself sob then, wailing on the floor of the station and finally letting myself be comforted by the loving arms that held me close.

Mother, I thought, a heavy stream of tears rolling down my cheeks. *We've done it.*

The rough wind stung my eyes, the skin of my face still red and sensitive from the morning's news. I licked my lips, the cold air chilling my cheeks.

The masked man has been caught. My hands trembled in my pockets. *The dead eyes that haunted my dreams almost every night are now behind bars, which means…*

My thoughts were cut short by the familiar presence at my side, my face whipping around to meet Rowan's, the collar of his coat flipped up in an attempt to keep the bitter cold at bay.

"Ah, the stench of privilege," he drawled, my shoulders loosening at the small smile on his lips. His eyes flitted up to the station's towering presence. "Must be a special occasion. You'd never let me get this close."

A sad sense of solace pulled at my lips, his green eyes dark but not as threatening as they had been when we'd first met. He had of course heard the news by now, Rin publishing an article about my mother's murderer as soon as he'd received my phone call. The Black Press had become the most popular paper in a single day, being the first to receive the details of the crime of the decade.

My eyes found Rowan's again, the hitman staring up at the statue behind me, King Alpheus' strong gaze overlooking the streets of the First.

"They sure do keep that thing clean."

"That *thing* is our monarch."

"It's a statue." He shrugged, his sharp stare falling from the metal symbol to me. "So who was it? The killer?"

"He's a criminal affiliated with one of the two gangs that burned away in the fire." I swallowed harshly, my voice still unsteady as I spoke. "He had no records in Nieve, an unscripted immigrant which made him hard to trace. He had been conducting business overseas, smuggling illegal goods back over the border. Once he returned and found his colleagues gone, not even their bodies left to bury, he made it his mission to find the man responsible.

"By then Silverstein was back overseas, the criminal becoming livid once he connected the corporal to the crime at hand." I clenched my fists, nails digging into my palms. "So he turned his fury to the monarchy as a whole, settling on murdering the Viscount.

257

"But on the night that he chose to infiltrate, the Viscount wasn't there, and he had been spotted by his wife." A soft breath escaped my lips, the pain of losing my mother no longer a dull ache but a fresh cut. "My mother. He killed her and disappeared, fleeing back overseas until two years ago, once he was sure he wouldn't be found.

"Apparently he claimed that he had abandoned the life of gangs and organized crime after fleeing Nieve." I crossed my arms over my chest, my body trembling despite the layers of clothes I wore. "I suppose the guilt became too heavy for him to carry, because he turned himself in."

"He what?" Rowan's voice was questioning, eyes narrowing as I explained.

"After reading about Silverstein in the papers he turned himself in, wolf mask in hand. Something about how his tormentor was finally brought to justice, so it wasn't right for him to keep his hold over my family. In the end it was a simple story of revenge. One that ruined my life just as it ruined the lives of many others." A sad smile made its way to my lips, sorrow a feeling far heavier than anger.

"I see."

I nodded at Rowan's words, eyes staring down at my black boots. As painful as reliving all of this was, the relief that sat just a finger's reach away would be worth it. I deserved to let this go.

"So tell me, Valeria. Do you honestly believe that?"

My posture went rigid, gaze shooting up from my feet to the boy before me, his lips pressed firmly and eyes murky.

"What..." I swallowed the fear in my throat, anger pricking my eyes. "What the hell are you on about?"

"None of this feels off to you?" His eyes had narrowed, prying past my skin and into my soul. "I mean sure, your little story makes sense, but why would he step forth after all this time?"

"I told you—"

"Men like that don't just suddenly have a change of heart. I know because I'm one of them."

My lips trembled, anger cutting through the deeply rooted exhaustion, my blood burning through my veins. *He doesn't know what he's talking about.* My breaths became shallow. *He doesn't know anything!*

"Even if he had planned on coming clean after holding off for so long, it would've taken longer than a week."

"You don't know that." My voice was weak, much too fragile to sound convincing.

"I just know that something here isn't right. The same thing goes for Silverstein's case. I've been investigating things myself, and something doesn't line up." His words weren't threatening or mocking, but desperation bit at every syllable, as if he were begging me to wake up from a pleasant dream and face reality with him. "There is an unseen factor here, and we just keep walking over it."

"Why won't you just let this go?" I whispered, my strength abandoning me.

"That's rich coming from you!"

Rowan gritted his teeth, arms tensing beneath the fabric of his coat. He must have noticed the shift in my posture, my hands stiffening in the pockets of my coat, because his eyes fluttered shut, a deep exhale leaving his lips.

"Look." He brought a hand up to rub at his forehead, his eyes pleading. "You said it yourself that we could end up as friends one day. Then, as someone that you've confided in, *trust me on this.* Please just"—he paused, his fingers hesitantly taking my sleeve in his grip, his stare as soft as he could manage—"don't be a pawn."

His jaw twitched as he swallowed, the boy seeming to choke on his own words.

"You've never been this accepting of the truth handed to you. You've always looked for another lead, another side to the coin. Why are you just taking the simple way out when you *know* that something is missing?"

"Why can't you just be happy?" My eyes had pricked with tears, fists clenching at the weakness in my voice. "Your arsonist was caught, my mother's killer is standing trial—why are you looking for something to ruin it all? I'm tired, Rowan."

His gaze trembled, falling from mine as my voice cracked.

"I'm tired of getting my heart torn apart."

We were silent, the boy dropping my sleeve from his grip, his hands returning to the cold pockets of his coat. The rare moment of clarity in his eyes was gone, sealed over with a fresh layer of steel as he turned his back to me.

"Do what you want." His words weren't angry as I had expected them to be, just bitter. "You're not my problem anymore."

My lips trembled, brows furrowing in anger at his cold words. As much as I wanted to deny it, it hurt to hear those words from him. He and I were two very different people, leading two very different lives, but for a short few months he had been my colleague. He had been my friend.

"Just do yourself a favor."

His words were picked up by the wind, but I still heard them, my lips quivering as he disappeared into the winter fog.

"Look that man in the eyes and tell yourself he killed your mother."

Chapter 17

ROWAN'S WORDS HAD PLAGUED MY mind, infesting every spare moment of my life. It had been two days since our conversation outside the station and even though I had already shut him down, he was all I could think about.

I groaned, shifting in my bed after another sleepless night. Papa had yet to come home, spending the last few days in the station, the trauma of that night as clear as yesterday now that the killer had been caught. It was hard for him to sleep within these walls, to pass through the room where his wife had been murdered. It would take all of us a little while to return to normal.

I pulled myself out of bed, threading my fingers through my tangled hair. The bags under my eyes were worse than ever, my dreams no longer overrun by nightmares but with a deep-seated sense of dread that stemmed from the assassin's words. *The killer has been caught, his arsonist had been put behind bars, so why was he so adamant about ruining my sense of peace?* I sighed, rubbing tiredly at my face. Maybe he needed the chase, the thrill of the case. Now that it had finally been solved after all these years, he couldn't move past it. I knew for a fact that I had a similar feeling. I was happy that the people responsible were brought to justice, but this case had been my life for so long. It had reached a point where hunting my mother's killer had become a part of my identity. A bitter smile found my lips, my face turning to stare at the thin girl in the mirror, her cheeks hollow and eyes heavy with a sorrow far beyond her years. I just felt—dead. If I'd looked in the mirror that morning and found a ghostly corpse in my place I would've hardly been surprised. I looked enough like one already.

I guess I can finally understand Papa's worries.

I pulled my night shirt over my head, the chilly winter air slipping through the cracks of the estate, tracing circles across my exposed skin. My stitches had finally been removed, Flint and I spending an entire night trying to gently pull out the medical threads. Now all that remained was a thin scar, stretching across the right side of my ribs. Rowan had been careful while patching it up, leaving me with a discreet mark rather than a jagged reminder.

My hands worked swiftly, buttoning up my white work shirt easily, the cold fabric tickling my skin.

"You've never been this accepting of the truth handed to you, you've always looked for another lead, another side of the coin."

I pursed my lips, his words still heavy on my mind. *"Why are you just taking the simple way out when you know that something is missing?"*

"I'm not." My voice was firm, eyes moving to stare at the mirror as I spoke.

I'm not. My hands clenched at my sides. And even if I did decide to face the killer, to stare him in the eyes, it wouldn't be because of Rowan's words. It would be for myself, to finally get closure on what had happened to our family, on what I had seen.

That is all it is. I grabbed the deep blue uniform jacket from my dresser, hurrying out the door before my reflection could glare at me any further.

I just want closure.

"Absolutely not." My father's decision was firm, eyes as tough as stone as I clenched my fists at my sides. I had stomped up the stairs and into his office as soon as I arrived, not taking a moment to leave my coat at my desk.

"Papa just let me see the man. I won't even speak to him," I tried again, a frown pulling down on my lips. "I should be allowed to see him myself!"

He was always so hardheaded, a trait of his that I had inherited as well. Despite Victor and I being twins, Papa always treated Victor as if there were years between us, ignoring the fact that I had always been sharper and stronger than my softhearted brother throughout our youth. In his head I was still his little Vally, unable to take care of myself or complete the simplest of tasks without my brother's aid.

"Has Victor gone to the prison?"

"No, so don't give me that look."

He sat back in his chair with a groan. While that steadied the anger on my tongue, I was still upset. I had the right for closure.

"Valeria, believe me. These past few days have been the hardest ones of my life." Papa sighed, rubbing tiredly at his brows. "Every time I enter that dark cell I see her lying there again, her skin pale and cold. I see you and your brother frightened and trembling in that cupboard."

My hands relaxed at his words, a pit of guilt forming in my chest at my father's vulnerability. It wasn't fair of me to press him.

"Please Valeria, just trust me to handle this. I don't want you to go through this with me."

My lips pressed into a firm line, my father's tired gaze enough to melt through my stubbornness. There was no use arguing with him, it would only make us more tense around each other and at a time like this I wouldn't want to contribute to any of his stress.

"Alright Papa, I understand."

I rounded his desk, pressing a kiss to my father's cheek before leaving his office, the weight of Rowan's words still pulling down on me. *I am healing now.* I forced the image of his dark eyes from my mind. *I don't need to worry anymore.*

My steps sped up as a familiar figure came into view, my brother's back stiffening as I buried my face between his shoulder blades.

"You're here early." He turned around, a frown overtaking my features at the dark bags under his eyes. He must've been feeling it too, the memories from that night coming back stronger than ever.

"Are you feeling alright?" I asked, stepping up on my toes to fix his hair, brown strands uncombed and messy.

"Not really." He sighed, hands resting at his back as I fixed him up. "How obvious is it?"

"Extremely."

"Thanks, that really boosts my self-esteem." He scoffed, but I had gotten him to smile nonetheless, which was enough for me.

"Don't worry." I pulled away, much more satisfied with his appearance. "You're still handsome."

"You're just saying that because we're twins."

"I am kind of obligated to, aren't I?"

I gasped as his hand snaked behind me, pulling on my ponytail just hard enough for me to jolt. I scrunched my nose at him, an annoying grin on his lips.

"What were you talking to Papa about?" He changed the subject before I could retaliate, scooping up a stack of files from the desk on our left.

My lips had parted, but the words didn't escape me. I didn't want to worry Vic, and bringing up the prison would only spoil the peaceful air between us. He was my safe space and I was his. I couldn't be selfish and ruin that.

"Nothing," My lips spread into a smile, my brother's blue eyes finding my own. "Nothing important anyways."

"Well if that's the case, I should go. Papa's been, you know..." He struggled with the words, my heart tugging.

"Busy?" I said, my brother nodding solemnly.

"So I've been handling a few of his cases."

That explains it, I thought, eyes moving back to the bags under his eyes.

"They're pretty big." Victor rubbed at his face tiredly, deep blue irises finding mine again. "For example, we've finally got some new information on the thieves that broke into Raul Martin's estate."

My blood ran cold, hands going rigid at my sides.

"Did I end up telling you about the case?" He furrowed his brows, eyes narrowing at my surprised reaction.

"Yeah." I cleared my throat, forcing my stance to relax. "A bit here and there."

"Well, we think it's the same pair that terrorized Laury James Young, the politician."

Not good. I nodded slowly at my brother's words. *Not good at all.*

"We're sending out some Silvers to interview shopkeepers in the area, to see if they spotted any suspicious activity."

"That sounds like a lot." I rubbed at my neck, muscles sore from the tension of the situation. "Anything else?"

"Not on that case, but"—he discreetly peered over her shoulder, leaning in closer to my ear—"we might have a lead on Alias Black."

My body instinctively pulled back, eyes wide in shock.

"What?" My voice was louder than intended, my brother glaring at me as I collected myself. "How? He's never been seen by anyone."

"Until about two weeks ago." He grinned, the files creasing in his tight grip. "A dark-haired man in his early- to mid-twenties was spotted leaving the apartment of Dally Lough, a crooked merchant in the Fourth. Lough's mutilated body was found by his brother the very next morning.

"The suspect was spotted slipping out of Lough's apartment at around ten p.m. two weeks ago by a bar's busboy. A stupid mistake on the killer's part."

That was the night we interviewed Marvin Reese. A thick lump sat in my throat. He had been running late, appearing after a *"long day at work."*

*How could he have been so careless? So impulsive? So...*I stopped myself, blinking at the absurdity of my own thoughts. He had killed someone, murdered them in cold blood, at the end of the day he was a killer that needed to be punished for his crimes. In our deal I had agreed not to slip any unknown information to the force—I wouldn't tell them his name or give them his address, but I certainly wouldn't lie or sneak around for his benefit. Although the thought of Rowan on the execution block was an unpleasant one, it was the cruel reality of all that he had done.

I won't save you Rowan Marrow. I can't. I bit my lip, avoiding my brother's eyes. *But I won't go out of my way to sentence you to death either.*

"I have a meeting in ten but let me know if you want to help with any of the cases."

Victor sighed, one of his hands pulling me into his chest and squeezing briefly before he disappeared down the hall, leaving me cold and alone. *And impossibly conflicted,* I thought, letting my eyes flutter shut.

That feeling didn't last too long though. Two warm hands clasped mine, the kind eyes of Louisa Tate meeting my own.

"Have you had breakfast, Val?" Lou asked me, a soft chuckle leaving my lips as she brushed a stray hair behind my ear. "You look tired."

"I am tired." I sighed, but smiled at her nonetheless. It felt good to be honest with them again. All the lies I told had gathered beneath my feet, threatening to swallow me whole every night as I slept, so while this feeling of serenity was only temporary, it comforted me. It was nice to talk openly for once.

"Good morning!" Oliver's voice filled the space of the fourth floor, Flint's quiet figure walking at his heels.

"Good morning." I beamed, happy to see them all here. "Another drop off?"

"I thought your father might find some use of these." Oliver held up the thick stack of books, grunting as he set them down on a nearby desk.

"Good morning, Lieutenant Tate." Flint nodded his head at Lou, the girl ruffling his hair as she grinned.

"You hear that, Ollie? Jones here knows how to address me *respectfully.*"

"Only because he hasn't been exposed to your puzzling stupidity for as long as I have."

"I could dismember you *so* easily, it's almost pitiful."

Oliver stiffened at her morbid words, a sad sigh emitting from the girl as she stared off.

"Hello, My Lady."

I tore my eyes away from Lou and Oliver's amusing display, Flint's kind eyes already on me. He took a step forward, eyes flitting to the bickering pair before leaning in toward my ear.

"And your wound? How has your recovery been?"

"Surprisingly well." My gaze had brightened, the boy's hands resting at his back. "Thank you again. You're always there to save me when I need it most."

His lips parted, brown eyes swirling with something that I couldn't identify, but before he could get another word out, a hand laced through mine, pulling my attention back to the pair.

"Val, Nana's patience has finally run out." Lou's olive eyes were urgent, my own body stiffening. Nana Tate was the only person stronger than Lou, that old woman holding more ferocity in her fingernail than the two of us combined. "She expects to see you and Vic by the end of the month or she will come here to get you herself."

"I will definitely find time to stop by," I said, the girl giving me a hard look. I furrowed my brows, staring at the stack of books that Oliver had laid out on the table behind us.

"*The Art of Dreaming*?" I read the title, fingers trailing over the deep green cover. The leather-bound book was a thick one, its title and credentials outlined in gold.

"Yes." Oliver peered over my shoulder, his analytical eyes squinting behind his glasses. "It's a philosophical collection of thoughts and theories by Raymond Grey."

"He lit himself on fire!" Flint said excitedly, my eyes widening in alarm.

"To, quote, *experience pain in its most mortal state*," Oliver said quickly, moving his eyes from the book to me. "A real fun fellow. He believed that one should not base their expectations only on what they choose to believe. Nothing in this world is truly impossible."

My eyes narrowed, Oliver's words sitting heavily in my throat. Something about that didn't sit well with me, making my stomach churn with an anxiety so intense it shook the very core of my being.

"The world is limitless!" Oliver's voice boomed, vibrating through my chest. "And the most impossible things are often our cruelest realities."

"Hey." I flinched at the hand on my shoulder, Lou staring at me with concerned eyes. She must've sensed my unease, her grip soft yet secure. "Let's get some air, yeah?"

I nodded slowly, her strong hand taking mine and leading me through the vast halls. My heart thumped violently in my chest, Rowan's words louder than they had ever been before.

*What if...*I gripped my chest, my breaths ragged. *What if he's right? What if something is wrong?* I panted heavily, the building slowly tipping. *What if this was set up by a bigger presence, by the real killer? What if he was watching us right—*

"Val!"

I gasped, my lungs sucking in air greedily as my legs shook beneath me. Lou grunted, catching my trembling body and leading us softly to the cold floor of the station.

"Val, breathe for me." She brushed the sweaty hair from my face, her fingers cold against my burning skin. "Please, just breathe."

I gripped her hand tightly, my knuckles going white as my nerves settled, an unsteady tremor still running through me.

"Damn it, Valeria." Lou exhaled shakily, pulling my face into her chest, her heart thumping wildly beneath the fabric of her shirt. "You always give me the worst scares."

"I want to see him, Lou." Her grip on me stiffened, my uneven breaths pressed against her shirt. "I want to see the killer."

"Val, are you sure?" She loosened her hold on me, my body slowly straightening up. "What did the Viscount—"

"It doesn't matter what he said." I stared into her eyes, my hands finding hers. "Lou please, help me do this."

Her pink lips pressed into a thin line, eyes swirling with a deep ocean of concern.

"I don't know how much longer I can go on like this," I whispered, fingers trembling in hers. "I need to see him. I need closure."

The station had grown silent, only the sounds of our thumping hearts filling the space between us. Lou had always been a pillar in my life, a beacon of happiness and strength that was always there to cheer me on. I'd always been on the receiving end of our relationship, and I hated that, but in that moment more than ever, I needed her. I needed her to pull me to my feet and tell me to *go*.

"Alright." Her voice was quiet, more restrained than it usually was. "Alright, fine. I can sign up for a shift on the island in the next day or two. You can come along with me then."

She winced, my body slamming back into hers, my arms wrapping around her neck.

"Thank you," I whispered, her own arms securing snugly around my waist.

"I said I'd always be there for you, didn't I?" She sighed tiredly, but I could hear the smile in her voice. "I can't exactly take that back."

I let myself be enveloped in her warmth, Lou's soft hair tickling the skin of my face. I was going to end this cycle of suffering, as painful as staring that murderer in the face would be, I had to do it. I needed to prove that this sense of peace was not a fleeting one.

The metallic rumble of the prison gates sent a chill up my spine, the sound scratching up my skin. Nieve's Imperial Prison was the most secure place in the kingdom besides the King's Palace, itself. No Silver could get in without a great deal of paperwork—just as no criminal got out unless it was in a body bag. The salty air whipped my hair around, the thick smell of the ocean comforting despite where we stood. The

Imperial Prison was built on a tiny island that sat a ways out from Nieve's seaside. Surrounded by jagged rocks and miles of sea, it was the ideal place to keep the kingdom's most twisted criminals.

The guards at the front gates saluted as Lou passed them by, the action bringing a smug smile to the girl's face, her hands resting at her back. My own rested at my sides, jittery fingers clenching and flexing as I tried to steady my pounding heart. Although I had prepared the past two days for this meeting, my mind had gone blank, replaced with the irrepressible instinct of fight or flight.

It had taken a lot of sneaking and a few of Lou's intimidating glares to get me here, the guards not daring to meet my eyes as the two of us strolled through the metal cage. Papa would surely find out eventually, but for now my presence within the vicinity was a secret, one that would be well-kept at least for the next few days.

"Are you sure you still want to do this?" Lou's voice was hushed, eyes staring ahead as we walked through the frigid building. "There is no shame in turning back."

"I need to do this," I said firmly, my nails digging into my palms. "This isn't just about me anymore."

I need to see it. I licked my lips, our heavy boots clamoring up the strictly guarded stairs, the metal clanging with every step. *I need to see his eyes.*

We had been led onto the fifth floor of the prison and taken down a twisting hall, a single door occupying the secluded wing.

"Please refrain from speaking with him before his trial," a guard muttered on our right, unlocking a series of locks, five different keys in her possession. "Not that the bastard has said much since he arrived."

"Understood." Lou gave the woman a nod as she pushed the door open.

A thick wall of glass separated us from the man in the room, his head lying in his arms as he sat at the wooden desk in the center of his cell. The man must've been in his early forties, his brown hair just beginning to streak with silver. His skin was a sickly pale, trays of uneaten food spilled by his door, the faint smell of rotting meat forcing its way through the thick barrier.

"You have visitors, Chet." The guard's voice boomed, her tone deep and commanding. The criminal shifted weakly, my lips pursing at the man before me.

This is him. My palms stung as my nails drew blood. *The man that so boldly snuck into my home in the dark of night. The man that killed my mother.*

"Chet Reisonschvatt," the guard said.

I winced at his name, the guard becoming impatient at my side.

"You will lift your head in the presence of Her Grace."

The man stiffened, his shoulders rolling back as he lifted his face, the expression he wore hard and empty as his eyes finally met mine.

"A shift in perception," Oliver had preached in one of his lectures about a year prior, Flint and I listening in at the door. *"A change in how you see the world. This change can be triggered by something as simple as a conversation with a friend, or a passage in a book."*

My hands fell limp to my sides, my heart no longer pounding in fear but stopping completely in my chest.

"Or you could be changed by a situation so ground shaking"—I gagged, fingers clamping over my lips—*"that it trembles the core of who you are completely."*

"Valeria, are you alright?" Lou's strong hands gripped me as I stumbled to my knees, her eyes wide and alert. "Open the doors."

The guard looked at us in bewilderment, her surprise quickly melting away at Lou's deadly glare.

"Open them now!"

The doors creaked open, Lou helping my stumbling body through them.

It wasn't him. Hot tears collected in my eyes as my vision blurred. *Why wasn't it him?*

"We're getting you home, Val. Don't worry," Lou whispered to me, but I didn't want to hear it.

I need to get away.

"Just hold on a bit—"

Lou stumbled back as I ripped myself from her grip, my boots slapping against the cold floor as I bolted through the prison, the tears I had tried so hard to suppress now spilling over in heavy streams.

I pushed my way through the endless crowd of guards, heavy sobs wracking my chest and my body burning. *Rowan was right. He was right, and I was a fool.*

My steps didn't stop. Even as the prison shrank at my back and I got closer and closer to the shore, I kept running, only stopping when my shaky legs finally gave out, sending me tumbling into the rocky sand at my feet. I lay there, heart throbbing in my chest as the sand mixed with my salty tears, strangled sobs escaping my trembling lips. My fingers dug into the ground, the nausea from earlier clawing itself back up my throat, burning bile falling from my lips and drawing pictures in the earth beneath me.

Why? Tears dripped from my cheeks onto the sand. *Why is this happening to me?*

Am I not allowed to live in peace? Is my only purpose on this earth to roam as a miserable creature, to chase an unattainable reality that will always exist just beyond my reach?

My body quivered, clothes wet from the moist ground and the unrelenting wind chilling me to the bone. My teeth sunk into my bottom lip, eyes carefully drifting across each of my fingers, my fists clenching as I counted ten. *There's no mistaking it.* I gritted my teeth, pressing my forehead into the sand. *This is real.*

I had sat there unmoving for a while more and screamed, emptying my burning sadness into the earth until my voice was raw and all that remained beneath my skin were the faint flames of hatred and a half-beating heart.

Distant cries in the background forced my body upright, my arms moving to wrap around my shivering body. *How cruel this world is.* I stared out at the crashing waves, feeling the salty spray that floated up into the air.

"Valeria!"

My name sounded strange, wrong.

Lou's ragged pants grew louder as she approached. "Valeria, I knew we shouldn't have come, that this would be too hard for…" Lou's tear-stricken eyes met mine, the girl stopping where she was at my empty gaze.

If this is what life set out for me—if my path is to seek justice until my dying breath—then so be it.

"Are you…" Lou swallowed, words tentative as she stared into me, my gaze tired, feeling more vacant than it had ever been before. "Are you alright, Valeria?"

No words escaped me, my eyes focusing back out to the crashing waves. My throat had grown hoarse and scratchy with strain, a new weight—one much heavier than any before it—pressing down on my chest. *They will pay.* My lips twitched, Lou's eyes still on my back.

Whoever did this to us, whoever did this to me, will pay their dues in blood.

May God have mercy on the guilty. My cold eyes met Lou's again, the girl's brows knitting together nervously before extending a tentative hand to me.

Because I surely won't.

Chapter 18

IT HAD BEEN A WEEK since I discovered the truth.
That the man sitting in the Imperial Prison had not committed the crime at hand.

Despite the sheer horror of the mistake, I hadn't let the truth slip past my lips. Not to Papa or Vic, not to Lou or Oliver, not even to Flint. As much as I hated keeping such a secret, I had an unshakable feeling that I was being watched. Like I could endanger any one of them just by whispering a few truths.

And although I hadn't shared the information with a single soul, I had somehow ended up on the doorstep of the only soulless creature I knew, Rowan's unruly figure answering the door at the fifth knock.

"And you're sure?" Rowan had asked, a steaming mug of tea clutched in my cold hands. "You're positive that it isn't the right guy?"

"Yes," I whispered, my voice quiet. "It's undeniable."

Rowan sighed, rubbing at his face. My body sunk further into the black sofa, the soft fabric hugging my icy skin. He had asked out of courtesy—I knew that, but I still appreciated the gesture. He had known what happened as soon as he opened the door, his green eyes steady, expectant.

"His eyes." I spoke slowly, the throbbing pain within me now reduced to a dull ache. "The eyes of the man who killed my mother were not those of a petty criminal. They weren't angry or broken, but the eyes of a heartless killer." My tired gaze moved to meet his, Rowan's brows furrowing as he stared down at me. "Cold and calculating."

"I knew it was too easy," he muttered under his breath, hands fingering his thick black hair. His eyes hesitantly found mine but quickly dropped to his feet, as if the words he wanted to speak refused to come out. The silence of the room was heavy, but at that point, nothing else could weigh me down. I was done, finished, much too tired of this world and its injustices to waste any more of my tears.

My attention was caught by the sound of tearing, eyes widening as Rowan ripped the notes from his drawing board, the carefully-strung papers falling worthlessly to our feet.

"Hey." I sat up, placing the cup down at my feet. "What are you doing?"

"Starting from square one." He crumpled a ripped piece of paper in his hands and tossed it onto the floor. "We've been going about this the wrong way. This sort of criminal isn't one that we can force out into the open. We'll have to beat him at his own game."

"But…" I stammered, finally standing to my feet, a hand gripping one of the fallen papers. "But all of our work—all the time we spent investigating. Aren't you angry?"

"Angry? Why would I be?" A bewildered laugh escaped him, the boy rolling up his sleeves. "Frustrated? Maybe. Tired? Most definitely. A tiny bit impressed? Shamefully so."

I narrowed my eyes at his words, but felt strangely calm, the crushing pressure in my chest lifting for the first time all week.

"This is part of the process, Chief. Not every case is as simple as counting to ten. Besides"—he shrugged, finally turning from the board to face me—"what's a few more months stuck with you? I've lived through worse."

The smile that twitched across my lips was small, barely visible, but Rowan had spotted it, his shoulders relaxing. I still couldn't understand him, this blood-soaked boy. The same hands that had wrapped my bandages had slit the throats of women and children alike, killing men in their sleep and carving their bodies into festive shapes and decor. A part of me hated him and always would, the justice-seeking noble within me refusing to look past his reputation. But the victim in me—the part of me that ached and screamed—she was more accepting. She was probably capable of doing a lot more than I'd ever admit. And while I wanted nothing more than to hold her head down below the surface, to drown the terrified child in the cupboard and move on, I couldn't. Because while I didn't trust her, I trusted her anger.

After all, it's what would help me finally solve this murder.

The days spilled into one another as Rowan and I spent every night bustling about his apartment, throwing ideas and theories back and forth, my tired body slipping into Flint's apartment just as the sun came up. Flint was still living in our estate, the riots and protests ravaging the streets of the lower neighborhoods unrelentingly. I had told Papa that I needed space, some time to cope with the sudden arrest and to let go of what had happened to our mother, and while he was reluctant, he eventually agreed, loosening the harness on my back.

But even with my newfound freedom, I found myself burning out quickly, my drive to solve the case flickering as a candle would. Drilling the facts of the case through my mind every night and thinking about it all morning had started to affect me mentally, the floor continuously swaying beneath my feet from dusk till dawn.

Once home I would lie alone in my room, watching the hands on the clock slowly trek across its face. Waiting, watching—for what, I didn't know. Hours would elapse in that manner, my worn gaze boring into the ticking thing. Perhaps I thought if I waited long enough, sleep would finally take me. Maybe then I wouldn't have to lie there and endure the agony of *being*.

I yawned, my hands lazily tracing over a few thin files as I sat at my cramped office desk.

It's much too early for meaningless work. My hands found a random mug of coffee at the edge of my desk, the cup sent down from the heavens, appearing suddenly in-between my scribbling sessions. I blew on the billowing steam, bringing the cup to my lips and taking a generous gulp. My face scrunched immediately, gagging at the sickeningly-sweet liquid, the murky stuff full of so much sugar that my teeth throbbed.

Victor. I seethed internally, shuddering at the sugary aftertaste. *That damned boy and his nasty tricks.*

I shakily set the hellish cup at the edge of my desk, as far away from my work as I could manage. My irritable temperament was soon interrupted, Lou's bright eyes catching mine.

"Good morning, Val!"

"It was a good morning, wasn't it?" I sighed, eyeing the drink with as much hatred as my tired body could muster. Lou's brows furrowed, attempting to follow my gaze, but ultimately deciding to shake off my behavior.

"I just needed some help sifting through the record room and wanted to ask—"

"Done!" My chair screeched back loudly, hopping to my feet in excitement. "Anything to get me out of this paperwork."

"Glad to see you so enthusiastic about dusting shelves."

"Always for you, Lieutenant." I grinned, ducking around her, a breathy chuckle escaping her smiling lips.

"Just keep it discreet, yeah?" Her steps matched with mine, the two of us rushing down the long hall to the doors of the archive. "The Viscount wouldn't be too happy with me distracting you from your duties, and I really like my job."

"Do you?" I asked, linking my arm through hers.

"Of course." She scoffed, flipping the end of her loose ponytail dramatically. "Who doesn't love flaunting their authority and scaring the deputies?"

"You know, you're a lot scarier than you look."

"That's nice to hear."

The cold air of the storage room licked at my skin, chilling me past my coat. A strange ache had found itself beneath my skull, but it was nothing more than a faint discomfort. I rubbed at my forehead, following Lou's steps, the girl grunting as she reached for a high row of records. She blew the dust off them before handing the record to me.

"You start here and continue to the right." She sighed, dropping the heavy load into my arms and dusting her uniform pants off. "I'll start from the other side of this row."

"Yes ma'am," I said, a grin pricking her lips as she turned her back to me, moving to the other side of the vast room. I winced, blinking as my head throbbed again, but I ignored it, sitting on the floor with a huff and laying the old case files out before me.

About two hours had passed, my groggy body dragging its way across the storage racks row by row, organizing the files in alphabetical order. The uncomfortable feeling at the back of my head had morphed into a full-on throbbing pain, my hands gripping my hair, nails digging into my scalp. My vision had blurred, my ears full of fog as I stumbled to my feet, hazed eyes slowly drifting over the tilting room.

"Valeria?" A hand gripped my shoulder, Lou's concerned gaze coming into focus. "Are you feeling alright?"

"Honestly"—I rubbed at my eyes, a ragged breath leaving my lips—"not really, no."

"Maybe you should take the day off? Go home and rest?"

"Yeah." I stumbled over my words, rubbing at my tired eyes. "I think that—that would be best."

Lou's hand slowly slipped from my shoulder as I passed by her, my feet still steady despite the heavy weight on my brain. My head felt tight, like someone had filled both of my ears with water and clamped my nose shut, pushing an immense amount of pressure between my ears.

The cold street cleared a bit of the fog away, but it was still present, blurring my vision every few minutes as I stumbled through the streets of the First. I had told myself to go home, to return to the estate, but somehow my weak form had made the two-hour stumble back to the Fourth, the familiar metal stairs of Rowan's apartment towering overhead. My disoriented figure staggered up the steps, stopping at the fifth floor, trembling knuckles hitting the door twice. My brows furrowed as it swung open, unlocked and unguarded.

That isn't right. I swallowed harshly, my hand resting on the pistol at my hip, stepping slowly into the apartment.

"Rowan?" I called out, blinking as my vision blurred again. I wiped harshly at my eyes, the living room looking normal enough. The hand at my pistol relaxed, my feet leading me easily to his bedroom.

"Rowan?" I knocked softly before gripping the doorknob. "Rowan, are you…"

My body froze, eyes wide in terror and hands as rigid as steel. For his bedroom floor had been soaked in crimson, the sticky stuff splattered aimlessly across the walls, painting my vision red.

"R—Rowan?" My voice was below a whisper, fear holding my vocal cords in its deathly grip.

I staggered over to the desk, eyes facing the ceiling as I tracked through the thick puddle of blood, gripping the hard wood once I reached it. I forced myself to bend down, peeking behind the desk and finding it empty. I swallowed hard, straightening back up shakily.

"Where the hell…"

The hair-raising scream that left my lips could've cracked the windows of the building, fear flooding through me so vigorously that my heart must have stopped for a second or two. Because when I turned back around to face the doorway, I was far from alone.

I had always told myself that if I were to ever come face-to-face with my mother's killer, I would have to be restrained, for the rush of anger and hatred toward the man would be too great for me to handle.

But now as the cold, dead eyes of the killer stood at the door, his form large and monstrous, his arms long enough to reach out from under my bed and grab me, all I felt was fear. The pistol fell from my frozen grip, his wolf mask the same as it had been all those years ago, skin-like and splattered with velvety red.

He advanced toward me without hesitation, a strangled screech leaving my lips as I stumbled back, flinging my body over the desk in an attempt to get away. My head hit the back wall, but I hardly felt a thing, a horrible screech ripping through my throat as I was grabbed from behind.

"Valeria!" His voice was inhuman, scratching down my back like the sound of the metal prison gates.

My hands were desperate, clawing at him as I screeched, the urge to vomit flooding through me as I was pulled close to his chest, his dark clothes bloodied. In a final attempt to survive, I twisted myself from his grip, grabbing the letter opener on Rowan's desk and plunging it into the man's shoulder, his hands digging into my waist.

A pained yell left his lips, but I gave him no time to recover, ripping the thin blade out and moving to strike again. But before I could his grip on me tightened, and all I could do was scream as my back was slammed against the wall, hands held over my head.

"Listen to me!"

I squeezed my eyes shut, his heavy voice distorted in a terrible way, scratching against each syllable like grinding metal.

"You're dreaming. This isn't real!"

I had abandoned reason from the moment our eyes met, terror taking the reins as I screamed and screamed, the man pressing against my legs as I tried to kick.

"Whatever it is you're seeing right now." He grunted, fingers tightening on my wrists. "It isn't real! Look at me."

"No," I whispered, hands held over my head. Even if that were the case, even if what I had seen were just a nightmare conjured up by my foggy mind, it felt real to me. "I can't."

"Look at me." His voice was more forceful this time, as if he would pry my eyelids apart himself if he had to.

My lips trembled as I took in a breath, eyes reluctantly fluttering open. I swallowed a scream at the sight before me, the masked man's bloody form standing right before my eyes.

"Valeria—"

"No," I whispered, turning my face away from his, the fear too heavy in my lungs. "Please, no."

My heart hammered through my ears, eyes opening and closing as I tried to collect myself, panic setting in as I began to tremble once again. Whether this was real or not, I couldn't bear what stood before me for another second.

"I can't." I struggled against his hold, gritting my teeth before slamming my head back against the wall. "I can't do this!"

"Hey, hey!" He tried to stop me, black dots dancing around my vision as my head made impact again. "Just look at my hand!"

My head fell limply to the side, blurry eyes focusing on the man's hand as he held it out to the side.

"How many fingers are there?"

"Please." Hot tears slid down my cheeks, my shaky hands clenching above my head. "Please, don't make me—"

"Valeria, answer the damned question!"

I flinched, teary eyes focusing on his hand. "One, two, three"—I breathed heavily, my heart thumping wildly through my chest—"four, five." I froze, swallowing harshly before parting my lips again. "Six."

"Six." He sighed in relief, his voice still sounding off but not as intense as it had been before. "You're dreaming, Valeria. Someone must've slipped you something when you weren't looking."

I turned my eyes to the floor, unable to stare at the monstrous man in the face, even though he was just a projection of my fears.

"Okay." He sighed, my teeth sinking into my lip as his posture shifted. "I'm going to let you go now—"

"No, please." My whisper was pained, tired eyes squeezing shut once again.

"We need to figure out who drugged you," he said, but it still wasn't Rowan's voice. It wasn't his face in front of mine. "Where were you up until—"

"Rowan, please!"

He stopped at my tears. My strong voice and unwavering stance had reduced to nothing before his eyes. In a mere second, my raging heart had diminished to ash, the little girl in the cupboard now trembling in his grip.

"I need you." I struggled, swallowing harshly as I avoided his gaze. "I need you to knock me out until it wears off."

"What?" His hands gripped me more firmly as he spoke, my body jolting. "Chief, this could be a new lead! This is valuable—"

"I can't do it!" I yelled, my voice cracking midway. My eyes opened again, focusing on the gushing wound on his arm, the bloody letter opener discarded at our feet. "If I have to see his face again, someone is going to get hurt and I"—my lips quivered, fresh tears streaking my cheeks—"I don't want to hurt you anymore."

He was silent, a deep exhale wracking through his chest as I cried, soft sobs leaving my lips.

"Fine," he breathed, a hand resting against the side of my jaw. "But don't blame me if this hurts."

I shook my head, a shaky exhale escaping me as he pulled back his fist.

"Thank you."

Chapter 19

MY FEET SAUNTERED STEADILY DOWN the cobblestone streets of the Fourth, the dim street lights illuminating the early hours of the night. We had reached the midpoint of December, Nieve's bitter cold finally having purpose. Rowan and I had decided to take a short break from the investigation, giving me some time to mentally heal after that whole ordeal.

Rowan had knocked me out cold—one strong hit to the jaw was all it took to send me tumbling into his arms. I didn't wake up until well into the night, heavy eyes fluttering open to find Rowan's figure sitting silently at my side, only leaving to sleep himself once I was fully awake.

I had been drugged—*Dream Stitched,* as they called it in the Underworld. Somewhere throughout the day I had ingested or inhaled a form of hallucinogen, its effects more intense than I could ever imagine.

A shiver skimmed over my skin, the familiar brick apartment complex coming into view. I pulled my cap lower over my eyes, swallowing harshly as my feet clambered up the stairs to the fifth floor. As badly as I wanted to return to the case, I had been reluctant to make the long walk back to Rowan's apartment, my fingers trembling unsteadily as they gripped the handle. I swallowed hard, forcing the remaining fear from the forefront of my mind, my hand twisting the doorknob and pulling the door open.

"Rowan?" My voice was hesitant, eyes hesitantly peeking into the dim apartment. "Ro—"

A deep sigh of relief left my lips, the dark-haired boy appearing at the entrance, hands clutching a few dirty dishes.

"Are you waiting to be invited in or something?" he asked, eyes slipping from mine as my nervous heartbeat steadied. I shook my head gently, stepping into the apartment's warmth and shutting the door behind me. Papa had stopped asking for my whereabouts as much, my father becoming much calmer since the alleged killer had been caught. I didn't have it in me to tell him the truth, and even if I were to, I doubted he'd believe me. It was my memory as a child against a confession and mask as evidence. I wouldn't get very far.

"Any new thoughts on the case?" Rowan called from the kitchen, the sound of running water accompanying his muffled voice.

"Not really." I sighed, slipping the thick brown coat from my shoulders, a careful hand loosening my uniform tie. "I still can't figure out why that guy would confess to a crime he didn't commit."

"He could have been threatened?"

"I thought of that, but still." I shook my head, pursing my lips in thought. "There are few things worse than being publicly shamed and sentenced to death."

"That isn't necessarily true." Rowan appeared from the room behind me, wiping his wet hands on a towel. "There are things far worse than death."

"Well aren't you a lovely little ray of pitch black."

"Are you naturally this hard to deal with, or do you try?" He threw the towel at my face, the moist fabric muffling my words of protest.

"You're one to talk," I mumbled, wiping at my face with my sleeve. Our words had fizzled out, leaving the two of us in a thick silence. Rowan's eyes had grown heavy, and while he was good at masking his emotions, I could see it—a sense of unease.

"Have you figured out who drugged you?" He took a seat on the deep brown lounge chair, eyes focusing on his hands.

"No," I said, voice small. "I didn't leave the station that entire morning, and I doubt anything happened there."

"Why do you say that?"

"Because it's the *Imperial Station*." I scoffed, the boy lifting his eyes to mine. "The whole purpose of that building is to protect people."

"Which people?"

"All people!" I furrowed my brows, my grip on the couch tightening. "Every citizen of Nieve's Capital City from a child in the Seventh to an old man in the First."

"So you are refusing to even consider it as a possibility because of your blind faith in your coworkers?" His voice wasn't mocking as it often was, but urgent, my eyes narrowing. "I hate to break it to you, Chief, but not everyone is as morally bound as you are."

"You don't know what you're talking about." I sighed, uncomfortable with the sudden shift in conversation. "Slaughtering people mercilessly doesn't make you some expert on behavior. Heartlessness doesn't equate knowledge."

"But it does give me a broader view of the board." Rowan's eyes weren't angry, but tough, the vivid shades of green forcing their way through my head as he stared. "You are focusing on one chess piece, closing in on the King, when in reality he's almost completely useless, just a distraction for the Queen, who moves almost freely across the tiles, who has the power to control the *entire game*."

"What the hell is that supposed to mean?" I was tired of these half explanations and metaphors, my mind exhausted beyond anything I could imagine.

"I'm trying to tell you to open your mind to the possibilities," he said carefully, still holding something back on his tongue. "But that isn't what I wanted to talk to you about today."

"What is it then?" I laughed bitterly, utterly unamused. "How I'm incapable of recognizing good intentions from bad ones? I hate to break it to you—I was a trainee myself, and a damn good one at that."

He ignored my words, leaning his elbows over his knees as he contemplated his words.

"When you were"—he licked his lips, eyes flitting from mine—"*under the influence,* what exactly did you see?"

My throat tightened, the constricting image of the masked man still raising the hairs on my neck. After I had woken up in his apartment, I hadn't said a word, locking myself in Rowan's bedroom and slipping out into the bitter cold before he could awaken. I couldn't relive those moments so soon.

"I know you must have envisioned me as—well—not myself." He trailed off, brushing the loose strands of hair back from over his face. "But how vivid was it?"

"The same as that night," I said quietly, swallowing the lump in my throat.

"The exact same?"

"Yes." My voice came out much softer now, as if speaking too loudly on the matter would summon the masked man. "An *exact* copy."

"Describe him to me."

"Rowan." My shoulders stiffened, pupils shrinking with dread.

"Just…" He put his hands up, struggling with what to say. "Just do it, okay?"

I sunk further into the cushions, lips trembling as the unforgettable image of the man crawled its way to the front of my mind.

"He was tall." My voice trembled, fingers ripping into the soft fabric of the couch as the killer's face burned through my mind. "A towering giant of a man. And his arms"—Rowan furrowed his brows, leaning in closer—"they were long enough to grip you from beneath your bed and strangle you in your sleep. He had a strange, almost monstrous build, heavyset and strong. And the mask…" My eyes widened, Rowan sitting up as my posture went rigid.

"What is it?" he asked, narrowed eyes glinting in the pale lights of the room.

"Seeing it again made me realize something." I swallowed harshly, my face slowly turning to his. "It didn't look like a mask at all. It was almost like the fabric morphed with his face, like it was part of his skin."

My fingers found my hair, threading through the roots.

"No, that can't be it. That wouldn't make any sense!"

"But what if it does?" He moved from his chair, crouching at my feet as my breaths became uneven. "Valeria, tell me. How sure are you of what you saw that day?"

"You're seriously going to question my sanity after all we've gone through?" I yelled, but it was more of a cry, broken and afraid, desperate for him to stop where he was.

"I'm not questioning your anything." He stared into my eyes firmly, lips pursing before they parted again. "I'm simply stating that you yourself are no longer a stranger to this world of lies and illusions."

My stomach dropped at his words, realizing very quickly where this was going.

"Rowan, don't," I pleaded, my mind on the brink of insanity, hands shaking at my sides. "Don't say another word!"

"Valeria, you have to listen!" His hands slammed down on either side of me, the two of us staring reluctantly at each other as we caught our breaths. "How do you know that what you saw ten years ago was *real*?"

When Victor and I were kids we had always played around a bit too roughly, collecting new scars and bruises by the end of every week. I remember one particular incident clearly, our bare feet beating against the cold floor of the estate as we raced down the steps, Victor hot on my heels. I had turned back to look at my brother then, a mistake I would learn to regret, a single misstep sending me toppling down the steep expanse of stairs, my back slamming onto the ground floor of our estate. That sudden impact had managed to knock every wisp of oxygen from my lungs, and I lay there unable to move, my vision blurring as my brother screamed somewhere in the background.

That feeling manifested itself within me once again, my body struggling to remember how to breathe, unable to speak, and completely helpless.

"It has to have been," I whispered, the sound of my heart drowning out everything else in the room. "Rowan, it has to have been real. My mother—"

"Your mother was murdered by an unidentifiable man." Rowan's words were firm and clear, his gaze reluctant but steady nonetheless. "One who somehow drugged you before—"

"Stop it." I pushed his chest away from me, shakily stumbling to my feet. "Stop it right now."

This isn't happening.

This is not happening to me.

"If you are going to sit here and tell me that the thing I saw ten years ago—the thing that lurks in my dreams every night—isn't real, you might as well just kill me and get it over with."

"Valeria—"

"You have to be wrong." I shook my head, feeling sick to my stomach.

There has to be something that we are missing. I grabbed my coat from the floor, Rowan yelling after me as my steps picked up. *This couldn't have been a figment of my imagination. It couldn't have been a lie!*

I had run down the stairs of the building, the metal steps clanging as my boots hurried down without restraint.

I'm not crazy. My breaths were ragged, muffled curses echoing from behind me as I shoved my way through the street. *I couldn't have dreamt him up.*

*If he wasn't real, then...*My stomach lurched, a hand moving to clamp over my mouth. A shudder escaped me, my lips trembling as Oliver's words forced their way back into my mind.

"Nothing in this world is truly impossible." A whimper left my lips, eyes filling with the stinging tears that I hated so much.

"The world is limitless!"

I had sat there outside in the cold, arms clutching my body as a few loose tears slipped down my cheeks. I was too tired to sob, to scream or cry. Instead all I could do was sit there and let the winter wind dry my eyes. My body didn't move for quite a while, the cold emptiness of

December comforting in a way I hadn't expected. Only when the first few snowflakes of winter littered my lashes did I stand once more, the pale crystals reminding me that as hollow and frigid as my heart felt, it was not the only thing lost to ice.

Chapter 20

"Valeria, darling. Come in here, would you?" The sweet voice of Nana Tate echoed from the kitchen, her words as warm and bright as they always were. "Pour yourself some tea dear, and I'll have some biscuits out in just a second."

"I really am alright, Nana." I smiled, catching a glimpse of her familiar silver curls. "I just had a short shift today and thought it was about time that I visited."

"Did Lou threaten you?"

"Yes ma'am."

"Good, I raised her well." She huffed, finally meeting me with open arms.

Nana Tate was a petite woman in her early seventies, her bright smile and kind olive eyes matching Lou's. While even I towered over her small frame, she was tougher than any Silver in the Imperial Force, her words sharp and concise, eyes catching the faintest changes in a person's demeanor. And of course, she had a killer right hook.

"What did I say about going and getting so grown?" She sighed, squeezing me in her warm embrace. "I bet you have all the boys on your heels."

"Not interested."

"And she's smart too." Nana pulled away grinning, staring up at the sky. "Your mother would be proud."

My smile wilted, the topic of my mother more sensitive than ever since my argument with Rowan. I had avoided anything case-related since then, my focus shifting to lifting my brother's spirits and reading at The Wild Iris bookstore.

"Is something the matter?" Nana's wrinkled face drew together in concern, a weak smile forcing its way to my lips.

"No, I just—"

"Don't lie to me, Valeria."

I stiffened, her knowing eyes seeing right through me. I pressed my lips together, taking a seat at the worn brown table, Nana's cozy home standing in the Second District long before it bustled as it did now.

"It's about Mum."

Her eyes drooped in sorrow, colorful irises swimming with a depth I could never hope to understand.

"Rather, what happened to her." I swallowed harshly, the next words heavy on my tongue. "Do you think that children"—my nails dug into the fabric of my pants—"when they're afraid and alone—do you think they might imagine things that aren't really there?"

"Of course."

My fingers clenched the floral fabric of the tablecloth, knuckles going white beneath the table. Nana's expression softened, the woman brushing back her long curly hair before placing her hands onto the table.

"But what determines reality and fantasy to you, Valeria?"

"What do you mean?" I furrowed my brows, tired of the meaningless questions that awaited me at every corner. "Reality is the truth, what stands right in front of your eyes, what's really there."

My lips trembled, not with sadness or anger, but with a deeply rooted exhaustion, a weariness that consumed my soul, coating my heart like the thick Nieve fog.

"Fantasy is only what we want to believe."

"Then let me correct you."

I stiffened as Nana's hands took mine, her calloused hands proof of a long and difficult life.

"Reality is the truth that we choose to accept, what we choose to believe. Fantasy is the limitless sky above that."

"But possibilities aren't concrete." I pursed my lips, frustration breaking through the surface. "They only exist within our minds."

"That's very true." She laughed breathily in agreement, a soft fierceness lighting up her eyes as she leaned in closer. "But why should that mean they aren't real?"

A chill ran over my skin, my heart throbbing at her words. My lips quivered, a small smile overtaking them as I sighed, bringing Nana's hands up to my lips.

She never ceases to surprise me.

"Whatever you are questioning—whatever you are unsure of—is still the truth, just a different side of it." Her hands squeezed mine. "Now all that's left is opening your heart to the possibilities."

Her wrinkled eyes fell from my face to my neck, a wave of sorrow washing over her expression.

"That was Marisol's, wasn't it?" Her hands moved, gently brushing the black pendant at my neck. "That necklace was your mother's."

"Yes," I breathed, squeezing the cold metal in my grip. "I never take it off."

"It's beautiful. I remember when she first got it." She laughed, my lips twitching into a grin at the sound. "Quite the peculiar choice of flower, but very pretty nonetheless."

"Peculiar? In what way?" I furrowed my brows, straining to stare down at the dark charm.

"Usually it's roses or orchids in jewelry." She shrugged, silver curls bouncing. "I've never seen a black dahlia used before."

"A black dahlia," I murmured, holding the charm tightly in my grip.

So that's what it is, I thought, my thumb grazing the sharp petals. I furrowed my brows, grip tightening on the charm.

Why does that seem so familiar?

My narrowed eyes moved from the necklace to Nana, my shoulders stiffening as her eyes widened, the faint scent of smoke grabbing her attention.

"Oh my!" She jumped to her feet, startling me to mine. "The biscuits—I forgot the tray in the oven!"

A laugh bubbled through my lips, followed by another, my body swaying forward as I was brought to tears, the frantic woman scolding me as I grinned, wiping the tears from my eyes.

Open my heart to the possibilities. My shoulders relaxed for the first time in what felt like weeks.

That didn't mean the truth wouldn't be frightening—that what I would find wouldn't tear me apart—but I wanted to know. I needed to see both sides of the coin.

"You seem giddy." Vic's voice strained, my brother's upper body disappearing into the attic, my waiting figure at the bottom of the retractable ladder.

"Do I?"

"Eerily so." He huffed, handing me a bulky box. I pursed my lips as its full weight was given to me, huffing as I set it down by the staircase. Victor had decided to go through our attic, hoping to clean it out and renovate the tiny space into a makeshift reading room.

"Is all this really worth it?" I grunted, gripping the next box that was handed to me. "You can't even stand upright in there."

"It'll be fine." He waved his hand lazily at me, eyes bright with excitement. "Besides, Papa said I could paint it however I please."

"Why do I have a feeling that you're just going to store your toys in there?"

"They are train models, not toys," he corrected me, hair bouncing as he ducked down to give me a look. "And what if I am, hmm?"

"No shame in it, just don't try to cover it up with *reading room*."

"Yes, it wasn't very convincing, was it?"

"Unfortunately not." I laughed, my brother's eyes squinting as he grinned.

My smile slowly dropped, Nana's words giving me the courage to ask the burning question.

"Hey Vic?" My voice was small, fingers picking at a stray splinter on the wooden ladder.

He hummed from above, hands rustling as he waited for me to continue.

"What do you remember about that night?"

The rustling stopped, Victor's blue eyes peeking out from the roof.

"About *that* night?" He slowly came down a few steps, hands gripping the sides of the wooden structure. "Not much, honestly. Most of my vivid memories are from after the crime, not really during it. Like when Papa found us, he…" His words stopped, my brother growing silent as he swallowed heavily.

I wasn't the only one then. I sighed, my eyes momentarily falling shut. Even though he didn't often show it, thinking about that night was hard for him too.

"So you don't remember anything?"

"Not really, just that you protected me." Victor leaned his back against the ladder, bright eyes heavy with a sense of sorrow.

"We protected each other."

"No V, you protected me." He shook his head. "You took the burden of that night upon your shoulders the moment you clamped your hand over my eyes. I don't think I've ever thanked you for that."

"Quit it, will you?" I sighed, rushing into his chest. His arms wrapped around me without hesitation, the familiar smell of linen and coffee mixing with the faint scent of cigarette smoke. "Dramatic thing."

I jumped at the loud rumble that echoed around the room, my eyes turning up to squint at my brother.

"You think Papa will be back anytime soon?" he asked, trying to suppress his grin. "Because I'm starving, but having dinner without him just doesn't feel right."

The two of us burst into a fit of laughter, my brother grinning sheepishly at me as I pulled away from his embrace.

"If it's Papa we're talking about, then he'll definitely be late." I laughed, crossing my arms over my chest. My brother's squinted eyes widened, his posture straightening as realization hit him.

"There actually is one thing that I remember from that night, just because it was so absurd!"

I furrowed my brows, a strange sense of dread twisting my stomach into knots as he spoke.

"Old Reliable stopped working!"

There it is. My heart caught itself in my throat, the organ still beating.

The possibility.

"What do you mean, stopped working?" I asked slowly, my brother's brows knitting together at my expression.

"That old golden clock just froze." He shrugged, turning back around to climb up the ladder. "I remember glancing up at it as we came down the stairs and being completely disoriented by the fact that it stilled."

We really had been drugged. I stumbled back, my mind racing.

But how? How would two noble kids that never left their mother's side get drugged? As rowdy as Vic and I were, we never strayed too far from our mother, so *when—when would it have happened?*

"Now, give me a hand with the—"

"I'll see you later, Vic!" I yelled behind me, already clambering down the stairs. "Don't wait up for me!"

Rowan had been right. He had tried to tell me, and I had just pushed him away. I had chosen to see one tile on the chess board while he had the full view.

My boots stepped into the bustling street, a gloved hand moving above my head at the familiar black outline of a cab.

"Taxi!"

"Rowan!" I panted, running up the stairs of his apartment complex. I had the taxi driver drop me off at the outskirts of the Fourth, not wanting to disclose the assassin's address, leaving my freezing body to make the thirty-minute run to his building.

"Rowan, you were right!" My voice echoed up the stairs, feet finally stumbling onto the fifth floor. "Ro—" I tensed, the door unlocked and cracked open.

No. My heart hammered in my chest, palms beginning to sweat despite the cold.

Not this again.

I closed my eyes, taking in a deep breath. I didn't think I was drugged, my mind clear and gait steady. I swallowed my fear, swinging the door open and slamming it shut behind me. My shoulders slumped, feet staggering forward at the sight before me. Rowan's apartment had been torn apart, the shelves toppled, books ripped and discarded at my feet, bloody stains smeared sporadically along the wall.

"Rowan?" My voice came out as a whisper, my eyes searching the house wildly, the breath stopping in my lungs at the dark-haired boy sitting at the center of the common room, the couch overturned and table discarded, two of its legs splintered and cracked.

"Rowan, what happened?" I ripped the gloves from my hands, ready to examine the boy. "Who—"

"Leave."

I froze at his voice, his tone icy and detached, just as it had been that night in the alley.

"Not another step."

"Rowan, what the hell happened?" I whispered, his back still facing me. "Did someone—"

"It would do you well to walk away." The blood stilled in my veins, a dangerous edge to his voice. A shiver ran down my back as he turned his body, lifting his murderous gaze to me. "I don't really care who I kill right now."

My eyes fell to the pocket watch in his grip, his hands bloody as they trembled at his sides, fists completely torn open.

"Hey Rowan," I said quietly, the boy wincing at the sound of his own name. "What time is it?"

"You tell me." His dark eyes were foggy as they met mine, pupils dilated to an impossible degree. "The damned thing won't tick."

He's drugged. I swallowed harshly, taking a tentative step back. His shoulders rolled back slowly, the boy standing unsteadily to his feet, his twitching hands sending panic through me.

"Hey." My voice shook as he stood to his feet, his posture stiffening. "Just sit right there, and I'll get you some water."

He ignored my words, his bare feet taking another swaying step in my direction.

Don't panic. I tried to steady my pounding heart, but it was no use. I was a sheep in his den, and Rowan was no longer a lion but a monster, with teeth and claws that would tear into anything in sight.

"Rowan, sit." I tried to steady my voice, feet slowly backing up toward the door, not daring to move my gaze from his. "Ro—"

I screamed, the boy bolting toward me. My hands had just grazed the doorknob, barely twisting it when I was slammed back against the wall, my head spinning at the impact.

"Ro—" I gasped, his hand grabbing my throat and squeezing, eyes staring down at me vacantly as I struggled in his grip.

No. I tried to pry his fingers from my neck, but he didn't budge. My hands clawed aimlessly as panic set in.

I am not going to die like this. I kicked as hard as I could, his body pressing against me easily as I struggled. *Rowan Marrow is not going to kill me!*

My eyes had begun to bulge, lungs screaming for air as they burned, my hands numbing as the world went in and out of focus.

He didn't even flinch, his eyes expressionless as they watched the life drain out of me—as if he needed to see it—like he needed to watch it happen.

He's drugged. I tried to think, my eyes rolling to the back of my head. *He's in a nightmare, and I*—my hands fell limply to my sides—*I must be the monster.*

The strength had left my body, the last bit of control wasted on my hand as I weakly lifted it, holding my fingers up in front of his face.

Count. My eyes fluttered shut, hand trembling. *COUNT THEM, ROWAN.*

His grip loosened all at once, my body hitting the floor with a heavy thump, tears pricking the corners of my eyes as air burned through my desperate lungs. Rowan stumbled back, his eyes blinking fast as I heaved onto his floor, warm vomit rushing past my lips as I choked, my body too weak to stand. I shakily turned my tear-stained face to his, the unreadable expression on his face morphing into one of pure horror, bloody fists shaking at his sides.

"V..." His lips trembled, eyes wide with a childlike panic. "Valeria, I—"

"It's okay," I croaked, throat swollen and burning, my arms shaking as they held up my weight. "It's fine, Rowan."

He sat there, watching in silent terror as I collected myself, my throat throbbing where his hand had been. *He could've killed me.* My chest ached as I sat back against the wall. *I could have died.*

My eyelids drooped heavily, fear coursing through me as my body gave out. *I can't fall asleep here—not with him still like this.* Fear slammed against my chest until our eyes met again. His hair was a mess, having pulled at it anxiously in every possible direction. His lips quivered as he avoided my gaze, but above all his eyes were heavy, weighted with a regret that I had never seen before. My eyes fell shut, my body giving into exhaustion. *He won't hurt me again.* The thought carried me off, my body succumbing to strain and exhaustion. *I don't know why, but I'm sure of it.*

When I had woken up again, I was no longer at the apartment's front entrance, but back in Rowan's room. I furrowed my brows, looking around quickly, spotting my coat and work vest sitting neatly on the desk beside me, leaving me in my uniform shirt and station-issued pants. A sigh of relief escaped me—the boy had been sensible enough to remove the vomit-soaked clothing from my unconscious body but was careful not to go any further.

I parted my lips to speak, pausing at the sharp pain that came from my throat. I shakily stood to my feet, taking a few slow steps to the mirror hanging on his bedroom wall. I turned my head away quickly, the purple outlines of Rowan's fingertips frightening to look at.

I swallowed hard, wincing at the soreness it caused, before slowly walking to the door. It was morning now from the looks of it, a few pale rays of sunlight seeping through the snowy fog outside. The hallucinogens should have worn off by now.

My steps were silent as I closed the bedroom door behind me. My eyes drifted across the mess of an apartment and stopped on Rowan's still figure, the boy still sitting in the center of the living room, pocket watch in hand.

"You're awake." His words were hesitant, a steady tremor running through his hands as he spoke.

"So are you," I said softly, the pain in my throat intense but not impossible.

He was silent, gently placing the pocket watch at his side, his white tank top soaked through in sweat. I stood unmoving as he shifted, slowly turning to me but avoiding my face, knowing exactly what he'd find on my neck.

"Rowan." I swallowed slowly at the ache in my throat, ignoring the pain for his sake over mine. "What happened?"

His hard eyes stared at the wooden floor of the common room. Whatever he had seen had shaken the usually-stoic man, completely shattering the unwavering emptiness in his eyes.

"Look, I know these things are hard to talk about," I said gently, flinching at the image of the masked man that had burned itself into my mind. "But please, what did you see that frightened you so much?"

That made you look at me like that?

I swallowed hard, the silence in the room much too heavy for my strained limbs to handle. I let out a breath, turning my back to the boy, pausing at the sigh that left his lips.

"When I was a child"—I turned back to look at him, Rowan's fists trembling at his sides—"I lived in the Seventh with my mother. We had nothing, barely owning the clothes on our backs."

He stopped, slowly flexing his hands, almost forcing them to lie still in his lap before his lips parted again.

"It wasn't easy, but at the very least I had somewhere warm to sleep every night, my mother pulling me into her chest even as Nieve's wind chilled every crevice it could find.

"When I was ten years old I was sitting in an old backroom that my mother had rented for the night, waiting for her to return home from whatever work she had managed to find." His lips pulled into a smile, one much too sad for a man his age. "I remember staring out of the tiny cracked window and looking at the distant lights of the First, thinking that someday I was going to take her there.

"Pathetic, wasn't I?"

I said nothing, my hands moving to wrap around my cold body as his eyes met mine.

"My mother had finally returned from a job at some bar in the Seventh," he said slowly, moving to stare at his hands. "I remember because she smelled of tobacco and liquor, her skin sticky with sweat as I ran into her arms for the first time that day.

"She had swayed unsteadily and stumbled to the mat at the corner of the floor, urging me to eat whatever she had brought, her body too tired to take another step. So I sat back, letting the flickering lights of the other districts guide me to sleep."

My bones stiffened at the sudden pause, Rowan's quiet gentleness hardening in a matter of seconds, chilling the room instantly.

"That was the last time I would speak with my mother. Because the next time my eyes opened, it wasn't the lights of the First that flickered before them, but the raging flames of a fire, burying the Seventh District in a hellfire so thick that I'm sure the devil himself stood impressed."

The Nieve Disaster. I flinched at the thought. *The fire that lit up the kingdom in shades of yellow and red.*

"I had shaken my mother awake, grabbing her hand and leading her swaying body down the steep steps of the building, the flames licking at our feet as we ran." His hands clenched, knuckles going white as he recounted that horrid night. "But by the time we had moved to escape, the building was already engulfed in flames, the two of us managing to scramble to the second floor before we were trapped between the walls of smoke and fire."

"So how did you…" My throat throbbed, the question heavy on my tongue. "How are you alive?"

"Just as the flames had begun to sear our heels, my mother put herself between my body and the raging fire, breaking an old window with her bare hands and yelling for me to jump." He swallowed harshly, a faint sheen of sweat coating his forehead, the hallucinogen's earlier strain leaving him tired. "I didn't want to leave her, to abandon my mother, but her nightgown had already caught the flames, the liquor on her skin making her a perfect human torch. And as I sat there on the window's ledge, I turned my head back to her and watched."

His eyes were faraway, staring off into some memory that I couldn't see.

"I watched her burn alive."

"Rowan." My voice was barely audible, the sheer horror of his words sending the hairs on my neck upright. "How could you bear that? Her screams, her agony?" My own mother flashed through my mind, my stomach lurching despite it being empty. "How did you *survive?*"

"She didn't scream." A bitter smile spread across his lips, the forced expression twitching as he blinked. "In fact, she didn't even cry. Instead, she stared me in the eyes and smiled.

"Her dress had encased her in fiery flames, her last bit of strength spent breaking that window." He shook his head, chest rising and falling with every ragged breath. "I know I shouldn't have looked. I shouldn't have turned back around to see what had become of my mother, but I couldn't help it. And when my eyes met hers, she smiled.

"And I remember thinking to myself…" My hands clenched as his voice swayed. *"How could anyone ever be as beautiful as her?"*

His eyes had finally turned to me, angry tears trickling down his face in heavy streams. My heart throbbed in my chest, feet moving on their own toward the crying boy.

"Don't," he said, trying to give me a hard look, but the tears had already fallen, his chest shaking as he tried to restrain his sobs. "Don't come any closer. I'm still a bit—" His words cut off as I gently grabbed the back of his head and pulled his face into my stomach, letting the fabric of my shirt soak up his tears. He had stiffened at first, fists resting at his sides, but as my hands trailed through his hair, his shoulders began to shake, Rowan collecting himself into my pale work shirt like a child.

I trailed my fingers through his hair carefully as he calmed down. His black strands were softer than I thought they would be—smooth and clean, the quivering of his body reminding me of a distraught kid. Broken and alone.

A lot like myself.

He swallowed harshly before pulling away from me, his eyes avoiding mine as I took a seat across from him on the floor.

"While that was how everything started"—his voice was quieter now, calmer—"what I saw earlier wasn't my mother or the fire. It was the man that found me afterwards.

"I had fallen from the second story of that flaming building, breaking an arm and bruising myself badly." He unconsciously touched his left arm, my eyes spotting a lengthy scar that trailed up his bicep. "Orphaned kids don't find honest labor easily, especially in the Seventh. I was roaming the streets looking for work when some rich guy stopped his car on the side of the road and picked me up.

"He took care of me, gave me a place to stay, even taught me how to play." His puffy eyes drifted to the worn piano in the corner of the room. "But the minute I was out of a cast, everything changed."

"He drugged me for the first time and set me loose into the streets with a blade in my trembling hands. That's when I learned that the things the human mind can conjure up when under the influence"—he shook his head, as if to rid himself of the memory—"can be truly horrifying.

"When I came to I was sitting in a pool of blood, three grown men lying by my sides, all three of them torn apart savagely."

I tried to ignore the familiar flashes of the crime scene photos, the many victims of Alias Black often mutilated beyond recognition, the overkill so full of anger and hatred that even seasoned killers could not bear to look.

"After that I worked as a private hitman for the man until he died," Rowan said, avoiding my eyes. "By then I was already sixteen years old, alone in the world with no money or family. Killing was all I was good for.

"I swore to myself that the minute I was out of his disgusting grip, I would *never* be dependent on anyone ever again." His fists clenched so tightly I was sure the bones ached. "If I am to be condemned to hell either way, then I will pave my own path there. I refuse to be dragged there by anyone else."

I swallowed hard at the words, a shiver tracing up my cold skin. The bitter hatred in his eyes was enough to drown the both of us, and the longer I listened and stared, the deeper I sunk.

"If I could go back and change anything, I wouldn't have waited for him to die though." His eyes had gone blank again, a chilling expression overtaking his features. "No, I would've strangled him myself."

As sick as his sins made me, and as angry as I was for the innocent lives he had taken, I couldn't help but find myself sitting heartbroken on the floor of his apartment asking myself, *Why?*

Why couldn't we have met a few years earlier?

"You were right, by the way," I whispered, his eyes clearing and moving to mine. "That's what I came to tell you. Both Victor and I were drugged that night."

"Was I?" he asked, his expression unreadable. "I'm sorry. I didn't want to be. And I'm sorry for"—his words cut out, eyes tentatively glancing at my throat—"putting my hands on you. For both times."

My wrist sat heavily in my lap, the memories of that night in the alley still fresh. Rowan and I weren't friends. Honestly I didn't think we could ever be. My family and I were destined to chase guys like him to the ends of the earth while he was fated to kill those at my side whenever they got in the way. Such was the natural order of predator and prey, both roles applicable to either side. But whether I wanted to acknowledge it or not, I cared for him, as a colleague if nothing else.

"I'm sorry too." His brows furrowed at my words, a weak smile overtaking my lips. "For sticking you with that letter opener."

His lips pricked into a smile, hands moving to wipe at his eyes. "For your information, that wound was infected."

"You should've cleaned it better." I shrugged, Rowan's eyes as dark as they'd always been, but a bit clearer. His amused gaze fell from my face to my chest, eyes narrowing as he stared.

"Excuse you." I brought a hand to my chest, the assassin giving me a hard look before reaching out himself, taking the pendant into his hands.

"It's bloody."

"Is it?" I sighed, wiping at the intricate petals with the collar of my shirt. "It's a black dahlia, by the way," I said, more to myself than to him. "Which apparently is a strange flower to have jewelry for."

"Black dahlia," he repeated slowly, eyes staring off behind me.

"It sounds familiar, doesn't it?" I pursed my lips and stood. "I'm thinking of asking my father about it when I get home."

"Or you could talk to your professor, or that reporter kid."

"Okay, Oliver I can understand, but Rin?" I froze, furrowing my brows at the boy. "Why him?"

"Flowers are a secret language. There could be some double meaning behind that."

I blinked hard at his words. "A secret…"

My hands loosened, falling limp at my sides as everything finally fell into place.

Black dahlia.

"Rowan." My voice was unsteady as I rose to my feet, staggering toward the door.

Black dahlia.

"What is it? What happened?" He stumbled to his feet, moving to grab his coat, but I was already out the door, bracing the bitter cold in my thin uniform.

Black dahlia.

"Valeria!" His voice echoed at my back as I scrambled down the metal steps, panic coursing through me as everything finally cleared.

Black dahlia.

"B.D."

B.D. was a writer, one who had eyes inside and outside of the monarchy, someone who stood for the voices of the less fortunate, who knew the truth behind the fire and needed to be eliminated.

B.D. stands for Black Dahlia.

The Black Dahlia was my mother.

Chapter 21

I‍T HAD STARTED TO RAIN, the cold streets of Nieve icing over as the rain pounded down, soaking my clothes through. But even though my lips turned blue and my vision blurred, my mind had never been clearer.

The door to our estate slammed open, my work boots tracking mud into the house as I staggered through, breaths uneven and wild as I stood at the door of the common room. The very same room my mother had been murdered in, and the same room where her killer would be brought to justice.

"Valeria, what happened?" My father's brows came together, eyes wide as I stood dripping at the doorway, my body completely steady despite the cold. "Where the hell is your coat?" His eyes widened, the cigar dropping from his fingers at the sight of my neck. "Who put their hands on you?"

My father took a few quick steps toward me, but I backed away, his brows knitting together.

"Valeria, *now.*" There was a dangerous edge to his voice, but I was done teetering around my words. "Tell me who hurt you, and I'll take care of it."

"Is that how it works?" My voice was nearly silent, quieter than it had ever been—it wasn't sadness that held me down, but anger. "When someone breaks the law—when someone *hurts* someone else—as the Viscount, it's your job to take care of it, isn't that right?"

My father's pale eyes narrowed, the man before me still riding off the surprise of my unruly appearance.

"Valeria, whatever you're trying to say"—his eyes bore intently into mine—"just say it."

"Tell me I'm wrong," I whispered, a shiver finally pricking my skin as my insides trembled. "Tell me that you have an explanation for everything."

"Valeria, what are you—"

"Don't play stupid with me, Papa." My voice shattered, lips trembling as I spoke. "I'm tired of playing these games!"

"Then why don't you just ask what is clearly sitting on the tip of your tongue?"

"We were drugged, weren't we? That night she died." His eyes remained steady as I spoke, but I was no stranger to masking my emotions. "You somehow managed to slip something to us so we wouldn't recognize you when you killed her. *Hard decisions have to be made for the betterment of the people.*" His words felt different to me now, making me sick to my stomach. "She knew too much about too many things and had decided to expose the corruptions of the nobility to the public."

"I don't know what you—"

"Shut up and let me finish!" My voice was venomous, broken eyes staring into the man before me. "You had ten years to talk, ten years to spare us from our endless paranoia and suffering, and you did *nothing*. Now it's my turn to speak."

His jaw clenched, the man falling silent as I steadied my trembling fists.

"You weren't out working that night—*no*, you were in the house with us. Hiding behind a wolf's mask and the hallucinogens. That's why Vic and I lived. We were drugged heavily enough that even if we had woken up in the middle of the night, even if we had snuck down the stairs and witnessed the murder, you would still be completely free of suspicion. She was your wife after all, *the Viscount's Jewel.*

"You know, I think I would have died on this earth without ever knowing the truth if it wasn't for one tiny factor." That's when it happened—my father's surprised face had begun to harden, his feet carrying him toward the small bar at the fireplace's side. "Not everybody died in that fire, and while Silverstein had committed horrors of his own, it wasn't his dogs that Marvin Reese saw outside his window.

"The Viscount is the monarch's right hand, his commanding voice and authoritative presence." I quoted my father. The words that were once so endearing and exciting were now heavy with the scent of blood, red and sticky with his sins. *"The King's watchdog."*

A bitter smile twitched on my lips, a hand moving to push back my soaking hair as the man's hands moved, unscrewing the top of a crystal bottle, pouring its golden contents into a decorative glass.

"He was talking about you that entire time, and I was too blinded by what I chose to see as possible instead of fathoming the impossible. Silverstein shouldn't have been caught with that pin—no, he probably didn't even know what it was, but *you* did. And as soon as I came over to you with questions, you knew exactly what I was planning on doing and planted false evidence in Silverstein's house, leaving me to find it.

"And I played right into your hands, didn't I?" I laughed coldly, tears of anger pricking at my eyes. "Oh, you must've loved seeing me all lost and confused, picking up your breadcrumbs eagerly as the years dragged on."

I jolted as my father's hand slammed against the wooden bar, the sound echoing throughout the vast estate.

"If you're so sure of everything"—his voice was lower, filled with a thin sense of serenity that threatened to shatter like a sheet of ice— "then why don't you just ask the damned question?"

A heavy lump sat in my throat, and as hard as I tried to swallow it down, it stuck, refusing to dissolve as my lips parted.

"Did you…" My voice shook, the words painful despite everything I knew. "Did you kill her?"

"Speak clearly and with conviction." His voice was rough, the man finally staring at me like a cop instead of my father. "I didn't teach you to mumble."

"You killed her." My voice didn't slip this time. The man before me was no longer my father, but a criminal. A killer. "You killed our mother, didn't you?"

The silence between us was deafening, the only noise between us being the pathetic sound of my shattering heart.

"Why?" I whispered, gritting my teeth as he brought the glass to his lips, the amber liquid glowing by the fireplace. "Why did you do it?"

"Did you not just answer that yourself?" His words angered me, a tired sigh escaping my father as he rubbed at his face. "As clever as you are, Valeria, there are things that even you cannot understand."

I had expected to be afraid, to break down at his feet and sob, but I was not the little girl hiding in the cupboard anymore. The pounding of my heart was not my fear, but my burning desire for justice. The rage within me had bubbled over, and my father didn't flinch as I advanced toward him, pulling the unlicensed pistol from my hip and pressing it against his forehead.

"Answer me, damn it!" My hand trembled, finger shaking as it gripped the trigger. "You had your time to play the caring father, the noble Viscount—you mocked me from the sidelines for the past ten years and now it's your turn to tell me why!"

"I didn't play any part. You and your brother are my life. Your mother was my greatest love, I—" He pursed his lips as the pistol pushed further into his skin, my eyes overflowing with hatred.

"Don't talk about my mother like you loved her," I said through gritted teeth, my father hardly flinching. "If you cared about her, if you cared about any of us, you wouldn't have done what you did!"

"I did what was necessary for the survival of the monarchy." His eyes bored holes into mine, the icy blue matching my own. "*That* is my job, that has *always* been my job, and that is what you will never be able to understand. And you were wrong." He brought the glass back up to his lips, eyes never moving from mine. "I was never going to harm you or your brother, whether you saw the unfortunate event or not."

"Then how did the hallucinogens end up in our system?"

But by the time the words left my lips, I had already figured out the answer.

"She knew." My voice was below a whisper, gun shaking in my trembling palm. "She knew that she was going to die and she stayed anyway."

"Your mother understood what she had done and what had to be done for the sake of the monarchy," he said firmly, the glass slamming back down against the table. "Hard decisions need to be made for the betterment of the—"

"Don't try and justify your actions with cheap noble words," I yelled, his words falling silent again as the gun's barrel pressed further against his head. "You *killed* her, Papa! You murdered your own wife before our eyes. You ruined us!"

"I did my job. I protected the King. I got rid of the gang issue. Hell—I ended sixty percent of organized crime in a single night! Yes, it may have cost some innocent lives, but everything I have ever done was for the *greater good*. Your mother threatened that balance. If she had exposed the truth behind the fire, the riots now would have only been the beginning!"

"But you can't do that!" I yelled, his words making my stomach churn. "You don't get to sit here and decide who should live and who should die. You don't get to play God!"

We had grown silent once again, my heavy pants and the clinking of ice being the only sounds that filled the common room. I flinched at the muffled yells outside, my head turning toward the windows.

"You should go join the celebration," my father said.

I stiffened as his hands clutched the gun's barrel, moving it away from his head easily. *He's not even intimidated.* I gritted my teeth, watching the man sit back in his chair with a tired huff. *As much as I hate him, he knows I can't do it.*

"What the hell are you on about?" I swallowed hard, my throat suddenly dry. A grin stretched across my father's lips, the man turning to look at me.

"You brother was able to close a pretty big case today thanks to you."

My fists clenched, a weak attempt at stopping the tremor from running through them.

"We had a minor lead on a black-haired man who had been spotted near recent murders," my father drawled, satisfaction blatant in his tone. "Murders carved up by the individual Alias Black."

My limbs went numb at his words, the metal hilt of the gun much colder now against my skin.

"So we waited patiently, spreading officers out over all of the districts, sitting and watching, until a similar description was made again, this time the killer leaving a woman's house in the Second. We had a Silver of ours track him, slipping a little something into his drink."

The police had drugged him. I shook my head slowly, flinching as my father stood back to his feet. *They purposefully Dream Stitched him.*

"And as he stumbled home, you wouldn't believe how surprised I was to find my daughter climbing the steps of his apartment building, leading us right to the door."

He grinned, my heart stilling in my chest.

"Our little *Spider Lily.*"

My body went cold at the name, fear twisting itself up my throat.

He knows. I stumbled back, feeling sick to my stomach. *He has been watching me from the start, from the very beginning.*

"How..." My throat dried up, the strong voice that rattled the walls of my home earlier completely abandoning me. "How do you—"

"Don't worry, darling. Everyone has their secrets," my father said gently, but his eyes were razor sharp. He had me right where he wanted. "You seem more than capable of handling a little truth, so let me give you another hint. Your brother should be out by the station right now."

I furrowed my brows at his words, my feet already staggering toward the entrance.

"Didn't you hear?"

I broke through the front door, my soaking body running through the icy cold.

"Victor just caught the infamous Alias Black."

Chapter 22

EVERYTHING SOUNDED FUZZY, LIKE THE world itself had been put out of focus, my ragged pants the only sound echoing through my mind as my boots beat across the cobblestone streets. My heart lurched into my throat at the huge crowd of citizens and reporters alike surrounding the entrance of the station, adrenaline burning through me as I rammed into them headfirst. I grunted, pushing my way through the rowdy crowd, camera flashes blinding me as I reached the front, my hands falling limply to my sides.

"Let's go!" My brother's barking voice echoed across the square, his kind eyes now hardened to steel. And in his grip, a beaten and hand-cuffed Rowan Marrow, a steady stream of blood running down his busted lips. A junior officer moved to grip his secured arms hesitantly, flinching as the killer turned his head back and grinned.

"No need to tremble, little mouse. I mean, you must be painfully curious as to what sort of horrible ooze runs through the veins of *Alias Black*." The assassin's words slithered past his lips, catlike gaze unwavering even beaten and bound. "Go on, cut off a few limbs if you're tempted to take a look. I'm a monster, remember? *I'm sure they'll grow back.*"

I flinched as he was grabbed by his hair, Victor slamming the killer's face into his knee without a single glint of remorse. An unsettling laugh left the hitman's lips, blood dripping down his nose as he stared my brother in the eyes.

This can't be real. This is impossible. My heart hammered violently in my chest, the boy spitting warm blood onto the station's steps. *There's no way they could have caught him.* My eyes scanned over the team responsible, brows furrowing as I spotted just a handful of fresh officers aside from my brother. *He could have easily murdered them all.*

That was when those familiar green eyes shifted from the ground to me, the dark orbs calm and collected despite the abuse he had just endured. *He could have killed them, and yet, he hadn't.*

Because Victor is my brother.

Rowan's sweaty hair fell in front of his eyes, the boy giving me a nod before being dragged away, three Silvers pinning him down. Before my mind could fully process my decisions, my feet pounded up the stairs in pursuit of my brother.

"Vic, what—"

The words were jolted from my mouth as two junior officers held me by the arms, keeping me from approaching my brother.

"What the hell do you think you two are doing?" I growled, pulling against them as hard as my tired body could, but they wouldn't budge. "Victor!"

My brother's back had stiffened at my voice, any hope within me stomped out the minute his eyes met mine, the vivid blue orbs now pale and icy, matching our father's. He put a hand up, the two guards releasing their grip on me, sending my body stumbling forward. He stared at me in silence, the rage rippling through the air around him palpable. Like heat waves surrounding a flame.

"Vic, listen. Papa, he—" But my words were cut short, the hurt in his eyes deeper than any apology could ever reach.

"Out of all of the horrible things that you could have done to me"—his voice trembled as he spoke, what was left of my heart crumbling into dust—"this is by far the worst."

My mouth had gone dry, all the guilt that I had carried with me over the past few months—all the lies I had told to attain the truth—coming back all at once and pulling me beneath the surface.

"We were supposed to tell each other everything, and you..." He couldn't even look at me, his nostrils flaring in anger as he roughly wiped the moisture from his eyes. "You *lied* to me, to all of us!"

"Vic, I know I haven't been honest." My lips trembled as I spoke, tears pricking my vision. "But you have to trust me, I—"

"Oh, that's rich!"

I flinched as his voice boomed, a horribly cold laugh rumbling from his chest as his eyes watered.

"*Trust you?* Valeria, I was the first person to stand at your side! No matter how crazy your ideas were or how reckless you got, I was there from the very first breath."

My body trembled as he yelled, my brother's gaze so empty and broken, so full of hatred toward me that I found myself praying for the ground to open up beneath my feet and swallow me whole.

"And for some ungodly reason you *still* turned around and linked arms with Alias Black?" he yelled, hands moving to pull at his roots. "Am I some sort of joke to you, Valeria?"

"That isn't it at all!" My voice broke, hands grabbing at his coat in my desperate grip. "Vic *please*, I was just trying to protect you!"

His lips trembled, arms aching to pull me into his chest and forget about this mess, to pretend like this had never happened. But our connection had been frayed, and no matter how much time passed, or what I did to regain his trust, nothing would ever be the same.

A few flashbulbs went off behind me, my brother turning his teary face away from the prying eyes of the press before reluctantly flitting back to me.

"I know that you've always been smarter, V." My heart throbbed at his words, his eyes filled with a vulnerable anger. "I know that you've always been the more resilient twin, but you're *still* my sister. You were mine just as much as I was yours, so why couldn't you just let me protect you?"

315

Were. I shook my head, a million different apologies on my tongue, but none could escape me.

"Why didn't you come to me?"

I had done the worst possible thing to my brother. I had lied. I had lied and ripped his heart out, feeding it to the wolves right before his eyes. And yet I knew that he still wouldn't be able to hate me. Instead Victor would spend the rest of his life wondering what exactly had gone wrong and how he should have fixed it. That's why, with a heavy heart, I parted my lips once more, freeing him from the string that bound us to each other's side, that made us a pair.

"These issues, my decisions." I swallowed any remaining strands of hesitation as I spoke. "They have *never* been your responsibility."

Victor's hands had gone limp at his side, my brother's eyes freezing over completely as I shivered under his stare.

"Fine then," he said, words cut like steel. "Just as you won't be my responsibility now. Cuff her."

My brows drew together, eyes widening as the two officers twisted my arms behind my back.

"Wait." My voice was breathless, the Silvers grunting as they held me back. "Victor, wait a damn minute!"

"Father and I bought you a train ticket. You leave for the North tomorrow morning. Until then you'll be left in a holding cell." My brother didn't spare me another glance, stepping down the white marble steps easily as I was dragged away.

"Let go!" I kicked one of the guards hard, the young boy tripping over my quick feet. The other officer was a lot tougher, her grip on my arms fierce, the metal handcuffs digging into my wrists as I struggled.

He has to know the truth. I struggled against her grip, thrashing wildly. *He has to know what our father had done!*

"I said, let me—" I ripped myself free, a strangled gasp leaving my lips as I stumbled down the marble stairs, slamming my head against the last tile, the world around me instantly drenched in darkness.

The next time my eyes opened, I was no longer in the streets of the First, but in a cold, leaky cell, a thick coat covering my shivering body. My eyes squinted, a pained moan leaving my lips as I touched my throbbing forehead, fingers coming away bloody.

"You awake?" A familiar voice echoed from a few cells over, my sore body creaking as I leaned toward the bars.

"Try not to move too much," Rowan said from somewhere behind me. "You hit your head pretty hard."

I swallowed harshly, the reality of our situation feeling much more real now.

You idiot. I laid my head on my knees, tired shoulders sagging as I stared down into my lap. *All these years the killer was sitting across from me at the dinner table, and I had been oblivious.*

Father had drawn all the right cards. He easily disposed of his wife and had the perfect witnesses to the crime. My account on the man that did it was never even questioned, never dissected. I was the only one who saw the killer, after all, my hand clamping over my brother's eyes before he could see the monster himself.

My father had orchestrated the perfect crime and escape.

"You knew, didn't you?" I asked suddenly, my voice a quiet echo. "That it was my father. You knew from the moment we got back from Silverstein's estate."

"Actually, I had my suspicions since we spoke with Marvin Reese."

My lips trembled, the last few embers of shame and anger fighting to stay aflame. "Then why the hell didn't you—"

"I couldn't take the risk."

I paused, his words softer than they had ever been.

"I couldn't say such a thing if there was even a slim possibility that I was mistaken. I had to be completely sure."

A bitter smile trembled on my lips, my throbbing head lifting from my knees to rest against the cold wall. "Because I'm *weak.*"

"No," Rowan's voice was gentle, quiet. "Because he's your father."

I swallowed the weight in my chest, my eyes much too tired to cry. I had nothing left. I had thrown everything away in pursuit of this case, and now that I had all of the answers, part of me wanted nothing more than to go back to being blind, to being completely unaware of the ugly truth.

"You'll be okay." Rowan's words were quiet but sure, the assassin's voice bouncing off the walls of the empty jailhouse. "*He* can't stay upset with you forever."

"Is that right?" A bitter laugh left my lips, a dull gaping hole where my heart used to be. "Because right now I feel like every important thing in my life has just slipped through my fingers."

Rowan was silent, my head leaning back against the cold stone wall once again, eyes falling shut.

"That coat you're wearing." My shoulders stiffened, eyes opening at his words. "It's your brother's."

Tears I didn't know I had collected themselves in my sore eyes, trembling lips burying into the thick fabric of Victor's coat. He must have come in to check on me when I was out cold, wrapping the coat over my shivering body.

He still loves me. A shaky breath wracked through my chest. Even if we would never be the same, just knowing that was enough for now.

"I don't..." My voice trembled, the words barely above a whisper. "I don't know what to do, Rowan. Now that I know it all, now that every card is on the table." My fingers clenched the fabric of my brother's coat. "Where do I go from here?"

"It's unlike you to be brought so easily to a standstill."

"I'm afraid."

"What is there left to be afraid of?" I had expected his words to mock me, but they were sincere. "You have all the tools now. You can see every square on the board." His voice strained, the boy shifting in his cell as he spoke. "All that's left is to take the next step."

"And where will I end up once I do?"

The two of us sat in silence, my lips pressing together as the nothingness between us dragged on. It was unfair of me to ask him for such answers. He had lost just as much as I had.

My worries were not his concern.

"I don't know." His voice was quiet, my eyes moving to stare through the thick bars at the sound of it. "But if it doesn't lead you to the light, you won't be alone, Valeria."

He paused, the air in my lungs coming to a standstill.

"I will sit with you in the dark."

My chest tightened, his words unknowingly tugging at the organ in my chest. For some reason he was able to calm my pounding heart, soothing the tension in my bones as I hugged my knees close. The atmosphere between us was oddly comforting despite the dark and dreary place, because for the first time since we had met that night on the roof, Rowan Marrow was not a monster in my closet. *He is my friend.*

"Don't be too hard on yourself, Chief." Rowan cleared his voice, the sound of clanging chains echoing from his cell. "All things considered, this whole confrontation could have gone worse."

"How exactly?" The weight had abandoned my voice, hands wrapping the large coat over my form completely.

"The vicinity could have been on fire."

"That wound is still a bit too fresh."

"No, but really." I could hear the smile in Rowan's voice. "Sometimes good people make bad choices"—his words were careful, unsure as they reached through the bars of his cell and into mine—"but that doesn't necessarily mean that they themselves are bad. Just that they're human."

"And I suppose you're the same?"

"No."

I grinned at his blatant admission, rubbing a hand over my face.

"I'm a rotten bastard inside and out."

Our soft laughter had fallen silent, the subtle click of a lock echoing through the vacant holding cells. Whoever was about to walk in was hesitant, the door creaking open tentatively before slamming shut.

Who... I furrowed my brows, hands moving to grip the bars. *Who would...*

My eyes widened at a flash of curly hair, hands tightening on the bars at Lou's puffy eyes, her lips pressed into a fine line.

"Lou, I—"

"Don't." She turned her face away from mine, hands trembling at her sides. "Don't say another word or I'll end up regretting my decision even more."

I narrowed my eyes, brows coming together as I stared at her, shoulders going rigid at the keys in her unsteady hands.

"I told you." A sigh slipped past her pink lips, the tan skin of her face flushed from crying. "I told you I'd be by your side no matter what, didn't I?" And despite the"—her gaze shifted down the hall, closing in on Rowan's cell—"*questionable* decisions you've made, I have to believe that you had your reasons. I have to believe that I can trust you."

My heart skipped a hundred beats in my chest, her bloodshot eyes still managing to look so warmly at me despite the obvious hurt swimming within them. Her hands moved to rest against mine, their warmth melting through the icy grip of the cell.

"Listen," Rowan's voice cut in, Lou's eyes narrowing instantly. "I hate to ruin such a romantic moment, but—"

"Oh yes, that reminds me," Lou said. "The killer stays in his cell."

"Hang on, now." Rowan stumbled to his feet, hands clanging against the bars.

"Lou, I'm not asking you to risk your job, your reputation—everything you've worked for," I stammered, the girl shaking her head, gripping my hands tightly. "I'm asking you to drop the keys and walk away."

"No. Val, just listen!" she pleaded, my shaky lips pressing into a frown. "Oliver got his hands on a truck. We can leave! The three of us can move to the seaside, to Kairi even. We'll cut our hair and change our names. We can hide from this mess for the rest of our lives if that's what you need. Just let us do this with you!"

"This isn't just about me anymore." I pulled away from her hands, wanting nothing more than to run into their waiting embrace. "The nobility have taken advantage of too many, stealing the lives of the dead and ruining those of the living. This is so much bigger than I am."

"No." her curls bounced as she shook her head. "I don't know what happened—what led you to this killer's doorstep—but whatever you're planning, I can't let you do it alone."

"I won't be." I smiled, eyes drifting down the hall.

She turned, looking over in Rowan's direction, her head pressing against the bars with a heavy sigh. *Lou is so kind. She is so good.* A bittersweet smile made its way to my lips.

She's exactly what Nieve needs.

"Besides, this is going to get messy." I swallowed hard, my father's ruthless words filling my head. "The people will need someone they can trust at my brother's side when all of this is over."

"That's why we have you," she whispered, and I bit back the urge to cry.

"Lou, please."

My voice was softer, tired eyes pleading with her. Who knew if we would ever see each other again, if I would even survive by the end of this story? But I needed to know one thing for sure.

"Take care of him for me."

She held my gaze, countless conflicting emotions swirling within her green irises, but not a single word left her trembling lips. She gave me a reluctant nod, a heavy sigh of relief leaving my lungs as she turned her back to me, letting the metal keys hit the floor. The scraping of her boots grew faint as she disappeared back into the depths of the building, leaving my cold hands to clutch the cell's metal bars.

I swallowed the pain in my chest. The fantasy of leaving this life behind in pursuit of a new one was tempting, but I didn't deserve that.

At least not until I set things straight.

My fingers snaked through the bars, grabbing the rusted metal of the keys. My shaky hands worked surprisingly quickly, unlocking my cell door and slipping down the hall to Rowan's in the matter of seconds.

I looked away guiltily as his face came into view, the boy's lip busted open, a large purple bruise forming over his left cheekbone. His green eyes were illuminated by the uneven cracks of light in the holding cell, the orbs staring into mine intensely as the keys trembled in my grip.

"Come on," I muttered under my breath, hands too jittery to hold the keys straight.

"Valeria." His fingers extended toward me, but I pulled back.

"Just give me a moment." I bit my lip, trying to push the correct key through only to have it clatter to my feet.

"Hey, if you need—"

"I said I can do it!" I yelled, Rowan's parted lips falling shut at the desperation in my voice. *If I can't handle this much pressure, if I can't open one damned door*—I gritted my teeth, fingers tense—*then how am I ever going to succeed in bringing my father to justice?*

I closed my eyes, swallowing harshly before picking the metal keys up and trying again.

"Just…" I breathed, blinking hard as the ground tilted beneath my feet. "Just give me a second to—" They fell from my trembling fingers once again, but this time Rowan was ready, his steady hands catching them easily.

"*Breathe.*" His voice was smooth, soothing, like the gentle murmur of the ocean.

"I have to bring this to light, Rowan," I whispered, taking the keys from his warm hands. "If my father was capable of killing his own wife, imagine who else he would cut down in order to preserve his ideals."

"And you will." His eyes stared steadily into mine beneath his thick brows. "You won't be doing this alone."

I paused, hesitantly lifting my eyes to his, wincing at the wounds that littered the tanned skin of his face. His life as Rowan Marrow was over, his identity now exposed to the public. He was a dead man walking, and it was my fault.

"You'll help me?"

"I don't have very much else going on in my life right now." He shrugged, a grin twitching at the ends of his lips. "Besides, we made a deal, didn't we?"

I clenched the cool metal in my hands, my heartbeat picking up at the confidence in his words. I forced the tension from my shoulders, hands finally relaxed enough to slide the key in, the door opening with a quick twist. He stepped out of the cell, closing the door behind him before meeting my eyes again. *We are going to finish this, no matter where it leads us.*

Our silent steps headed for the door, eyes scanning every cell as we passed, discovering that we were indeed the only two people in the compound.

"By the way," I said, the image from the station flashing through my mind once more, "I know you could have killed him."

Rowan's movements stiffened, as if he had expected these words eventually.

"My brother. His squad was composed of new recruits, children." The words sat uneasily in my mouth. "You could have killed them all."

"I could have, yes." He nodded slowly, and when his face turned to look down at me, it had changed, his dark eyes glowing one shade brighter. "But that doesn't mean I should have."

I swallowed harshly, a heavy warmth spreading through my chest at the faint glint in his eyes. *We can do this.* My hand moved to softly grip his sleeve, his gaze dropping tentatively for a moment, but he didn't protest. *All of this will be over soon.*

Chapter 23

OUR BODIES FLITTED FROM SHADOW to shadow, creeping further and further from the First District every second that passed. The Silvers on duty would have noticed our disappearance by now, meaning that Rowan and I were wanted criminals, him more than myself.

It didn't help that our faces had been plastered on every paper, the media booming with the capture of Alias Black and the Viscount's daughter's slipping sanity.

I pulled my cap lower over my eyes, Rowan tilting his head toward the towering brick building, the words *The Black Press* painted in big black letters at the front.

We had managed to contact Rin Ryugazaki by using a random telephone booth to call the publishing house and asking for him personally.

"If this ends up being a trap, I'll take the personal liberty of snapping that camera boy in half," Rowan muttered under his breath. He had been against the idea from the start, but his reluctant feet trudged behind me nonetheless. "This plan is stupid."

"Yeah, well this stupid plan is keeping that empty head on your shoulders."

"Empty, huh?"

"Completely and utterly vacant." I couldn't suppress the smile on my lips as my eyes met a familiar pair of almond ones, Rin's slender figure hidden in a dark corner at the end of the street.

"I just want to tell you that you're out of your mind," Rin whispered viciously as soon as we were within range. "And *you*, you tricked me into letting Alias Black into the archives!" He whipped his head around to face the hitman. "Must be interesting to read articles about your own horrifying murders."

"I don't know if I'd say that." Rowan shrugged, eyes razor sharp despite his cool expression. "I've never really cared for the paper."

I told Rin everything, from the very beginning until the last few moments in the cell, his lips pressed together firmly as he listened, sharp eyes contemplating my words carefully.

"And you have no concrete evidence?"

"He doesn't even believe us." Rowan scoffed, Rin's eyes narrowing at him.

"Well excuse me for thinking that this is all a bit sudden!"

"No evidence, just a confession," I admitted.

Rin's eyebrows lifted at my words, my body shrinking back into my coat sheepishly.

"Untaped."

"Damn it, kid." Rin rubbed at his forehead, thinking hard.

I had known that this was a stretch, that actually getting my father behind bars for what he had done would be more difficult than pointing an accusing finger.

But still—I swallowed my anxiety, Rin's deep eyes still staring off—*I have to at least try.*

"At the end of the day it comes down to your words against his, which isn't that strong of a bet considering he's the Viscount and you're the crazy girl who Alias Black abducted."

"*Oh,* it's abducted now, is it?" Rowan's lips twitched into a threatening grin, teeth baring. "Don't you and your sniveling reporters have anything better to do than hash out lies?"

"I don't know. Shouldn't you be carving up a baby or two?" Rin narrowed his eyes, a cold laugh booming from the green eyed assassin.

"Actually, my preference is overcompensating young men with clunky cameras to hide their tiny—"

"Would the both of you just shut up and let me think!" I yelled, the three of us pausing at the eyes that followed us. The boys grew silent at my sides, glaring at each other as I sighed in frustration. "Any way that you look at it, the people will end up siding with my father over me."

"Well, that depends on which people."

My head snapped up at Rin's voice, Rowan shrugging at my side.

"He isn't wrong," Rowan said. "If you start at the bottom and slowly rise to the top, not only will you have strength in numbers, but a very livid and dedicated mob."

"Fine then." I huffed, pulling my cap lower as the streets grew busy. "Where do we start?"

"The Seventh," Rin said, eyes flitting from our faces to the bustling roads behind us. "Start at the Seventh District."

It had been one day on the run, the Seventh District serving as our home for the past few hours. I wish I could've said that it wasn't as horrible as the rumors, as the stories that slithered out of its depths, but I found the Seventh to be exactly what I had dreaded, the streets reeking of gasoline and urine, corpse-like people inhibiting the grimy streets.

Word had traveled fast of the Viscount's sins, sparking a quiet storm in just a few short hours. But gossip of our presence had also reached the crooks and crevices of the Seventh District, eyes staring heavily wherever we walked.

"They won't rat us out," Rowan had told me, stuffing his hands into the pockets of his coat. "I don't even think they have telephones in these parts."

"That's horrible."

"It's just how the monarchy was structured." He shrugged, eyes lingering over the dirty streets of the district. "Those with hard beginnings would be forced to live in the slums, never given the opportunity to rise to success legally. While those born rich would die even richer."

His words had left a rancid taste on my tongue, the feeling only intensifying as we turned the corner, a small crowd of men and women surrounding us like a fleet of ships.

"Hey, Blue Blood."

I froze at the title, turning my back slowly to face my accuser.

"It's true, isn't it?" The man's face twitched with anger, his eyes those of an animal. "The fire wasn't started by a gang." He turned to the crowd, his thinning hair patchy and unkept. "It was started by one of them!"

"Drop it," Rowan cut in sharply, my hand moving to rest on his arm.

"*Oh,* you've charmed yourself quite the serpent, Your Grace." The balding man grinned a toothless smile, but his eyes were heavy with a burning hatred, one so strong it seemed to amplify the entire crowd. "All it takes is one rich skank to—"

Rowan's hands were quick, pulling his coat back and grabbing the hilt of his blade, my hand catching his just as he unsheathed it, the accuser taking a stumbling step back.

This anger, this hatred—my eyes scanned the gathering mass—*it is what we want, after all.*

Rowan's narrowed eyes peeked down at me, the hitman relaxing the tension in his shoulders at my collected stance.

"I would advise against starting a fight you can't win," he said shortly, the balding man snarling at Rowan's words.

"All of us against the two of you?" The angry man grinned bitterly, the crowd growing denser at our sides. "I like my odds."

"Come on, now." I shivered at the sudden shift in Rowan's voice, a threatening chill spiking the air in a matter of seconds. *"You know better than that."*

"Yes, all of those rumors are correct," I said loudly, every set of angry eyes moving from the assassin to stare down at me. "It's all true. My father exploited the vulnerability of the Seventh to get his own form of justice, killing hundreds of innocent people in the process."

Although I knew that to be a fact, saying the truth out loud left me sick, nauseous with the reality of what my forebearer had committed.

"As horrible as that was, it's already happened. Nothing could ever bring back those who passed due to that heartless crime." I lifted my eyes from the balding man in front of me, moving to stare out into the growing crowd. "You cannot bring them back. Now the question is—what will you all do next?"

Heavy murmurs ran through the sea of people, Rowan giving me a reassuring nod before I spoke up again.

"We have a plan."

"We aren't following you into a battle we know we'll lose." A woman stepped forward from the crowd, a sobbing baby strapped to her back. "While your only punishment would be a smack on the hand, this sort of thing could cost us our lives."

"That's why you'll follow *him*."

Rowan stiffened at my right, all eyes falling onto the hitman.

"You know you're basically telling these people to follow the devil into hell, right?" Rowan whispered under his breath, their intense stares enough to sear past our skin.

"Don't give yourself that much credit. I'd say you're a middle-class demon."

"And you'll stand with us?" a young boy asked, his blond hair matted with dirt, blue eyes narrowed and angry. "You'd betray your own father?"

"The man I am leading to jail is not my father." I had expected the words to hurt, a frightening feeling filling my chest when they didn't. "He is my mother's killer. He is the arsonist that burned the Seventh to ash. I do not consider this an act of betrayal, but of justice."

And although the cheers that erupted from the crowd were comforting to hear, a thick lump of dread had found itself a home in my throat, the ominous feeling heavier than all those broken eyes.

The First District was crawling with Silvers, an early curfew enforced to all of its inhabitants. An old phone booth in the Sixth had gotten me in touch with Oliver, the frantic boy letting me know that he and Flint were being heavily watched, my father probably waiting for any indication of my return. As difficult as that made things, part of me was relieved. At the very least they would be safe.

A public confrontation is what we had decided on, choosing to attack up front at full force. With enough people backing our story and pushing for change, the station would have to issue a proper trial by law. I would be caught after that of course, put back into my holding cell or placed under house arrest until the trial. My words wouldn't mean much on their own, especially with my sanity now being questioned, but if Victor and I could sit down and talk, even for just an hour, then maybe I could get him to see the truth, to see both sides of the coin.

With a voice like Victor's on our side, we would surely win the case.

I stiffened, another vaguely familiar face passing me by, forcing my attention back to the situation at hand. We had collected quite a crowd, a group of almost three hundred people traveling up to the First with us in inconspicuous groups. Rowan and I had decided to split up, stopping at different shelters in districts Six through Four to pick up bags of wearable clothing. Now we were all here, blending in completely with those hurrying down the crowded streets of the First.

"Going ahead." Rowan's warm breath brushed past my ear as he passed me, his silent figure disappearing into the bustling sea of coats and winter hats. I swallowed my nerves, hands clenching in the pockets of my coat as I waited for the next step.

Rowan would draw the crowd, the protest commencing as soon as the officers would start closing in.

It's going to be fine. My eyes flitted anxiously across the crowd, observing the nearby Silvers, their pristine badges glistening as they moved.

Nobody needs to get hurt. We're just going to—

A hand dug into my shoulder harshly, my fingers moving to grab the thin blade from my sleeve, unsheathing it as I whipped around.

"V, where have you—"

My brother's soft eyes were wide with relief, the expression melting away instantly as I brought the blade to his throat. His lips parted, but before he could say another word, a voice boomed across the square, drawing the attention of us both.

"Ladies and gentlemen, people of Nieve!" My lips fell apart at Rowan's figure, the assassin climbing onto King Alpheus' pedestal, the metal statue covered in snow.

"I am the voice of justice. I am the voice of those pushed into the shadows, of those discarded in the slums, of those burned to ash and blown away to be forgotten!" Rowan's hair whipped wildly around his head, the snow speckling the black locks as it whistled in the wind. "We are tired of being erased, we are tired of being dubbed less than, and we will not stand for injustice any longer!"

The crowd had solidified then, the police growing weary as the mass of bodies grew and grew, my brother's grip on me loosening at the sight.

"Viscount Kenneth Ross Anson"—Rowan's teeth bared as he spoke, eyes hot and venomous—"is a liar and murderer!"

"What?" Victor whispered, his voice laced with confusion, but I couldn't tear my eyes away from Rowan.

"He started the fire in the Seventh ten years ago! The heinous crime of arson was treated as his own little vanity project, the sick bastard boasting his efficiency without fail," he belted, the crowd below him swelling with every word. "Kenneth Ross Anson is the epitome of our corrupted government, the man going as far as to kill his own wife for the sake of his name!"

Rowan's eyes met mine briefly before shooting his fist into the air, the crowd mimicking his movements.

"Will we stand for this type of leadership any longer?"

"No!" The sound echoed across the cobblestone streets, my brother flinching at the mass of it.

"Will we grow tired and submit?"

"Never!"

I never would've imagined what happened next, the tone shifting so quickly that I barely caught it. Somewhere within the crowd an officer set off a pistol, sparking a full-on frenzy, Silvers and citizens tearing into each other outside of the station doors.

My heart dropped as people broke through the lines of officers, their hateful gazes glowing bright as their feet slapped their way through the station's doors, bodies hitting the ground as shots rang through the air around us.

I bit my lip, prying myself out of Victor's hands, Rowan's voice echoing from somewhere near the front of the square. My boots crunched through the snow as I bolted up the station's steps, panic heavy on my heart.

This was supposed to be a peaceful protest. My lungs burned as I ran, breaths ragged. *A show of strength and unity, not violence!*

I glanced to the side, Lou's straining figure holding back the crowd, her deep eyes meeting mine for a brief second as I passed her, grunting as I cracked open the station door and slipped inside. I rushed up the steps, the first floor of the regal building completely torn apart, bodies of Silvers and citizens alike lying across the fine marble floors.

I shut my eyes as I climbed the stairs, the empty eyes of a dead woman lying trampled against the steps staring up at me, a gushing bullet hole in the side of her head.

By the time I reached the fourth floor, I had expected the worst, pulling my father's office doors open to find him sitting back in his fine velvet seat, a square glass of whiskey clutched loosely in his hand.

My breaths were uneven, violent as I tried to steady my racing heart, the man not even taking a second to raise his eyes to me.

"It's a beautiful color, isn't it?" He held up the glass to the faint lights of the room, the soft colors of amber glistening into soft browns. "It reminds me of your mother's eyes. She was a beautiful woman. You take after her quite well, except you have my colors." My father's eyes squinted as he smiled sadly, but I wouldn't budge.

Not after everything. Not after all he'd done.

"You obviously have a lot to say, so why don't you get to it?"

"I want…" My voice had begun to shake, but I gritted my teeth, refusing to weaken before the murderer. "I want you to stand trial."

"Stand trial?" His lips had twitched into a smile, but it didn't reach his eyes. "For protecting the monarchy from those heathens? I don't think so."

"You're the only heathen here." My father's eyes hardened at my words, my fists trembling at my sides despite the conviction in my voice. "You had everything, and you decided to throw it all away. You don't even feel any remorse, do you?"

"Of course I do." His tone was sharp, eyes finally meeting my own. "But I have control over my emotions. I am not a reckless child, Valeria."

"A heartless psychopath is what you are."

"Then do it."

I narrowed my eyes at him but soon tensed at the realization of his words, my hands moving to rest on the concealed gun at my side.

"I could see the outline of that pistol in your coat from the moment you walked in here, yet I didn't flinch, or scram, or shoot you myself." He paused, placing his own gun out from behind his desk. "Because you aren't here to hurt me."

I pulled the pistol from my hip, cocking the gun without hesitation. My father smiled at me, his eyes softening for the first time since I had confronted him.

"You won't. You can't."

"Oh, but I want to."

"No, you don't." He set his glass down with a sigh, fingers grazing the rim. "Your anger wants you to, but you've never been one to lose yourself to it."

"Shut up."

"You know, darling. I find it awfully amusing how you stand there and berate me, your own father"—he tapped his glass, relentless gaze meeting mine—"while you so easily turned around and shook hands with the most revolting murderer in the kingdom."

My fingers tightened on the trigger, lips trembling as he took a swaying step toward me. "Stay where you are."

"But he'll be dead soon enough." My father ignored me, moving to stare into the fireplace as he stepped forward again. "With the crimes he's committed, his head will be rolling at our feet in the matter of days. Perhaps we'll string his body up outside the station so the rest of the vermin can watch him rot." An unsettling smile twitched on his lips at the thought, the flickering flames reflecting in his eyes. "It would be a fitting ending for such scum. All that will remain of that savage killer are the twisted tales to his name."

I flinched at his words but refused to drop my eyes from the madman.

"Soon Rowan Marrow will be nothing more than the faint wisp of a nightmare."

He turned his face back to me, silver hair reflecting in the flickering light of the room, his eyes widening as they met mine.

"*Oh, you must be jesting Valeria.*" I dropped my gaze at his words, stomach churning. "What's with that expression? Could it be that you've actually decided to confide in Alias Black, of all people? To trust *him?*"

"I don't trust anyone anymore." The words were quieter than I would've liked, my father's grin widening.

"But that isn't really true, is it?" My lips quivered at the booming laugh that escaped the man. "I'm a bit disappointed, Valeria. At the very least I thought you had more sense than that."

"Shut up!"

"Do it then." His smile dropped, bitter eyes icing over. "Kill me, Valeria. Put a bullet between my eyes just as I killed your mother." The pistol trembled in my grip, my father baring his teeth like a rabid animal as he spoke. *"Without a second thought.* Do it!"

"Stop—"

"I said do it!"

I jumped as his hands slammed onto his desk, a smile twitching at the ends of his lips.

"You won't. Do you know why?"

My feet stumbled back as he threw the chair back, advancing toward me with quick steps.

"Because you're *weak.* Because you are nothing more than a fragile little girl."

"I am not." My breaths trembled as I spoke, tears pricking my vision. "Damn you, I am not!"

"Small and frail, hopelessly naive!" He trailed on, my heart pounding through my ears. "You never had the spine to do what was needed for your country."

I jumped as he gripped the glass, sending it flying across the study, the fine crystal shattering into countless shards.

"What I had to do for this country! No"—he slicked back his hair, turning his hateful gaze to me—"you are nothing more than a child. A child who decided to take things too far."

The fear that infested my bones was all too familiar, my eyes recognizing the true form of the masked man that preyed upon my dreams every night.

"Foolish, senseless, naive—"

A gunshot rang through the room, a scream leaving my lips as my father dropped dead at my feet, dark sticky crimson spilling out from beneath him.

I whipped my head around, eyes wide at Victor's wild gaze, his pistol still hot to the touch.

"Are you alright?" Victor panted, words strained as he tried to catch his breath, my eyes still wide in horror. The gun slipped from my sweaty grip, clambering to the ground with a dull thump, the Viscount's warm blood kissing its metal.

"Victor, you just…" My words stumbled, Victor's body slumping forward unsteadily. "You killed—"

My jumbled thoughts were cut short as my brother's side slammed into the doorframe, my eyes widening in horror at the sticky red liquid that trickled from the edges of his lips.

"V," he breathed, my hands lunging for him as he fell, sending us both to the ground. "I think I'm in trouble."

No. My hands searched his uniform, stopping at a wet patch of fabric at his right side, my hands pulling away a deep red. *No, anything but this.*

"Help." My voice shook as I looked around anxiously. "Somebody help us!"

Glass, broken glass. The air was thick and burning in my lungs as I gasped, clinging to my brother as I tried to breathe. *He's been stabbed, impaled, something!*

"Victor, stay with me." My breaths were shallow, the pool of blood around us widening by the second despite my pressure on the wound. "This can't be real," I whispered, my red hands trembling violently as they gripped my brother. "Please tell me this isn't real!"

"It's okay," he forced out, his pupils dilating as they focused on me. "This is okay. This is fine. This is…" His bloodied lips finally trembled. "This is perfect."

"No." I shook my head hard, my lungs burning in my chest. "No, it isn't. Please don't." My voice broke, hot tears spilling over my cheeks. "Please don't leave me here alone."

Warm tears stung the corners of his eyes, a weak smile forcing its way to his lips as he stared up at me, the blood on my hands still warm.

"I'm sorry, Victor. I swear, *I swear* I will never keep another secret from you ever again, *just don't leave me.* Victor, you can't—"

"What you said." His voice was much quieter now, like the ocean after a harrowing storm. "About Papa. I didn't want to believe it but"— he paused, taking in a shaky breath—"I remember."

"Victor, it doesn't matter anymore," I cried, the heavy tears blurring his face. "Nothing matters except you, so please—"

"When Papa found us that night, his eyes were different."

I furrowed my brows at his words, my brother taking in a shaky breath.

"They weren't frightened or even surprised. Because he already knew."

My breath hitched at his struggling words.

"He knew what he had done."

"Victor, please stop. Focus on your breaths, I..." I stumbled over my words, my hands trembling as they pulled away coated in his blood. "I can't stop the bleeding!"

"I shouldn't have..." He exhaled, eyelids growing heavy, ragged breaths wracking through my body as I gripped his hands, his fingers no longer trembling. "I shouldn't have doubted you, V."

"You can make it up for me later, just *please*," I whispered, my tears dripping down onto his face. "*Please don't die.* I don't care about justice. I don't care about the greater good. I care about you, Victor." My words were heavy, the weight of dread pushing down on my chest at every ragged breath. "So *please, don't leave me here to bury you.*"

"Dramatic thing," he whispered, his hand weakly squeezing my arm, leaving a bloodied print against the pale fabric of my sleeve. "Please..."

My shoulders fell forward as they shook, Victor's lips trembling at the desperate sobs that wracked through my chest.

"Please, forgive me." My brother's bright eyes took one more moment to look at me, the few tears they held trickling down his face. "Valeria."

His chest had stilled, the grip of his fingers falling limp, and I sat there and cried, cried as if the ferocity of my anguish might bring him back, as if the sheer force of my grief would pry his eyes open once again.

Rowan had appeared after some time, watching silently as I dissolved into the kind of despair that gripped me by the throat and pulled me beneath the surface. My screaming sobs had echoed through the empty building, sounding through the streets below and leaving Silvers and civilians alike completely suspended in time, my throbbing wails carrying the despair of the moment through the icy air and freezing them in place.

Heartbreak was heavy in the deep Nieve fog, the city itself mourning the loss of Victor Kaede Anson, heir to the title of Viscount.

My brother.

Chapter 24

IT HAD SNOWED THE DAY we buried my brother, the weather fitting considering the fact that winter had always been his favorite season. His small palms would press against the cold glass windows of our estate as a child, the boy sitting and waiting with wide eyes every morning, from the very start of December until the first snow.

I had said a few short words at his funeral, nails digging into the skin of my palms to keep from falling to my knees and shattering completely. For the past few days I hadn't been able to do anything myself, Lou and Nana taking it upon themselves to bathe and dress me, Flint coming by every day to watch me eat, frowning when I rarely took in more than two bites.

Anytime I ate it would end up climbing back up, my body refusing to survive without him.

Without my other half.

But today there was no snow, only heavy grey clouds as we stood for my father's funeral. I had worn the same dress as for Victor's, not wanting to show up at all but being dragged there nonetheless. Unlike Victor's funeral, there were very few who came to send the Viscount off. While my brother was praised as a hero, my father would be forever used as a cheap villain. As a reminder of Nieve's corruption in the hands of those sworn to protect us all. My father was shunned by the kingdom, all medals and awards stripped from his name, leaving him to exist forever as a warning to those who would think of themselves above the law.

The guest list consisted of Nana, Lou, Oliver, Flint, and my grandparents, the heartbroken pair standing through the entire service without saying a word.

Rowan had disappeared without a trace, vanishing into the midwinter air after the night of the riot. Not that he'd have been invited. His face was hung up almost everywhere, the once infamously mysterious assassin becoming the most wanted man in Nieve.

"Val?" Lou's voice was gentle, a soft hand resting on my arm. "It looks like it's going to rain soon. Let's head inside, okay?"

The wind had strengthened, lifting the ends of my dress as it howled through the streets of the First. I stared blankly at my father's gravestone, only lifting my eyes when Lou took my hand in hers, lacing her fingers gently through mine.

"Valeria?"

"I think..." My voice was a hoarse whisper. "I think I want to stay here alone for a bit."

Lou said nothing, nodding silently before letting her hand slip from mine, a few curls coming loose from her tight bun as she followed the others out of the cemetery, leaving me alone with my father.

I swallowed harshly, the cold licking at the exposed skin of my hands as I stood alone, staring at the gravestone, even his name feeling foreign to me. *It's strange*—the wind died down, abandoning me in its wake—*how a raging heart can blister and burn, and in a single moment, suddenly turn to ice.*

I wanted to be angry. I wanted to be hurt, to scream, to dig him up and demand he answer for all he had done, but all my emotions had abandoned me. From the moment my trembling body had stepped out the station doors—my brother's blood still warm on my skin—I had felt empty. The bright blue of my eyes had become vacant, unrecognizable, leaving me with no trace of my brother.

Cold emptiness. That was all I felt.

I loved Victor, after all. I loved him to death.

But for some reason, in the end I did not die.

"How?" Even my voice had changed, as if someone else were speaking from beneath my skin. "How could you do this to us?"

I had yet to cry for my father, all of my tears used up on Victor's untimely passing. But despite that—despite all of the horrible things that he had done—there was a bitter emptiness in my chest every time he crossed my mind, the ache different than that of Victor's.

A wet droplet hit my arm, trickling down to my elbow before falling off, followed by another and one after that. I closed my eyes, the rain pounding heavily, my shivering body hoping that it would wash away the pain.

Why? I swallowed harshly, the bitter cold becoming an extension of my existence. *Of all the things this world could have stripped me of, why did it have to take my brother?*

I furrowed my brows, eyes fluttering open as the rain stopped around me. I turned my head up, tracing the wide rim of a black umbrella, Rowan Marrow's still body gripping the handle, his hair slicked back and clothes soaking through.

"You'll get sick if you stay out here too long."

"Rowan." My whisper was barely audible over the pounding rain, his white dress shirt completely drenched. "You haven't left?"

"Not yet." His quiet words were muffled through the rain, green eyes flitting to mine. "My train leaves in a bit, but I realized that I never got to say goodbye."

"Oh." I swallowed harshly, hating that word with a burning passion. "Goodbye then."

"Valeria." My name was breathless on his lips, his hardened exterior left cracked by the rain. "When you…" I turned my eyes back up at his hesitation, the boy flinching at the emptiness that met his gaze. "When you think of your father, how do you feel?"

The faintest embers of anger flared up within me, irritated by his brutal question, but I was tired, far too tired to yell or curse.

"I don't know," I said softly, my heart clenching in my chest. "I feel heavy. Conflicted, not like how I feel about…" I drifted off, my brother's name still too painful on my tongue.

They were dead. My entire family had gathered beneath my feet. They had left me behind to bury them, to mourn for them, to carry the weight of their lives—their sins—on my shoulders until I'd lie down beside them. *And it isn't fair.*

"I…" I whispered, gripping the fabric of my shirt as my chest tightened. "I don't understand what it is. But it hurts."

*My mother was gone, but I learned to cope. My brother had left my soul split, half of my heart resting in the coffin with him, but my father— my father, he…*My nails tore through the skin of my palms. My father was a killer, a liar, so then *what is this ache?*

It hurt. So much so that I could barely speak from the weight of my grief.

And yet not a single tear could escape me.

"Rowan, what is this?" My lips trembled, a hand moving to grip the umbrella, pulling his body down toward my own. "What am I feeling?"

He looked down at me with tormented eyes, the boy soaked to his bones with the icy rain, and for a fragment of a second, I thought I might ask him to stay. But I didn't. As tattered and broken as I had become, I wasn't that foolish.

I don't know how long the silence between us extended, just that his gaze held onto mine with a sadness I hoped to never understand. For the sublime emptiness in the green irises that had always frightened me now mirrored my own.

"I couldn't tell you." Cold raindrops ran down his face, but despite the sorrow that swam within them, his eyes remained dry. "No one can ever really grasp another person's experiences or perceptions. Only you can tell me what you're feeling."

His hands slipped from the umbrella as he spoke, the boy standing upright into the hammering rain, his black hair matted to his face.

"But if I were to speak for the majority of the world"—he leaned toward me once more, cold lips pressing faintly to my cheek, eyes remaining unchanged even as he turned his back to me, stuffing his hands into his pockets—"I'd say that most people tend to cry when their fathers die."

I furrowed my brows, blinking fast as my hands moved to my eyes, finding them wet. Tears unknowingly slid down my face, mixing with the rain that had remained on my skin.

It hurts. My lips quivered, a ragged breath escaping me as Rowan's back disappeared into the pounding rain. *Despite whatever he had done, at the end of it all, he was still my father.* My shoulders shook, hot tears streaming down my cheeks in heavy streams. *He was still my Papa.*

The rain had thrashed against our rooftops for the next week, Rowan's train long gone to who-knew-where by the time it finally ceased. And while the heaviness in my heart would never simply disappear, the rain had washed away some of my hatred, leaving me ready to accept the cards that my father had dealt me.

Ready to heal.

Epilogue

THE TOWERING MOUNTAINS OF THE North blurred at my side, the endless stretch of grassy fields retaining their lush shade of green despite the dropping temperatures. Winter was fast approaching once again, the train's window cold beneath my fingertips. We would reach Nieve's Capital in a few hours, then it would be the simple matter of a short cab ride until I was back on the familiar streets of the First District. *Back home.*

It had been three years, after all—three years since I had walked the uneven cobblestone streets of the First District. The concept of time had become a blur, my constant travel throughout Nieve's borders leaving me more exhausted than I had ever been. *But I've been grateful for the distraction.*

It was in the silence that my thoughts settled, where the gaping hole in my heart would ache, reminding me exactly whom I was and the weight that came with the blood in my veins.

"You plan to return, don't you?" the Crown Prince had asked me a month prior, the rough Nieve air biting at my cheeks as we stood out by the Palace gates. I had been summoned in regards for a diplomatic mission up North, King Alpheus himself requesting my presence for the affair.

"Maybe." I had turned to look at the Prince, his pale hair blowing in the breeze. *"Truthfully, I haven't decided yet."*

"I see." His chocolate eyes had slipped from my own, my hands moving to rest respectively at my back.

"You disapprove?"

"No, nothing of that sort." He shook his head, arms crossing over his chest with a deep exhale. *"I just—I worry for you, Valeria."*

"You shouldn't waste time worrying over me, Your Highness."

"It's not something I can help." His kind eyes drifted to mine, my posture stiffening at the sincerity of his words. *"If I were to station you back in the city, it wouldn't be easy for you. You'd face prejudice from the people and hostility from the nobility."*

I dropped my gaze, focusing on the gleaming marble tiles as he spoke.

"They would cast you as an outsider."

"I am well aware. Still..." I turned my face up to the sky, the vivid blue above the Palace unlike anywhere else in the kingdom. *"As dark and deep as the shadows of the Capital are, I cannot abandon it. Believe me, I've tried. It is a part of me—perhaps the part I hate most, but a piece nonetheless."*

I turned to face him once more, Caelum's eyes heavy as they stared into my own.

"So with your permission, I think I'd like to go home."

He was silent, the Prince staring past my skin and into the hollowness underneath. While I could never forget what I represented and where I had come from, the Valeria Anson from before was dead, her body buried alongside her brother's in the lonely cemetery of the First. In a sad way, that thought comforted me.

I didn't know if I could bear the weight of her misery. The reality of what she had become.

"Very well, Valeria." The Crown Prince had smiled softly at me, extending a hand in my direction. *"Then from the bottom of my heart, I wish you a kinder existence."*

"Viscountess Anson?"

My tired eyes fluttered open, moving across the office space of the train car and meeting a pair oh-so-bright.

"Is everything alright?"

"Yes." I sat up quickly as Flint slid the door shut at his back, my words quieter than they used to be. "Just resting."

Flint nodded, his usually-messy curls combed back, the boy pressed into a clean button-down shirt and a pair of uniform pants, the silver imperial badge at his chest glistening in the light.

It was hard to accept how much the two of us had changed in the past few years, our roles reversing in almost every way. The boy that I had saved all those years ago was now the line that kept me tethered to this earth. That kept me grounded when everything around me had crumbled to ash.

It had taken me two years to properly function on my own again, the kingdom taking its own time to heal after the Viscount's sins had been brought to light. I had left the First soon after my father's funeral, the familiar halls of my home and twisting streets of the Capital serving as unbearable reminders of all that I had lost. It was only after six months in the soundless mountains of the North when I had reached my limit. The world was painful to face—it would always be—but I could not live in isolation any longer. If I had spent one more moment in those silent fields, *I would've torn myself apart.*

"You should sleep. We'll be pulling into the Capital before nightfall." Flint stared down at me gently as he approached, my hands moving the thick stack of files from the forefront of my desk.

"Is that an order, Silver?"

"I have no authority to issue those to you, but I would highly recommend some rest." Flint shrugged, a smile tickling his lips. "Knowing Captain Tate, I would expect quite the reception upon your arrival."

"Yes, Oliver had the courtesy to call ahead and warn me." I sighed, rubbing my hands over my face as Flint laughed, hands resting at his back. "I really wish she wouldn't go to such lengths."

Captain Louisa Tate. A smile unknowingly pulled at my lips. *The Chief of Nieve's Imperial Forces and head of the Capital.* After the last

Viscount's demise, new rules had been implemented into the justice system. The country's fate would never again be left to sit in the palms of a single individual. Instead, the responsibility of the kingdom was to be divided, to sit on the shoulders of many instead of one. Lou had been my brother's right hand at the station, his second-in-command from the very beginning—it was only natural that she fill part of the hole he had left behind. She had no noble blood in her veins, yet was the best choice the King's council could have made. She was the perfect candidate for Captain, coming from humble beginnings herself, yet excelling through the ranks with a speed that no other Silver could ever hope to match. She was a good fit for the people, a bright light searing through Nieve's weighted darkness.

I, on the other hand, had been given a choice.

As heiress to the Anson bloodline I could either step down from the role thrust upon me or accept the title and forget my past. To leave my father and his sins at my back and plunge headfirst into the future.

And so I had become Viscountess, the cord between royalty and the people, my assignments focusing on internal affairs within the kingdom rather than criminal ones.

"Valeria, if you…" Flint's words were careful, his eyes hesitant as I turned my face back to him. "If you need more time away from the First, we don't have to go back so soon. Captain Tate wouldn't mind."

"I know." I clenched my hands before me, the once-bulging scar on my palm now a subtle reminder of a deal I made all those years ago. "But I can't just keep running away. I can't avoid the station forever."

My role as Viscountess had kept me in a constant state of motion, my days divided between the snowy mountains of the North, the raging waves of the South, and the Palace gates, leaving me very little time to visit the Capital. The main city was no longer my responsibility, the burden of the seven districts residing with Lou.

I had gone back to the First a few times over the last three years to visit my family's graves and attend Lou's inauguration, but even then I had avoided the station like the plague, the mere sight of the familiar double doors and marble steps sending my stomach into knots.

Even after all these years, there was something unsettling about the towering marble building to me now. It was as if the place I had once called home was stripped away completely, leaving me as an imposter on my own doorstep.

I didn't know if I was ready to go back—if I was ready to walk through the very halls where my brother had taken his final breaths—but whether I was ready or not didn't matter.

I refused to hide any longer. It had been long enough.

"I think it's about time I went home, Flint." I smiled weakly at the brown-haired boy, eyes heavy with a sudden sorrow. "I don't—I don't think I can bear to be alone anymore."

"You wouldn't be." His voice was tender, the boy taking a seat across from me. "If you want to go somewhere else, it won't be alone."

Flint's eyes had softened, but the boy staring at me now was no longer the kid I found in the sewers. His once-thin frame now towered over my own, his strong hands steadier than mine could ever be.

He tentatively took my tense hand in his, careful fingers lacing through my own.

"I'll stay." His words were gentle, eyes tentatively meeting mine. "If you want to go, I'll stay with you, Valeria."

My heart quickened beneath the fabric of my shirt, lips parting but falling shut before a word could escape them, the scratchy voice of the conductor echoing throughout our car. I dropped my eyes from Flint's, my cheeks warm for a reason I couldn't recognize.

"We'll be stopping again soon." My voice was unsteady, hands restless in his gentle grip. "I think I'm going to go stretch my legs for a bit."

"Do you want me to accompany you?"

"No, I..." My words were quick, his hands gently releasing my own. "I can manage."

He parted his lips to protest, but fell silent as he met my eyes.

"Stop looking at me like some wounded animal." I crossed my arms, the boy freezing under my gaze. "I'll be fine."

"That's not—I didn't—" He paused, spotting the small grin on my features. His expression relaxed, the boy letting out a gentle chuckle before nodding. "I can never win against you."

I furrowed my brows at the words, a warmth filling my chest.

"Alright." He repressed his smile, the same familiar dimples peeking through. "I'll be here when you return."

My heart steadied, shoulders relaxing at the sight of them. As much as he'd changed, he was still the same boy. *He is still my Flint.*

The lavish train car resided near the engine, the renovated space used by high-ranking nobility and royalty as a mobile room during long travels. I had become accustomed to life on the tracks, my role within the kingdom keeping me on my toes. I slid the heavy door open, nodding to the guards stationed outside my car, before advancing through the main part of the train.

I gripped the scratchy cushioned seats as I made my way toward the back, the train's path unsteady despite the speed we were traveling at. Nearly every seat had been filled, the train station a madhouse of bustling families and traveling children now that the holiday season was at our backs. I spent the past winter as I had the past three years— behind a desk, my nose buried in official paperwork and diplomatic documents.

The colder months were always the hardest to cope with.

But this year had been different, the numbness that would arrive with every snow failing to show itself, leaving whatever was left of my heart to bleed across the floors of my vacant office in quiet agony as winter waged its yearly war on the outside world. That's when I had decided it was time to come back. To come home.

My body jolted forward as the train took a sharp turn, eyes widening as I noticed where my feet had carried me. I had walked through the rest of the carts, reaching the very end of the train, the only thing separating my swaying body and the winter wind being a rusted metal door.

I licked my cracked lips, twisting the heavy handle and pulling it open with a grunt, shrinking back into my coat at the gust of wind that greeted me. The cold stung at the skin of my cheeks, painting my nose bright red, but I stepped out into it nonetheless, bare hands moving to grip the balcony's icy railing as I left the car's warmth.

The black train tracks extended out from beneath me, the lush greenery from further north existing as a mere whisper the closer we got to the Capital, jagged ice coating every crack and crevice it came across.

How heartbreakingly beautiful.

My hands squeezed the frozen railings despite the bitter cold, my hair blowing ahead as the train sped down its tracks. People always told me that he was never destined to stay. That my brother was a mere shooting star in my night sky, and that I should be content with the time I had been given.

But I don't believe in things as trivial as fate.

I closed my eyes, my breath painting the frigid air white.

I refuse to believe that destiny could be so cruel.

Time heals all wounds—wasn't that what they'd always say? That the more time one would give themself to heal, the fainter their scars would grow. But frankly, I didn't want time to heal my wounds. If I were to grow old and my scars faint, I feared I'd forget him. Forget the color of my brother's eyes, the mischief in his smile, and the softness of his embrace.

No, I'd rather my wounds bleed eternally.

In truth I didn't think I'd ever fully recover from what had happened to me—to my family. As hard as I tried to forgive and forget, the gaping hole in my chest would forever ache. For my brother, if for no one else.

The creaking of metal at my back forced my tired eyes open, limbs stiffening momentarily at the sound of our even breaths, the rushing wind quieting down only for a moment.

Click.

My lips lifted weakly at the familiar sound, eyes tearing up for a reason I couldn't identify as the words found themselves on my tongue.

"You're coming back too, aren't you?" I turned slowly, a familiar pair of green eyes glinting as they met mine.

"That does seem to be the case." Rowan shrugged, stuffing the rusted pocket watch into his coat, his cool expression spoiled by the faint tenderness in his gaze. His hair had grown out, the dark locks now tied back lazily, a few loose strands framing his face.

I swallowed the heaviness in my throat, the two of us standing in the gentle stillness of the balcony.

"Why?"

He slowly met my eyes, every shade of sorrow swirling within them as his lips parted.

"Because, as ugly and tainted as Nieve is"—a few specks of snow littered his hair, decorating the strands like stars in the night sky—"I just couldn't stay away for too long. This is my home, after all."

He feels it too then.

As drenched in sin as the kingdom was, it was still my home. Where I had grown up, where I had played, where my brother's body rested. I could not just abandon Victor there.

"What's your excuse?" he asked, stepping out into the cold, gloved hands gripping the railing at my right.

"I think you said it best." My shoulders relaxed slowly, the frigid air numbing my face. "Besides, where else would I go?" I exhaled, my breath painting pictures in the winter breeze. "There is nothing left of me. I am but a remnant."

"Don't."

My brows drew together at the softness in his tone, the hitman refusing to meet my eyes as we stood side by side.

"Don't give yourself that excuse. If you do that, you'll never piece yourself back together. And I don't want..." He stopped, the words catching themselves in his throat. "I don't think your brother would've wanted that."

My grip tightened on the railing, the dull ache in my chest sharpening for the first time in years. It had been a while since I'd felt such a pain.

"Well then." He shifted the topic, raising an eyebrow as he met my gaze. "Aren't you going to arrest me, Viscountess?"

"I'm afraid I'm off duty at the moment." The smile that found itself on my lips was faint, but real, Rowan's own pulling back.

"How unfortunate."

My eyes fell shut, the two of us standing in the gentle nothingness of the moment.

"I've heard that the Seventh has been given resources to heal." Rowan shrugged into his coat as the wind picked up, the air stinging my cheeks. "That the Viscountess facilitated aid to the outer regions and appointed a private team focused on the eradication of Dream Stitching."

"You've been keeping up with the news, haven't you?" I raised an eyebrow, but the teasing expression slipped from my face at the sincerity in his gaze. "I just"—I squeezed the railing—"I thought the people had suffered enough. It was about time that someone took responsibility for their pain and worked to make a difference."

It was time I owned up to my predecessor's mistakes.

"You've done well, Valeria."

The words were weighted, heavier than I had anticipated, a whisper tickling the back of my mind, begging to escape into the night air.

Have I?

"The snow." His voice broke through the brief silence. "It was heavier than usual this year."

"Don't try to start small talk with me, Rowan."

"It's not like you're making this reunion any easier, Chief." He huffed, a soft chuckle escaping me. It felt good, talking with him again. He had been there for it all, from my valiant start all the way to my tragic end. He had read through every chapter of my book.

"But I couldn't say." I shrugged, following his eyes to the piles of snow that passed us by. "I didn't catch any snowfall this winter. I was…" I swallowed the sudden weight in my throat, my brother's bright eyes flitting through my mind. "I was far too busy."

351

"That's a shame." Rowan stared off, the train's tracks icy beneath us. "You might just catch the last snow by the looks of it though."

I turned my head up to the sky, the billowing grey clouds a testament to his words. Something stirred within me, my brother's ghostly palm pressing against my own at the thought of winter's last snow.

"That would be lovely."

He nodded silently, stuffing his hands into the pockets of his coat, the outline of his fingers moving as they traced the golden watch. There was something on his mind, and the longer we stood out in the cold pretending to be two normal people, the heavier it got—the more the past scratched at our backs, begging to escape our lips.

"Do you..." He caved first, which would have surprised me three years ago, but not anymore. I had grown accustomed to swallowing the past, drowning it before it could devour me whole. "Do you regret it?"

He didn't have to specify his words for me to understand them.

"No." The word was certain, more than I thought it would be. "At first I thought I did—but no, I don't think so anymore. The life I lived up until three years ago had been nothing more than a dream, one that went on for far too long." I turned to face him, his gaze fixated on the blistering horizon. "I had to wake up and face reality at some point. So thank you, Rowan Marrow."

"For ruining your life?" He had tried to jest, but I could see through it, and for the first time since I had known him, I saw it in his eyes. *Remorse.*

"For waking me up."

He looked away at my words, loose strands of his hair blowing back as we stood there side by side. I knew more of Rowan Marrow than most would ever discover, and I was sure he knew every secret of mine, yet as we stood there, we had never felt more like strangers.

Strangers with memories.

"Do you want to hear something absurd?" I asked, the boy raising an eyebrow at the whispered grin on my lips. "Back then, on that day." I stared off as I spoke, my father's funeral feeling like a lifetime ago. "For a sliver of a moment I had almost asked you to stay."

My confession sat between us, the wind carrying any hesitation or embarrassment into the clouds with it.

"Do you want to hear something crazier?"

I turned my head up to look at him, swirling irises tentative with something I couldn't describe.

"If you had asked me then, I think I would have."

His hair blew back wildly in the wind, the boy and I staring at each other in a comfortable silence as we sped along the track.

The smile that pulled at my lips was a strange one, full of a tickled amusement that I hadn't expected. Rowan grinned, wiping at his face as a laugh escaped me, followed by another, a few of his own rumbling from within his chest, leaving the two of us in tears, grinning like idiots.

"Good God, what fools we've become." He shook his head, shoulders loosening beneath the fabric of his coat.

The train had begun to slow, the blistering wind relaxing a bit as the two of us collected our bearings.

"Should I be worried about your return?" I turned to look at him, hugging my coat closer.

"Hm?"

"I would appreciate a friendly heads-up should bodies start piling again once I'm back in the Capital," I clarified, the boy moving to lean against the railing as I spoke.

"I don't mean to disappoint you, Your Grace, but I think Nieve will have to survive without my services." He met my eyes, the harsh green tired and worn, exhausted from the life he had led. "I don't have enough hatred left in me to keep up that life."

"A domestic life, huh?" I raised an eyebrow. "I never thought you'd be the type."

"It's pedestrian, I'll admit, but my previous job has left me with the means to retire." He shrugged, my eyes rolling at his shameless remark. "I think I'll pursue the life of an underpaid employee, a pianist perhaps. It's simple and steady but I think…" He paused, something almost painful in the way he looked at me. "I think that's something I need right now."

He felt it, even if he would never admit to it—I could sense it in his words. The weight of all he had committed was pressing down on his shoulders just as my father's sins clawed at my ankles, threatening to pull me below the cobblestone streets. I could not forgive Rowan for what he had done—it wasn't my place—but just knowing that there was something there, something stirring within his chest, was enough for now. *At least until I catch him myself.*

"That being said, once a bastard always a bastard, am I right?" He smiled softly, the atmosphere between us strangely warm despite the bitter weather. I laughed softly, my cold hands moving to the safety of my pockets.

"Right."

The train had gradually begun to slow, the twisting mountains of the North seeming further than they had been a few moments prior.

"Well it looks like this is my stop," he said, my brows furrowing.

"Your stop?" My body turned to face his. "Aren't you—"

He had cut me off, a gloved hand extending to point at the sky. "Look."

I squinted, following his gaze, my limbs falling loose at the swirling white specks that sprinkled the air around us. My lips trembled at the soft throb in my chest, one that had gone silent for so many years, I had feared it had disintegrated completely.

Winter's last snow. A wistful smile overtook me, the silence of the balcony peaceful as the cold lips of winter left their mark. My hand moved from the warmth of my coat, the early evening air sinking its teeth into my skin as snowflakes littered my palm, kissing the pain away.

"Thank you," I whispered to no one in particular, Victor's smile pricking the corners of my eyes.

There it is. My palm pressed against my collarbone, my mother's necklace warm as it dug into my skin. *That feeling again.*

Victor was still here, still with me. My brother's honeyed eyes and soft words whispered in every snowfall, in every spoonful of sugar in my tea, and in every train ride through Nieve.

My lips parted as I turned my head back to my right, dread jolting my blood as I found myself completely alone.

My brows knit together at the sudden emptiness of the balcony, the hitman disappearing into the wind like a faint dream. Or rather a memory.

"Rowan?" His name was breathless on my lips, my body stumbling back into the train's embrace, the sudden heat thawing my bones. My anxious eyes flitted across the bustling aisles, passengers moving to their feet as the train came to a stop. A brief flash of raven hair caught my attention from within the masses, my unsteady body pushing through the crowd.

"Rowan, wait!" I yelled, weaving through tired husbands and yawning wives.

This isn't the Capital's stop. My heart hammered in my chest as I pushed into the next car. *What the hell is he—*

I stopped, passengers moving around me as I froze in the center of the aisle, my eyes locking with his through the window.

"Rowan!" I shoved myself into an empty aisle, prying the window's glass open with a grunt. "Rowan, where are you going?"

"Hell, most likely," he called from the worn metal platform, his body being the only still one amongst a sea of suitcase-lugging people. "But I have a few stops to make first."

I furrowed my brows, nails digging into the skin of my palms as the train unloaded. "But you—"

"Don't worry, Chief." I paused at the softness in his gaze. "I will see you soon enough."

My words fell silent, the tension in my hands melting away as I held his gaze.

Of course. I closed my eyes momentarily, regaining my bearings. *Of course he will.*

A sad chuckle left my lips, a bittersweet weight blurring my vision. His lips pressed together at the sight of me, the boy shaking his head.

"Don't waste those tears on the likes of me, Valeria."

"It's not something I can help."

He tipped his head back as he laughed, the lighthearted sound sparking shivers up my arms as it was carried up by the wind.

"Careful with those words." He grinned, eyes glinting in amusement. "You might end up charming me."

"Wouldn't want that now, would we?"

I smiled, the boy staring tenderly at me. My lips trembled gently as I held his eyes, the worn rumble of the train's engine jolting our attention back to the present. I squinted as the wind tickled my cheeks, winter's stinging touch seeping in from the open window as the train trudged forward.

"Goodbye, Rowan Marrow."

"No." His steps sped up, leaving prints through the snow as he leapt from the platform, holding my eyes as the train rolled down the tracks. "See you soon, Valeria."

My lip quivered at his words, hands moving to grip the edge of the open window as the wind blew through my hair.

"I expect a good chase, Viscountess!" Rowan yelled, his voice muffled by the wind. "Don't go easy on me now!"

I matched his grin, shaking my head at his words. "I wouldn't dream of it!"

But as the train picked up speed and Rowan's figure became just another speck in this vast and vacant world, I had a feeling that I would not see him again. Perhaps I had hoped.

The warmth that had collected itself in my eyes spilled down my cheeks unknowingly, leaving hot streaks to tickle my skin.

Goodbye, Rowan Marrow. My hand clutched at the fabric of my shirt, my heartbeat steady beneath it.

Goodbye, my friend.

Acknowledgments

I'D LIKE TO THANK LOST Island Press for giving me this incredible opportunity and choosing to believe that the emotionally written and sporadic first draft I submitted back in December could have eventually amounted to this novel. I'd like to thank Mel Torrefranca who has been my guide through the world of publishing and an incredible voice of support throughout this process. Thank you to the entire Lost Island Press staff, from the editors and proofreaders to those in marketing and cover design. You truly are the sweetest and most passionate people.

Thank you most of all to my family. To my grandma, Safta Sara, who is the spark behind my imagination and who painted my childhood with her endless stories. To my parents, who have always shown me constant support. To my mom, who rearranged her schedule so I could sit for hours in the library as a child, to my dad who followed through on every little thing I needed, to my uncle Eli who insisted I read from a young age, and to my siblings, who endlessly terrorize me with their love and foolish antics, always leaving me with a funny scenario or two to write about.

I'd also like to take a line or two to thank all of my friends who listened to me rant and scheme and obsess over the process of writing this novel. I don't know if I could've been half as patient with myself as you all were.

And of course, thank you to all the people who've found themselves in the pages of this story. Your time and support is of immeasurable worth to me.

Lastly I'd like to thank all the incredible authors whose words have guided me from the moment I was able to read them. Your stories are what crafted me as a person, and for that I am forever thankful.

About the Author

SHIRA BEHORE is a young adult mystery and fantasy author from Central Florida. She first began stitching together worlds and characters at the age of eight and has been writing stories ever since. When Shira isn't typing away on her laptop, she's likely to be found buried in a book, working on a painting, or planning new videos for her YouTube channel. She can also be found obsessively scrolling through Google Flights, getting ready for her next adventure.

youtube.com/shiwrites
instagram.com/_shi_writes